COWBOY WOLF
TROUBLE

KAIT BALLENGER

sourcebooks
casablanca

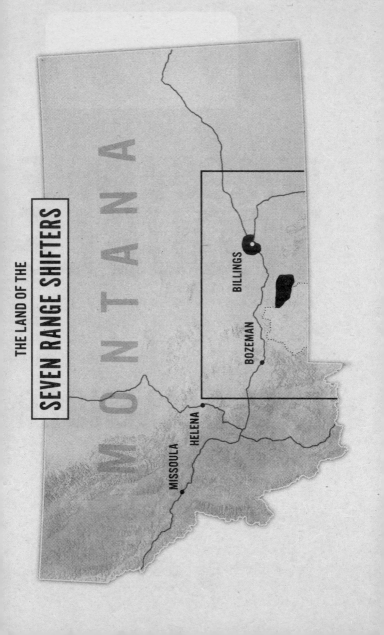

THE LAND OF THE

SEVEN RANGE SHIFTERS

MONTANA

MISSOULA

HELENA

BOZEMAN

BILLINGS

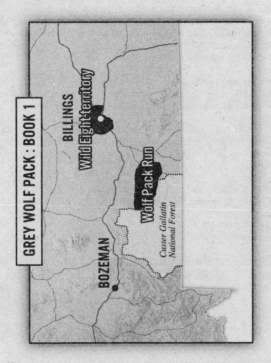

Copyright © 2019 by Kait Ballenger
Cover and internal design © 2019 by Sourcebooks, Inc.
Cover image by Craig White

Sourcebooks and the colophon are registered trademarks of Source-books, Inc.

All rights reserved. No part of this book may be reproduced in any form or by any electronic or mechanical means including information storage and retrieval systems—except in the case of brief quotations embodied in critical articles or reviews—without permission in writing from its publisher, Sourcebooks, Inc.

The characters and events portrayed in this book are fictitious or are used fictitiously. Any similarity to real persons, living or dead, is purely coincidental and not intended by the author.

All brand names and product names used in this book are trademarks, registered trademarks, or trade names of their respective holders. Sourcebooks, Inc., is not associated with any product or vendor in this book.

Published by Sourcebooks Casablanca, an imprint of Sourcebooks, Inc.
P.O. Box 4410, Naperville, Illinois 60567-4410
(630) 961-3900
Fax: (630) 961-2168
sourcebooks.com

Printed and bound in the United States of America.
OPM 10 9 8 7 6 5 4 3 2 1

Chapter 1

IT WAS MORE THAN A HUNGER FOR FRESH STEAK THAT filled Wes Calhoun's belly. Violence brewed in the night air, and he sensed it. As he prowled through the stable, rays of moonlight lit his path, flooding in through the open doors. The scent of freshly baled hay, mucked stalls, and the oiled grooming polish he'd brushed into the foals' coats this morning hung heavy in the air.

When he reached the wrought-iron gate of Black Jack's stall, he paused. He had half a mind to turn back now. Just a pivot of his foot, and he could walk back into Wolf Pack Run and listen to the voice of reason. He could already hear the roar of Maverick's rage. When the Grey Wolf packmaster returned from the western packlands, he wouldn't take Wes defying his direct orders lightly. But as hard as Wes's logic yelled his life would be a helluva lot easier if he marched his ass back inside, he couldn't do it.

Kyle would be waiting, and Wes needed to know. For the Grey Wolves. For the safety of the Seven Range Pact. For his own twisted reasons.

Black Jack let out a frustrated huff, the heat of the horse's breath swirling in a visible dance around his face.

Shit. Wes jumped back, anticipating the blow before it came.

The horse reared up on his hind legs and kicked open the old stall gate with elegant ease. The weight of the massive beast fell back to the ground with a thud of his hooves, his long, black mane whipping about his face. The fierce mustang trotted out of his stall and pegged Wes with a look of *I haven't got all night*, as if it were normal for a horse to regularly escape his hold. Though Wes supposed for *this* animal, it was.

He was damn near untrainable.

A devilish smirk crossed Wes's face as he placed his hands on Black Jack's shining coat and mounted the horse bareback. Black Jack had never been very good at following the rules.

And neither was he.

As soon as Wes's leg was over his back, the horse bolted out the open stable door and into the night. Wes buried his hands in the mustang's mane for leverage, leaned forward, and gripped hard with his muscled thighs, trying his best to move with the galloping beast. The cool night air washed over his face. The fresh scent of the mountain evergreens, hinted with pine and cedar, filled his nose along with the earthy dampness of moss upon shale rock. The encroaching cold of the coming winter's first frost hung in the air.

Yes, this was what he needed, despite the trouble it would cause him. With each pounding leap, Wes felt all four of Jack's hooves connect with the cold mountain ground as they bounded into the trees, running with an abandon that only fueled Wes's defiance. Maverick refused to see the danger right in front of him, but Wes knew firsthand what waited in that darkness.

Black Jack bounded through the mountains with speed and agility the likes of which Wes couldn't replicate, even as his wolf. When Wes finally caught Kyle's scent on the distant breeze, he pulled back on the wild horse's mane, and they skidded to a stop among a dense band of evergreen trees. His ears pricked for the slightest hint of noise. Nothing but the sounds of the forest. It was a quiet October night. With the light of the supermoon bright in the night sky, hunger filled Wes, and the forest's cacophony of sounds echoed in his ears—birds snuggled in their nests, a far-off stream just starting to slow and ice around the edges in the mountain cold, a nearby fox hunkered in wait for an approaching hare.

Quickly, Wes dismounted, then inspected Black Jack with a firm stare. "Stay close."

The horse let out a pissed-off huff and started to rear up on his back legs. Wes's eyes flashed to his wolf's, and he leveled a don't-fuck-with-me stare at Black Jack.

Not tonight, bud.

The horse released an angered whinny before stomping off to forage on the remaining autumn short grass.

Wes rolled his eyes before he headed down the mountainside on two feet, slipping through the familiar pines in search of the clearing where he and Kyle had agreed to meet. The surrounding noises of the forest filled his wolf with keen, sharp awareness. He stepped through the opening in the tree line and into the clearing.

Kyle waited for him. "How goes it, my man?" Kyle extended his hand and his other arm for a brotherly half shake, half hug.

Wes towered over Kyle by nearly four inches. With a bandanna under his flat-brimmed hat and tattoos peeking out from underneath his heavy winter coat, Kyle looked like the city slicker he was. Judging from the abundance of clothing, he must have driven up on the nearby highway. Something about the oddity of that raised the hairs on the back of Wes's neck in warning suspicion. A lone wolf from Los Angeles who'd moved up to the mountains several years earlier, Kyle maintained close ties to the Wild Eight but had never sworn in. Wes saw Kyle for exactly what he was: a two-faced snitch who played any side to fuel his raging coke addiction.

True men, fierce werewolves and warriors who fought real battles, formed the Grey Wolf Pack versus the violent wolves who comprised the new members and associates of the Wild Eight, men who were now barely better than loosely organized street thugs. They were lost and weak in the absence of Wes's leadership. It was *his* fault. *His* decisions that had led to the demise of his once-mighty pack and the shared dream of freedom they'd fought for.

Seven mountain ranges surrounded Billings for seven shifter packs—grey wolves, black bears, bobcats, grizzly bears, coyotes, lynx, and mountain lions alike. Since as far back as their history was written, the shifters who roamed Big Sky Country and called Montana's vast mountain ranges their own relied on the Seven Range Pact to govern their law, enforced by the Grey Wolf Pack's rule.

Wes's great-great-grandfather had formed the Wild Eight faction, the eighth and only illegitimate pack among these mountains. Residing in downtown Billings, the Wild Eight had wreaked havoc on the inner city and the humans dwelling there in opposition to the Seven Range Pact's sanctions. But with Wes's surrender as packmaster of the Wild Eight, the war within their species had become dormant. The packmaster of the Grey

Wolves, Maverick Grey, interpreted this to mean the eventual dissolution of the Wild Eight in the absence of a Calhoun to lead, the end of their civil war. But Wes knew better. The Wild Eight would resurge, even in his absence. And when they did, they wouldn't stop until they'd claimed Wes's life for his betrayal.

"How's life?" Kyle asked, as if they were there to shoot the breeze.

Wes ignored the question, pulled the cash out of the pocket of his jeans, and held it up for Kyle to see. "You said you had information for me."

"Always down to business, huh, Wes?" Kyle swiped under his nose with an obnoxious sniff. He was jonesing alright. "So I was at the clubhouse the other day when I heard Donnie saying that there's a new alliance forming."

Wes's eyebrows climbed toward his hairline. "Between who?"

Donnie's name alone pissed off Wes. All too quickly, his one-time loyal friend had jumped in as the Wild Eight's packmaster in his absence. Under Donnie's leadership, the Wild Eight had become street scum.

Kyle leaned forward and whispered as if they weren't alone. A sly grin crossed his lips. "Word on the street is the vamps."

Wes saw red. *Lies*. He shoved Kyle squarely in the chest. "You call me all the way out here to tell me this bullshit? You think this is funny?"

Kyle backed up. He threw his hands up as if in surrender. "I shit you not, man. That's the truth." He laughed. "Donnie went to that side of town the very next day for a private meeting, if you catch my drift."

Wes raged. No, it couldn't be true. If it was, that meant everything he had worked for, everything he had sacrificed, was for nothing. He knew Donnie was scum. He knew every member of that pack was in some way scum, but there had been a time when he'd been one of them, when he'd thought better of them, *expected* better. He may have led the rebellion against the Grey Wolves to live by his own rules, but he *never* would have allowed the Wild Eight to betray their own kind. Not with the likes of those bloodsuckers. He'd given up everything to ensure that.

If Donnie was partnering with the vamps, that meant the peace the Grey Wolves had enjoyed after Wes's surrender would soon be over. For the Seven Range Pact, this would mean war.

Wes crossed the clearing to where a small stream ran. He crouched down, reached into the icy-cold water, and splashed some on his face. But it didn't help. The moonlight hit the water, causing his reflection to stare back at him. He was one of those monsters. He'd been their leader, the worst of them all. All before the night he'd trekked up this godforsaken mountainside and surrendered himself to Maverick. The blood of his father and an innocent woman had still been fresh on his cowboy boots. His anger and shame filled him like an empty vessel, screaming for release. Hunt. He needed to hunt. His tendency for violence, the impulsive rage he barely contained, was how he'd thrived as their packmaster for so long.

During the daylight hours, the physical labor of herding and caring for the Grey Wolves' wild horses and yearlings and working with his hands on their cow-calf operation kept Wes busy, unable to dwell on the wrongs of his past. But when night fell, hunting was his only release, and with the supermoon blazing in the night sky above him, calling out his wolf, he intended to do exactly that.

"Any more news on this, and you report to me, understood?" As the words left Wes's lips, he caught a familiar scent on the breeze. A mixture of whiskey, the gasoline of the cars in downtown Billings, and the musk of a male werewolf. The snarl that rumbled in Wes's throat was barely contained. He'd recognize that scent anywhere.

Wes honed in on the sounds flanking the clearing. The occasional rustle told him the Wild Eight wolves were nearby, hidden in the darkness of the trees. Now that he was aware of them, he felt their eyes on him. Kyle had sold him out, the ignorant little shit.

Slowly, Wes stood, his anger simmering. He would battle them, spill their blood for ever daring to attack him, which they clearly planned to do. But one sharp move would alert them, and he needed to gain the upper hand. First, he'd take out the weakest link in a show of ruthless dominance, a reminder that *he* was still alpha, their leader or not.

Prowling toward Kyle, he extended to his full height. He placed his hands squarely on either side of Kyle's neck, as if he were about to pull him into a brotherly hug. His eyes trained on the area of the tree line above Kyle's head where he now sensed movement. His wolf threatened to burst from beneath his skin as he felt an approaching presence from behind.

They would attack when his back was turned. It was typical of Donnie's tactics and of what the Wild Eight

had now become. When *he'd* been packmaster, Wes
had never been so cowardly. Ruthless, brutal, wild, and
unpredictable, but never a coward. He smiled. Their cow-
ardice meant they still feared him. That was why they
needed to attack when they thought his defenses were
down. Though they had waited three years, he'd always
known they wouldn't stop until they saw him dead.

But clearly, though time hadn't lessened their fear, it
had made them forget that Wes never let his guard down.
Kyle reached for his knife, but Wes easily blocked it.
With one swift move, he twisted Kyle's neck until it
snapped. Kyle crumpled to the ground.

Wes didn't think. His wolf tore from his skin in a
painfully satisfying release, shifting bones and sinew.
Another wolf darted from the trees behind where Kyle
had stood. Wes didn't recognize the newbie's scent.
But it was no matter. In a bounding leap, Wes collided
with the other wolf midair. They landed in a mix of
snarling teeth and tangled limbs. The other wolf lunged
for Wes's throat. It took all of two seconds for Wes to
overpower the lesser beast, pinning him to the ground
with his paws. *He* was the alpha. *He* had been their
leader. But they had attacked when his back was turned,
a weak strategy unbecoming of his legacy. And for that,
he would spill their blood without remorse.

He ripped into the other wolf's throat. Blood dripped
from his sharp fangs in a salty, iron-filled heat. Wes
didn't stop to think. He had only one true target. He
rounded in search of Donnie, who crouched in wolf form
at the other side of the clearing. Both wolves snarled.

Slowly, they circled each other. Wes charged. The
two wolves collided in a clash of claws and teeth. Wes

sank his fangs in first, ripping into the fur of Donnie's shoulder. Donnie yelped in pain. In retaliation, Donnie caught Wes's front leg in the weight of his powerful jaw. Pain seared through the limb. The bite knocked Wes off-balance. Donnie used his front paws, along with Wes's momentum, to slam Wes onto his back, sending the two rolling in a fit of limbs and snarls. Paws to chests, they rolled until Wes emerged on top.

Donnie lunged forward, teeth snapping, but Wes knew how to end this. Donnie would hide behind his wolf as long as Wes let him, because he was a coward, because he feared the increased pain of his human form. But Wes knew pain. As Nolan Calhoun's son, he'd known pain his whole life, and he didn't fear it. He embraced it.

Without warning, Wes shifted, his paws changing to hands that were against the fur of Donnie's chest. He gripped the snarling beast, digging and crushing Donnie's throat with his large hands. Steadying his feet on the ground, Wes lifted the snarling wolf by the front scruff of his neck, his hand threatening to crush Donnie's windpipe with one sharp squeeze.

Donnie shifted beneath his hands, clutching at Wes's grip against his throat. Bloodlust coursed through Wes's veins. He had killed so many times in his life and never thought twice. But the fear, the hurt, the betrayal reflected back in Donnie's eyes stopped Wes short. He couldn't bring himself to crush the other wolf's trachea. Wes hated what Donnie had become, loathed it with every fiber of his being, but his enemy had once been his friend, his brother.

Wes's betrayal of their pack, then Donnie's attempt on Wes's life. Wounds deeper than knives had cut both of them to the quick. Now, they would be even.

"This is your one and only chance," Wes growled. "Next time, I'll kill you." Wes released him.

Donnie crumpled to the ground, gasping for air.

From the enraged look in Donnie's dark eyes, Wes half expected the bastard to attack him again right then and there. Donnie shifted back into wolf form, and Wes followed suit.

A loud howl suddenly echoed through the forest. Wes and Donnie froze. The scent of the Grey Wolf pack-members who were on tonight's patrol drifted on the night air. Immediately, Donnie and his men sprinted from the clearing, scattering into the darkness behind Wes in several directions.

Cowards.

Lips curled into a snarl, Wes bolted toward the trees. He may have spared Donnie, but he held no loyalty to the new members. His opponents made no attempt to hide now. He heard them, smelled them, tasted their filthy blood in his jaws. He hunted them anew, because if Maverick ever found out Wes had spared the life of a former friend on Grey Wolf packlands, the Grey Wolf packmaster would kill Wes himself.

Wes barreled behind the Wild Eight wolves at full speed, darting around trees, over rocks, under low branches. He acted on pure instinct. He and his wolf fused into one tonight. He felt it in the marrow of his bones, and his wolf was hungry.

The gamy scent of livestock drifted overhead. The Wild Eight wolves were headed toward a ranch at the bottom of the mountain. Wes saw them now, two of them up ahead. An old wooden ranch fence lay beyond.

They leaped over the fence, Wes close on their heels.

Clearing the fence, he ran forward without hesitation until, with a loud metallic snap, pain shot through his front leg and paw. A yelp tore from his jaws. Uselessly, he tried to pull his paw back, only to find metal digging farther into his fur and flesh. The pain was hardly worse than the realization that the Wild Eight wolves' scent now trailed in front of him, retreating, and he couldn't follow.

A trap. The rancher had set a fucking trap. *Damn it all to hell.*

Blood poured from the wound. But it would heal. Wes could deal with the pain. It was how he was going to get the hell out of this trap that concerned him. His fellow Grey Wolves likely wouldn't find him for hours. Their focus would be on the Wild Eight wolves, not keeping tabs on him, and it would take Black Jack at least an hour to track his scent. He snarled. The night was quickly taking a turn for the worst.

About thirty yards away, a porch light flicked on, blazing and searing his nocturnal retinas. As the sound of the Wild Eight's paws against the ground faded away, the noise of a different challenge thudded in his ears. Approaching footsteps followed by the quiet click of shotgun shells being loaded into the barrel. *Shit.*

Adrenaline pulsed through him. Pack law forbade human knowledge of their kind. His choices were limited. Kill to save himself and preserve his kind as pack law allowed, or shift and risk them all for the sake of one human life. The hair on his haunches raised as his wolf prepared to fight.

Shame and regret immediately filled him. No, he couldn't. Not again. He had already taken one innocent human life too many. Three years, and he still felt as if the blood were fresh on his hands...

As the footsteps drew closer, an internal war raged inside Wes. Teeth bared, he ignored the pain coursing through his paw and focused on the only real decision he had.

The only choice that ensured his survival.

Damn that idiot brother of hers.

Naomi Evans's breath swirled in the cold autumn air as she fumed at her brother's stupidity. The bulky weight of her father's old breechloader pulled against the already-stressed tension in her shoulders. She loaded two buckshot shells. As soon as she'd heard that trap snap closed, she'd known Jacob hadn't listened to her. She'd warned him that animal traps were *not* welcome on her ranch. That hadn't sat well. Jacob was still sensitive that their father had left the ranch to her, the biologist, instead of him, the born-and-bred cowboy. She shook her head. Since the day their mother birthed him, Jacob had been determined to be a thorn in her side, but she hadn't expected him to step over the line. She'd made her message clear: her ranch, her rules.

So much for that.

The sound of her shotgun's barrel clicking into place resonated in the almost dead silence of the Montana mountainside as she walked out into the night. The summer crickets had long since left, leaving nothing but the occasional owl's hoot or the rustle of the wind.

A deep sigh shook her. She didn't want to do this. But there was no other choice now. She'd either have to call the Defenders of Wildlife to come collect it, or put that pesky beast out of its misery, depending on how bad its wounds were. Though now a rancher like her father before her, she had respect for the surrounding wild-life, something that the worldview of her Apsáalooke heritage and her interests as a former biologist had cultivated in her.

She'd tried everything. Extra fencing, chicken wire, a blow horn, warning shots, you name it. Everything the local environmental and animal protection groups suggested. But nothing had worked. She couldn't afford to lose any more livestock, and the carnage left behind had been unlike any she'd ever seen. The thought made her shudder. From the dismembered carcasses, this one was some sort of alpha brute, or worse, a whole pack.

She stared out into the abyss of her ranch's land with nothing but the swirls and bursts of twinkling stars and the stark white moonlight overhead to light her path, but the cold seeped into her skin at the thought of the wounded animal on her property.

A small rustling noise sounded. Immediately, she hoisted the gun to her shoulder. Adrenaline pumped through her. She should turn back now. Something inside her screamed this with pure certainty. There was little she could do for the animal at this point. Unless she wanted to get herself mauled, she couldn't free it from the trap, and she didn't need to see the extent of its injuries to report it to the Defenders of Wildlife. But she wanted to look this beast in the eye. As gruesome as the remains it left behind had been, the biologist in her marveled at a predatory animal that could hold such power, and the size of its tracks indicated this wolf to be some sort of anomaly—way larger than typical for the kinds that roamed this mountain range.

"You couldn't stay away, could you?" she whispered into the darkness, the question as much for herself as for the animal.

A snarl answered back. She crept toward the noise, eyes glued to the rustling animal just out of reach of the porch light. Only movement and a vague outline to her eyes, but she knew it was him.

As she reached the edge of the darkness, her eyes adjusted to the lack of light. The grey wolf lay hunkered down in the dirt. *Canis lupus irremotus*, her mind instantly cataloged. A Northern Rocky Mountain grey wolf. Yet much larger than what would be typical for the species, especially since their reintroduction to the wild. They'd been almost extinct barely twenty years earlier. The trap anchored the wolf's front paw. Around the wound, blood pooled black in the moonlit mountain dirt. From the looks of him, the Defenders of Wildlife would be able to patch this beast up and then hopefully release him back into the wild. Maybe by then, he wouldn't be as fierce and brazen about slipping fences to eat livestock.

She stepped forward. At the sight of her gun, the wolf snarled again.

But she held the gun steady for her protection. She may not want to kill the creature, but if it came down to his life or hers, she'd pull the trigger, no matter how it would break her heart. As she examined the large, majestic beast before her, a heavy weight pulled on her conscience. Animals like this withered in captivity if not treated right. "Sorry, bud. I didn't want to do this," she mumbled.

The wolf's golden eyes held her gaze for a prolonged moment. It examined her with equal curiosity. When it finally broke eye contact, the air surrounding the wolf suddenly shifted and bent. Fur retracted and limbs shifted.

Naomi's breath caught in her throat. Two seconds ago, she'd been face-to-face with a large, angry grey wolf. Now, a man crouched before her. Before she questioned her own sanity and whether she'd accidentally mixed the glass of cabernet she'd drunk at dinner with medication she'd somehow forgotten she'd taken, she lifted her gun again, clinging to her only means of protection.

His deep, gravelly voice rumbled through her chest. "Don't shoot." He lifted a hand in surrender.

Gun at the ready, she stepped backward. "Get up." She said it because she wasn't entirely sure what else to say.

He remained on the ground.

She brandished the gun. "I said, get up." She fought to keep the terror and shock from her voice, though her heart pounded against her chest.

Slowly, he extended to his full height. Instantly, she regretted her demand. Now, at the end of her gun's barrel stood a man—a very large, very naked man.

"I'm not going to harm you." His gaze followed hers to his bloodied arm. "We're at an impasse."

Funny, considering he was the one in her animal trap. "I'm the one holding the gun, asshole," she retorted.

Slowly, he nodded. "Fair enough."

She stood there, gun poised on him, unmoving. Her breath swirled around her face in the cold night air. She'd barely been prepared to kill a wolf, let alone a man. As she calculated her next move, he stood naked before her, both hands lifted in surrender. The trap clamped onto his forearm failed to faze him, despite the blood running down his arm. The expression on his face remained unaffected, distant, rather than panicked or aggressive.

She needed to subdue him. Right?

Briefly, she considered calling the police, but she quickly reconsidered. Predominantly white law enforcement had never been kind to her people. And a young Apsáalooke woman reporting a naked, unarmed Caucasian man caught in a wolf trap seemed like a recipe for harassment. Her idiot brother was out of town for the week—so there'd be no help there. She could call someone from the Nation, she supposed, but the nearest tribal police on the res were an hour away, and they didn't hold sovereign authority outside their lands. Not to mention she'd be damned if she needed a man to save her. This far into the mountains, it was just her and her father's shotgun on this one.

"Where did the wolf go?" she asked.

The slightest lift of his eyebrow questioned her sanity. But not in the way she'd been hoping.

"That's not humanly possible," she breathed.

He smirked as if she amused him. "Good thing I'm not human."

Suddenly, the eyes of a wolf stared back at her, though he was still a man. She stumbled back in fear. He lunged, and she pulled the trigger. The shot rang in her ears, echoing through her ranchland. A hard, heavy weight hit her square in the chest, and she felt herself falling. The starlight blurred before her eyes until everything faded into black.

Chapter 2

WHEN NAOMI WAS THREE YEARS OLD, SHE HAD NEARLY drowned. Her parents had taken her into the mountains to explore and see the Yellowstone River. She remembered the way the white waves of water crashed against the rocks. Her mother's voice had called out to her to stay away from the edge. She could still feel the slip beneath her small purple sneaker before she plunged into the water.

The river had engulfed her, and for a moment, all sound ceased to exist. The current had twisted and pulled her under. And then she had heard it. The sound of her mother's screams on the surface. And though she didn't know how to swim, she had kicked.

When she'd resurfaced from the water, the park rangers had said it was nothing short of a miracle. But Naomi knew the truth. She'd saved herself. In that moment, she had decided that she would be a fighter.

Even as she floated through the darkest confines of her subconscious mind, the will to break free moved through her, driving her like an invisible hand as she struggled to resurface from the darkness.

The beeping sounds of hospital machinery rang in her ears, the memory sharper and more piercing than a knife. The sun streaming through the nearby window beat down on her face, but it did nothing to warm her. Cold. She felt so incredibly cold. Cold enough that she shivered from head to toe. Staring at the empty hospital window frame, she knew what came next. She fought not to turn her eyes toward the bed, not to be reminded of the way his body had become crippled and withered.

But she lost.

Her gaze turned toward him, but not of her own accord. Her father lay in the hospital bed, half-lidded eyes staring up at her as the chorus of machines screeched their terrifying cry. The light inside those eyes began to fade. Terror gripped her. She heard it then. The sound of her voice screaming, howling like a madwoman for the nurses to come. But even then, she'd known it was too late. And that was when the weight of it had hit her.

The sounds of the hospital, of her screams, quieted, transitioning into a constant ringing in her ears as the final light faded from his eyes. Dead flat. Until they weren't…

Yellow eyes, sharp and piercing. A wolf's eyes.

Naomi came to on a jolt of energy and fear. Dreaming. She had been dreaming. Closing her eyes again, she slowed her breathing. A gentle sway moved beneath her as she lay on her stomach, her spine curved in an upside-down U. Where the hell was she? Her head throbbed, and her thoughts somehow felt fuzzy. Was she on a horse? The oily scent of coat polish permeated her nose, and from the gentle sway, it certainly felt like it. But she didn't trust her disoriented head. Hadn't she been at home just moments ago? As she attempted to push herself up, a soft tug pulled at her wrists. She shifted until her wrists were in front of her face. Loosely tied rope wrapped around her wrists. Panic flooded her. She scrambled in an attempt to sit up. Immediately, she slipped from where she'd been perched, and her back hit the cold mountain ground with a hard thud.

"Shit," a nearby male voice cursed.

The moon above bathed the normally pitch-black forest in pale moonlight. A horse's hooves leading up into thick, muscled legs stood less than a foot away from her; its coat was as dark as the night sky. *Equus ferus caballus*. A black American mustang, a typically free-roaming species. She scrambled to sitting despite the ache in her shoulders from the fall. It took her all of two seconds to ascertain she'd been riding passed out on the back of the horse. And this horse was decidedly *not* free-roaming.

She didn't think. Jumping to her feet, Naomi darted into the trees. She had to escape. Had to get back to her ranch. Her feet flew over the hard mountain terrain as she ran downhill. Ten yards in, a rock caught the toe of her boot, and she toppled into the dry autumn leaves. She started to scramble to her feet again.

And that's when she saw him, looming in front of her. Her captor.

He sat on the back of the dark horse, hands clutched in the beast's mane, those same yellow wolf eyes narrowed in her direction. Thankfully, he was clothed now. Or at least wearing pants and little more, as it were.

He rode before her as a man. But his eyes told the true story.

"Werewolf." The word fell from her lips.

"Glad we've gotten that out of the way," he said.

She jumped at the deep rumble of his voice. His voice was human, but those dangerous yellow eyes...

He dismounted the horse, and her eyes widened as she took in the full sight of him. Mangy blond hair brushed beneath his chin, wild and unkempt. He stood unnaturally still, wolf eyes ablaze through the darkness. Harsh, brutal features comprised his face. Jagged cheek-bones, a bladed nose, an angry slash of a mouth, and a strong jaw lined with a thin layer of coarse blond stubble clenched tight. He watched her with relentless intent. Violent battle scars marred the skin of his chest, high-lighting the bloody wound at his shoulder from where her shot had grazed him, and the deep slashes of the now-removed wolf trap in his forearm only served to make him appear all the deadlier.

Wild, fierce, virile.

Dangerous.

In her work as a biologist, she had developed a brief, flirting fascination with large apex predators. After she'd finished her degree, she'd accepted a brief summer internship at a large-cat rescue in northern Florida, where she'd worked with the rehabilitated predators up close. She'd been captivated by the lan-guid way they moved, their ability to become so still in anticipation before they struck or lunged at prey, a trait common among predators across varying species. Being so close to such strength and power had filled her with both excitement and fear. She remembered once observ-ing a cougar crouch in anticipation of catching a live rabbit that had been released into its cage. The intense, deadly look in its eyes had both thrilled and terrified her. Making her want to draw closer while also being thankful a cage had stood between them.

She had no such protection now.

It was the cold, ferocious intent in his golden wolf eyes that paralyzed her, that held her captive. Even in this form, he was lethal, standing well over six feet, his body unforgiving muscle and sinew that moved with predatory fluidness.

Few would have called him handsome. Terrifying seemed more accurate, yet she couldn't pull her gaze away. She didn't want to.

He wore nothing but a pair of loose jeans covered with riding chaps. The combination hung low enough on his hips to serve as a reminder there was nothing underneath. Her eyes followed the trail of blond hair on his muscled abdomen. The material covering him seemed so precariously perched there that it sent a wave of embarrassed heat straight to her cheeks.

Slowly, she shifted her legs underneath herself until she crouched over the tree roots. Though she naturally loved the outdoors, having grown up on a ranch, she'd never been a very fast runner. But she had to fight, had to try. She knew these mountains. She could find her way to her ranch, even in the dark. Right? He took one step toward her, and even that small movement was predatory, not fully human.

And she was his prey.

She didn't think.

She bolted again. She made it all of two strides before the large weight of him collided with her side. She toppled to the ground face-first, hands still bound, but she wasn't going down without a fight. She tucked her bound hands under her chest and army crawled forward. One large hand locked around her ankle and wrenched her back toward him. She screamed, thrashing and kicking against his hold. She fought with every ounce of strength she had, but he subdued her with ease. She'd known the escape attempt would be futile, but she couldn't have lived with herself if she hadn't tried.

She kicked him again.

"Oh no, you don't." He prowled up the length of her body until he pushed flush against her, his arms pinning her chest to the ground.

She was skilled in a knife fight. Despite her bound wrists, she reached with both hands for her blade, the one her brother, a decorated veteran, had trained her so well with, only to find it wasn't there.

Her opponent held one arm against her breastbone, and the other went to his belt. "Looking for this?" He held her knife up with a dark smirk.

Naomi froze. Adrenaline gripped her hard and fast. She immediately recognized the Ka-Bar her brother had given her. Jacob still held loyalty to the brand from when he'd been in the Marines. With it, she held her own, thanks to Jacob's training, but without...

Her heart thumped upward into her throat like a jack-rabbit. Her captor's face hovered inches over hers, those wolf eyes staring at her with such intensity that it paralyzed her. Every inch of her burned with awareness at how close he was, that if he turned into a wolf again, he could kill her with ease with one bite of his powerful jaws.

This was one fight Naomi knew she wouldn't win.

<hr />

"You killed my sheep." The sharp words bit through the night air.

Wes stared down at the human woman beneath him. Their noses were close to touching, and his body pinned her to the ground, yet the accusation fell from her lips without so much as an ounce of fear in her voice. He had no idea what she was talking about.

Focusing on the words proved difficult. Hard as he tried, his thoughts gravitated to the feel of her. How long had it been since he'd felt a woman beneath him? Small, taut breasts pushed tight against his chest, leading to a soft, feminine stomach that tapered into full hips.

As if the curves of her against him weren't doing enough funny things to his head, he breathed in the deep scent of her as his eyes scanned the black coils of hair across her shoulders. His head clouded with the way her delicious smell tantalized his nose. Fresh-cut grass, baled hay, the open air, and the subtle smell of bitterroot flowers. They grew wild across the mountain plains in these parts.

His cock had immediately responded. He'd been ignoring the blood flowing further south in his body all evening, an unfortunate male side effect of adrenaline and battle. Or fortunate, depending on how he looked at it. But up this close and personal to her, the ache in his dick couldn't be ignored.

What was wrong with him? She'd pointed a gun at his head. Had that shotgun not been nearly as big as she was, she'd have blown his arm off. And now his body responded to her like this?

He knew he was one sick bastard, but it was still jacked up.

Until her words interrupted, he'd been so focused on the plump curve of her lips that he'd almost lost himself and kissed her.

"You slaughtered my livestock." Her voice was feminine but deep in a way that stirred low in his belly. To his ears, the noise sounded incredibly human and unintimidating, yet it raised his hackles. For a woman whose life he'd spared, then saved from the hands of the Wild Eight soon to be prowling her lands, her thanks had been shooting at him and now blaming him for petty ranch theft.

"I didn't kill your livestock." Slowly, he pushed into a plank position above her, then stood. He'd take his chance with her running again if it meant escaping the hazy fog her scent flooded over his brain. He tried not to notice the sudden chill down his front or the way his cock ached for the return of her sweet body heat against him.

She scrambled to her feet with some difficulty, considering her hands remained bound. Her full lips pulled into a scowl. "Evidence says otherwise. After all, *you* were the one in the trap not far from the sheep's pen. Not to mention I smelled it on you just now."

"Trust me, sweetheart, if I wanted a mutton steak, I'd take a chomp out of my pack's flock." He didn't know which made him bristle more: the accusation that he'd murdered her flock, or her implication that he smelled like the inside of a damn barn. Which he likely *did* at the moment, considering he'd spent the morning herding a couple hundred of the Grey Wolf calves into the barn so his packmembers could begin preparing to take them to market soon, but that was beside the point. "If it's the blood you're referring to, that's the blood of my enemies. Not your precious lambs."

She struggled with the bindings at her wrists, attempting to remove them but with no luck. "I won't take your word for it."

"You're a feisty one, huh?" He shook his head. What the hell had he gotten himself into? She was a pistol, and he *liked* irritating her. Every time those gorgeous brown eyes blazed in challenge, his head filled with naughty thoughts. He'd always had far too much appreciation for feisty women.

"If you wanted cooperation, maybe you shouldn't have abducted me from my pasture."

"You had a gun to my head," he said.

"You ate Lambie," she countered.

When the frustration on his face made it clear that he had no clue what she was blabbering on about, she sighed. "My sheep," she elaborated. "A wolf has been killing them. I can tell from the tracks left behind. My guess is that's why I caught you in the trap my idiot brother set."

"You name your livestock?" His gaze swept over her. From her faded jeans, cowgirl boots, and worn, overlaid suede jacket, she looked as if she knew her way around the ranchlands. Her dark hair and skin suggested she was Native American. Thanks to the language she'd muttered earlier, and considering their proximity to the reservation, he guessed Crow tribe. Crow Agency was only a short drive from here.

"Just one: the sheep that you slaughtered two weeks ago. His name was Lambie, and he was a sweet, gentle ram. My father gave him to me when I was ten. The only thing worse would've been if you killed our family ranch dog, Blue. You're lucky he's with my brother right now, or he would have taken a good chunk out of one of your back legs."

Wes stared openmouthed at the woman before him. He wasn't even sure where to begin. Who the hell did she think she was, Little Bo-Peep? Call him ignorant, but as far as he knew, no rancher in their right mind named their flock like they were house pets.

When he'd been stuck in her trap in wolf form and she'd stared down at him, apologizing for holding her gun on him, he'd imagined the Wild Eight wolves turning around in search of him but instead finding her, and something inside him had snapped. In that moment, he'd been back *there* again. The memory shook him as he imagined himself in that godforsaken bedroom, blood dripping from him and an innocent woman…

He closed his eyes and released a long exhale. He hadn't been able to bear the thought.

So he'd shifted in front of her. *Pack law be damned.* He'd done it both because he had no other way to escape the trap he'd been locked in—not without opposable thumbs—and also to warn her. The Wild Eight were bound to circle back looking for him, and with their blood pulsing from the night's battles, if she managed to get in their way, an innocent human female like her would serve as nothing more than a bloody diversion to them. He knew he and the woman weren't safe. Not even now that they were hidden in the forests of the Grey Wolves' territory again.

She was a stranger to him, but he'd be damned if he'd allow those monsters to kill another innocent. Though he *should* have taken her life as pack law dictated when she'd lain passed out in front of him, he couldn't bring himself to kill an innocent. Not again.

If he'd thought he'd had his ass in a sling before this, Maverick was going to lose his shit when he brought this woman back to Wolf Pack Run with him. But he wasn't allowing her to walk free. Not by a long shot.

Finally, he managed to find his words. "What's your name?"

She watched him with wary eyes, sinking into the shadow of a towering pine as if that would shield her from him. "Naomi K. Evans."

"What's the K stand for?" He couldn't help but ask. She'd offered the initial after all.

"It stands for Kitty." She shrugged a pair of slender shoulders. "My parents were *Gunsmoke* fans."

Naomi Kitty Evans? He lifted an eyebrow.

"Well, *Miss Kitty*," he chuckled. "I didn't kill your damn sheep."

"You try having several of your livestock maimed and exsanguinated, then find some freak wolf-man in your pasture and see if you believe he's innocent."

Wes froze. He ignored the freak wolf-man remark in favor of more pressing issues. "Exsanguinated? You mean bled dry?"

"That's what exsanguinated means," she quipped.

He grumbled. He knew damn well what it meant. "I didn't kill your sheep," he repeated.

Though he had a sudden suspicion of who, or more accurately *what*, might have. Tonight was getting worse by the second. If they expected to live through the night, they needed to hunker down—and fast.

"Sure." Her voice was doubtful. "And what else were you doing on my land?"

"Chasing other wolves."

At this, she eyed the tree line as if they would spring forth from the branches at any moment. It was a very real possibility. She inched farther toward the pines. The moonlight cast shadows on her face. A faint spark of hope glimmered on her pretty features.

"If that's the case, you can give me back my blade

and let me go. I need to get back to my ranch. You haven't wronged me, and I haven't wronged you…" Her eyes fell to the wound on his shoulder and arm. "At least not intentionally. We can call this a truce."

Black Jack let out a flustered huff, and Naomi jumped at the sudden noise. Wes watched her with careful eyes. Despite her outward bravado, she was more terrified than she was letting on, which meant this little human woman wasn't reckless and strange—she was brave.

He shook his head. "I can't let you do that. We need to get to the nearest shelter, and fast. If you value your life, you'll come with me." When she didn't answer, he sighed. "We'll get you back to your ranch as soon as possible, but there are other wolves prowling all over these mountains tonight. Soon enough, they'll be at your ranch, too, and believe me when I say they won't show you so much kindness."

"I wouldn't call it kind—"

"Get on the damn horse, woman!" he ordered.

She was impossible.

When she still didn't move, he allowed his eyes to flash to his wolf's. He hoped a little reminder of his true nature would force her to think about the threat the other wolves had posed to her. He meant to keep her safe from them, protected.

In response, she trudged toward Black Jack. That was more like it.

Stepping toward her, Wes unknotted the rope he'd used to tie her wrists, but touching her forced him to pause. She quivered beneath his hands. *Shit*.

When she moved to pull away, he captured her hands in his, cradling them. He rubbed his thumb in a gentle circle over her skin to soothe her, the same movement that had served him behind the ears of many a scared, skittish horse.

"For tonight, you're safe as long as you're with me." He aimed for a whisper, but it was more of a growl.

An emotion he couldn't recognize flared behind her dark-brown irises. The color was so dark, they were almost obsidian in the moonlight. She snatched her hands away as if he'd wounded her. But the pain was his. He felt the pain of her fear, her blatant rejection of his attempt at kindness, in his chest. She thought he was a monster, and the reminder of his true identity seared through him. He would never escape the truth of his past.

Wes Calhoun, nefarious supernatural outlaw and former packmaster of the Wild Eight. He'd been their leader. The worst monster of them all. For years, he'd shed blood without remorse, killed without consequence, and hadn't regretted it for a second.

He'd do well to remember that.

With one last reluctant look in his direction, she turned to climb onto Black Jack, trembling. She still put on a brave face, but there was no missing her terror.

Better terrified than dead. Even if she was somehow entangled with the Wild Eight and the vampires. He pushed the feeling aside and breathed in the deep scent of Naomi's hair. Without a doubt, she was scared of him. He licked his chapped lips as he offered her a leg up in place of the absent stirrup.

No more than he was of her.

Chapter 3

A STRONG HAND GRIPPED NAOMI AND PULLED HER BACK.
She found herself facing her captor. She'd been about to
climb on the "damn horse" with his aid when suddenly,
he'd yanked her back again. He signaled the horse with a
hand gesture, and immediately, the beast reared up. Her
shotgun fell from its perch on the horse's back and into
a nearby bush. The dark horse galloped at full speed into
the forest, leaving them stranded on the mountainside.

"What are you—?"

Her captor clapped a hand over her mouth. Something
dangerous flared in those golden wolf eyes. She started
to swat away his hand, but then she heard it.

A chilling howl echoed throughout the forest, confirming her worst fear.

Wolves. And from the warning gleam in his eye…
more wolves like him.

Before she could wriggle free, he scooped both arms
around her, one bracing her back and the other beneath
her behind. Sweeping her into his arms with ease, within
seconds, he'd carried her several feet toward an oak and
pressed her back roughly against a large, hollowed-out
depression in the bark. His movements were swift and
gentle but belied by his firm and unyielding strength. He
hoisted her leg around his waist, one large hand cupping
her ass as he pressed ever closer, both stopping her from
running and pinning her with the muscled weight of his

body. Pushed this flat against the inside of the hollowed tree and shaded from moonlight by its tremendous shadow, they were hidden from view.

He pulled her knife from his belt. She stiffened, but immediately, he pressed the hilt of the Ka-Bar into her hand. Her fingers eagerly tightened around the grip. But he must have felt her tense, because he chose that moment to meet her gaze head-on again. She wasn't sure what she saw in the depths of his golden wolf eyes, but it spoke volumes, in the way only the eyes of an animal seemed to be able to communicate straight to the soul. He held her gaze with such a sure, steady confidence, it was as if he'd whispered: *I'll protect you. You have my word.*

Slowly, she nodded. She couldn't help but trust him. In a single look, he'd confirmed what the more pragmatic part of her mind had already suspected—if he'd wanted to hurt her, he would have by now. He'd had more than ample opportunity. Granted, he had rushed her, which had caused her to fall, consequently knocking her out before he'd dragged her up the mountainside on the back of his horse, but she had drawn a shotgun on him.

Trusting her instincts, she relaxed into him. They were so close that they were pressed flush against each other. In the silence and darkness engulfing them, as she listened for the slightest noise with a heady mixture of adrenaline and fear, her senses came alive. Every touch, every sensation heightened. She could feel every slow breath he drew as the corded muscles of his chest moved against her breasts, the steady beat of his heart, and the warmth of his hips pinning her and creating a delicious pressure between her legs.

It'd been years since a man had held her in an embrace

like this. Clouds shifted until a moonbeam streamed into
their hidden cove within the tree. They were so close
together in the gentle moonlight that she saw the planes
of his bare chest clearly. All thick, rounded muscle and
sinew. The thin, silvery scars of past battles, though ini-
tially alarming, served to make him all the more rugged
and manly. One particular specimen marred the skin
of his right pectoral in a jagged gash. With her hands
braced upon his naked chest, her fingers itched to reach
out and touch the puckered flesh, to feel the warm heat
beneath her palms.

His skin was so warm that she felt as if she'd been
wrapped in the blissful embrace of a heated blanket on a
cold winter's day, a cup of steaming cocoa in her hands.
The wide breadth of his shoulders dwarfed her with
their impressive size. She wasn't a rail of a woman. She
sported her fair share of healthy curves. Curves his large
hands seemed more than capable of handling and holding with ease. With acute awareness, she felt his palm
still bracing the curve of her bottom. She fit within his
hand as if she'd been made for him.

He must have been aware of it, too. As the minutes
stretched on, the rock-hard length of his erection grew
and strained against the fabric of his jeans, rubbing
against her center. The sweet, aching pressure softened
her cleft until she felt herself slicken. His nostrils flared,
and briefly, she found herself wondering if he smelled
the wet heat between her legs with his wolflike senses.

The feel of him pressed against her tantalized her, but
it was the heat in his gaze that drew her in. Those golden
wolf eyes, so animal in appearance, yet full of human
knowing. They bored into her with stunning intensity

as he drew closer. The tip of his nose brushed against hers. Their lips were so close, they breathed the same air between them, the heat of their breath swirling in the cold autumn air.

Slowly, he brought his palm up to cup her cheek. His fingers splayed open, and the rough pad of his thumb tugged gently at the skin of her lower lip.

Something flickered in his dark gaze, something raw, animal, hungry. It roped her in, making her forget all reservation and filling her with so much desire, it was near criminal. Instinctually, she leaned in.

And that was all the encouragement he needed.

His mouth claimed hers in a kiss that was as brazen and unforgiving, as terrifying and tantalizing as the electricity between them. She fell into the destruction before her, into him and the carnal desire between them that she knew would tear her to pieces even as the pleasure put her back together again. He parted her lips, meeting not even a hint of resistance from her. He was inside her then, his tongue, his kiss, his taste consuming her until there was nothing but him. The woodsy scent of his skin filled her nose. The heavy, muscled weight of him pressed against her breasts and center, heavy and swollen with need...and the taste of him. Man, the taste of his kiss. He tasted like hot apple cider, tangy with a hint of masculine spice that warmed her from the inside out.

And she couldn't get enough.

In an instant, something told her she couldn't have stopped the electricity between them even if she wanted to. It was as if some gravitational force pulled them together, so strong and ruthless, she was helpless to fight against it. The ache between her legs grew, his erection still pressing against her center. Without thinking, she writhed beneath him. A purring growl rumbled deep in his throat. That noise alone would leave her wanting for days.

He ground against her, the aching bead of her clit hardening with each delicious, torturous movement. She whimpered and moaned in pleasure, the sounds stifled only by his kiss. That unforgiving, relentless, unstoppable kiss. She couldn't remember a time in her life when a kiss had ever felt anything close to this.

The pressure built. Her nipples tightened and her breasts grew heavy as she continued to melt into him. Just when she felt certain she would shatter to pieces in his arms, suddenly, he froze, his lips lingering in a gentle brush against hers.

Her heart stopped. She heard it, too.

A rustling near the clearing. A jolt of fear shot through her, drowning out her arousal.

Then a voice. "The horse's scent goes that way. Let's go."

The sound of the voice, no matter how human, chilled her to the bone. Thank goodness. He'd sent the horse away to lead the others off their trail.

More rustling, followed by the sound of several sets of paws hitting the ground. Then the forest fell silent again. Yet still they waited. With the heat between them deadened by fear, the minutes dragged on at a snail's pace.

Finally, he released her. "They're gone," he whispered. "I'll get Black Jack. He'll have rounded back to throw them off his scent by now. Stay here." He shifted to wolf form, his blue jeans dropping to the ground, before she could tell him there was no way in hell he was leaving her alone in the trunk of this tree. Quickly, he slunk off into the darkness. She remained where she stood, still as a statue and feeling every bit the sitting duck.

Finally, when she felt certain he wasn't returning at any moment, she inched out of hiding. If she climbed the tree, she'd be safer than tucked away in the rotted-out part of the oak's trunk. She retrieved her father's old shotgun from the bushes where it had fallen and propped it against the tree base. Just as Naomi began to feel her way around the edge of the trunk for a place to grip onto, a menacing growl sounded at her back.

She twisted toward the sound, grabbing and lifting the shotgun to her shoulder. Her heart stopped, and she struggled to breathe. A wolf equal in size and stature to her captor emerged from the darkness. She knew immediately it wasn't him from the ferocious look on its face and the lack of the distinctive black markings around its neck. Sharp fangs dripping with saliva glinted in the moonlight.

Slowly, she inched away into the shadows, gun braced in challenge.

The wolf prowled closer, refusing to retreat. *Shit*. She had no choice.

The shotgun kicked against her shoulder as she fired a warning shot at its paws. Dust flew everywhere. The buckshot hitting the ground clouded the air with dirt. But the wolf didn't retreat as she'd anticipated.

It lunged.

A pair of heavy paws hit Naomi's shoulders. The wind flew from her lungs. She slumped backward into the base of the tree trunk. Pain seared through her as the animal's claws ripped into her skin like tissue paper.

Holding the shotgun in front of her like a shield, she struggled against the wolf. It thrashed and snarled above her, fighting to push past the gun at its throat.

Blood trickled down her shoulder. Spittle from the beast's snapping jaws dripped into her face. It was only inches away from her.

If only she could reach her knife…

She screamed, though she knew no one heard her. *Shit*. She couldn't hold on much longer. Her muscles burned with exertion as her strength wavered.

Just as her arms gave, the weight of the wolf on her chest lifted with a sudden jolt. Renewed sounds of fighting followed. Flesh tearing. Jaws snapping. Naomi scrambled over the cold ground into a sitting position, aiming her shotgun in front of her.

But she didn't need it.

Her captor had returned. Faced against the wolf that had been on her chest only moments earlier, he stood directly in front of her. He held a protective stance—tail raised and bristled with legs spread wide, teeth bared in warning—as if he were guarding a mate.

Each time the attacking wolf moved closer, her guardian advanced. Slowly, the beasts squared off in a careful killing dance. Step for step. Until finally, her guardian lunged.

The two wolves collided in an all-out brawl. Teeth tore into fur and bone. Within seconds, her guardian had the other wolf pinned. He ripped into the furry flesh of his opponent's throat, striking the final blow. His back heaved with the weight of his kill. The fog of his heated breath in the cold night air twisted in a murky cloud around his face. Blood dripped from his muzzle.

But he had won...

Naomi scrambled to her feet, gun lowered at her side. Her guardian—not her *captor* now—was a terrifying, beautiful sight to behold. Bathed in the moonlight, his grey fur reflected silver with tufts of black surrounding his face and haunches. Through the darkness, the blood on his muzzle appeared near black as well. The large beast loomed over the carcass of his opponent with a fierce, predatory grace. He was breathtaking.

And he had saved her life...

"Thank you," she whispered, her words releasing on an exhale.

The wolf's golden eyes held her gaze for a prolonged moment. He trotted into the shadows. When he returned, human, his jeans hung low on his waist, he grabbed her wrist and pulled her toward his horse.

"We need to get out of here *now*," he warned.

This time, without hesitation, she got on the damn horse.

"For tonight, this is camp."

Black Jack's silky mane whipped about in the breeze as Wes led him into the Grey Wolf quartering stable. He closed the door shut behind them, sealing out the whistling autumn wind. He patted the large steed on its hindquarters. Tucked away in the mountainside, the stable was a far cry from the state-of-the-art buildings of their ranch at Wolf Pack Run, but it would do for now. The massive cow-calf operation at Wolf Pack Run spread over more than 125 acres and boasted more than its fair share of modern amenities, but there was no way he and Naomi could safely reach the main compound tonight.

He'd need to treat her wounds—and his own—but first, he'd secure their lodgings for the night. It was doubtful, *highly* doubtful, a member of the Wild Eight would be so brazen as to track this far onto Grey Wolf lands, and Wes had purposely taken Black Jack into the knee-high waters of the Shield River to better eradicate their trail, but he wouldn't take any chances.

Making quick work of securing the place, Wes barred the stable door, then retrieved his revolver, her rifle, and her knife from his saddlebag. He trusted they would know if the Wild Eight approached. Black Jack was as good a watchdog as any. Wes placed the weapons within arm's length of where he intended to curl up on the floor and sleep once he'd tended to her injuries. No matter how minor, they'd need to be cleaned to prevent infection. Humans, he knew, were fragile.

Clicking on a row of nearby heat lamps to give some light and warmth, he turned and surveyed the sight before him. The ambient light cast a soft, fireside glow upon the stone floor and iron stall gates. The scent of manure and saddle polish hung heavy in the air.

Black Jack trotted to the far end of the small five-stall row. Sniffing each pen, Black Jack took his time picking out his favorite space, since he was the only horse currently putting the stalls to use. When he'd made his selection, he nudged the gate open, moving past the terrified human woman shivering in the center of the stall block.

Damn, if this night hadn't gone straight to hell in a handbasket…

Wes had attempted to assess Naomi's injuries as he'd ridden hell-for-leather. The scent of her blood had been sharp in his sinuses, but none of her wounds had appeared critical. She'd been scratched across her left shoulder, and there was one gash in particular that made him want to resurrect that Wild Eight scum just to tear out his throat all over again. But overall, she seemed okay.

Though he'd gone and kissed her. He'd lost himself in the moment and had been drawn in by their closeness. She'd leaned in to him, melting against him in a way that had nearly undone him. That kiss alone had sparked some sort of fire in his chest that he couldn't even begin to address. Not now.

He watched as her eyes darted around the stable with a confused, hazy gaze. Wes had seen that distant look before in many men post-battle. Their eyes glazed like someone had placed a dark filter over the world around them, obscuring reality from their reach until all they saw was a world haunted with the worst of their ghosts. Traumatic shock.

Wes didn't blame her. That Wild Eight member had aimed to kill her. He didn't want to think about what might have happened if he'd not circled back to her when he did. Her wounds were superficial but likely painful nonetheless. He should have known better than to leave her alone, even armed with the shotgun.

He'd intended to take her to the safety of Wolf Pack Run, but after their fight with the Wild Eight wolf in the clearing, he hadn't wanted to gamble his chances on her life. With so many Wild Eight running loose in the Grey Wolf packlands tonight and Black Jack burdened by two riders—thus making Wolf Pack Run another several hours' ride—he'd thought it best they hunker down until morning. The Grey Wolves maintained several spare quartering stables throughout their lands, this being the closest to Naomi's ranchland and their previous location. It was a far cry from safe with the Wild Eight still roaming the forest, but it was a preferable alternative to continuing on through the woods and risking further assault.

Crossing the stable to Black Jack's pen, Wes retrieved a flask of whiskey and a spare clean shirt he kept there. Hardly antiseptic and gauze, but for now, it would have to do. He exited Black Jack's stall, coming to stand before her. As she stared up at him with those wide brown eyes, he watched her struggle with her words, opening and closing her mouth several times before finally pointing toward him, then the stable door. "So you are a… And that other wolf was a.…" She stammered until her voice trailed off.

"Werewolf," he offered. And yes, she was *clearly* in shock, because they had covered this already. He crouched beside her, eyes darting to her shoulder to indicate the scratches there. "May I?"

Slowly, she nodded. She stared off into the ether, her eyes still glassy. "Werewolves…are…real." She spoke each word with careful precision, testing the weight of them on her tongue.

"We are. Pretty much any supernatural critter you can think of is real. But all you need to worry about up in these mountains are shifters." Ride northeast into Billings, and that was a whole different matter. But he decided he wouldn't spring that on her, at least not tonight. He poured some of the whiskey onto the clean T-shirt. "This'll hurt," he warned.

"Shifters?"

Moving with careful precision so as not to scare her, he eased the material onto the cuts. She released a sharp hiss. He hated to hurt her. Though the wounds were superficial and would heal within a week or two at most, he didn't want to cause her discomfort.

"Like me," he answered. He made a circle with his finger to indicate the surrounding mountain ranges. "There are seven legitimate shifter packs throughout the state. The foothills of the Beartooth Mountains, where our ranch begins, is the entry into Grey Wolf territory. Our land is here in the foothills, throughout the Custer Gallatin National Forest and the Absarokas, and extends outward all the way to various parts of western Montana. Out west, there are dozens of other subpacks among those lands, both Grey Wolf subpacks and the other shifter packs...grizzlies, black bears, bobcats, lynx, mountain lions, and coyotes." He dabbed the drying blood away from her skin, leaving the surrounding skin a blushed shade of pink.

She released a long, shaky breath. It shouldn't have, but the sound tugged at his loins. He wondered if she'd make the same sound when she...

"You mean to tell me all the wildlife in Montana are actually part human?" She looked down the row at Black Jack with growing horror spreading across her features.

Wes chuckled. "No. But there's a fair few of us. Mostly apex predators." He nodded to the now-cleaned wound on her shoulder. "Probably best to let that heal in the open air. Covering it will only prolong the process."

She continued to watch Black Jack, who paced around in his stall as if the space thoroughly displeased him. Nothing but a fresh mucked stall with brand-new hay every day would do for the mustang. Spoiled bastard that he was.

Pocketing the flask and tucking an edge of the shirt

so it hung from the back pocket of his jeans, Wes sauntered over to Black Jack's pen. Snatching a brush off a nearby storage shelf, he tossed it about in his hands. "Black Jack here ain't nothin' but a wild mustang. I'd say I broke him myself, but that'd be a bold-faced lie. He may allow me to ride him, but he has a mind of his own and only listens when he damn well chooses. He's hardly obedient." He clicked his tongue, urging Black Jack over to the edge of the stall gate.

In response, the horse snapped at Wes's fingers, clearly fuming about his less-than-desirable sleeping arrangement. Wes tore his hand away and frowned at the beast before he glanced back toward Naomi. She watched the exchange with intrigued eyes, the shock of battle beginning to dissipate.

"He'd likely be nicer to you." Wes extended a hand toward her. "It might calm you both." And at this rate, he needed to find some way to help calm her enough so they both managed some sleep. Otherwise, he and this slight little human were in for one long night.

Considering the heat that had passed between them in the clearing, he had an idea or two about what indulging his urges might entail. A good, honest roll in the hay. He smirked at the euphemism. He'd lay out a saddle blanket, then strip her of her clothes, using nothing but his body to keep her warm. He imagined spreading her legs wide before him and pleasuring her with his mouth until it wasn't fear that made her tremble and cry out. He reckoned she'd taste as delicious as she smelled, and that would only be the beginning of his fun. That one flicker of her desire that he'd caught in the clearing wasn't nearly enough. He would take his time and enjoy every second of savoring her…

But beautiful and tempting as she was, and as much as his lower half protested otherwise, he wasn't about to take advantage of her. That kiss had been a mistake. She was clearly still in shock. Further, Grey Wolf Pack law strictly forbid human-werewolf relationships, both for the pack's protection and to maintain the purity of their shifter bloodlines. Not that he'd ever been one to listen to Maverick's rules—tonight being clear evidence of that—but considering the mess he'd gotten himself into, that particular prospect would only make a bad situation even worse.

A grim shroud of emotion settled over him at the thought.

Distance was best for both their sakes.

For a long moment, she eyed his extended hand, until finally, she reached out and took it. The touch sent a jolt of electricity through his skin, as if his arm were being charged by a live wire. He ignored the temptation of the feeling and led her in front of Black Jack's stall, passing her the brush.

"He'll be more amiable to you, stubborn brute that he is. He still hasn't gotten over having a wolf as a rider." Wes shrugged. "He comes by it honestly. I'm just as stubborn."

At that, Naomi's full lips curved into a small, Mona Lisa smile. She reached her hand out toward Black Jack, who sniffed and nibbled his wet lips over her knuckles, checking if she had any food, before he stepped forward, offering his large head and the side of his massive neck to her. Wes watched as she brushed her hands through the dark horse's mane. With each brush stroke, they both visibly relaxed, the weight of the evening lifting from them.

She was a tried-and-true cowgirl, alright, looking suddenly very much at home in the warm glow of the stable as she brushed through Black Jack's mane. Wes leaned back against the next stall over and watched.

She was trouble. Even his damn horse liked her.

When Black Jack had finally gotten his fill of attention, he flicked his dark tail and turned his large rump directly toward Naomi, preparing to do his business.

"Have some manners," Wes grumbled at the horse.

"I've mucked up my fair share of manure. I'm no stranger to it." Naomi smiled and handed the brush back to him. As she did, her eyes caught on the wounds at his shoulder, and then her gaze trailed to his forearm as if she were just remembering he'd been hurt, too. "Oh no. Your injuries are far worse! I shouldn't have let you care for me when you were injured yourself. Here, let me—"

He shook his head. "We heal quickly. You don't have to—"

She'd tugged the shirt from his back pocket before he finished his sentence. She extended her hand for the flask tucked in his other pocket. Reluctantly, he passed it over to her. From the intent look in her eyes, it was clear she wasn't going to take no for an answer. He didn't have the heart to tell her that the risk of infection for werewolves was extremely low. Their bodies healed with what humans would consider miraculous ability, both inside and out.

She pointed to where he'd set the weapons on the floor, indicating he should sit.

He flashed her a smirk and touched his forehead to feign the tip of his cowboy hat. "Yes, ma'am."

She smiled, coy and sweet. Every bit the sweet, fragile human woman she was. It softened his hard heart far more than it should have.

He took a seat where she'd indicated. Moments later, she sat down beside him, pouring the whiskey on a new, fresh section of the T-shirt.

Her buckshot had mostly missed him, but one of the pellets had pierced the soft junction of tissue between his shoulder blade and his collarbone. That held little consequence, compared to how the jagged teeth of the wolf trap had pierced his forearm. But with the rate at which he healed, it was already beginning to scab over.

She turned toward him. Bracing a hand on his bicep, she held herself steady as she dabbed the alcohol-soaked T-shirt over his skin. Her eyes darted to his face, searching for a hint of pain, but he didn't show her any. Up this close, the scent of her overwhelmed him in the best of ways. He smelled, tasted nothing else. His eyes transitioned to his wolf's without his consent.

A sharp little intake of breath escaped her lips as she tore her gaze away. He wondered briefly if she'd seen the heat in his eyes, seen what her proximity did to him.

"Why here?" she asked, nodding to the door.

From the sudden change in subject, he sensed she'd seen every bit of what she did to him. Yet she didn't retreat. He watched her as she worked, rubbing the dried blood away. "Well, I figured sleeping in a spare stable was better than the cold gro—"

She shook her head. "No. I mean why do so many shifters make their homes here? Because western

Montana is a natural habitat for the atypical Northern Rocky Mountain wolf? Because of the proximity to Yellowstone down in Wyoming?"

"That and force of habit. We've been here for centuries."

"Centuries." She rubbed gentle circles at the edges of the wound and down lower onto his chest, cleaning the dried blood away. His cock stiffened with each movement of her palm drawing closer to the steady beat of his heart.

He tore his gaze from her and focused on a spot on Black Jack's stall to distract himself while she worked. If he didn't look away now, he'd do something they both might regret in the morning, sweet as it would be. He chanced a look at her again. She chewed her lip in fascinated interest. Damn if he didn't long to nibble on that himself.

"And your pack is…?"

"The Grey Wolves," he supplied.

To this day, it felt strange on his tongue. Though they *were* now his pack, he still felt like an outsider, and his past still haunted him. When he'd joined the pack, Maverick had made him swear his life with the Wild Eight was behind him. Wes had kept that word and never returned to his birth pack, and the Grey Wolves had accepted his surrender without further condition. But as hard as he tried, he couldn't escape himself. He'd always be Wes Calhoun, the man his current packmates had once sworn as their enemy.

"So why did that other wolf attack us? It was a grey wolf, too. Wouldn't it be your packmate?" She found the last clean section of the shirt and poured the remaining whiskey over it.

Wes shook his head. "By species, yes, but it wasn't from the Grey Wolf Pack. That was a Wild Eight wolf. They're the Grey Wolves' enemies."

"If they're werewolves, too, and you're the same species of wolf, why are they your enemies?"

"We likely wouldn't be if it wasn't for humans and their damn need to control everything."

She paused. "You mean to tell me I'm not the only human who knows of your existence?"

"No, you're not." Though outside the Execution Underground, she was likely one of the few. The human-run clandestine organization was into some serious Area 51 high-level secrecy shit. All the way up into the highest echelons of the government. "But if you hadn't set that trap, you wouldn't be here."

"My brother set it, not me." She clutched his hand in her own, holding his forearm steady.

He raised an eyebrow.

"I was trying to find a more peaceful solution. My brother has different ideas about how to run the ranch. We have an average-size cow-calf operation. Mostly run by me with the occasional help of a few hired ranch hands. It was our father's, and my brother is still pissed our dad left me in charge. He's a born-and-bred cowboy."

Wes was only vaguely aware of her words or the burning sensation of the alcohol over his wound. His focus zeroed in on the feeling of her palm in his. When was the last time he could honestly say he'd just held a woman's hand in his? The sweet, supple softness of her skin against his was doing unimaginable things to his head.

Her eyes darted to Black Jack again, who had taken

to kicking all of his hay to one side of his stall. "So the other humans. Who are they?"

Wes blinked several times as he gathered his thoughts about him. "You sure are full of questions."

"You try being abducted from your pasture by a man who is part beast and tell me you wouldn't have questions," she challenged with a hint of a smile tugging at her mouth.

If he was honest, something about her sass heated him to frustration—and far baser urges. It involved a gentle snap from one of those riding crops hanging on the wall, and that round ass bent bare before him. The thought made him instantly hard again. *Damn it*.

Cooped up in this stable so close to her, his sensitive nose latched onto her scent like a lodestone. He blew out a long sigh. *Down, killer*.

"There's an organization called the Execution Underground," he answered. "It's an elite group of humans who hunt supernatural creatures like us. They do so under the guise of protecting humanity." Having come over with the Europeans in the 1600s, the human hunters never hesitated to kill their kind if and when it suited them.

"And what do they have to do with this?" She stroked the material over his forearm. She must have assumed the strain in his voice to be from the wound.

"They place rules, regulations on supernaturals, on packs like us. Some of us want to cooperate to keep the peace, like the Grey Wolves. Others don't want to roll over and play dead without a fight."

"Like the Wild Eight?"

He gripped her hand tighter, but not for the reasons

she seemed to think. "Yeah, that's what they say they're about: freedom for shifters. But they're really no better than a well-organized street gang. They only look out for their own interests. They cause trouble that eventually comes down on the rest of us." He saw that now in a way he hadn't years earlier. The way the actions of the few affected the many. "And they won't stop until they claim my life."

Her eyes grew wide. "You must have done something to really piss them off then."

"You could say that." That was all he intended to share on the topic. "All you really need to know is that for tonight, you're safe with me. I won't let anyone harm you, and once this blows over, we'll get you back to your ranch as soon as possible." With one last squeeze of her gentle hand, he forced himself to pull away from her. Any more of this, and he wouldn't trust his better judgment to hold him back.

Pushing to his feet again, he gathered a saddle blanket from the storage shelf and tossed it to her. She caught it and stood, stepping away from where she'd sat beside him. He returned to the spot he'd claimed as she crossed to the other side of the stable. "Now, unless you plan to be running on little more than air in the morning, I suggest you get some sleep."

Chapter 4

THERE WAS NO WAY IN HELL SHE WAS GOING TO SLEEP.
Naomi watched as he latched Black Jack's stall closed
and moved to turn on another row of nearby heat lamps.
Whether the man was her captor or guardian or a bit of
both, she wasn't sure. Especially after that kiss he'd laid
on her, though she was fighting hard not to think about it.

The lamps cast an orange shadow, part warm glow
and part darkness. The color highlighted the golden
undertones of his skin, showing where he'd been kissed
by the sun on more than one occasion. It made the white
slashes of the scars across his chest look even more ferocious. Naomi imagined he spent a fair amount of time
out in nature. Even in human form, he seemed to belong
there among the trees and the mountain foliage and the
rushing streams. The thick muscles of his body and that
suntanned skin spoke of long days on a farm or ranch
like her own. She'd inferred as much when he'd referred
to his flock, though she'd yet to learn how a werewolf
could live like a born-and-bred cowboy.

Black Jack watched the man, his dark, orb-like eyes
both resigned and slightly annoyed. As her captor moved
around the stable, plugging in all the heat lamps in hope
of raising the freezing temperature of the space even a
degree or two, his movement was somehow languid,
predatory, and she was surprised it didn't alarm or upset
his horse more than it did.

"You're an alpha." The words toppled from her lips before she stopped herself.

He turned toward her and raised a blond eyebrow.

"Call it a hunch," she said.

"You're a quick study."

She shrugged. "I'm a biologist."

His cold eyes met hers. In this light, she'd yet to see their color now that he stared back at her with a human's gaze, not a wolf's.

"A rancher biologist?" A smirk curled his lips.

She held those mysterious eyes without fear. Probably not her smartest idea to hold the gaze of an alpha wolf. That signified challenge, but she wasn't about to be mistaken as weak. "Former biologist, by trade anyway."

He hooked his thumbs through the loops of those damn jeans. The thin trail of blond hair at his navel that led further south to his...

Well, for her hormones, apparently all it took was saving her life, an unexpected kiss, and hauling her off like some sort of wolf caveman to turn her into an adventurous vixen. Cross-species mating be damned. She'd never thought herself the type to be interested in dark and mysterious, yet here she was, her nipples tight at the thought of how he'd felt above her, against the oak tree, then when she was nestled in his lap atop that wild mustang. She still didn't even know his name.

But she supposed it *had* been a long time. Her last encounter with a man had been with David Lawrence, the PE teacher, when she'd been teaching biology on the res several years ago. Before her father's passing, before she'd taken over the ranch. Sparks hadn't flown, and needless to say, it was a one-time occasion she hadn't been looking to repeat. She had the feeling that wouldn't be the case with a man like the one before her.

"Around these parts?" He quirked a blond eyebrow in her direction.

She gathered the impression that the thought of her studying wildlife like him amused him.

"Partially. I went to California for my career briefly. It's a more biologically diverse landscape than here." She shrugged. It was a clear attempt to brush him off, but she could tell he wasn't buying it.

"And?" He leaned against one of the stalls. "What had you runnin' away from these mountains aside from *biological diversity*?" he mocked.

He'd caught her fib. She knew what he was thinking. Montana—and the Beartooth and Absaroka Mountains near Yellowstone, in particular—could hardly be described as anything other than biologically diverse.

"I answered your questions. You answer mine. Fair is fair, Miss Kitty."

She frowned at the awful nickname and crossed her arms over her chest. "Why do you assume I was running?"

"People come up to these mountains to get away from their lives. Tourists from around the world pay good money to spend time on these lands, to get a little taste of playing cowboy on a ranch for a few days and breathe some fresh air. Those of us lucky enough to be born out west don't willingly leave mountain views like these, not unless there's a reason to run away."

"And how would you know? Have you ever run from something?" She gave him the once-over. From the plethora of scars and tattoos she'd seen across his chest, she wouldn't be surprised in the slightest.

"This isn't about me." A dark smile twisted his lips. Sexy, yet somehow slightly sinister.

Her female parts went on high alert.

Down, girl.

For a moment, she toyed with the idea of telling him the same lie she told everyone else, that she'd simply wanted to see the world beyond the scope of these mountains, but somehow, she knew that those searing eyes would see right through her. What could it hurt to tell him? They would only know each other for the night. "I was running away from the ranch. It's my family's, and I'm the oldest. I've known I would be responsible for running it since I was a kid, but I don't know… I guess I thought maybe if I created another life for myself before that happened, I wouldn't be stuck there."

"You wanted to be a biologist, not a rancher."

She shrugged again. "Maybe. I don't know. Honestly, I earned my master's in biology at MSU in part because I liked it, but also because I figured that whenever I was forced to come back to the ranch, at least it would be somewhat applicable. If I was going to run the ranch, which I knew eventually I would, I needed to be better trained, better prepared, better…everything. The men in the ranching and farming industry hardly have tolerance for women in the trade, let alone a woman of color. Even though I'm half-Caucasian by my father, my skin and features don't afford me any privilege. If I didn't know my way around the hard work of a cattle count, our ranch's reputation would have suffered. So, really, I don't know. I never had enough room to figure that out."

The irony of that wasn't lost on her. She lived in Big Sky Country. There was enough room, enough space and sky and stars for everyone, it seemed. Everyone except for her. She'd always been too caged by the weight of a future already decided for her.

"Then you ran off to California when you finished school?"

"Only for three months before my father got sick. Pancreatic cancer that spread throughout his body. He was gone within a year."

"I'm sorry," he said.

She nodded. "So I came back, and I've been running the ranch ever since."

He crossed his arms over his chest. "But you wanted California?"

"For a little while, but that wasn't the life for me."

He pegged her with a hard stare. "And what is the life for you, Miss Kitty?"

In the dim lighting of the stable, with the cold mountain winds whistling beneath the wooden doors, it felt like a deeply personal question.

Her brow furrowed as she averted her gaze. Her whole life, she'd always been told what was expected of her. It had never mattered if she wanted to run the ranch or not, if she wanted to keep these mountains as her home. That was simply what she'd been *supposed* to do. And since her father's death, she'd never once stopped to question it. She wrung her hands together. Finally, she managed a whisper of a response. "No one's ever asked me that before."

A sort of sad contemplation filled his steely eyes. He watched her as if he saw straight through her, as if he already knew the answer to her heart's hardest question before she did. "Well, Miss Kitty, rancher and former biologist…" His tone was mocking, instantly cutting the tension between them. She wanted to slap the smugness right off his handsome face. "I'm back to my original suggestion… Get some sleep. You'll need it."

He grabbed a saddle blanket for himself from the shelf and padded toward the middle of the stable. He sat down on the cobblestones, allowing his back to sink against one of the stalls, and tossed the blanket over his lap. He gestured toward the other side of the stable a little more forcefully than necessary.

Gritting her teeth, she did as she was told and marched to the other side, where she sat down on the cobblestone floor. The cold of the stones seeped into her bottom, even through the relative protection of her jeans. She pulled the saddle blanket over her and lay back, staring at the wood-beamed ceiling. Her suede jacket hardly protected her any better from the cold than her jeans did.

A shiver ran through her.

Might as well try to sleep, since he wasn't letting her go.

She lay there for what seemed an eternity, counting the ceiling beams and listening to occasional purring snores from Black Jack. She tried to sleep, but between the freezing-cold cobblestones beneath her, the sound of the mountain winds whipping around outside, and the thought of the heated kiss she'd shared with her captor, sleep failed to claim her. The kiss was the proverbial elephant in the room—or stables, as it were. Neither one of them seemed willing to broach the topic.

It was just as well. She chalked it up to nothing more than being caught up in the momentary forced closeness. He probably hadn't mentioned it because it didn't mean a thing to him.

But she'd enjoyed it, though he was a werewolf and a stranger. She tried not to let that thought make her stomach all kinds of queasy.

After a long while, a frustrated grumble broke the silence in the stable. "Come here."

She rolled over and looked toward her captor. She'd thought he was asleep by now. "Excuse me?"

He was lying on his side, propped up on one elbow and facing her. "You heard me. Your teeth are clattering louder than a whole chain gang. Come here."

She glared at him. "If you think I'm sleeping next to you, you're insane."

"If you want to freeze your sweet ass off all night, suit yourself." He rolled onto his back and placed one arm behind his head.

She glared at him. From the looks of it, he was probably used to any woman readily jumping into bed with him, captive or not.

He patted the space next to him with a satisfied smirk. She knew full well how warm he was, and he damn well knew it.

"Woman, I haven't got all night," he said, repeating his words from earlier.

Damn him. Anger fueled her, because she didn't want to freeze all night, because the part of her that was still hung up on the passion in that kiss *wanted* to be beside him, stranger or not.

Pushing up off the floor, she stomped over to him, making it clear that despite the necessity, she was clearly dissatisfied with this arrangement. She lay down beside him, shoulder to shoulder, pulling the blanket over her. Even with only their shoulders touching, she was already a bit warmer because of his close proximity.

Before she could stop him, one large arm snaked beneath her waist and lifted her. She gasped. With one arm across her shoulders and another in the crook of her lower back, he pulled her flush against him, until their legs were tangled together. Her breath caught. The warmth of his body was a sweet, burning relief, and immediately, her eyes grew heavy. She wanted to protest, but she could barely find the words. His eyes held hers.

This close up and in the glowing light of the heat lamps, she could see a pale rim of greenish-grey around the blue of his irises. There was something wild and untamable in that deep color.

"You saved my life from those other wolves," she whispered. "At least tell me your name."

For a long beat, his deep, blue gaze held hers as if he were gauging her reaction to what he would say next. Finally, he replied, "Wes Calhoun." He brushed a gentle hand over her shoulder, sweeping the dark tendrils of her hair away. "Sleep now, Miss Kitty." The deep grumble of his voice wrapped around her, melting her into his heat.

Wes Calhoun: gorgeous, infuriating, deliciously warm.

She should have been terrified—of him, of the threat of the other wolves still out in the forest. Yet somehow, she wasn't. She felt safe, protected in his arms. He hadn't hurt her, though he'd had plenty of opportunity in the past several hours. In fact, he'd saved her life. That had to count for something. Didn't it? The part of her that wished he'd kiss her again thought so.

She pondered all this as she finally allowed herself to drift slowly to sleep.

———~~~———

Wes couldn't sleep. He lay there for hours, listening for the sounds of the Wild Eight as he memorized the sharp lines and smooth curves of Naomi's face as she slept. This slip of a woman felt far too good in his arms for his liking, and the scent of her hair and skin this close was pure, unadulterated torture—and Wes *knew* torture. But he couldn't very well allow her to shiver all night. It was just below thirty degrees Fahrenheit outside the stable, cold enough that a human could freeze, given enough time. And he hadn't risked shifting in front of her just to let her die in the cold.

How had he gotten himself here?

When dawn finally broke and the temperature slowly started to rise, he couldn't stand it any longer. Laying her down on the cobblestones, he quickly stood and covered her with the extra saddle blanket, hoping she didn't wake. She stirred, wiggling and snuggling into the blankets where she'd been in his arms only a moment earlier. Her lips parted ever so slightly, and her eyelids fluttered. For several long moments, he continued to stare down at her from a safer distance. Then he managed to tear his gaze away and head out of the stable.

The first light of the morning peeked over the horizon. Vivid swirls of orange, pink, and purple with occasional hints of gold washed over the autumn browns. The fiery colors of the skyline contrasted with the blue mountain ranges in the distance.

Wes gathered a few spare logs he kept near the

stables for nights and mornings like this and built a small fire. Finding himself a soft patch of dead grass, he sat beside the smoking embers and watched the sun rise. He breathed in a deep draw of mountain air. The cool moisture filled his lungs and mixed with the peaty smoke from the embers.

For all intents and purposes, the pastures where he managed the Grey Wolves' wild-horse contract and the stables at Wolf Pack Run where he served most of his relegated pack duties were more his home than his apartment inside the main compound would ever be. He spent his days tending to the horses in the pastures or the main stable and running wild through the mountains. Inside Wolf Pack Run, he still felt chained down by the weight of decisions. Out here, he was free. Most days, the colors of these mountains allowed him to forget the blood that still lingered on his hands and boots.

But today, the mountain terrain didn't provide him shelter.

The image of those lifeless grey eyes from years past still haunted him, burning behind his retinas until that was all he could see.

He tore his gaze from the sunrise and glanced over his shoulder to where Naomi lay sleeping on the stable floor. When he'd encountered her the night before, she'd been rightly terrified of him. She'd barely had the wherewithal to fire that shotgun when they'd first met. He shook his head.

The past is the past. Maverick's words played in his head.

Except when it wasn't.

In search of a distraction, Wes examined the wound

where a single pellet was still embedded in his shoulder and the marks on his forearm. The blood had coagulated, but his arm and shoulder still hurt like a son of a bitch.

He deserved as much.

A gust of wind swept over the grass and circled into the stable. Naomi stirred, and her scent carried to him on the breeze. The smell was intoxicating, enough to make him hard instantly, but that hadn't been why he'd allowed her to live. No, her scent hadn't saved her. It'd been his own twisted form of redemption. Because as he'd stared into her terrified eyes last night, he'd found himself at a crossroads—and he'd surprised even himself with the decision he'd made. Maverick would tell him it was the right thing to do, despite his initial fury. Wes supposed Maverick's moral compass had always worked better than his own, but he wasn't so sure. Because as he'd held her all night, he'd recollected how everything he ever touched spilled blood.

Was he protecting her or damning her to a darker fate?

He stoked the fire and watched the embers crackle with heat.

The road to hell was paved with blood from his good intentions.

Naomi woke to rays of sun shining directly into her face. She sat up with a start, shielding her sensitive eyes. Her tired bones ached, and everything in her called out for more sleep. After allowing a moment for her eyes to adjust, she lowered her hands and squinted into the light. She was sitting on the floor of the stable with the saddle blanket still over her. The door was wide open, allowing the sun to stream in.

So it hadn't been a dream…

She glanced beside her. Wes was gone.

A heady rush of adrenaline shoved away any remaining sleepiness. Because now was her chance…

Wes might have had the one-up on her at night, but daytime was her turf. A fresh wave of fear at what she was about to do washed over her. Pushing herself up from the hard cobblestone floor, she slowly inched toward the stable doors. She prayed on all that was holy and spiritual that her footsteps didn't make a sound.

When she'd slipped through the stable doors unaccosted, the burst of fresh mountain air rushing into her lungs felt like the first regained breath of a drowning woman. A handful of trails surrounded her, leading to steeper hills or back down the mountainside. Judging from where the sun sat slightly to the west, it seemed to be past noon. She had never slept this late before. She'd always woken up with the sun's first rays to begin working on her ranch chores.

With shuffled steps, she eased farther out onto the mountainside, scanning her surroundings. The last smoking logs of a campfire sizzled nearby, as if they had recently been stomped out. She was alone. Unguarded. Her heart swelled. Wolves were nocturnal creatures by nature, and Wes had said they'd be safer come morning. With her knife returned to her, she could hold her own if she ran into any other wolves—or so she hoped.

She steeled herself. She could do this. She could escape, find her way home.

With as much agility as she could muster, she darted down the mountainside.

She made a break for the trees, running faster than she'd ever run in her life. Her heart thumped like a jackrabbit's inside her chest, and she gasped for breath as the brisk mountain air seared her lungs. If she could just make it to the tree line. Then, even if he found her missing, she'd have a head start.

When she reached the forest, she nearly collapsed with relief against a nearby maple. Black Jack let out a frenzied whinny in the distance. She turned her head toward the noise. She was almost in the clear.

A large hand slammed into the tree bark above her head, stopping her in her tracks. She let out a terrified shriek. Wes stood over her. With one arm resting overtop her head and the other beside her as he leaned over her, she was caged between him and the tree trunk at her back.

He wore a Stetson. The hat brim tipped over his brow and cast his face in shadow as his eyes raked over her from head to toe. She'd thought he was impressive in the darkness, but that was nothing compared to the light of day. Scars from his life's battles—as well as the healing wounds he'd sustained at her hands and in defense of her—marred the surface of his smooth skin and made her want to draw closer with aroused interest for the powerful muscles underneath.

The sunlight breaking through the treetops overhead caught the light undertones of his hair. The golden hues matched those of the mountain light. The color was barely darker than the pale material of his Stetson but somehow lit from within with gold. It matched the coarse, closely trimmed hair of his beard. She imagined the bristle against her sensitive skin. Her nipples tightened.

"You didn't think I'd make it that easy on you, did ya?"

"Can't blame a girl for trying," she sighed.

"Now that you're awake, we'd better get a move on." Retreating an inch or two, he gestured to where Black Jack stood several feet away. The horse trotted up beside them, then resumed grazing on the short grass.

Naomi glanced over her shoulder toward the woods. Wes had already proved once that running wasn't an option. She'd barely made it several feet last time. Could she manage to get away on his horse?

He seemed to realize she was weighing her escape plans, and a grim chuckle rumbled in his chest. "You come get on the horse willingly, or I'll throw you over my shoulder and haul you the whole way myself."

She shook her head again. "No, not unless you're taking me home." One night under his protection. That's what they'd agreed, which meant it was high time she headed back to the ranch.

"Suit yourself."

The next thing she knew, one muscled arm wrapped around her waist, and her feet lifted from the ground. He slung her over his shoulder as if she weighed little more than a bale of hay.

Naomi let out an involuntary shriek. She kicked her legs, her boots repeatedly pounding against his stomach, but the blows didn't seem to faze him. "Put me down!" she hissed.

Slowly, he climbed the mountainside, his horse following. "Not until you agree to behave." He didn't even sound winded from carrying her.

Before she could give further protest, he slapped her on the ass hard enough that her breath caught. Not enough to seriously hurt her, but enough to leave a burning red mark on the skin beneath her jeans. A rush of desire flooded between her legs.

Renewed vigor drove her. She kicked and pounded her fists against his back. For several minutes, they continued like that. She shrieked and cursed, using the most creative profanities in her vocabulary, until finally, he dropped her onto her feet again.

"You really want to leave?" He crossed his large, bare arms over his chest.

"Of course I want to leave."

"Then go."

She blinked several times. *What? Just like that? Then why had he…?* For a moment, she thought he was mocking her, but his face held nothing but seriousness. "Is this some sort of a trap?"

He let out a low, throaty laugh that both pissed her off and did unimaginable things to her lady parts. *Damn him.* Her instincts were going haywire and betraying her. He may have saved her last night, but now he was nothing more than a psychopathic freak of nature holding her captive.

"No trap. If you really want to go, go on." He gestured for her to make her exit.

Slowly, she stepped away from him. When he didn't immediately charge her or rip her to shreds, she took a larger step. She was several feet away before she picked up the pace. Though her feet moved forward, she could scarcely believe it. This was really happening. He was really letting her go.

"Just don't come crying when the vampires keep bleeding your livestock dry," he called after her. "Or when they decide to drain you, too."

She stopped dead in her tracks and spun to face him. "Excuse me?"

"You heard me." A slight smirk curled over his lips.

She'd never wanted to punch anyone more in her life.

"Just like you see in the movies. Nasty fangs and all. Unfortunately for their prey"—he gave her a pointed look—"which would mean humans like you, they can hide their fangs. What the movies get wrong is that while they're nocturnal, they can go out in the sun for limited periods. Blend in as well as you and me in a crowd, and the only thing that kills them is chopping or ripping their heads off."

She gaped at him.

"Those bloodsuckers pick off their fair share of humans down in Billings once they tire of feeding from a willing host. When the opportunity presents itself, they can barely resist, well fed or not, and they'll take men and women alike. Doesn't matter. Humans don't stand a chance against their strength. All it takes is one bite, and they can drain you dry, no chance of survival. Honestly, I'm surprised they've left you alone this long."

Before she could stop herself, she took several steps toward him. "*Vampires?*" she repeated. She couldn't manage to wrap her head around it.

He gave a single nod. "What else did you think was killing your sheep? A bear?"

She crossed her arms over her chest. "That's a perfectly plausible assumption." Her eyes narrowed, and she gave him an anger-filled once-over. "A mangy wolf is more like it."

His smirk only deepened. "It wasn't me that killed…"

He snapped his fingers several times. "What was its name again?"

She scowled. He was mocking her. The heels of her boots dug into the grass beneath her feet. "Lambie," she ground out: "His name was Lambie."

"Right, Lambie." That damn smirk of his returned. "I didn't eat Lambie, or any of your livestock. And last I checked, bears don't drink blood." As if that settled it, he turned and climbed back up the mountainside, following where his horse had trotted off to, without so much as another glance over his shoulder.

She stood there, gaping. *No. No. This can't be true.* Sure, she'd known all along that the carnage left behind from the attacks on her livestock was not that of a normal animal. Her livestock had been completely drained of blood. No normal predator did that—at least none native to these parts—but logic had told her the killer couldn't be anything but. With the events of the last twenty-four hours, Wes's explanation seemed better than any other. And if that were the case, what did that mean for her own safety? Vampires? In her pasture?

She shook her head. No, it wasn't worth it. The ranch's finances may have been at risk, but no livestock was worth dying for. So what if the creatures took a few of her flock? Even if they cut into her calves and hurt her income, they wouldn't be able to get too many before the animals went to market soon.

For several long moments, she just stood there. An internal war of wills raged inside her.

Damn it.

Naomi marched back up the mountainside and followed Wes. When she found him among the trees, he was rubbing polish over a brown leather saddle, which Black Jack appeared beyond displeased to be wearing.

She took a step back. Until now, she had assured herself that Wes and the other shifters he'd mentioned were some sort of genetic anomaly. She'd hypothesized that the shifters were a cross-species of human and animal that biologists like herself hadn't begun to predict or understand, or maybe even creatures genetically manipulated *by* scientists. But vampires? That kicked any chance she had of evolutionary explanation off a cliff.

Though the tales and spiritual beliefs of her mother's people alluded to creatures beyond physical explanation, Naomi had never really taken such stories to heart. Much as with her father's Christian religion, in her mind, those creatures were metaphorical and symbolic. Something she respected but didn't subscribe to herself. The reality Wes proposed was too supernatural for her tastes. "And what makes you think vampires bled my flock?" she asked.

"I don't *think* that's the case. I know." He poured another drop of polish on the cloth and rubbed it over the saddle's horn. "You're just going to have to trust me on this one."

She laughed. "And why in my right mind should I trust you?"

"Aside from the fact that I saved your life?" He tossed the brush and polish into his saddlebag. "Wolves are the natural enemies of vampires. It's the way of our world. Centuries ago, shifters were blamed for the human deaths caused by the vampires. It made our species vulnerable, hunted. We lost innocent men and women. Shifters and vamps have been enemies ever since. As a pack, we Grey Wolves have chosen to align ourselves with humans, as their protectors, in an attempt to clear our species' name with the humans who hunt our kind.

"We patrol Billings and protect the humans there from the vamps and the Wild Eight when we can, and we also make sure the vampires don't move into the western part of the state. Our subpacks out there don't have as many trained warriors, so they and the local humans would be easy targets for the vampires to attack. We can't let them do that. Population density is low enough there that human deaths would draw plenty of attention from the Execution Underground."

"The human-run organization you mentioned?"

"The very one. Human deaths mean more sanctions from the Execution Underground for our pack and others, so we don't want the vamps getting a foothold there." He ducked underneath Black Jack and adjusted the underbelly straps of the saddle. The horse grunted and stomped his feet. From the angry gleam in its eye, Wes was lucky he wasn't standing behind the beast.

"If anyone under our pack's protection has issues with vampires, we'll take care of them. If you're willing to do what it takes, I can get you that protection." He cleared his throat. "The way I see it, unless you want your whole flock to disappear, I'm your only chance to get those bloodsucking pests in check. Nobody wants those fuckers out of Billings more than I do."

"You said only one night and then I'd be home."

"No, I said you'd be safe with me *for the night*, which you were, and we'd get you home as soon as possible, which we will."

"That's misleading, and you know it."

"You weren't exactly in a mood to listen to reason last night." He held a bridle out for Black Jack to bite. The horse obeyed but nipped at his finger as he did it. Wes either didn't notice or was so used to the horse's behavior that he didn't care.

She scoffed. "You try being in my position and behaving *reasonably*." She said it as if it was a dirty word. *Reasonable. Ugh.* He sounded like her idiot brother, trying to convince her to sign on with any investor that pounded on the ranch door. She and Jacob had decided together that the only way to bolster the ranch's financial profit was to turn the home where they'd grown up into a farm-to-table bed-and-breakfast. The old farmhouse was far too large for just her anyway, and Jacob had his own place.

Ranching by nature wasn't the most profitable of businesses, especially calculating overhead costs, but it was a different era even since the time of her childhood. They had an average-size ranch, about two thousand acres. But every day, small farms and cow-calf operations like theirs were being swallowed up in favor of massive corporate CAFOs, where the animals were treated with little respect, and disease and mess ran rampant, cutting quality in favor of big profits. If she and her brother wanted their father's legacy of pure, clean ranch and farm life to live on—which she did—the ranch needed new vitality and life. But for the changes she and her brother envisioned, they needed a fair amount of money, something they sorely lacked. The little bit they'd had in her father's estate, set aside for this very investment, had been allocated to his medical debt, leaving them up a creek of financial issues without a paddle.

It's this or let the ranch go under, Naomi. We can allow investors and still maintain the legacy of the ranch. Be reasonable. Her brother's voice echoed in her head.

She refused to accept any old offer that walked through her door. She *would* find an investor, one who would allow her to maintain the integrity and heart of the ranch, of their family home, but she needed the *right* one. In his fear of losing everything, Jacob was in too much of a hurry to accept an offer. His love was blinding him. It was just a matter of time until they found the investor she wanted. She was certain.

Wes shrugged. "I didn't say your concern wasn't warranted." He pulled back on the reins, and Naomi stepped closer to a nearby tree as he guided the animal forward several feet.

"What do I have to do to get the pack's protection?"

"You'll need to follow my directions and come with me. We'll likely have three moons before you can return to your ranch."

"Three moons? What the hell does that mean? And what about my ranch? My livestock? Who's going to care for them in my absence?" Managing the ranch was her sole responsibility. She had a few ranch hands who helped out on a part-time basis, but that was hardly enough to keep the operation afloat in her absence.

"It's how wolves measure time. Three nights. In that time, the Grey Wolves will likely put a patrol on your ranch to watch over the place, see if there really are vampires attacking your flock, corroborate your story. I'll send some ranch hands to care for your livestock while you're gone. Then you'll need to swear fealty to the Grey Wolves."

Naomi's eyes widened, and she shook her head. "Uh-uh. No way. I am *not* becoming your pack's human pet…"

"You won't be a pet. All it means is that you're loyal to the Grey Wolves, that your goals are aligned with ours."

"And what do *you* get out of all this? Out of helping me?" She had no idea what his endgame was.

"The Wild Eight have teamed up with the vampires. They won't stop until I'm dead. I won't stand on the sidelines for this. If I figure out why the Wild Eight and the vampires are targeting you, it may save my own life."

She wanted to ask why the Wild Eight wanted him dead, but that was a question for another time. This was already too much to take in. She paused, attempting to process what he was telling her—and what he wasn't. Really, what choice did she have? "And when this is all over?"

"No more vampires will be exsanguinating your flock, and you'll be free."

Free. The word slammed into her, filling her with hope for her survival, more hope than standing so close to a werewolf who could murder her with his bare hands should have allowed. "If I do this, you'll really let me go?" she asked.

"I'll take you home myself." He mounted his horse.

She followed him, fully expecting him to ride away without her. He had saved her life, and somehow, she knew he would do it again. She couldn't say that of anyone else she'd ever trusted.

He pulled back on the horse's reins. The mustang came to a stop, and Wes twisted back toward her. For a moment, he simply lingered there, staring at her as if he was taking her in. With his wolf eyes ablaze and his

Stetson shadowing parts of his face, he looked far too mysterious, too dangerous to trust.

Finally, he extended a large hand down to her. "You coming or not?"

If what he said was true, then she had no choice. Her family's ranch—the life her father had built for their family on that small patch of land and its success—had meant everything to her father. It was his personal piece of heaven. She'd sworn to him before he died that she would take care of it at all costs. She wasn't about to let it be destroyed by big corporations, vampires, or whatever else came along. Her choice was to go with Wes or to risk her life in the forest with the pack of werewolves at her heels, and where would that leave her, even if she did manage to get back to her ranch?

A mischievous grin crossed his face. "If you don't want to get on the horse, I can always spank you again…"

She scowled. *Damn him.* "I'll get on the horse."

Before she could change her mind, she hooked her foot in the stirrup and placed her hand in his. He tugged her up into the saddle in front of him with ease. As she settled into the saddle, he gave the horse a swift kick, and within seconds, they were racing up the mountainside.

Maybe she was stupid, reckless, careless even, to trust him. But if what Wes had said was true, she had bigger problems than the infuriating wolf at her back.

Chapter 5

SHE SHOULD HAVE STAYED INSIDE AND CALLED THE
Defenders of Wildlife.

That thought plagued Naomi as they rode up the
mountainside, the freezing wind whipping past them
amid the hoots of nearby owls and the rustling of the
surrounding forest. Nothing but the moon lit their path.
They'd been riding since midafternoon, but with Black
Jack carrying the weight of both of them up the mountainside, the horse had slowed down spitefully, grum-
bling and huffing every few steps in protest. He'd already
tried to buck them off—several times. She was beginning
to understand why Wes called him an "ornery bastard."

She rested her weight further onto the horse. If she
had a dollar for every "should have," she would have
enough money to improve the ranch's dismal finances—
without the investors she had been courting.

"You can go to sleep if you're tired." Wes's deep
voice thundered through her, wrapping around her like
warm velvet. It was the first time he'd spoken since dark
had descended. His voice was the kind women longed to
hear on the other side of a late-night phone call.

Her body ached from her initial fight against him and
subsequent escape yesterday, compounded by sleeping
on the cold, hard floor of the stable and the pounding
headache that had started shortly after she awakened
and wouldn't relent. It had eased some after Wes had

stopped and hunted down a hare they'd roasted over a small fire he'd built, and they'd refilled their canteens in a nearby stream. She was thankful there was food and drink in her belly, but that was the only thing she'd eaten all day.

Between the slow, steady sway of the horse beneath her, her aches and pains, and the pervasive cold, she struggled to keep her eyelids open. A sleepy escape from the stress of her situation sounded like sweet relief.

Despite the cold at her front, the wolf-man behind her radiated heat as if she were snuggled next to a glowing fire. A very hard, half-naked glowing fire. The thought of his bare chest pressed at her back heated her face.

There was nothing her weary body wanted more than to curl up into the warmth at her back, but after their run-in with the other wolf last night and the threat of *vampires*, she wasn't chancing sleep in this forest, whether Wes watched over her or not. She attempted to distract herself.

Warm-blooded like the true Canis lupus irremotus, she noted. *But unusually warm, suggestive of an extremely high-needs predatory metabolism.* Mammals needed to feed often and heartily, unlike cold-blooded species. What fueled that metabolism? His reference earlier to his flock had indicated his diet remained consistent with that of a grey wolf, but would it be rude to ask?

"Not much farther," he said.

Suddenly, without command, Black Jack increased his gait to a speedy canter as if in the last dash of a long race just before the finish line. The shift in speed caught Naomi off guard, and she slipped from the saddle. She let out a terrified squeak, anticipating the impact with the ground.

Wes caught her midfall. With deft precision, he wrapped an arm around her waist, pulling her in to him until her bottom pushed between his thighs and her back fell flush against his chest, tucking her closer in to the heat of his body. Not too close for comfort, but far too comfortable for her liking. And if the sight of him nude in the darkness hadn't been enough indication, the hardened length now pushing between her ass cheeks suggested the males among his species were…blessed.

At least he was.

He wasn't beautiful in the traditional sense, more ruggedly masculine. Rough around the edges. But he had the animal reflexes of a cat. Or a wolf. And between his legs, he resembled more of a…

"…horse," he said, finishing her thought.

"W-what?" she sputtered. If it hadn't been for his warm grip on her, she might have fallen off the saddle again in the sudden fear that maybe he could read minds.

"A rancher who doesn't know how to ride a horse," he grumbled.

She felt him behind her, shaking his head with disbelief. The warmth of his breath hovered just above the top of her head.

She frowned and gripped the horse's hearty body to steady herself. She raised her voice over the wind. "I don't usually ride this long up a mountainside without a break."

Having learned to ride western style long before she had started grade school, she knew she was an excellent horsewoman. Sure, it wouldn't have been the first time she had fallen ass over teakettle off a horse, but she wouldn't admit it. Not to him.

She gripped the sides of the horse's large neck, hoping

her steadied position would prompt Wes to release her. But the grip of his arm around her waist held firm with a steady, unyielding strength.

They continued at a quickened pace for several minutes. When they broke through the tree line, he nudged the sides of their horse, and they picked up further speed as they bounded toward a steep ridge.

When they crested the top, Naomi gasped.

A dip in the landscape led down into the foothills of the Beartooth Mountains. The ranchland revealed through the trees stretched for miles. From this vantage point, she noted a small, isolated village in the distance. A development of log cabins spread over the vast plain, centered around what looked like a massive fortress, complete with stables, a barn, and several other buildings.

Her mouth fell open in disbelief. The encampment was isolated enough by the sheer size of the landmass that the packmembers lived within plain sight. The lights from several of the cabins glittered in the darkness as if some sort of magic hung in the air.

"What is this place?" She breathed out the words on her exhale.

"Welcome to Wolf Pack Run." Wes slapped the horse on its behind, and it raced down the incline toward the village. The wind whipped through Naomi's hair.

Pack…

Her eyes widened, the word resonating within her. Of course. Wolves were pack animals. She knew this, and he'd mentioned his pack before, but the reality of encountering more than one of his kind twisted her stomach even as fascination gripped her.

Black Jack steered down a slope in the incline and along a path that appeared to be a back route into the village. They didn't encounter anyone…or *anything* for that matter, for which Naomi was grateful. From his clear alertness despite the late-night hour, she'd ascertained that Wes was likely nocturnal, either by habit or by nature. With this clearly being his pack's home, there had to be others like him roaming the night. The list of questions in her head abounded, but she remained quiet.

When they finally reached the fortress at the center of the complex, Wes dismounted. Naomi followed suit, thankful to feel her feet hit the ground. Pleased to have their weight off his back, Black Jack gave a happy, playful buck on his hind legs before he trotted off. Where to, she didn't know, but Wes seemed unconcerned by the horse's independent behavior.

Wes led her through the back doors of the lodge and then guided her down a few wood-paneled hallways until they reached another door. Pulling a ring of keys from his jeans, he unlocked it and ushered her inside.

As the door slammed shut behind her, Naomi took in the immaculate apartment. Mahogany furniture and kitchen cabinets with black-and-blue labradorite countertops. The open floor plan revealed a well-stocked kitchen, leading into an open living-room space with modern black leather furniture. Across the room was the door to the adjacent bedroom. The skull of a bull, hung on a nearby wall beneath a dried bull's hide, gave the place a touch of western appeal amid the modern decor.

Wes dropped his keys on the countertop. They hit the stone with a clatter that made Naomi jump. Turning toward her, he leaned onto the back of the couch, crossing his arms over his chest and studying her before he crossed the apartment to open the bedroom door.

She eased inside. A California king bed frame built of cedar sat in the center, its mattress covered by a mountain-patterned comforter and sheets. A matching side table and dresser completed the furnishings. The room struck her as bare, somewhat empty of the signs of life found in someone's well-loved home. But for the time being, the bed was the most beautiful sight she'd ever laid eyes on.

"You can sleep here for now."

He stood on the opposite side of the bed frame. Both their gazes fell to the large expanse of mattress between them. An awkward tension hung in the air, considering the closeness they'd shared the previous night.

"I'll give you the bedroom and take the couch until Maverick returns and decides how we'll address your vampire problem," Wes clarified. "In the meantime, our medic will want to dig your shotgun pellet out of my shoulder."

She grimaced. "Sorry about that."

He smirked. "Not the roughest kind of foreplay I've had."

That sexy grin scorched her from the inside out.

Oh. My.

"Not that Grey Wolves and humans can mate. Pack law strictly forbids it," he added. He shook his head as if he wasn't certain why he'd shared that last bit. "Get some rest." Without another word, he closed the door.

For a moment, she lingered, staring at the door. Though she knew she was safe from the Wild Eight and the vampires here, or so she hoped, the nauseous pit in her stomach deepened. Her knees shook, threatening to collapse beneath her. It was the first time she'd truly felt alone with herself, her thoughts, and every one of her fears since she'd met him—and all of those tumultuous emotions crashed over her. The comfort of the bed called to her. She climbed onto it and collapsed into the warm embrace of the sheets. Wrapping herself up in the childlike safety of the blankets, she finally allowed tears to fall down her cheeks.

She would allow herself this moment of weakness, because she *wasn't* weak. She had never been weak. She was a fighter. Tonight, she would cry. Tonight, she would be angry.

And tomorrow, she would help Wes save her ranch and destroy the monsters who had done this to her.

"This'll hurt."

Wes hissed as Austin poured a large splash of whiskey over his shoulder. The blood from the fresh wound mixed with the fiery liquid, forming a sticky mixture that clung to his pectoral muscles. The gashes in his forearm had healed clean, but Austin had needed to use his scalpel to cut through the healed tissue of Wes's shoulder. The Grey Wolf medic had just finished removing the wayward pellet.

"Did you forget your antiseptic out in the barn?" Wes asked through gritted teeth. When he'd called Austin in to help tend his wounds, the medic had been out at the chute, catching the cattle during the head count to vaccinate them. The pain in Wes's shoulder throbbed in a steady rhythm. The initial wound had been bad enough, but then he'd carried that all-too-attractive rancher up the mountainside to Black Jack while she'd been passed out, sending the shell deeper into the flesh of his shoulder. It's not as if she weighed all that much, but the searing pain had wrenched through his limbs and down his torso nevertheless.

"I reckoned you'd need it." Austin passed him the bottle. His thick Texas drawl lengthened all the vowels in his slow, steady speech.

Wes grabbed the whiskey bottle by the neck and chugged. The smoky, fiery drink burned down his throat, drowning out the pain for a moment. He took another swig.

With his free hand, he gripped the edge of the kitchen countertop where he sat. Right now, he and Austin were the only packmembers inside his apartment, but considering the human woman lying passed out on his bed, that wouldn't be the case for long. Word spread fast through the pack. The only bigger gossips in these mountains than little, old granny quilting groups in Billings were his packmates.

Wes watched as Austin threaded a medical needle. The recessed lighting in the kitchen was reflected in Austin's dark curls and glinted off the needle as he concentrated. A moment later, that needle was grazing Wes's skin.

"You know the drill." Austin pushed the first stitch through Wes's skin.

Wes winced as he swore.

"Many more stitches, and you'll be one large scar." Austin pulled the needle through.

Wes felt the stitching cord wiggle beneath the surface of his skin, like a snake slithering through thick grass.

He frowned at Austin, though he knew the medic was right. Scars covered his torso, rough evidence of the life he'd lived.

His eyes darted to his closed bedroom door. How had he gotten himself into this mess?

"What drew you out in that neck of the woods anyway? You weren't on land patrol or vamp-huntin' duty." Austin broke his concentration and met Wes's gaze. The question had clearly been burning on the tip of the medic's tongue.

Wes released a long sigh through his nose. "I told you. Hunting."

"You're expecting me to believe you happened to be out in the woods huntin' on a night when Wild Eight members show up? You reached 'em before patrol." Austin broke eye contact and returned to his work. He positioned the needle over Wes's chest for the next stitch. "Don't lie to a man with a sharp object poised over yer heart."

Wes answered with silence. He wouldn't be lectured. He was already sure to get that from Maverick. As Austin worked, the quietness of Wes's apartment pressed down on them. In the silence that stretched between them, Wes heard her. In the next room. The faint sound of her breathing as her chest rose and fell. And her scent still invaded his nose, alluring and disturbing and oddly…soothing. Getting himself into this situation when Maverick would already be red with rage had been a piss-poor choice, but if Kyle's information proved true, they had a lot bigger problems, and the exsanguination of Naomi's flock meant she was somehow connected.

The pack was screwed on all sides.

By the time they were several stitches in, Wes had downed a fifth of the bottle. As another stitch went through, the door to his apartment burst open with a resounding bang. Colt strode in as if his feet were being held to a fire pit.

"What the hell were you thinking?" he roared. "Going against Maverick's orders. Are you trying to get us all killed?" His steely-grey eyes blazed with fiery anger, the same color as the revolvers of the gun manufacturer for which he was named.

Wes frowned. "By who?" He gestured around the room with the hand that held the whiskey bottle. "No one followed us here. Wild Eight, vamps, or otherwise."

Austin cleared his throat before he muttered under his breath, "I reckon he means Maverick's 'bout to lose his shit over this." And it wasn't only Wes who was likely to get reamed. The consequences would likely flow all the way down the chain of command, with Colt being the top target.

Colt paced the room, shaking his head like a madman. "Where's your sense of duty to this pack?" Whenever the Grey Wolf high commander let loose and yelled, there were always questions of duty and honor and service to one's pack.

Wes growled. Screw Colt's sense of duty. Of course Colt was the perfect soldier. He'd been nursing from the pack's teat since he was a pup. The differences between them were like those between a wild mustang and a thoroughbred show horse.

Wes had had to be broken in the hard way. Colt had been groomed for this. He was loyal, brave, and obedient to a damn fault.

"Don't blame me because Maverick was wrong." Wes brandished the whiskey bottle in Colt's direction. "I told you all the Wild Eight would resurface, and not a damn one of you listened, Maverick included."

Colt froze. Austin stopped fiddling inside his medical kit and turned a wide-eyed look at Wes.

"The Wild Eight are back. They've recruited new members. They're organized, and they want my life for my betrayal." Wes took another swig of whiskey as he allowed the weight of his words to sink in. "And I have news of what they're planning, but Maverick hears this first."

Colt's jaw tightened. His fists clenched at his sides. He knew firsthand what that meant. This shit was serious. Despite the angry, jerking tic of his temple, Colt nodded calmly. "And the human?"

"I was chasing the Wild Eight off our packlands. They ran onto her ranch." Wes flashed him a cheeky grin and swallowed another swig of whiskey. "Wolf trap."

He had saved her because he couldn't live with the guilt of more innocent blood on his hands. Leaving her there vulnerable to the Wild Eight—or worse—had been the only other option, and condemning her to death that way would have been the same as if he'd killed her himself. The dark mixture of guilt and pain Wes carried in his chest flared at the thought of the past.

Colt shook his head. "If you had listened to me in the first place, you wouldn't have been in that situation."

Wes set the whiskey bottle down on the countertop with a thud. "I'm free to come and go as I wish. Last I checked, I don't take orders from you, Colt. You're not Maverick's second."

Colt tensed at Wes's words. Colt not being second was a matter of technicality, and they all knew it. It was only a matter of time before Maverick made it official.

Austin snatched the gauze tape from his medical kit and ripped off a piece with his teeth. "Colt's right, Wes. Not yer brightest moment. Not with Maverick gone. It leaves us open, vulnerable." Austin placed a square of gauze over the gunshot wound and ran the tape over one edge.

Wes gave him a look that said *Whose side are you on?*

In response, Austin pushed ever so slightly on the wound until Wes let out another hiss. Colt's side. Clearly. Yeah, probably best not to piss off the guy with access to all the good pills and who carried the sharp medical supplies.

Wes released a long sigh. "Nobody said my record was full of bright moments."

A snarky laugh sounded from the open doorway. Blaze stood in the hall outside Wes's apartment door with a smug grin on his face. He was wearing one of those flamboyant Hawaiian shirts, a bad habit he'd picked up while spending several years working in Silicon Valley. The SoCal wolf liked to remind them frequently that Silicon Valley was farther west than any part of Montana, but that didn't make his ways stick out any less among the Grey Wolves, a pack of tried-and-true cowboys. Blaze was a damn tropical peacock. This particular shirt was near-fluorescent orange with an array of awful blue seahorses patterned across it.

"Maverick is going to flip when he gets back." The Grey Wolf techie's grin widened. His teeth were blindingly white against that California tan.

Wes snarled in response. "Stay out of this, Blaze."

Annoying shit that he was, Blaze had been on a mission to piss Wes off as much as possible since the first day Wes had stepped into the compound.

Colt was still shaking his head. "I'm calling Maverick now. This needs to be addressed. We need a strategy."

Blaze threw his hands up in surrender and laughed. "This is way above my pay grade. I'm out." He wandered farther down the hall, muttering under his breath about them being total pussies.

Colt immediately rounded on Wes again. "I'll alert Maverick to the situation, but until Maverick returns, she is *your* responsibility." Colt stalked toward the door. He paused in the doorway, his mouth cinched tight and his nostrils flaring with barely suppressed rage. He left without another word, but Wes knew Colt would take care of contacting Maverick.

He might have been kissing Maverick's ass to earn second, but he was a good man, a good soldier, a fierce wolf.

Austin ripped another piece of tape, and his eyes darted toward the closed bedroom door with a look of concern.

She'd likely be passed out asleep for a while. Her body needed to recover from everything it'd been through in the past twenty-four hours.

Wes shrugged with his good shoulder. "You heard Colt. I brought her here. Until Maverick says otherwise, she's my responsibility."

Austin nodded slowly. His face went from serious to somber.

Wes frowned. "What?"

"Nothin'." Austin shook his head.

Wes quirked an eyebrow.

"So assumin' for a moment that she's innocent…" Austin released a long sigh as he taped the last piece of gauze in place. "Just remember you're one of the good guys now."

Wes almost laughed. It was more of a morbid chuckle. If Austin only knew the half of it. "Everybody thinks they're the good guys, Austin." Wes knew that firsthand. He'd always thought himself the hero, until he'd realized he wasn't.

Austin pulled off his gloves. "Know-what-I-mean?" The phrase rolled together in that smooth Texan drawl.

In other words, *Play nice with the fragile human. Don't hurt her, you brute.* Austin was too nice to say it in those terms, but Wes got the message loud and clear. Austin had always had the biggest heart among them. It's what made him a damn good medic and an intense but fair fighter.

Wes slid down from the countertop, his bare feet landing with a smack on the marble flooring. "I didn't hurt her when she had a gun to my head. I have no intention of starting now."

Austin nodded. "If you say so." He closed his medical kit. He seemed to realize he was fighting a losing battle and headed toward the door, kit in hand.

When Wes heard the door latch shut behind Austin, he padded to the bedroom door. Slowly, he inched the door open, just far enough that he could see Naomi still unconscious on top of his bed. The small difference that opening the door made caused her scent to flood his apartment. He should have known better than to bring a human back to Wolf Pack Run. If he'd learned anything from his past, it was that humans caused nothing but trouble.

And now he was lusting after a human female he *should* have killed…and he was stuck with her by his side until further notice, all because he'd chosen to save her rather than to allow fate to take its course. Apparently, he was a glutton for punishment.

In his Wild Eight days, nothing would have stopped him from bedding a woman like her. But if there was one other thing his brief stints with humanity had taught him, it was that he ruined everything he touched. He had spent too long spilling the blood of enemies and friends alike for it to be any other way. What was the point of saving her just to destroy her?

He breathed in the deep scent of her. Scanning the black tendrils of her hair lying across his pillowcase, he chugged another drink of whiskey. He had worked hard to abandon that life. He had no intention of going back now.

Not even an hour later, the door to Wes's apartment burst open. He didn't bother to sit up to see who it was. From the rigid rhythm of the footfalls as the steps approached, Wes could tell it was Colt. Only Colt's footsteps sounded like they were timed, as if he were a damn soldier marching in formation.

His packmate's voice rang from the open doorway. "He's ready for you."

Wes stretched out on his sofa where he'd been lying before he pushed himself to his feet. He'd been trying to catch some shut-eye, but that task had proven impossible. Not with Naomi's scent invading his apartment and his confrontation with Maverick imminent. His mind refused to settle.

He scratched at the five-o'clock shadow covering his cheeks. "That was fast."

Colt folded his arms over his chest. "He rented a car. He said he'd send for Trigger tomorrow."

Wes's eyes widened. *Shit.*

Never once had Wes seen Maverick get near anything with an engine. Chalk it up to force of old habits or paranoia over his movements being tracked, but the tried-and-true cowboy took his horse wherever he went. Speed and efficiency be damned. He even rode that ornery beast all the way to the bottom of the northern coyote packlands in Wyoming twice a year.

If Maverick rented a car just to get back to Wolf Pack Run, he was fit to be tied...

...and Wes may as well be a dead man walking.

At least, the Wild Eight or the vamps wouldn't get to him if Maverick did first.

Wes released a long sigh through his nose. "Let's get this over with then."

When they stepped out into the hall, Colt turned to the left, though his personal quarters were to the right, as if he were about to lead Wes to Maverick's office. He stopped midstride, catching his mistake. From the dark look in Colt's eyes, they were both back there again. The night when Colt had hauled Wes in at Maverick's request. Wes's hands had been bound behind his back with rope and chains.

"I know the way." Wes nodded over his shoulder to indicate the human woman still asleep in his bedroom. Someone would need to guard her during his brief absence. "I'm not Maverick's prisoner." Wes clapped a hand on Colt's shoulder and gave him a dark smile. "Not this time."

Wes left Colt waiting outside his apartment, dutifully guarding Naomi until Wes returned. Colt wouldn't dare trust even a harmless human woman among his precious pack, perfect soldier that he was.

When Wes reached the door to Maverick's private chambers, he didn't hesitate. He'd take his punishment like a man. He threw open the doors and stepped inside.

Maverick's private chambers sat directly in the center of Wolf Pack Run. The alphas' mansion was at the center of the complex and Maverick's room in the center of that. Should Wolf Pack Run ever be under surprise attack, their packmaster would be guarded by more than one hundred lesser wolves.

The vast two-room space was divided between a regular office and the technical room, which contained all the high-powered computer equipment and technologies the pack possessed. A short adjoining hallway led back into the packmaster's private suite. They were the most luxurious quarters inside Wolf Pack Run, allowing no one to forget exactly who gave the orders within its walls. Though most of the time, the room simply served as Maverick's quiet personal office, during times of war, these two rooms became central command.

Maverick stood behind his one-of-a-kind executive desk, his palms splayed across the desktop, supporting his muscled weight. The handcrafted, stained maple gave the legs of the desk the appearance of small tree trunks. The solid piece of furniture fit well with the dark coffered wooden ceiling. During the daylight, the dark colors of the room made it warm, comforting. Now, the dark-shadowed beams and low lighting promised no mercy.

He didn't bother to look up as Wes entered. Wes stood before him in silence.

"I'm not even going to ask what you were thinking, because *clearly*, you weren't." Maverick's biceps flexed with barely contained rage as if he were fighting to keep from destroying the desk beneath his hands. "You disobeyed me. I told you to forget the tip from Kyle. I *forbade* you to have any contact with the Wild Eight and their associates. And now…" The growl that escaped from Maverick's lips was feral.

"I gave you your life." Slowly, Maverick lifted his gaze. His wolf eyes blazed with unchecked aggression. It was the same look he'd given Wes all those moons ago, back when they'd been enemies—which from the looks of it, they might have become once again. Had he been in full wolf form, Maverick's teeth would have been bared. His lips were one twitch away from snarling. "What's to stop me from taking it now?"

Wes didn't answer. Instead, he picked a spot at the edge of the desk and stared at it, refusing to meet Maverick's gaze. He had broken his promise to obey the packmaster's orders. With his history, he knew Maverick would never take that lightly. Had he been in Maverick's place, the consequences would have been deadly.

Maverick slammed his fist onto his desk with a resounding bang. "Answer me."

Wes lifted his head, meeting Maverick's stare head-on. "I wasn't thinking. I was acting, and I was right."

Maverick straightened to his full height. Slowly, he rounded his desk to stand before Wes. When he stopped, they were nearly nose to nose. Mirror images in size, in build, in strength, but opposed in all the ways that mattered. They were built to be enemies.

"The Wild Eight are back," Wes hissed. "Just as I warned you. I told you they would never remain dormant, and now not only have they gained strength, new packmembers, and greater numbers, but they've aligned themselves with the vampires."

If the news caught Maverick by surprise, he didn't show it. His nostrils flared and his jaw clenched tight as he inhaled a deep breath. "I don't care what you think you know. How *dare* you question my judgment? Disobey my orders?"

"I have followed your orders faithfully for three years, *Packmaster*"—the words spilled like vitriol from Wes's lips—"but I will not stand by as my life, as this pack, is threatened."

The burning rage in Maverick's eyes flamed. "That same leadership spared your life." He stepped even closer. For a moment, Wes expected him to clutch him by the throat. "I could have bled you dry, and I still can. Don't you dare forget it."

It was a half-hearted threat, and Wes knew it. If Maverick had wanted him dead, he'd had the chance—countless chances. They both knew that though Wes now called Maverick packmaster, in a fight, only Wes was Maverick's equal, and who would win would be the luck of the draw.

Maverick stepped away, turning toward his desk. The tension between them decreased to a low simmer. Maverick still wanted that fight, the ultimate battle of alpha males. Wes smelled it. But Maverick would never risk it. He was too level-headed for that. "As punishment, you will have no further involvement in this. Do you understand?"

Wes gritted his teeth. Short of death, it was the worst thing Maverick could to do him, and Maverick knew that. Worse than any physical torture. Wes was part of what the Wild Eight was after. This was personal. To be sidelined, frozen out without so much as a say or even an indication of future plans was nothing short of total emasculation.

"Maverick, they've partnered with the vampires. For the Seven Range Pact, this'll mean war. I know the Wild Eight's tactics better than anyone. Do you understand what this means?"

"I understand exactly what this means. Perhaps better than you do. You will leave this to me. That is a direct order." Maverick's eyes narrowed. "And if you disobey me again, I will show no mercy." His eyes darted in the direction of the doorway. "What about the human? How does she play into this?"

Wes ran a hand through his hair, gripping it at the base of his skull. "After the Wild Eight attacked me, I followed them onto her property. I got stuck in a wolf trap in the process. She had a gun on me."

"And then you chose her life over the safety of our pack? Bringing a human back to Wolf Pack Run?" Maverick clenched his fist as if to hold in his rage.

"She's proof of what the Wild Eight have been up to. Vampires have been draining her flock, and the Wild Eight knew their way around her land. And when have they ever gone after livestock before? She's connected."

Maverick's lips drew into a scowl. "You brought her here so I could clean up your mess?" He shook his head, reaching up to massage his temple as if he were a parent dealing with a rebellious teenager. "You only listen to my orders when it's convenient for you. You have no idea if this woman is innocent. Wild Eight running through her land and vampires exsanguinating her flock, yet you think she's not involved? What if they're targeting her because she's an accomplice? A weak link that needs taking care of?"

Wes hesitated. He'd been too focused on saving her, trusting her, to consider that maybe she wasn't so innocent. A seed of doubt planted in his mind. No, he wouldn't show it to Maverick, even if the packmaster's words gave him pause. His instincts said otherwise. Nevertheless, it served as the reminder he needed to keep his distance from Naomi, tempting as she may be. "I know she's not involved. Not directly, but her connection with the Wild Eight and the vampires, why they're targeting her, could give us valuable information."

"You know pack law."

"You can't kill her." Wes stepped forward, forcing Maverick to meet his eyes again. He needed to see the darkness that lay just beneath the surface, the darkness that as his former enemy, Maverick knew better than anyone. Wes lowered his voice to a near whisper. It was the closest Maverick would ever hear him come to pleading. "Maverick, I can't have any more innocent blood on my hands."

Maverick tore his gaze away and rounded his desk. "Perhaps you should have thought of that before you brought her here. We may have sworn ourselves to protect humanity, but not at the risk of exposing the entire pack."

"You can't kill her," Wes repeated.

"I can, and I w—"

"Then I offer myself in her place."

Maverick fell silent. He scrutinized Wes carefully. "Why does she mean so much to you?"

Over the past twenty-four hours, Wes had asked himself that question countless times. He didn't know her. But all it took was the thought of how terrified she'd looked holding that shotgun on him. Hell if he knew why, but he wanted, *needed* to protect this woman's life, even if it meant giving up his own. "I told you. I don't want any more innocent blood on my hands." It was the best answer he had to give.

Maverick circled around to the front of his desk again, standing inches away from Wes, forcing him to stare eye to eye. "You've really changed that much? In the old days, you wouldn't have hesitated to kill her."

Wes held Maverick's gaze, refusing to look away, though he wasn't sure he knew the answer to that question himself. If he was truthful, he hadn't changed. Sure, he didn't want to kill Naomi, but his reasons for offering his life in place of hers were purely selfish, because he didn't think she should have to pay for his defiance of Maverick's orders, because he really *was* certain he could never live with himself if innocent blood was spilled on his hands again. It was his own twisted way of saving himself.

Slowly, Maverick stepped back. "Three moons. She's your responsibility. We'll monitor her ranchland, send patrols to stake out the terrain, and evaluate if the threat the Wild Eight and the vampires pose to her is true. If she's innocent, I'll let her go, should she swear never to speak of our pack again. For your sake, Wes, I hope you're right, because if I find out you've brought a traitor into our pack, it will be both your blood feeding these lands."

Chapter 6

SHE'D KNOWN THIS WAS COMING, BUT THAT DIDN'T mean she had to like it. After Wes had allowed her to catch up on some sleep, to shower and see to her assorted scrapes and cuts, he'd announced it was high time for them to eat and for her to meet the pack. They'd walked the short distance to the mess hall, but Naomi had stopped in her tracks as they'd neared the large doors.

Isolated with Wes on the mountainside, her companion had, at times, almost seemed human. But inside the mess hall with dozens of other creatures, male and female alike, there would be no escape. Based on the wolf that had attacked her in the woods, her impression of them, save for Wes, wasn't one of friendly welcome.

"You're scared." The early-evening shadows darkened his features. He caught the trepidation in her. Those icy eyes seared straight through her. Every time he looked at her, she felt exposed, naked, raw.

She frowned, wishing she could deny it.

"I can smell your fear, and they will, too."

Wes's words sent a chill down her spine.

"You can do this," he urged.

"Of course I can. If I wasn't afraid of creatures stronger, faster, and harder to kill than me, I'd be an evolutionary failure." She picked up her gait in order to keep up with his strides as they walked. "Is this the part where you tell me I have nothing to be scared of?"

Wes shook his head. "No, you have plenty to be frightened of, but I want you to use it. Walk in there like you own the place. The Grey Wolves value bravery." He pegged her with that penetrating stare of his. "We all do."

A deep blush rose on her cheeks. He thought she was brave. She almost laughed. No one had ever described her that way. Reckless, yes. But never brave.

When they reached the doors, Wes glanced down at her. "Just lie low and you'll be fine." His hand was positioned on the door handle to the mess hall. "You ready?"

She opened her mouth to answer, but he abruptly tugged her toward him. Stumbling forward, she would have collided into his chest had he not caught her by the small of her back. He leaned in next to her ear. The heat of his breath brushed over her, sending a chill down her spine. "If you're brave enough to spend a night in my arms, you can handle this."

Heat flooded her face. She *had* wanted their closeness, once she'd been in his arms. But that was a different matter entirely.

When she pulled away, there was darkness in his gaze, mixed with a hint of humor. He winked, stepped away from her. "Ready or not."

He pushed the door open, and they stepped inside, where five long, wooden tables stretched the length of a western banquet-style room. Hanging lights in the style of old oil lamps lit the space. Old cast-iron wheels hung from the walls. Along with the curved wooden ceilings, the furnishings harked back to old mining times, to pioneers and cowboys long since passed. But Naomi had little time to appreciate the decor.

As she and Wes stepped farther in, a swift silence

rushed through the hall. The room was lined to the brim with bodies, and every eye turned toward them. She'd thought Wes's gaze made her feel as bare as the day she was born, but it was nothing compared to this. She moved forward, eyes defiant, following Wes. He prowled through the hall, oblivious to the stares, or unconcerned. Silence invaded the room, making it so quiet, she could have heard a piece of hay stuck to the side of her boot hit the floor.

Wes took an empty seat near another dark-haired wolf. The other wolf was younger, seemingly by several years. Closer to her brother's age—old enough to be a man with some experience, but still young enough to be too reckless for his own good. The black strands of his hair formed handsome curls.

Unlike Wes's, Curly's eyes were a warm, honeyed shade of brown when they met hers, not much darker than the light-brown shade of his skin. But his boyishly handsome features were pulled into a look of caution. More than half the other wolves were staring at her. Their expressions ran the gamut from shock to horror, from curiosity to downright gawking, and from mild annoyance to blatant aggression, the latter mostly from the males of the species.

The males of the species are always more aggressive to assert dominance, she reminded herself. Though in nature, a person was far more likely to be mauled by a female protecting her young than by an alpha male. Unfortunately, that offered little comfort. Naomi's eyes darted to a group of women sitting farther down the length of the table. Their outward appearance was normal, not as large and menacing as their male counterparts, but the occasional flashes of gold in their eyes told a different story. They were just as dangerous.

Wes sat down a seat's length from Curly and patted the bench for Naomi to sit between them. Slowly, she lowered herself onto the bench between the two werewolves. Her bottom connected with the seat, and she almost let out an audible sigh. At least she'd made it to her seat without being mauled.

The loud scrape of wood against varnished floor caused Naomi to jump. Three wolves across the table from them immediately stood, abandoning their plates and exiting the hall. Naomi's heart dropped. Her eyes shot toward Wes in search of reassurance, but he didn't seem to notice.

He picked up a nearby carving knife and sliced into the succulent-looking brisket sitting in front of him. Several other nearby platters were piled high with equally delicious-looking food. Mesquite corn on the cob, boatfuls of gravy, and biscuits nearly bigger than her fist. The smell wafted into her nose. The meal smelled divine. Her stomach grumbled with hunger, but she didn't dare move. Everyone in the mess hall, save for Wes, still stared at her.

He speared a large piece of brisket with his fork and shoved it into his mouth. Slowly, he chewed. When he finally looked up from his plate to notice all eyes were still on them, he slammed down his fork with a loud clatter. A low growl rumbled from his chest. A clear challenge to everyone in the mess hall. From the angry look on his face, he might as well have bellowed *What the fuck you lookin' at?*

Naomi's heart stopped.

Immediately, talk and chatter filled the room as if someone had turned off the mute button on a television and the sound had been left on full blast. A sense of relief filled her. Wes turned back to his food, grabbing a biscuit and then smothering it with gravy.

To her left, Curly still eyed her skeptically as he slowly returned to his food.

Naomi leaned over toward Wes. She lowered her voice just enough for him to hear her over the roar of the hall. "How am I supposed to get them to trust me?" She nodded to where the three wolves had been only moments earlier.

"It's not you. It's me. Trust me." He sliced more brisket and set it on the plate in front of her. "Eat."

She looked down at her food but didn't pick up her fork. Her stomach churned with nerves.

Wes nudged the plate again. "Don't tell me you're not hungry. I've never met a woman before whose stomach growls louder than mine."

Her head snapped toward him, and her eyes narrowed into a glare. Warmth flushed her cheeks as a small smirk curved his lips. He was egging her on. *Damn him*.

She tore her gaze away from him and glanced down at the food again. It looked more than appetizing, but her stomach was both filled with hunger and in a state of nerve-induced revolt. She wanted the food, but with her nerves as on edge as they were, she didn't rule out vomiting if anything went astray. "I'm not hungry at the moment."

"You feelin' nauseous, darlin'?" The voice, thick with Texas drawl, came from her left. Curly finally looked toward her, a half-eaten ear of corn in his hands.

She gave a tiny nod. "Sort of."

He set his food down and wiped his fingers with his white linen napkin. He twisted toward her, reaching inside his pocket.

Naomi scrambled back, ending up halfway in Wes's lap. She glanced toward the hand that had gone for Curly's pocket. He held a penlight between his thumb and forefinger. From the looks she'd gotten since they first walked in, she had fully expected him to pull a knife.

Wes slapped his fork down with another loud clatter and pegged Curly with a glare. "And *you* told *me* not to scare her." He shook his head. "Austin, Naomi. Naomi, meet Austin, our resident medic. He's about as harmless as it gets around here."

Austin lifted his free hand in a gentle sign of surrender. "I didn't mean to scare ya. Did you get hit in the head while he was haulin' you up here?"

"Yes."

"No."

The answers came in unison. Austin glanced back and forth between them.

Naomi rounded on Wes. "You jammed the butt of my own gun into my temple."

"No. I didn't need to. You'd already passed out from shock."

Naomi shook her head. "I've never passed out from fright in my entire life. He's lying," she said to Austin.

"Don't let her fool you. She just couldn't handle the sight of me nude." Wes lifted Naomi from his lap and set her on the bench beside him.

She scowled at him, and he shot her his infuriating smirk in return, only this time, a little softer than before.

Despite his demeanor in the stables earlier, something in that teasing half smile made him every bit as tantalizing as when he'd held her against him. And damn if she didn't find herself wanting to return the grin.

Austin shook his head. He lifted the penlight and shined it into her left eye. "Don't mind him. He has no filter." He checked the right eye. "Your eyes are dilatin' normal, and you've slept since then, so I'd reckon no concussion. Likely nerves." He nudged her plate closer toward her. "A little somethin' in your belly will help."

She nodded. "Thank you."

"Welcome, ma'am." He pocketed the penlight and turned away from her again.

"Where's your accent come from?" She asked the question before she could stop herself. It sounded pure Texas, but Wes had said the Grey Wolves stuck to Montana as their native lands. Austin didn't seem so intimidating. Not nearly as much as Wes.

A slow smile curled across Austin's lips. "Northern Texas."

Within a matter of minutes, he launched into telling her how he had come to end up at Wolf Pack Run. He was half coyote from his mother's pack in Mexico and half grey wolf from his father's family, who were Mexican American wolves who'd immigrated to Texas several generations earlier, but Maverick had allowed him to join the Montana Grey Wolf pack because he shifted into a grey wolf, not a coyote, and had some fine medical skills to boot. Austin spoke of how he sometimes missed the Texas lowlands, but never the dry heat. As they talked, Naomi picked up her fork and knife and took a bite of the brisket. The smoky beef flavor melted in her mouth, more tender than any piece of beef she'd ever eaten that hadn't come from her own pasture.

Brave. Wes's previous reassurance echoed in her ears.

Werewolves and vampires looming or not, maybe she could do this after all.

By the time Wes finished eating his fill, Naomi and Austin were chatting like two best friends snuggled up at a slumber party. Occasionally, he tuned in to snippets of their conversation. He told himself it was hard not to since he was sitting right next to them. It wasn't that he was in any way interested in this little human's life. Not in the slightest.

Austin talked mostly about his early life in Texas, a frequent topic of discussion he sprang on anyone who would listen. In turn, Naomi shared about her brief stint working as a teacher on the Crow tribe res, the few months she'd spent in California, and her life prior to running her family's ranch. Several times, Wes found himself wanting to ask her questions and chime in on the conversation, but he didn't dare allow himself the chance. As Maverick had highlighted, until they knew otherwise, there was still a distinct chance Naomi could be associated with the Wild Eight. His gut instinct said otherwise, but he wouldn't find himself scorned by a woman's betrayal. Not again. He needed to keep his distance.

To think he had questioned whether she could get the pack to trust her. Once they warmed to the idea, her looks alone would have half the alpha males in the pack fighting for her attention. Throw in the fact that relations with humans were forbidden fruit, and they'd be salivating like starving men.

Just as Wes was contemplating telling Austin to put his tongue back in his mouth and stop panting, the door to the mess hall burst open.

Wes's head snapped toward the noise. Malcolm stood in the doorway, his wolf eyes blazing. His eyes scanned the room until they fell on Wes, then Naomi. Unchecked fury burned in his gaze at the sight of her. *Shit*.

The mess hall fell silent again.

"So it's true." Malcolm prowled toward them. "You thought you could bring a human here unchallenged?"

Wes stood, stepping between Naomi and Malcolm. He crossed his arms over his chest. Malcolm's bone to pick was with him, not her. "You've got a problem? Take it up with Maverick. This doesn't concern you."

The wolf answered in a voice so deep, it gave James Earl Jones a run for his money. "You want to get involved with the Wild Eight again, fine. Be my guest. But don't expect me to sit by while you bring one of those wolf killers into our pack. Not after Bo."

Four months earlier, Bo, the Grey Wolf second-in-command and Malcolm's closest friend, had been killed by a hunter from the Execution Underground. A *human* hunter. Bo's death had left Malcolm grief-stricken, seething with unchecked rage and a burning hatred for all humans.

"You want to take your grief out on someone," Wes growled, "I'm your target, not her."

Malcolm drew back his arm. Wes saw the punch coming but didn't bother to block it. The blow collided with Wes's cheekbone, and his head snapped back. Pain shot through his cheek and radiated down his jaw. He bent over and clutched his skin where Malcolm had hit him. It would maybe bruise, but it would heal within a few hours.

Wes opened his mouth, prepared to ask the bastard if the punch he'd granted him satisfied, when a high-pitched female shriek pierced Wes's ears. While Wes had nursed his cheek, Malcolm had seized the moment to clutch Naomi by the wrist. The scent of her fear flooded Wes's nostrils.

He didn't think.

He grabbed Malcolm by the front of his shirt and threw the other wolf onto the wooden mess-hall table, pinning his fellow packmember with his superior strength. Naomi broke free of Malcolm's grip. Several other packmembers scattered.

A fierce snarl ripped from Wes's throat. "I gave you the punch. For Bo. But if you *ever* lay another hand on her, I will tear out your throat. Understood?"

Malcolm's wolf eyes flashed in anger, and his mouth drew into a tight line, but he gave a curt nod. With a rough shove, Wes released him and stepped back. Every eye in the room was on him.

He turned his back toward Malcolm and stepped away, expecting Naomi to follow.

"Wes!" she shrieked.

Wes spun toward Naomi's voice. But it was too late.

Malcolm drew his knife and thrust it in a downward arc toward Naomi.

Most would have thought to jump away from the blade, but Naomi had clearly been trained in basic self-defense. She stepped forward, ducking under the blade's arc. The move allowed her to block the downward trajectory of Malcolm's forearm with her own, defending herself from attack. She latched on to his wrist like a vise and twisted the metacarpals of Malcolm's hand in the opposite direction. With a sweep and a kick, she took out Malcolm's kneecap. He crumpled to the ground, likely in part from sheer surprise—he clearly hadn't expected her to fight back—as she stripped his knife from his hands. Within seconds, Naomi crouched on top of Malcolm with her knee poised against his throat and his knife in her hands.

"Coward," she hissed. "I'm half your size, and you need a knife?" She shoved the tip of the weapon beneath Malcolm's throat. "If you *ever* touch me again, I will cut your balls off with your own blade." She dropped Malcolm's knife onto the floor beside him with a loud clatter and then scrambled to her feet.

Holy shit.

Wes swallowed down his curse. No one in the mess hall moved. Malcolm gaped up at Naomi from where he lay on the floor, stunned to silence and completely put in his place. Wes didn't blame the bastard. She'd just taken down a werewolf twice her weight and strength, using her small size, speed, and the element of surprise against him. The woman was a veritable lioness in sheep's clothing.

And in self-defense or not, she'd just threatened one of the pack's alpha males. Maverick's warning of her affiliation echoed in Wes's head, the doubt in his chest growing.

He grabbed Naomi by the hand. "Let's go."

Pulling her along behind him, he barreled out of the mess hall with Naomi's hand still clutched in his. This situation was growing worse by the minute. He was digging himself deeper and deeper into a hole that he wasn't certain he could climb out of. If she was a traitor, Maverick would have both their heads.

In the years he'd been a member of this pack, never once had he raised a hand to another packmate. His past reputation had followed him through the Grey Wolf Pack like an unwanted stench that had taken him years to even begin to wash off. Couple his past with the current Wild Eight threat looming over them, and he might as well have been a pariah. He'd been careful never to pick a fight, to keep his head low, to ensure he didn't stir up trouble. Many members of the pack were still distrustful of him. He didn't need to give them more reason to be.

But when he'd seen Naomi in Malcolm's grasp, none of that had mattered.

And now the human woman he'd brought into their midst had just threatened an alpha with his own knife. Not that the bastard hadn't deserved that and far worse. He was lucky it had been Naomi to disarm him. Had Wes been on the other end of that blade…

Her hidden skills spoke to more training with weaponry than most humans could boast. All the more reason that she could, in fact, be involved with the Wild Eight and vampires. The draining of her flock could be a clever ruse. The situation of him stumbling by mere chance onto a human the Wild Eight was targeting smacked of far more than coincidence. He'd staked everything on her innocence, yet what if she…

His eyes caught sight of one of their ranching ATVs with the keys still in the ignition. One of the packmembers had likely ridden it over from their pasture and wouldn't be riding it back out in the dead of night. All the ranching equipment on Wolf Pack Run remained communal, owned by the pack as a whole, so there was no reason for Wes not to use the available vehicle to his advantage.

He climbed on, and Naomi followed without question. They rode out into the night and up a short distance into the mountain forests that lay just behind the main compound to one of the vacant mountain cabins used to house rare visitors. It was a short but safe distance from the mess hall, isolated enough from the main part of Wolf Pack Run that they weren't likely to run into other wolves for the rest of the night.

After they climbed off the ATV, Wes led Naomi up the pine porch steps and into the cabin. He switched on the inside lights, and the bright, recessed lighting illuminated the space. The small, one-bedroom cabin sported a recently redone kitchen with a marble countertop, a cozy living room with a flat-screen TV, a small bookshelf, and a fireplace. Farther inside, the master bedroom featured a large bathroom suite and an entrance to a porch with a hot tub off the back. Far and away better than the cold quartering stable of the night prior. Snatching two large blankets from the storage closet, Wes tossed one to Naomi before he cranked up the thermostat and lit the fire.

"Make yourself at home."

Wes wandered out the open door onto the porch. He needed air, fresh air, to clear the frustration from his head.

Naomi wrapped the blanket around herself and followed him with tentative steps. Wes stood at the edge of the porch, his gaze turned toward the never-ending

expanse of Montana sky. A small clearing in the trees
above allowed for a view of the heavens. Out on the
mountainside in Big Sky Country like this, every star and
constellation twinkled into view. A cool breeze brushed
over them. It was warmer tonight, as if they'd gone back
several weeks in temperature from the autumn cold they'd
started experiencing. But Wes still felt the hint of autumn
hanging on the breeze, the warmth fighting in a tempera-
mental battle with the Canadian winds to make the air feel
uncertain in a way only Montana weather could.

After several minutes of prolonged silence between
them, when his anger had finally simmered to a low boil,
he broke the standoff. "Are you trying to get yourself
killed, woman? It's your first night here." He didn't yell,
but stern censure filled his tone.

Still, Naomi's jaw dropped as if he'd slapped her.
"Last I checked, it was him on the ground. Not me."

"Exactly." He gripped a chunk of his hair. Maverick's
warning about her potential involvement with the Wild
Eight echoed in Wes's head. "Where did you learn to
do that?"

"My brother. He's a Marine," she said. "That wolf
pulled a knife on me. What was I supposed to do?"

"Maybe not make enemies your first night here by
going full-blown Wonder Woman on one of the pack's
alpha males?" he suggested.

She cocked her head to the side, confused. "You know
who Wonder Woman is? Isn't that a human thing?"

That's what she took away from this? Wes shook his
head. He turned away from her, tossing his blanket onto
the damp wood of the porch before he took a seat. The
sight of her struggling against Malcolm had twisted his

gut with both fear for her life and doubt about her innocence. "You're lucky Malcolm was so stunned by that little display that he didn't shift right there and tear out your throat. That knife would have meant nothing if he'd shifted. What part of 'lie low' don't you understand?"

"The part where I'm supposed to let someone stab me to keep the peace!" She dropped down on the blanket beside him with an ungraceful flop and drew in a deep breath. "I didn't ask for this." As she said it, her breath hitched on the last word.

Shit. He'd made her cry.

She was right. She hadn't asked for him, for this, for any of it. Yet here she was.

Unchecked rage blazed through him, directed at no one but himself. Somehow, the sight of this tiny human woman in danger was worse than a knife through his cold, dead heart. Not so dead now, he supposed, considering the way it had thumped against his chest at the sight of Malcolm's knife headed toward her.

He shook his head. What was wrong with him? He *shouldn't* care for her. He barely knew her. Yet seeing Malcolm attack her had terrified him.

There was only one other time in his life he'd ever been so scared...

Without thinking, he scooted closer to her so they sat nearly hip to hip and swiped one of her tears away with his thumb. She turned her head away from him with a pathetic-sounding sniffle, but he guided her chin back toward him.

"I'm sorry..." The words slipped out before he could stop himself.

It was the first time in his whole damn life he'd ever

apologized for anything. He was Wes Calhoun. Former packmaster of the Wild Eight, son of the nefarious Nolan Calhoun, and one of the deadliest wolves to walk these mountainsides. He apologized to no one.

Except, apparently, her…

They lingered there, his hand on her cheek. The moonlight and the glow from the cabin windows bathed them in a pale, gentle light, bright enough that he could make out the elegant details of her face, the slender curves of her body.

His cock hardened in rigid anticipation. He traced his fingers over the bandages she'd applied on her shoulders and throat, his touch whisper soft, a silent apology for those small injuries. Man, she'd be the undoing of him. He wasn't supposed to want her, to touch her. He'd taken her captive to protect her. He'd been down this path before, knew the deadly consequences, and yet…

He lowered his hand. They were playing with fire, and they'd both be consumed by the flame if he didn't cut the heat and tenderness between them now.

As his hand fell, she turned away from him, staring out over the mountainside, her eyes scanning over the land. While she wasn't looking, he subtly adjusted the erection straining against his jeans.

"How big is it?" She broke the momentary silence between them.

Wes froze. Apparently, he hadn't been as discreet as he'd thought, but he hadn't expected such a blunt ques—

"You do know the acreage of your own ranch, don't you?" she asked.

The ranch. She was talking about the Grey Wolf ranch.

A low chuckle passed his lips, the moment providing some much-needed levity. "Big enough to impress." *On both accounts*. "The Grey Wolf ranch is about 126,000 acres of operation, some deeded land, some state grazing lease. Our cattle herd is about 4,300. About 3,200 bred cows and 1,400—mostly heifer—calves, plus plenty of bulls, yearlings, and ranch horses."

Her jaw dropped. "You mean to tell me the Grey Wolves are sitting on a…hell, I'd estimate a seventy-million-dollar operation?"

He shrugged. "That's just the land and livestock. Likely more if you consider all the homes and additional utility buildings."

She gaped at him. "You guys could buy my ranch out in a second." She said it as simple commentary, but as she spoke, her shoulders lowered, and she folded further into herself. There was something she wasn't sharing.

If he hadn't been watching her so closely, the movement would have been barely perceptible. The slightest hint of vulnerability overtook her body language, and any bit of humor he'd felt from her previous comment disappeared. "I thought you wanted to preserve your father's legacy."

"I do." Her answer came swiftly, almost too much so, as if she were too eager to show it.

Clearly, she wanted that. She was here, trusting a werewolf she didn't know with her safety and her life in part for the sake of her ranch's well-being.

"But…" He waited for her to elaborate, to open up to him and speak freely as she had seemed to do with Austin in the mess hall.

She released a long sigh and pulled her legs up to her

chest, cradling them against her. "You're not supposed to talk finances with friends."

"Friends, huh?" He supposed it fit. Before she'd said it, he hadn't been exactly sure what he would call them. Enemies? Adversaries? Captor and captive? Disobedient werewolf monster and his sexy human pain-in-the-rear?

"Don't let the descriptor go to your head," she warned, drawing her attention back to him. "You're still a mangy wolf."

"As mangy as they come," he grumbled.

He allowed his gaze to wander over her. Bathed in the moonlight, with that small coy smile curving her lips, she was breathtaking.

He tore his gaze away and looked out over the Grey Wolf lands. If she had any idea how truly wild he was, she wouldn't be sitting beside him, so close that her scent wrapped around him. His eyes scanned the dark slanting hills beneath the foundation of the cabin. How different would this moment with her have been if he'd been born a Grey Wolf packmember, if his past wasn't so dark that he needed to keep her at arm's length?

The question seared into him, in part because the heart he once thought long dead already knew the answer.

———

Naomi stayed there beside Wes, sitting in silence for minutes that seemed to stretch into hours as they both stared up at the swirls of starbursts above. Her avoidance of his question about the ranch hung in the air, building heavy tension. She felt an aversion to answering the question as keenly as she felt the answer dancing on her tongue.

She'd never shared this part of her life with anyone. Yet somehow, she found she wanted to tell him. The events of the evening had left her feeling bare, and what fear could there be in opening up to him? In a few days, they would go their separate ways, and whatever was said between them would fade to a distant memory. And it already felt as if his eyes saw right through her.

She steeled herself. "We're an average-size calf-cow operation. Only two thousand acres. Our finances are hurting. We have plenty of overhead costs, yet not enough hands or cattle to truly turn a substantial profit or save a cushion for when the price of beef is low. We're getting by, but we've been trying to find investors to make the changes we need to keep the ranch afloat."

His deep voice was low, comforting. "That's nothing to be ashamed of, Miss Kitty. You're doing what you need to do to save your family legacy. That's admirable."

She shook her head. "No, it's not admirable. It's... it's one of my biggest personal failures." She released a long breath, the smoky heat of it twisting around her face in the cold mountain air. "It's my fault," she confessed. "We would have had the money if we hadn't had to use what was set aside in my dad's estate to pay his medical bills." She wrapped her arms tighter around herself both to keep warm and to hold herself together. "He didn't want chemo, and I pushed him into it. I didn't want him to die. I wasn't ready for it. And..."

Her voice trailed off, leaving the words unspoken, but as he had in the stables, Wes saw right through her.

"And you didn't want to be stuck on the ranch?" he finished.

Shame filled her. "I was so selfish. His death could

have been a dignified one, at home and peaceful. Not lying in a hospital bed, hooked up to all those beeping and whirring machines. But I begged and pleaded with him to consider chemo until he did. And for what? All so I could drive his legacy into the ground, escape the life he'd carved out for me with the hard labor of his hands, to say what he chose for me wasn't enough. That's why I have to save it, because it's my fault it's in its current state."

"Don't do that." His words were commanding but full of gentle understanding.

Her eyes shot toward him. "Do what?"

"Don't put yourself down for wanting more. It's your life. Your choice, Miss Kitty. And if you think it isn't enough, well, then it isn't, no matter what your father thought was best for you or how hard he worked to give you the life he envisioned. He worked for that because he cared for you and wanted you to be happy, but if you're not happy in the same way he was, you owe it to yourself to seek more." His gaze seared into hers. "You'll be miserable until you do."

The utter devastation in his eyes destroyed her. He shared her pain as his own. She could see it. "You say that like you speak from experience."

He looked away. "I don't know what it's like to have a loving father, but I do know what it's like to fail to meet your father's expectations, to be expected to uphold someone else's legacy that is both your origin story and so damn separate from your own, it hurts. I know how selfish and wrong you can feel for forging your own path, but you have to do it. If you don't, the resentment will consume you."

She wasn't certain how to respond. In that moment, he understood her on a deep human level, perhaps better than anyone she'd ever known. His gaze, how he saw through her, made her feel as if she was baring her soul. Her darkest failures and her biggest fears.

Pushing to his feet, he retreated into the cabin. She knew he wasn't ending their conversation, but he was protecting himself in a way she knew all too well, closing himself off. She watched through the window as he sat down beside the fireside.

A moment later, she joined him, rubbing her hands together in front of the dancing flames, basking in their warmth.

"I come here to think sometimes," Wes said as she sat down beside him. "For clarity. I think being out here in the woods gives me perspective on what really matters in life." He looked toward her. That stare made her feel so raw, so naked. A familiar fear scratched at the back of her mind, unwelcome yet so entrenched there that she wasn't sure how to overcome it.

"It's not ranching that I don't like," she confessed.

The orange flames of the fire reflected back in the pale blue of his irises. With the way those eyes seared into her, the flames only seemed appropriate.

"I love working the land," she continued. "But my whole life—after my mother passed when I was little, at least—it's just been me, my dad, and Jacob out there. My mother was pure Apsáalooke—Crow tribe, to a non-native like you. When I was younger, I had friends and extended family at the Nation, but you know how ranching is. It's a nonstop job, from sunrise to sunset, and I've gone days—hell, weeks—without having any real human contact. Even though my ranch is on the borderlands, I go once a year to the Crow Fair. It's a reunion where we honor our ancestors' lives as Plains buffalo hunters and introduce the young ones to our cultural heritage. But connecting with my community once a year is hardly enough. With my dad gone and Jacob living his own life, other than the help we have, I feel so alone. I know there's a possibility I could start a family of my own someday, but when does running the ranch ever leave me time to…?"

To meet a man.

A strong, attractive, and virile man. Like the one staring at her now, whose eyes bore through her with such intensity, it was staggering. She blushed and glanced down at her hands.

"I don't need a man to complete my life," she elaborated, "but I…need a family, time to make friends, the financial resources to hire more hands, and more opportunities to connect with my people. Not the isolation of ranch living."

"If you had those things, would the ranch be enough for you?" he asked.

She turned back toward the flames as a memory filled her mind's eye. Playing with her brother near the edge of their property. He was pretending to be a cowboy with an old piece of rope they'd taken from the barn, and she was running. Running as fast as she could, scrambling over the edge of the fence, splinters pricking her hands as she raced toward the safety of the forest. Jacob was three years younger and never fast enough to catch her. Just as she reached the tree line, the sound of her mother's red-apple-shaped dinner bell rang in the distance, and the spell was broken.

Even as a child, Naomi had known and recognized a powerful force drawing her to the land, these hills. Some western sense of adventure passed on to her from her father. It had dissipated after his death, and it'd taken the extreme circumstances of the past few days to be rediscovered.

"I think it would. I love these mountains. I can't imagine calling anywhere else home, and I want to preserve the legacy my father built. I think my father knew that about me even before I did." She turned back toward Wes. "That's what I want."

"Then that's something worth protecting, worth fighting for." His eyes were his wolf's again, staring back at her with that deep hunger.

"What about you? Do you like what you're doing here on the Grey Wolf ranch?"

"I mainly tend the stables, take care of the horses, train them." He turned away from her. "It keeps me sane."

"That's not what I asked."

Slowly, he leaned back on his hands, propping up the weight of his torso behind him. "It's the only thing my past allows."

She shook her head. "We all have a past."

"Mine is darker than most."

"It can't be all that bad."

At that, he smirked. "We come from different worlds."

It was her turn to shrug. "Last time I checked, humans could be pretty evil. War, nuclear weapons, genocide. Ever heard of those things?"

"Yeah, but when you're a human and a murderer, they lock you up in jail. You become an outlaw to society. In our world, they call that alpha."

He watched her with narrowed eyes as if he could see the gears turning in her head through her gaze. She'd recognized him as an alpha, and now she knew what that meant. She could tell he meant for it to faze her, but it didn't. The gold of his eyes flashed.

She shook her head and smiled. "Didn't your mother ever tell you not to play with your food?"

He raised an eyebrow.

"Don't you feed on humans?" she asked. "I mean, I know we just ate dinner and all, but I figured it was maybe like vampires."

He shook his head. "No. What would give you that idea?"

She pointed with two fingers to her own eyes. "Your eyes seem to flash every time you stare at me. You look hungry when you look at me."

A slight growl rumbled in his chest. "That's a different kind of hunger, Naomi."

Naomi. It was the first time he hadn't called her that awful nickname. The way he said it melted her insides like butter. Heat flooded through her center and outward. His words stirred something deep and low in her belly. She felt that heat burn all the way up into her breasts, her cheeks.

Wes tore his gaze away from hers. "We better get some sleep. I'll take the couch, and you can have the bedroom. We'll have a full day ahead of us come sunrise."

She nodded. As she stood and took one last look at him, a sharp pang hit her chest. She felt raw, vulnerable, open in a way she hadn't since she'd mourned at her father's hospital bedside. In the past hour, she'd been more honest with the man beside her than she remembered ever being with anyone, except for the man who'd raised her. Richard Evans had been honest and authentic almost to a fault, and she'd always returned that honesty. They'd had that special father-daughter bond she'd never been able to replicate with another family member.

She thought about what her dad would have said to her in that moment. He would have told her to tell the whole truth, because as truthful as she'd been with Wes, there was one part she'd left out. Yes, she wanted to keep the ranch. She'd always wanted that, even though she'd questioned if the dream was her father's or her own. But that vision of happiness on the ranch had changed in the past few days, beyond having a family and loved ones there to call her own. She'd always longed for a sense of adventure in her life, but she'd never before had a taste. Not until this.

And now, in a few days' time, when she returned to her ranch, that adventure would be gone for good as it rode off into the distance.

Chapter 7

"YOU A STEADY HAND IN HERDING CATTLE, MISS Kitty?" They were the first words Wes had spoken to her all morning.

Other than a weak *mornin'*, he hadn't said a thing to her. The moment she'd laid eyes on him as she'd emerged alone from the cabin bedroom, she'd realized that whatever honesty and openness had passed between them last night had dissipated. This morning, this was a man determined to keep his distance. She'd showered, changed into a fresh set of clothes he'd laid out for her (borrowed from one of his female packmates), and had been greeted afterward by the smell of fresh bacon and eggs sizzling in the kitchen. She'd been so consumed with chowing down on the contents of her plate with gusto that she'd somehow forgotten her manners and hadn't thanked him for making her a delicious breakfast or made any attempt at polite conversation. She was too caught up in feeling far more "human" than she had in days.

She swallowed the massive bite of eggs stuffed in her cheek with a strained gulp. "I've been herding cattle all my life, since I was old enough to ride horseback. I'm more than fair."

"Good." He stabbed his fork into another bite of egg. "How about other livestock?"

She raised an eyebrow. "What did you have in mind?"

He took a bite of his breakfast, chewed, and swallowed. "Well, I know better than to waste the skills of a perfectly good rancher, and I'll need an extra pair of hands this morning. It's past time I bring the wild horses into the chute and wean the colts. We had a couple of mares who were already bred when they arrived."

Naomi's eyes widened. If she hadn't already swallowed the bit of egg she was chewing, she might have choked on it. "The Grey Wolves managed to get a wild-horse contract? I thought you were mainly a cow-calf operation."

She had never met another rancher who'd managed to procure a wild-horse contract with the U.S. government. Typically, when droughts or a growing horse population got too large out west, the government would put a wild-horse contract up to bid for private ranches. In order to be awarded a contract, a ranch needed the ability to take care of at least five hundred wild horses, which meant they needed a helluva lot of land for the horses to roam and plenty of resources, particularly considering the hooved beasts were so rough on the landscape. Cow-calf operations were the main business in this part of beef country, and the bidding process for a wild-horse contract with the Bureau of Land Management was highly competitive. In addition to the amount of land necessary, the BLM required lengthy and exhaustive documentation, detailing a ranch's management process for the horses.

Wes shrugged, unfazed by her awe. "On our main ranch, we have cow-calf, yearlings, and now the wild horses, about 3,500 of them. I've headed up the project. Bid and negotiated the contract myself. The care and upkeep and managing the few hands that help with it is my pack responsibility. I talked Maverick into it. The contract may not earn as much per head as selling our calves in spring and fall, but it's steady payout, low on overhead costs, and less labor than cattle. We've got plenty of mouths to feed here, so we needed to diversify our profits without tying up more money in inventory."

Naomi blinked several times, taking in the sight of him as if she were seeing him clearly for the first time. The man before her was far more than a handsome wolf and a valiant warrior who'd saved her life. Clearly, he also had a mind for the ranching business and the skills to back it up. And if last night was any indication, he was also an incredible listener, a fierce friend. There was clearly so much more to Wes Calhoun than met the eye…and damn if she didn't want to see all of it, the good and the bad.

"I've never worked with wild mustangs," she finally managed when her initial awe started to subside.

"You've met Black Jack, so you have some idea. They're stubborn, ornery suckers. Black Jack's an extreme case though. He takes attitude and makes it a virtue. I had to pull him out of the herd because he was too much of a stud with the mares, and the BLM doesn't want even more colts they have to pay for, so I ended up purchasing him myself and breaking him. If you could call him broken."

Naomi grinned. She wouldn't dare call Black Jack broken or trained. The horse did as he damn well pleased.

"They're different from cattle," Wes continued. "They're skittish, and the slightest provocation can send them into a frenzy. You can help herd them into the chute, but I can't have you separating out the colts once they're in the pen."

She frowned. "Why? Because I'm a woman?"

He shook his head. "No. We Grey Wolves don't take too kindly to having any of our"—he hesitated to find the right word—"*guests* participating in dangerous activities or having weapons."

"And by guest, you mean prisoner?" And to think she'd thought she'd come here of her own volition.

He scowled. "Your words, not mine." He crunched down on a slice of bacon.

"What does it matter? I already have my…" She reached to her belt and realized that her Ka-Bar was missing again, and her shotgun had been lost in the melee as they'd escaped. Her eyes immediately fell in an accusatory glare on the wolf sitting across from her.

He didn't smile, but for a brief moment, she thought she saw a hint of amusement there.

"I'm glad you think this is funny," she snapped.

"Did I laugh?" he challenged.

"You didn't need to. I can see the amusement in your eyes." She'd yet to hear him laugh, and even with that smirking amusement twinkling in his eyes, she found she truly wanted to hear the sound. She watched him, gauging his reaction. He was different. The man she'd met in the Montana wilds was guarded here, edgy. Hell-bent on keeping her at arm's length.

He turned toward the stove, returning with the cast-iron skillet. "Here." He piled more food on her plate. "Eat more. A strong wind could blow you over." It was a clear attempt to avoid any playfulness between them.

She didn't protest. At least not verbally. If he wanted

it that way, then fine. Two could play at that game, and she knew how to play dirty. She mulled over how to crack his ironclad facade as she half-heartedly pushed her food around her plate.

Following breakfast, they rode the ATV back down the mountainside and through the heart of Wolf Pack Run. Despite her initial impression, it was less a development of homes and more a self-contained village that extended for several miles. As she watched the homes and buildings bustling with activity speed by from the back of the off-road vehicle, she noted with increasing interest a plethora of men, women, and families with young children, all so seemingly human in appearance that if she didn't know better, she never would have known the difference. There were even a few she thought looked familiar from the Crow Fair.

But her pleasant observation came to a halt at the same moment the ATV suddenly did. She'd thought they were headed straight for the isolation of the stables, but they had stopped outside what appeared to be some sort of warrior training field. This early in the morning, the training field was mostly empty, save for the nearby racks of weapons, and a few females watching off to the side. The field remained bare, except for the two battling wolves in the middle of it.

A man equal in size to Wes stood on the battlefield, barking orders at a she-wolf wielding a broadsword against him. Though their swords clashed, his sharp grey eyes watched her like a hawk, assessing her every move like a military commander.

"You can do better than that, Sierra. Push yourself," he demanded.

Anger and frustration filled the woman's face as she fought the male alpha wolf with vigor anew, pushing herself even harder than she'd been. Both of them were an impressive sight to behold.

"Colt," Wes bellowed.

The grey-eyed wolf's gaze lifted to where Wes and Naomi sat on the ATV.

In response, the female let out a resounding roar, throwing a kick into her commander's shield, causing him to stumble backward.

He scowled as he regained his footing.

She smiled wickedly. "If we'd been on the battlefield, I would have slaughtered you."

The wolf named Colt growled. "If we'd been on the battlefield, I wouldn't have taken my eyes off you," he said to his opponent. Stabbing his sword into the ground, he made his way off the field toward Wes and Naomi.

"I'll be right back," Wes said. "I need to see if Colt will lend us a hand rounding up the horses." He climbed off the ATV and met the other man halfway, their conversation descending into heated whispers as soon as they reached each other.

In the distance, Naomi watched as the she-wolf warrior exited the field. One of the other women handed her a water bottle that she promptly chugged. Her face was covered in a sheen of sweat. As she lowered the water bottle, her eyes caught Naomi's. The other females followed her gaze.

Oh no. The moment made Naomi harken back to every horrible run-in she'd had with cheerleaders in high school. They might as well have been a pack of rabid she-wolves, considering the way they'd treated her. As the actual she-wolves made their way toward Naomi, she stiffened, thankful Wes was close by and the keys were still in the running ATV. When the pack of women reached her, the one the commander had called Sierra stepped forward.

"You know your way around a broadsword?" she asked, her eyes darting down to the weapon in her hand.

Naomi's blood ran cold, although the question seemed to be more inquisitive than challenging. "No," she murmured.

"You certainly know how to use a knife," Sierra replied. "At least if what I heard about you taking Malcolm down in the mess hall is true."

Naomi raised both hands in surrender. "I didn't mean any offense by it, I swear."

Sierra turned her head to the side as if she were confused. "Offense? I would have given anything to see that bastard land flat on his ass." The smile she gave Naomi was genuine and warm, so much so that Naomi released a hesitant breath.

"Oh, thank goodness. I thought you all were about to throttle me for it."

The group of women chuckled, not with mean intent but with friendly welcome at the confusion.

"Not at all," a second one chimed in.

"Someone needs to teach these alpha males what's what," a third said.

"That's what we're out here for," Sierra added.

"Sierra," Colt called.

He and Wes had finished their conversation, and Wes was headed back toward them.

"And here comes the one who needs the biggest kick in the pants of all," Sierra muttered to Naomi.

"Except maybe for Maverick," another remarked.

Sierra scowled at the mention of the packmaster's name before she turned to head back toward the training field. As she and the other she-wolves moved away, she cast a glance over her shoulder. "I hope you stick around, Naomi Evans. We could use some more females like you here." The sentiment was echoed on the other women's faces.

"Thanks," Naomi said. Wes climbed onto the ATV, and as they sped off toward the stables, she cast one last smile at her warm welcomers. Naomi had the distinct impression that given time, she could easily befriend these women, werewolves or otherwise.

The Grey Wolf stables were truly a sight to be seen. This early in the morning with the sun barely peeking over the horizon, the massive complex bustled with male and female stable hands eager to get their work done. A cacophony of neighs and whinnies echoed throughout the space, and the smell of hay and freshly mucked stalls filled Naomi's nose as they entered. A few of the hands shot them curious glances as they entered but seemed to decide to keep to themselves after seeing Wes's face. He was all business, focused on the day's work like any true cowboy.

After Wes spent a brief moment showing her around, he allowed Naomi to take her pick from several horses. She chose a palomino mare by the name of Star, who, according to Wes, had been the horse of a wolf named Bo, the Grey Wolf second-in-command who had been killed several months earlier. The way Naomi figured it, a horse who'd lost its rider probably needed the attention and the workout. As she saddled Star, getting acquainted with the gentle mare, Wes busied himself with attempting to wrangle a saddle onto a pissed-off Black Jack.

As Naomi led Star out of her pen, her eyes fell on a shadowy figure standing backlit in the open stable doorway. As he stepped forward, she recognized him as the wolf from the training field Wes had called Colt. Colt's dark figure drew farther into the stable, and she noted the generous width of his shoulders and the limbs lined with muscle. These guys were seriously gorgeous.

If Colt's massive size wasn't enough to intimidate, the hawk-like nature of his stare beneath the rim of his black Stetson hat was. She wasn't sure why, but she had the distinct impression that nothing got past this particular wolf. Some of her brother's friends from the Marines had returned home with a similarly intense gaze.

Wes emerged, leading Black Jack by the reins. Apparently, he'd won the battle. Though from the look in the horse's eyes, there was no telling how long the minor victory would last.

Wes gestured back and forth between Naomi and Colt. "Naomi, this is Colt Cavanaugh, high commander of the Grey Wolf armies. When it comes to horses, he's the best at Wolf Pack Run, aside from myself. He's also one of the only wolves around here brave enough to give me a hard time."

"Put you in your place is more like it," Colt shot toward Wes. His tone was serious, but his eyes were full of mirth.

Naomi's eyes grew wide. She was still stuck on the "high commander of the Grey Wolf armies" part.

Colt extended a massive hand, and Naomi offered her own. His grip was strong and firm as they shook, yet surprisingly, not overbearing. It seemed calculated somehow, as though every move he made was strategic and carefully planned.

"Colt," she said, her voice more of an intimidated squeak than she'd intended. She cleared her throat and tried again. "Like a young horse. An appropriate name for a cowboy."

"Pleasure to meet you, Naomi." The high commander flashed her an easy grin. "You're all anybody on this ranch is talking about." The smile lit his face and changed it from hardened warrior to cowboy with rugged charm in seconds. It was the kind of white-toothed grin that could make the right woman weak in the knees.

Oh man, he was dangerous. Had she not been so enamored with the wolf standing beside him, her heart might have beat a little faster.

She glanced at the two men. Come to think of it, something about him reminded her of Wes. The shape of their eyes and the distinct way they creased at the edges when they smiled was near identical. She chalked it up to nothing more than shared wolf DNA.

Wes quickly launched into instructions. They'd be culling from roughly three hundred of the wild horses off one of the smaller herds, then corralling them into the chute to separate out the still-nursing colts. Colt would take one of the Grey Wolves' Rhino vehicles while Naomi and Wes rode horseback on Black Jack and Star, leading Colt's horse, Silver, along with them. According to Wes, though the mustangs were still truly as wild as possible, as the government and BLM intended, they'd been housed on the open plains of the ranch long enough to come running for food at the sound of a vehicle's horn, especially now as the weather grew colder each day, leaving the grass and foliage to dwindle and Wes to supply their food to keep them healthy.

Sticking with their plan, they rode out into the Grey Wolf pastures, following Colt in the SUV. When Wes signaled, Colt pulled the vehicle to a stop and laid on the horn. The loud, sharp beep rang throughout the hills. After a minute or more of the racket, Naomi covered her ears with her hands. This went on for several minutes until Naomi spotted the first horse off in the distance. The number multiplied as the herd rounded the hill toward the mountainside, barreling straight toward them. A sea of wild mustangs revealed themselves. The pounding of the large animals' hooves thudded against the ground in a display of raw power and strength.

Wes maneuvered Black Jack toward her, his satisfied smirk peeking out from beneath the brim of his Stetson. Naomi recognized it as the smile of a man who took pride and joy in working with his hands. Her father and Jacob got that same look when they worked the land.

"Showtime." Wes grinned before he kicked Black Jack into a gallop, heading straight toward the herd.

Naomi and Colt followed. The three worked together to move the herd eastward toward the chute. Naomi quickly learned what Wes had meant about herding cattle being vastly different from herding mustangs. For the first hour or so, it seemed every movement she made sent the skittish yet aggressive animals careening in the wrong direction. In due time, she found her footing, pulling her weight of the corral work as easily as the two wolves beside her.

It was past noon when they'd finally managed to

corral the horses into the chute, and Naomi was thankful for the extra breakfast Wes had urged her to eat. Shortly thereafter, Sierra showed up in one of the Grey Wolf pickup trucks, delivering them a basket of lunch, though she made certain to tell Colt—who, from what Naomi gathered during the conversation, was Sierra's older brother—not to think she'd make a habit of it. She made it clear her sole interest was Naomi.

The foursome shared the picnic lunch of pimento cheese sandwiches and a few Budweisers. As Naomi and Sierra made friendly conversation with the occasional interjection from Colt about everything from life at Wolf Pack Run to their favorite kinds of wine and their mutual love of B-rated romantic comedy movies, Wes remained quiet, distant, and seemingly caught up in thoughts of his work.

When they'd finished eating, Naomi leaned back onto the picnic blanket Sierra had brought and passed what remained of their break enjoying the playful sibling banter between Colt and Sierra that reminded her so much of her and Jacob. It had turned out to be a pleasant morning and a fine start to the afternoon. She found that the warmth and sense of belonging she felt among the ragtag crew made her heart a little tender. She never felt this way on her own ranch. Though she was friendly with the ranch hands, it was mostly just her out there, working alone. She didn't miss the silence.

When lunch was finished, Sierra made her departure. But not before she roped Naomi into a near-rib-crunching bear hug and whispered that she hoped Wes didn't scare her away, so Naomi would decide to stay at Wolf Pack Run. Naomi didn't get the chance to tell her that wasn't even in the realm of possibility before the female left without another word but with a conspiratorial gleam in her eye.

From the position of the sun, it was roughly three o'clock when Wes and Colt made their way into the chute. Once in the pens, Naomi stood near the chute and watched as the two cowboys sorted the horses down the alley. The mares and colts went into a pen on the right and the stallions into a pen on the left. One by one, Colt, who rode Silver, peeled the young horses off from the herd of mares. Meanwhile, Wes stood at the end of the alley, directly in the line of fire, prepared to swing the gate open or closed depending on whether a mare or a colt was running at him.

Watching the two men was mesmerizing. Each movement was careful, deliberate, calm, like well-practiced and incredibly courageous choreography. One wrong move, and any one of the horses they worked with could go off the deep end. Naomi had been on the wrong end of a horse bite a time or two, and it wasn't a pretty thing. That didn't even begin to cover the damage the beasts could do with the strength and weight of their muscled bodies if they decided to plow a man over. The mustangs were nothing like the calm, predictable cattle she was used to.

As she watched, her respect for Wes grew deeper by the moment. He'd not only saved her life and connected with her at the cabin, but he was tough, strong, brave, valiant, and seemingly afraid of nothing. He didn't even tense when the angry mares barreled down the alley toward him. When they'd finished, Naomi found herself more than a little enamored and amenable to the idea of being alone with him again.

Wes exited the shoot with Colt and Silver in tow, thanking Colt for his help. Colt tipped his hat to Naomi. "You're a good hand at herding," he said.

She grinned at the compliment. "You're not so bad yourself."

He and Silver started to head off. "Oh, Naomi?" Colt paused, several feet away from her, eyeing her from atop Silver. "Don't let the smooth cowboy side fool you."

She raised a brow. For a moment, she thought he was talking about Wes. "Yeah?" she asked.

Colt's award-winning smile disappeared, replaced by the look of a hardened warrior. It changed his whole demeanor within seconds to befit his title as Grey Wolf high commander. "It's Colt like the gun, not the horse," he said.

The words were enough to send a chill down her spine though she knew he was only riling her. Wes waved Colt away with a side comment about the commander being too big for his britches before joining Naomi. Resting his hands on his slender hips, he ducked his head low beneath his Stetson to shield his eyes from the afternoon sun. "So what do you think?" He nodded toward the pen still full of the now-sorted mares and colts.

She smiled. "You want the honest truth?"

He nodded. "Nothing less."

She released a long-held breath. "It's amazing, and I'm totally jealous. I enjoy working with cattle, but that's not nearly as much fun as these horses. What an adventure." She stared at the massive herd, her voice tinged with a hint of longing.

Wes's eyes never left her, observing her in that

careful way that made her feel naked. "There's something else you're not saying."

Barely forty-eight hours with the man, and it was as if he saw right through her. She dug deep inside herself, trying to find the right words to be open with her emotions in the way they'd shared in the cabin. It was something she'd never had with anyone since her father's death, and though she was eager to get back to that place with Wes, she wasn't used to the vulnerability of it. "It's just…" Her voice hitched. "I know I'll never have anything on my ranch like what you have here with Colt, Sierra, your pack. Even the close-knit community at the Nation is not like this. I guess I'm just tired of being alone."

He didn't shy away from her pain. Instead, he leaned in, the blazing in his eyes searing her straight to her core. It was as if his gaze said everything her heart longed to hear.

I know what that's like, and you're not alone.

She stepped toward him, eager to draw close, but he must have sensed her growing desire, because he turned away at the last moment.

He leaned onto the iron bars of the chute. "So you like the wild horses, huh?"

She nodded, trying not to be hurt by his clear attempts to keep her at a distance. He'd mentioned that their pack law forbade humans and wolves from mating, but somehow, the way he pushed her away despite the fire in his eyes made her think there was another reason aside from the pack law. He hardly seemed like the type to follow the rules.

"Yes, watching them run… It's a beautiful, exhilarating sight," she answered.

Wes grinned, smiling at her from beneath his Stetson

in a way that made her ache with need. "Oh, Miss Kitty, you ain't seen nothing yet."

———

"Stand back. Once one notices the gate is open and comes running, it'll be a stampede," he instructed. Wes stood at the chute gate, the cold iron latch clutched in his hand. With the young colts separated off their mothers to wean, he needed to release the mares back out into the open landscape. It was quite a sight to behold, wild mustangs running to the freedom of the Montana mountainside as they were meant to. It was one thing to see them galloping toward food, but witnessing them run with wild abandon toward their freedom was a whole different matter, and he intended to let Naomi enjoy it to its fullest.

"You ready?" he called.

Naomi stood several feet back from the gate, out of the line of sight. She smiled. The orange shade of the setting sun cast a warm glow across her ebony hair and lit up the brown tones of her skin. He'd been trying to keep her at arm's length all day. He'd worked not to notice how mesmerizing her look of concentration was as they'd worked, tried not to note what a hard worker and admirable cowgirl she was. So far, he was failing miserably.

"Ready," she called back. She bounced on the balls of her feet in anticipation.

Wes hit the latch and swung the gate wide. The release of the latch signaled the mares like the firing of a shot. A sea of mustangs shot forth from the chute, galloping out into the landscape. Wes turned and watched with appreciation.

It was a breathtaking sight.

And he didn't mean the horses. He couldn't stop the grin curling at his lips as he watched Naomi. Her gorgeous features were lit with enthusiasm and awe at the beautiful sight of the herd of wild horses galloping across the mountainside, their long manes billowing in the cold autumn wind.

"Do you see this? Wow!" she called out to him, her face wreathed with a smile.

Normally, he would agree with her. Even having worked with the horses for the better part of a year, he still thought they were an amazing sight. Yet he couldn't bring himself to partake of her joy. Instead, he stood at a distance, watching her with eager, hungry eyes like a starving man. Somehow, it felt as if he stood on the outside looking in, there but not truly present.

Never in the way he wanted to be.

It'd taken everything in him not to draw her into his arms last night as they'd sat beside the fireplace. He practiced the same restraint now. He wanted to kiss her with everything he was worth. But he couldn't. If his lips touched hers again, he wouldn't be able to stop himself. She'd end up laid out beneath him, with him claiming her in every way, and he couldn't allow that.

She was a human. In her arms, he was nothing but destruction.

But damn, if the way she'd bared her soul to him, told him her heart's desires and her deepest pains, didn't make him want so much more than the careful, calculated distance he'd placed between them. He *wanted* to open himself to her, to cast aside his shame and take off the mask he'd worn for so long that it felt as it were suffocating him. He longed for it in a way he was certain he'd never longed for anything in his life. It made him feel as if there were a growing, empty hole inside his chest. In this moment, watching her genuine smile lit by the afternoon sun, he felt that pain and longing so acutely that he struggled to breathe.

But he couldn't give in, despite how it pained him, because if he did, she'd see him for what he truly was. A violent man. A monster. A murderer.

No, he'd keep his distance, painful and torturous as it might be.

Better to let the pain consume him than to allow it to destroy an innocent woman like her.

Chapter 8

THEY RODE BACK TO THE STABLES IN COMPANIONABLE silence. When they arrived, they set about doing minor tasks in the now-empty building. The hands had long since headed in for the day. Naomi's body ached from the labor of a hard day's work, but still she pushed forward. She was well aware when she'd finally reached her limit.

"I need a break for a minute." Propping the shovel she'd been using against a nearby wall, she wandered outside.

In the distance, the sun was beginning to set. She stood for a long time, taking in the view as the sun painted the sky pale shades of tangerine and gold across the backdrop of blue mountain peaks and oncoming rain clouds.

A sudden interruption came in the form of a garbled mew. Somewhere close by, it sounded as if there was an injured feline, maybe even a cat that was dying. She followed the sound to an overturned bucket nearby, slowly lifting the edge. At first glance, she hardly would have called the yowling ball of fur that sprang forth a cat, but it hissed and spit just the same. A large, overweight tortoiseshell cat, orange and black in its distinctive markings, stared up at her from the mountain dirt.

Despite its hefty weight for an outdoor farm cat, its bones stuck out in odd places, and it had a hint of grey fur about its face, showing its increased age, which likely accounted for the fact that it could no longer be called cute…at least not exactly. Okay, maybe not at all. Though she supposed there was a hint of interesting sass in the feline's face.

Grateful for the distraction, Naomi scooped her reluctant snuggle buddy into her arms, petting and cooing at the feline as she made her way back to the stable.

When she stepped inside, still cradling the large mewling kitty, Wes was holding open Black Jack's pen, allowing the massive horse to exit his stall. Glancing up, Wes froze at the sight of her. Instantly, Naomi froze, too. She recognized the narrowed glare in his eyes. It was the same look he'd given her in the clearing. The one that said loud and clear…

…*We're not alone*.

"Don't move." He uttered the words with every bit of urgency he could impart as he glared at the intruder in their midst.

Naomi's eyes widened in alarm. "Please don't tell me there's a wolf behind me," she said breathlessly.

"No." His gaze fell to the gnarled monstrosity in her arms. "It's worse than that."

She followed his gaze to the massive feline, an eyebrow quirking in question. "You can't be serious?" She gripped the cat tighter, as if to shield the flea-bitten beast from him.

"Deadly serious."

"You don't like cats?" She asked the question as if *he* were the monster, rather than the deranged beast in her arms.

"I don't like that *thing*," he said.

She pointed to the blubbery ball of fur. "You mean this ca—?"

"Shhh," he hissed. "Don't say the *C-A-T* word. Peaches hates that. It will only make things worse."

"Peaches?" She glanced down at the hefty ball of patched, aging fur in her arms in confusion. The cat somehow managed to look overfed and decrepit at the same time. Its ancient yellow eyes, one larger than the other, were transfixed on Black Jack. Its mouth opened in a silent hiss, displaying a mouthful of rotting teeth complete with breath Wes knew firsthand reeked worse than the inside of the Grey Wolves' pigpen. From the alarmed look on her face, how anyone could deem the name Peaches appropriate seemed to fail even Naomi's tender heart…

Wes put forward a cautionary hand. "Just whatever you do, don't let go of her. I'm going to step toward you before he sees her."

Naomi looked at him as if he were insane. "Before *who* sees her?"

Slowly, Wes inched forward, attempting to place himself smack-dab in the line of fire to block the impending brawl.

But it was too late. At the sight of Wes's approach, the furred devil in Naomi's arms chose that moment to release a deafening yowl. The noise silenced the low chatter of the horses in the stable. Immediately, Black Jack's ears perked up, and his black eyes fell to where Naomi stood, holding his archnemesis.

Without hesitation, the horse bared his teeth and snarled. Actually *snarled*. The terrifying noise was rivaled only by the huff of an angry bull prepared to charge. Wes was fairly certain he'd never heard another horse snarl. Huff? Yes. Whinny? Yes. But snarl? No.

Then again, not every horse was Black Jack, and not every cat was that glorified hair-ball dispenser Blaze called a pet. Whether it was a catcher of rats or not, he'd told Blaze time and time again to keep that damn beast where it belonged—far from the stables. Wes didn't care where, though if he'd had his choice, preferably a dark trunk, a locked dark trunk without holes buried six feet underground.

The feline locked eyes with Black Jack. Their prolonged stare-down filled the stable with unspoken tension that called to mind every film Wes had ever seen featuring a traditional western standoff. But instead of guns, their weapons were claws, teeth, and hooves. The air was wrought with tension. Naomi, Wes, and the other horses remained the helpless, terrified onlookers.

The feline monster released another petrifying yowl in a challenge that sounded less like an aged cat and more like the pits of hell had opened and Satan himself was singing.

Realizing exactly to whom Wes referred, Naomi sought to rectify the situation. "Oh, quit it, you two." She cast a smiling glance at each of them. "I'm sure you can learn to be frien—" Naomi reached out a hand, attempting to stroke the battered brute cradled in her arms.

"Naomi, no!" Wes shouted.

The snarling cat twisted around and sank its tiny, sharp fangs into the meat of her hand.

Naomi yelped, releasing the cat, and exactly as Wes had feared, all manner of hell broke loose within the stable.

Free from Naomi's grasp, the satanic feline spawn hissed before lunging toward Black Jack, attaching itself to the horse's long face by the hook of its razor-like claws. Blinded by the fur covering his eyes, Black Jack reared up, prepared to charge.

And Naomi stood straight in the line of fire.

Wes dove for her just as she lunged toward him to escape Black Jack's path. They smacked into each other in a tangle of falling limbs. Naomi shrieked, her flailing arms making them career as Black Jack tore through the stable doors.

In his hasty exit, the horse knocked over the wheelbarrow full of manure Wes had finished mucking minutes earlier. The manure scattered, causing Wes and Naomi to slip through the damp grass as they stumbled out of the stable. Slipping and sliding, arms still flailing, they both landed—hard—on their asses, several feet away in the mountain dirt.

Both pairs of their boots were covered in horseshit.

In the distance, a terrifying yowl followed another snarl. Black Jack had now shaken off the furred devil and was chasing Peaches around the patch of grass outside the stables, biting and snapping at the cat's feet as it attempted to outpace the beast.

And as if sitting in the middle of the Grey Wolf pasture with his boots covered in shit, his horse running wild after a half-dead cat, and the human woman responsible for it sitting at his side complaining about him accidentally groping her weren't enough, the Montana sky chose that moment to open up.

Rain poured down on them in torrential icy sheets, soaking through their clothes within seconds.

"Shit!" Wes swore. "Get back in the stable."

Naomi finally turned toward him. Her eyes squinted past the raindrops. "What about the sweet cat?" she shouted through the rumbling of thunder.

The woman was the worst kind of bleeding heart.

"Forget the damn cat." The rim of his Stetson now curved down with the weight of the rain collected in its brim. The rain beat down on their backs like small drops of ice.

For once, Naomi did as she was told. By the time they managed to navigate their way around the manure, they were both soaked from head to toe. Wes left the stable doors open as they stripped off their mucked boots.

The day couldn't have chosen a worse way to end. He'd found himself in a perpetual state of misery ever since last night. Their ranch work hadn't helped. It had left him alone in his thoughts to dwell on every what-if of their previous interaction. And if he thought her scent had tortured him before, it was nothing compared to now.

He'd wanted nothing more last night than to lay her bare in front of the cabin's fireplace, filling her with the length of his cock and taking her until she cried out his name. He'd fully intended to do just that, until her hand had traced over one of the scars on his chest, a silvery, crescent-shaped scar hidden beneath the material of his shirt. He'd gotten that the night he'd killed his father, the night he'd spilled an innocent woman's blood. A human woman, just like her. So he'd broken the contact between them, because if he didn't, he would hurt her, destroy her, just as he had the only other beautiful thing he'd ever had in his life.

To make matters worse, thanks to Maverick's

warning and that little knife fight with Malcolm, Wes still wasn't entirely convinced of her innocence, despite something in his gut that *wanted* to trust her. The question of the Wild Eight and the vampires' deadly intentions itching at the back of his mind made him all the more conflicted.

"You're a magnet for trouble," he grumbled. The Wild Eight, the vamps, and him. He was exactly that to a human like her: trouble. Pure and simple.

He regretted it as soon as he said it. The words only served to relight an angry fire within her, and he was helpless against the draw of her flame, the passion she exuded from every pore. It somehow melted the ice around his dead heart in a way he'd never thought possible.

Hurt twisted her pretty features instantly, causing her to lash out. "*I'm* a magnet for trouble?" She stabbed a finger into his chest as she stepped toward him, advancing as she threatened him.

With her finger, her finger of all things. Like that was supposed to intimidate *him*.

"You're the one who brought me to this place. You're the one who led those Wild Eight monsters onto my land. You want trouble, look in the mirror," she hissed.

They stood nearly chest to chest, the tips of her taut breasts brushing against him as that damn accusatory finger pushed between his pectorals.

His eyes fell to the slender offending digit. This close and with his anger riled, he couldn't stop himself. His eyes flashed to his wolf's. "Unless you intend to follow through with that little threat, I suggest you take a large step back, Miss Kitty."

"And if I don't?" she challenged.

This woman would be the death of him. He gripped her wrist with his free hand, moving her small palm from his chest to his mouth. Close enough that her fingertips brushed the hair of his beard. "I devour that damn finger of yours and every other inch of you with it." He leaned closer, drawing so near, their noses nearly touched. "A night with me would break you."

"Don't flatter yourself." She tore away from him with a huff.

With a frustrated growl, he tore off his sopping-wet shirt, discarding it in a nearby pile of hay. Kicking off his water-filled socks, he trudged barefoot to a nearby saddlebag. He yanked it down from the wall and reached inside for the extra pair of clothes he always kept tucked in there in case of emergencies, or in case he didn't feel like being cooped up in his apartment all night.

"Here."

She turned, and he tossed a pair of boxers and a shirt to her, saving the jeans for himself. Though she had curves to enjoy, she wasn't large, and the jeans would likely fall off her hips anyway.

She caught the clothes, giving him a quick once-over. If he didn't know any better, from the frown on her face, he would have thought she disapproved. She made a point of narrowing her eyes at him. Her gaze darted over his bare torso, lingering on the plethora of scar-covered muscle and tattoos.

"You've already seen me naked." He flashed her a smug grin, referring to when they'd been in her pasture the first night they'd met.

Her face flushed red, and she averted her gaze. "It was dark."

He chuckled. "Not that dark." He turned away from her. He'd planned on saving his jeans for once she was distracted with her own changing, but somehow, getting her ire up gave him a sense of satisfaction. In part because he enjoyed watching her squirm.

Unbuckling his pants, he dropped them to the floor.

If she was looking, his ass was as bare as the day he was born.

"You're incorrigible," she hissed.

So she *was* looking. He chuckled again as he tugged on the fresh, dry jeans. Turning back toward her, he saw that she still stood with her back to him, not bothering to address the issue of her sopping-wet clothes. The woman was just as stubborn as he was.

"You've shared my bed," he challenged.

Naomi glanced over her shoulder toward him. All day, they'd both been skirting around what had passed between them the night before and the first night when they'd kissed, both of them painfully aware yet refusing to address it. Naomi's eyes grew wide as if she were surprised he'd been the one to break their silent standoff.

That made two of them.

But the silence between them had been killing him. Normally, Wes wouldn't have cared. In fact, before she'd come crashing into his life, he'd lived in silence, at least mostly. Isolated out in the stables, he'd only had minimal interaction with his fellow packmembers, and he preferred it that way.

Until her. Now he craved the noise. Her noise. The incessant chatter, the questions, the arguments, and especially the little intake of breath that escaped her lips every time he touched her, as if she were both terrified of him and aroused. It didn't matter whether it was the brush of his hand or that tight little body pressed fully against his. It happened every time. Every fucking time. And every time, it made him instantly hard.

He perched on the edge of a haystack. From this position, he watched her framed in the doorway of the stable. The door remained open, allowing in the sound and the smell of the rain. Everything about her—from her dark hair to her even darker eyes, perky little breasts, wide, rounded hips, and smooth brown skin—seemed fashioned specifically to tempt him. And those full pink lips drove him wild, making him want a taste of her.

He could think of more than one pair of pink lips he wanted to taste.

She crossed her arms over her chest, drawing his attention to the way her wet shirt clung to the curve of her breasts. "I'd hardly call a stable floor a bed, and if we'd both been in our right minds, that kiss never would have happened."

As if that were the end of their conversation, she walked into an empty stall, closing the wooden gate behind her. The paneling shielded her body from view from just below her chest downward. He should have turned away, but he couldn't help himself. With hungry eyes, he watched her strip off the wet shirt, revealing smooth, damp skin and a flash of a lacy black bra. She reached behind her, gently releasing the clasp to reveal her naked back. Soft shoulders tight with feminine muscle. The inky coils of her hair appeared even darker wet. They rolled over those strong shoulders like strands of midnight. His cock grew hard in an instant as he took in the sight of her.

Bending ever so slightly, she wiggled free of her jeans. With each shimmying movement, he became more aroused, leaving his cock as hard as a diamond. When she bent to strip her pants from her ankles, he swore. Damn if he hadn't seen the smallest hint of the side of one of her gorgeous breasts.

A few moments later, she emerged wearing the T-shirt and boxers. The stark white of the cotton contrasted with the dark tones of her skin. He wasn't entirely sure which he preferred. Her wrapped in his clothes as if she was his for the taking, or the sight of her naked back…

Naked. Definitely naked, he decided.

Crossing over to the wall, she reached for a saddle blanket and a canteen filled with water he'd given her earlier that morning. The hem of the oversized shirt rose, revealing the tight material of the boxers she was wearing underneath. On his narrow hips, they fit well; on her, they clung to that ample round ass, highlighting its tight curve.

The words left his mouth before he could stop himself. He couldn't resist. "Don't pretend you wouldn't haven't enjoyed it."

"Enjoyed what?" She returned to her spot on the haystack, laying out the saddle blanket to soften the spot where she sat.

"Me taking you. In front of the fireplace, on the ground in the stable, up against the tree in the forest. Take your pick."

"Don't flatter yourself." The words belied the flare of lust in her eyes. She chugged a swig from the canteen.

He had her, and he knew it. "I can smell your desire, you know."

She choked on the water and coughed until she caught

her breath. Abandoning the canteen, she braced her hands beside her. "Don't toy with me. It's not funny."

A devilish smirk crossed his lips. "Toys are for men who don't know how to use their hands."

Her cheeks flushed, and she tore her gaze away from him. "Fine. Don't lie to me then."

Wes scowled. A betrayer, a murder, a monster, yes. But never a liar. His father had been a liar. A deep growl thundered through his chest. "I may be a lot of things, but I'm no liar."

And he intended to prove just that.

Chapter 9

"WHAT ARE YOU DOING?" NAOMI INCHED BACKWARD from where she sat.

Wes's eyes shifted to those of his wolf. The golden yellow gleamed, and those black pupils focused directly on her. The growl that rumbled from his chest sounded downright feral, and sexy as all hell. She half expected him to shift right then and there. But he didn't. Instead, he prowled toward her. Her heart sped into overdrive.

From the look in his eyes, she was fairly certain she'd turned into Little Red Riding Hood, and the Big Bad Wolf was headed straight to devour her in all the dirty ways she'd dreamed that morning. She bumped into the stall post behind her, not even realizing that she'd backed up against it. He was only a few feet away now, quickly advancing on her. She gripped the saddle blanket for support.

"I am no liar." He slid his hands over the top of hers, clamping her fists onto the blanket-covered haystack and caging her with the massive breadth of his body.

Her breath caught.

"There it is." Something dark stirred in his eyes. One of the hands on hers slid up the length of her arm. In the wake of his rough fingertips, a trail of goose bumps peppered her skin. His hand caressed her arm, across her shoulder, then up the exposed skin of her neck before it came to rest on her chin.

Between him and the stall post, there was no escape.

She wouldn't have it any other way.

Heat flooded her center as the pad of his thumb gently tugged at the soft flesh of her lips. "I know you want me, because that happens every time I touch you…" His hand left her lips and smoothed down over the bare skin of her neck. "Every." Over the curve of her breast. "Damn." Down to the slope of her hips. "Time." He cupped her ass, pressing her against him. The hard length of him ground into her core.

She heard it then. The sharp intake of breath that escaped her lips. A heady mixture of impending danger and desire.

He was right.

Her legs dangled over the edge of the haystack she sat on, granting him easy access. His hands lingered on her thighs.

He slipped one hand between her legs, cupping her in his palm. With her legs spread, the thin fabric of the boxers she wore was damp with heat. A devilish grin crossed his lips. "I know you want me because I can smell it on you." He located her clit through the fabric, rubbing his thumb over the material in steady circles.

"Wes…" Her voice was breathy even to her own ears as her back arched, and she opened her legs further for him in clear invitation.

"Here." His lips brushed over the skin of her ear as he drew in her scent.

A shudder ran through her. "Wes…" she panted.

"Here." His mouth found the sensitive skin just above her breasts.

She ground her hips against the pressure of his hand,

the heat inside her growing. "Wes!" Her voice was desperate, pleading.

"And here." He dropped his head between her thighs, his lips brushing against her pussy through the soaked fabric of the underwear. He inhaled the scent of her sex, his lips grazing against her clit, promising all the heat and pleasure she knew he could give with his mouth. He hadn't even gotten her naked, and already she was on the verge of coming.

"I want to hear you say it." His hand returned to her center, circling her clit and probing her folds through the material. "Prove me a liar." He met her gaze. Those golden wolf eyes bore into hers, staring at her from between her legs.

She gasped for breath. "I…" Her back arched, and she struggled to hold herself upright.

He stood. With his free hand, he cradled her lower back, supporting her in his arms as she writhed at his touch. She was on the edge, nearly ready to shatter.

"Prove me a liar," he whispered. "If you don't want me, I'll stop. Right now."

"I…I…" She couldn't say the words. She *did* want him. Every inch of her pulsed with need. She eagerly pushed her hips forward, pressing her clit harder against his hand. "I want you," she panted.

"Fuck," he swore. He tore the wet fabric of the boxers aside, finally touching her beneath her clothes. The callused pad of his thumb flicked over her most sensitive flesh in one swift movement, sending her over the edge.

White-hot ecstasy rolled over her as she fell apart in his arms. Her orgasm came on rough and hard. She threw back her head and moaned, arching and bucking against his palm as she lost herself. She collapsed into him as the last waves of pleasure rolled through her. He hadn't lied about knowing what to do with his hands.

As she caught her breath, she lifted her head to meet his gaze. Their lips were so close to brushing; they hovered mere inches away. She'd told herself it was only heat between them that first night, a product of adrenaline and circumstance, but she knew now that was the worst kind of lie. It was more than heat. She wanted nothing more than to close the gap between them, to explore the budding fire of emotions kindled in her chest. Whatever it was, he wanted it, too. There was longing in his eyes as clear as day.

She leaned forward.

He turned away from her, offering no more than his cheek. "I'm no liar," he part whispered, part growled. He started to pull away.

"Wes." She reached for him.

He caught her wrist gently in his hand.

"Don't." The raw pain reflected in his face cut her to the core.

Without another word, he released her. He turned away and stalked out of the stables and into the rain. The door slammed shut behind him, leaving her in the sudden silence and stillness, his damp boxers clinging to the skin of her thighs, and her heart thudding as she stared after him.

—◦◦◦—

Wes tore out of the stable like a bat out of hell. He wasn't entirely sure where he was going. He just knew he needed to get out of there. Away from the scent of wildflowers on her hair, away from the feel of her smooth skin, the soft, slick heat of her pussy.

Away from her.

Without looking back, he stripped off his clothes and shifted. Run. He needed to run. As far as his legs would take him. He bounded up the mountainside. His emotions mixed into a powerful concoction, fueling him. Anger at himself and the whole damn situation. Frustration with his lack of control. Regret over the past that had dictated his life. And desire…for what he knew he couldn't have. For everything that was forbidden to him. She'd been wet for him. So wet. The moment when his thumb had circled her hot folds through the material and she'd fallen apart in his arms, he'd almost forgotten what he was, who he was. He'd spent the past years paying penance, ensuring he would never forget. Yet only minutes with her in his arms, and he'd lost himself. Until the weight of her trust had crushed him. He didn't deserve that trust.

The only thing that had ever been created from his hands was destruction. And when he lost himself to raw emotion, there was no other result. It was the only thing he was certain of.

If he stayed, this woman would be the death of him.

So he ran. He ran until his four legs ached, until darkness shrouded the trees. His muscles burned with the intensity of his pace, but he didn't care. He'd run until he couldn't run anymore. So the past wouldn't catch up with him.

He skidded to a stop somewhere in the middle of the forest long after the rain had stopped. Throwing back his head in agony, he howled at the rising moon. The sound echoed off the nearby pines. The long, drawn-out howl sent a flock of sleeping birds skittering away from their perch.

Every time he closed his eyes, he was back there. In that awful room. The coppery smell of blood filling his nose. He'd stood face-to-face with death before, having killed with his own two hands. But her death had been different. Because she'd been innocent. Because she hadn't deserved to die. Nolan and Donnie had lied to him, manipulated him, and he'd been too lost in a different kind of emotion that was as consuming, as powerful—and equally as destructive—to realize.

He knew what he needed to do.

Turning tail, he bolted back to Wolf Pack Run in a frenzied fury, running like a madman. When he reached the tree line, he shifted into human form and collected his discarded clothes, throwing on his jeans. The material reeked with the scent of her, with the tantalizing smell of her sex. He dragged the shirt off. It made his mouth water and his cock instantly hard.

Naomi. He trained his senses forward. He could scent her in the stables, hear her pacing the length of the packed floors. He'd wondered—briefly—if she might walk back to the main compound or if she'd hunker down and wait to tear a strip out of him. The latter, definitely the latter. And no more than he deserved.

This was his realm—the stables and rugged mountain terrain—and his fellow Grey Wolves knew that. And as Malcolm had seen, an attack on Naomi would constitute an attack on him. No alpha in this pack, save for *the* alpha himself, was fool enough to do that. Naomi would be safe within the stables for the time being.

He cut across the west pasture, past the mess hall and

neat rows of cabins, straight to the compound. He burst
inside the main building and tore through the halls. He
didn't stop until he reached the tech room adjacent to
Maverick's office.

Maverick would have had Blaze gather the intel
once Wes had delivered the news. Accessing the pack's
intelligence was something Wes had done hundreds of
times to keep himself up to date on the movements of his
former pack. And with Blaze as their computer expert,
he'd memorized the wolf's schedule like clockwork,
knowing the exact times the wolf was and was not in
his office. It's how he'd known that something was stirring among them, why he'd chosen to defy Maverick's
orders and meet with Kyle to learn exactly what that
something was. Now that Maverick had cut him out of
the fray, just after the Wild Eight had made an attempt
on Wes's life, it was more important than ever.

Not to mention that after everything that had passed
between them, he needed to know once and for all if he
could trust this woman. His instincts urged him to, but
Maverick's words and his past made him doubt those
instincts. Breaking into the data the Grey Wolves had
gathered would leave no place for doubt.

But this time was different.

Because if Maverick found out, Wes—and Naomi by
proxy—would be dead.

Slowly, he inched toward the control room. He needed
to know. He'd been telling Maverick for years that the
Wild Eight would resurge, and look where the hell that
had gotten him. The Wild Eight had teamed up with the
vamps. The thought alone sent his blood boiling.

At this hour of the night, the pack's satellites operated

on autopilot unless otherwise needed, and most of the alphas were on patrol, unless it was their night off. Ripping the door open, he expected to find the control room empty. Instead, he stood face-to-face with Blaze.

This time, his packmate's damn Hawaiian shirt was a startling flamingo pink with tropical palm trees at the bottom. "Coming to take my username for another spin?" A scowl curled over Blaze's lips.

Wes didn't respond. He contemplated telling Blaze he'd been looking for Maverick, but it would have been a bold-faced lie. Maverick was hardly ever in the control room, unless they were in active recon mode. And as he'd told Naomi, he was no liar.

And Blaze knew it, too.

He and Blaze may not have been enemies, but they were hardly friends. Blaze had taken it upon himself to use every opportunity to figuratively screw Wes up the ass ever since Wes had stepped into the pack. Blaze was annoying as all get out but ultimately a harmless thorn in his side, like an annoying fly that he couldn't shoo away. Not that Wes could say he blamed him. Had he suddenly been expected to be buddy-buddy with his sworn enemy, he would have thrown up equal resistance. Hell, Maverick had spared his life. He now called the man packmaster, but Wes still held a deep rivalry with the bastard, though that was now dampened by mutual admiration, by respect for the only man worthy to be called his rival.

Blaze stood from his desk chair, gripping the back of the leather seat. "You know what I'm talking about. You've been hacking my username to peruse files for the past several months. I've got a tracker set up that alerts my phone every time my log-in is accessed. You figured out my password."

Wes cocked an eyebrow. No sense trying to hide it then. "Blaze-ing Saddles? Really?"

Blaze chuckled. "You don't like my sense of humor?"

Wes shrugged. "Not particularly."

Blaze's frown returned, and he stepped toward Wes. "What happens if I tell Maverick about your little foray into the pack's classified files?"

Wes's jaw tightened. "We both know this isn't a fight you want to pick. That's not why you're here. You're an annoying ass, but you're not stupid enough to try to take me on, or you would have done so by now. We both know that."

A spark of anger flickered in Blaze's eyes. Wes had hit a nerve. Blaze was a valiant fighter, a superior warrior, but in a pack of equally impressive alphas, he was nothing more than average. Only his tech skills set him apart.

Taking on Wes one-on-one would maybe calm his anger, make him feel like a man.

But it would be a death sentence…for both of them.

"You think you know me so well."

"Tell me I don't," Wes challenged. "We both know what I want, but clearly, you want something, too, or you would already have told Maverick about this. Now I suggest you tell me what it is before I lose interest in this conversation."

A smile curled over Blaze's lips. "I think it's bull Maverick allowed you to be part of this pack. Had I been packmaster, I would have done you in myself, so you'd never have another chance to be involved in the Wild Eight and their bullshit. But who am I to question

Maverick's judgment?" He leaned against the desk of the control panel and crossed his arms over his chest. "Regardless of that, I don't think you're involved with the Wild Eight now. I think you really have gone Grey Wolf, and despite your past, I've always liked you. You're like a lovable bear I can't help but poke until he shows his fangs."

"The feeling isn't mutual."

Blaze's smile only widened. "I want a favor, Wes."

Wes raised an eyebrow. When Blaze didn't respond, another low growl escaped his lips. He didn't have time for Blaze's games. "It must be a helluva favor you need to risk Maverick's wrath on this. What kind of favor?"

Blaze's expression settled into one of serious business. "An open-ended one. You want me to give you my computer access and keep this all hush-hush from Maverick, fine. But I want an open-ended favor. To be cashed in whenever I need it."

It was a major leap of faith, to hand himself over to Blaze for whatever and whenever he needed. But annoying as he was, Blaze was far from stupid, and he held the upper hand here. If he sold Wes out to Maverick, the clash of the titans that would ensue would leave the pack bloodied and maimed. It may have been questionable who would win between Wes and Maverick one-on-one, but Maverick had the whole pack on his side.

Which meant, at the moment, Blaze had outpaced Wes.

"Fine," Wes agreed. "But I want you to tell me everything that's been going on with the Wild Eight and Naomi Evans."

Blaze stuck out his hand. "Deal?"

Wes took his hand and gave it a rough, curt shake. "Deal."

Blaze turned back toward his computer screen, typing in his log-in and quickly pulling up the files available on both the Wild Eight and Naomi. "After you told Maverick what happened yesterday, he had me do a search on the satellites in downtown Billings for any Wild Eight members and vampires meeting. There are photos that corroborate that what Kyle told you is true. The Wild Eight are in fact partnered with the vamps. But we think there's something else they're hiding. We just don't know what yet."

The sound of Blaze's fingertips clicking over the keys filled the small room. He jabbed the enter button, and a photo emerged on the screen. It was a night shot, from the looks of it, a dark figure feeding on a dead sheep.

What had she called it again? Lambie? "That's Naomi's ranch." The dark figure was likely a vampire. But what was it doing feeding on livestock instead of any of the buffet of humans it could take a sip from in Billings? Wes had been asking himself that ever since Naomi told him about her maimed flock in the woods three days earlier. Which meant she *had* been telling the truth, and he'd doubted her. Shame filled him. He couldn't hold on to such doubts. Now that he knew the truth, he realized how misplaced such doubt had been. He should have trusted his instincts.

Blaze nodded. "Maverick had me pull this up when he got back from the western packlands, before he even talked to you."

Which meant Maverick had known Naomi's story was true all along. Wes didn't need to convince him of

Naomi's innocence, because the bastard had known long before Wes had even pleaded with him to spare her life. No wonder Maverick had given her a chance to prove herself; he'd already known she was no danger to the pack. Wes had chalked it up to Maverick's compassion toward humans, to his insistence that they follow the ordinances of the Execution Underground, that they go above and beyond, working to protect humanity from both the Wild Eight and the vampires.

That attitude about their interactions with humanity had been what separated the Grey Wolves and the Wild Eight, what made them into sworn enemies. But if not trying to determine her innocence, why the hoax on Maverick's part? Why play it off as if her fate was in question? "And what's Maverick planning to do with this information? What's his endgame?"

Blaze laughed. "What do you think he was doing? Keeping you busy with the petty task of babysitting an innocent human. If it had gone as planned, the task would have at least had you tied up two more nights."

Wes raged. Maverick, his packmaster, his rival, his one-time enemy, a man he both admired and loathed, had treated him like a dog, throwing him a tasty bone to chew while he called the shots on an enemy hell-bent on taking Wes's life. The packmaster had gotten the best of him, one-upped him, and Wes had played into it like a fool.

"He has been gathering recon on her ranch," Blaze continued. "But there's been no movement or activity there at all. Not since we've been actively monitoring, not that it's been long. It won't be more than the additional two nights he promised before he's forced to admit she's both innocent and telling the truth and send her home."

"You get any more information on this, report it directly to me. Deal?"

Blaze shook his head. "No go, Wes. This was a one-time deal only."

Wes gripped Blaze by the back of his awful Hawaiian shirt, wrenching him to his feet. With his other hand, Wes grabbed the other wolf by the front of his collar. A feral snarl ripped from his throat. "You want open-ended favors, then fine, but that means I expect them in return."

Anger simmered in Blaze's eyes, but he nodded. "Fine. You cover my ass, and I'll cover yours, brother," he spat out.

Wes released him with a small shove. Stepping away from Blaze, he headed toward the exit. "Anything at all on this, and you let me know. Got it?"

He glanced over his shoulder, and Blaze nodded again.

His mind clouded with questions, Wes left the control room and Blaze in his wake. He needed to figure out what Maverick's endgame was. His life depended on it. In more ways than one. To protect himself should the Wild Eight come for him again, and because once he knew, he could take Naomi home.

He needed her as far away from him as possible. Before history had the chance to repeat itself.

Chapter 10

SHE HADN'T THOUGHT THIS THROUGH. NAOMI RODE UP the mountainside on Star's back. Of all the horses she could've chosen, she opted for the palomino mare she'd ridden while herding the wild horses. After all, Wes had identified the mare as Bo's horse. Since Bo, who had apparently been the Grey Wolf second-in-command until several months ago, was dead, his was the horse least likely to be missed. And she'd need to be as brave—or maybe *crazy* was the right word—as Wes to attempt to ride Black Jack on her own. Not to mention, Wes might miss the ornery mustang, though she couldn't imagine why.

Pulling on the reins, she slowed the mare to a steady mosey. The horse swayed with a gentle rhythm, the weight of the great beast rocking with each hooved step. At first, they'd ridden as fast as the mare could manage, dodging trees and the shriveling autumn undergrowth with ease as Naomi placed as much distance between her and Wolf Pack Run—between her and Wes—as possible. Now, as the forest grew dark, the decrease in pace became necessity. With no trail and the shadows of the trees elongating with each passing minute, Naomi's view was obscured.

She'd take her chances with anything if it meant getting back home. She'd find a way to address her vampire problem on her own terms.

The darkness closed in around them within minutes.

Naomi turned her face toward the treetops. Grey clouds crept past, darkening the forest and blocking the waning moon. The occasional moonbeam broke through the haze, reminding her that wolves had nocturnal vision, and she didn't.

She shook away the thought as she and the horse continued down the mountainside. No matter. They had a brief head start, if Wes even bothered to come look for her...which he would. Her injured ego flared. Just to make her miserable. Just to prove a point.

Not exactly the usual attitude after a woman experienced an orgasm of that caliber, or so she assumed. She had never come that strong and fast—and she'd thought she knew her own body well enough to know her sweet spots better than anyone. Self-love and all.

So much for that.

Her skin burned hot all over again at the thought. Somehow, she knew that the pleasure Wes gave with his fingers was no comparison to his mouth, to that infuriating, smirking mouth.

The mare shifted to step around a large log—that much Naomi could see—pulling her back to the present. The darkness heightened her senses. The aroma of damp earth from the earlier rain filled her nose. She leaned into the horse's movements, trusting the animal to get her at least to the bottom of the mountainside. The hoot of an owl in a nearby tree startled her nerves. She jumped, and the horse huffed a frustrated whinny. The equine chose that moment to come to a halt.

Naomi nudged the animal with the heels of her boots and shook the reins. "Come on, girl. We can't stop now." Her voice sounded out of place against the wind brushing through the thickets. She urged the horse forward again—another kick and a tug of the reins against the bit between the mare's teeth—but the animal didn't move.

Dismounting, she lowered herself from the saddle. Careful to keep the reins in her hands, she inched forward. Her palms smoothed over the horse's coat and up her neck until she cupped the great animal's cheek. "Shhh," she shushed. She patted Star's face. "Don't be like me and let a little ol' owl scare you," she cooed.

A rustle sounded from a nearby bush. Star whinnied again, raising up on her hind legs and kicking in a frenzied retreat, dragging Naomi backward with her. She tugged against the reins, fighting to keep the mare from bolting. The cloud parted in front of the moon. Dim moonlight lit the shadows of the forest just enough that they both could see. Star trained her dark eyes on the bushes several feet away.

And that's when Naomi realized it hadn't been the hoot of the owl that had spooked the horse.

On the other side of the clearing, a large wolf stepped through the brush. It wasn't Wes, and somehow, she knew it wasn't one of his packmates either. The moon illuminated the wolf's sharp canines as the werewolf growled. Naomi's heart thumped against her breastbone. Her breath grew quick and shallow. She dropped Star's reins and retrieved the hunting knife she'd stolen from the stables as the wolf lunged.

She slashed her blade through the air, slicing through the wolf's chest. The beast released a high-pitched yelp. It dropped its front paws to the ground, but the fight was far from over. Seconds later, it rounded on her again. There was no time to attack. She brought her arms up in a defensive position. The wolf's front paws hooked onto her arms. The werewolf stood on its hind legs, its front paws on her as it snapped its heavy jaws mere inches from her face, threatening to tear into her throat.

Lashing out, she kneed the wolf in the stomach. It fell backward onto its spine. Within seconds, it had regained its footing. Slowly, it circled her, each step careful and deliberate. She held her knife at the ready. Her pulse pounded in her ears.

The wolf lunged again. Naomi swung her arm. Her knife sank into the wolf's shoulder. But it wasn't enough. The werewolf's paws connected with her chest, knocking her clean off her feet. She fell backward. Her spine hit the ground. Wind rushed from her lungs.

She did the only thing she could think to do. She twisted the blade in the wolf's side. A yelp tore from its throat, and it released her. Long enough for Naomi to tear the blade from its hide and raise it overhead.

Before she could bring the blade down, the wolf soared off her, knocked to the side by an unforeseen force. Her eyes widened. Star had bucked the wolf with her back hooves, sending the werewolf flying across the clearing and into a nearby tree. Her breath billowed around her nose as she released an enraged whinny. Fiery aggression blazed in the horse's eyes.

Star charged. Within seconds, the horse was on the werewolf. The sounds of Star's heavy hooves striking the other animal rang in Naomi's ears. The wolf yelped several times, attempting to escape the blows of Star's wrath, but it was no match for the horse's mighty strength. Quickly, the yelps turned to keens of agony.

Finally, when the wolf lay still and silent, the horse

retreated, slowly returning to Naomi's side. She lowered her large head, sniffing at the blood on Naomi's arm and nudging her gently.

Naomi's eyes filled with tears. "I'm okay," she whispered to the beast.

Her vision swam.

No, she would not pass out. She would make it home tonight in one piece.

Slowly, she lifted herself to her feet, willing herself to stand. The knife still clutched in her hand, she crossed to the tree trunk where the wolf that attacked her lay silent and unmoving. She stood over the majestic, aggressive animal, admiring the patterns in the animal's grey fur.

She shouldn't feel remorse for the death of someone who had tried to kill her, yet somehow, she did. Slowly, she bent down, giving in to the irresistible urge to touch the wolf's fur, to feel it beneath her fingertips.

As she reached out to touch him, to her horror, the wolf's bones shifted and suddenly her fingertips were inches away from the face of a man. He lay against the tree trunk, naked and unmoving. His eyes were open, dark irises staring up at the starry nighttime sky. She reached out and brushed them closed.

A growl rumbled, and she snatched her hand back. But the sound came from behind her. A chill rushed down her spine. Slowly, she turned. Two more snarling werewolves prowled into the clearing. Wild Eight, she guessed, and there she stood, lingering over the body of their packmate, his blood on her clothes. Her hand tightened around the hilt of her blade. And she had thought she didn't need Wes to protect her.

She thanked God she hadn't dropped the knife.

A feminine scream pierced Wes's ears. He tore through the trees atop Black Jack, riding faster than he'd ever ridden in his life. He had to get to her. Had to reach her. She was innocent, and he'd caused her to run. If she died, he would never forgive himself.

The pain of his past mistakes twisted his insides. He couldn't live through the guilt. Not again. He'd give his own life in her place if that's what it took.

Wes released an echoing howl, signaling to the other Grey Wolves that he had located both Naomi and the Wild Eight. Hadn't they taken enough from him? His pack, his life, his love? And now they wanted this innocent woman.

Mine. The word echoed, wild and full of raw possession.

He burst through the trees and into the clearing, the evening's patrol members on his tail. He leaped from Black Jack, dismounting in one swift move. As the Grey Wolves surrounded the clearing, their sheer numbers made it clear that the Wild Eight wolves had no choice but to surrender. The sounds of the Grey Wolves snarling echoed in a terrifying chorus. Jaws snarled and snapped, prepared to tear flesh. The Wild Eight wolves froze and shifted into human form. They'd been circling Naomi and Bo's palomino mare, Star. Naomi clutched a knife in her hand, and her shirt was torn. They'd hurt her. *He'd* hurt her.

Wes would bleed them dry.

Colt's voice rose among the snarls. "Subdue them."

Naomi stumbled toward Wes. He caught her in his

arms, quickly pushing her behind him so he could shield her with his body. A crowd of Grey Wolf guards and warriors had formed around the prisoners.

Colt pushed to the front of the crowd. "You." He pointed to one of the guards in wolf form. "Alert Maverick immediately," he ordered.

The wolf gave a gruff huff in response before turning tail and darting off toward Wolf Pack Run, a long echoing howl tearing from him. But Colt's gaze never faltered from the prisoners in front of him. The Wild Eight wolves hung their heads in submission.

Colt crouched and gripped one of the prisoners by the hair, forcing his head up. "State your purpose for coming here." The threat in his voice made it abundantly clear that if the answer didn't satisfy him, there would be consequences later.

"Bite me." The Wild Eight wolf spat into Colt's face.

With strained movements that spoke of Colt's amazing ability to contain his wrath, he wiped the spittle away. The spark of cold anger in those grey eyes said the Wild Eight wolf would be dead as soon as he ceased to be useful.

"He's obviously Wild Eight. Who gives a shit what his plan is?" The voice sounded from the other side of the crowd. Malcolm stepped into the circle, shaking his head. He made his way toward the prisoner. "Just kill him already."

Colt stepped toe to toe with Malcolm. "Not until Maverick gives the word."

Malcolm lifted his hands in surrender. "If you say so, Commander." He took a step back, and that's when his gaze fell on Naomi, tucked away behind Wes's arm.

A devious smile crossed his face. "Then again, you're right, Colt. Why don't we use him for information?"

Wes snarled. He'd seen the malicious desire for retribution in Malcolm's eyes as he'd looked at Naomi. Whatever Malcolm intended, Wes would kill the bastard. Black Jack snarled in evident agreement and bared his teeth.

Before anyone could stop him, Malcolm crouched beside the prisoner, wrenching at his hair and forcing his head upward as Colt had done only moments ago. But Malcolm took it a step further. He gripped the prisoner's hair by the scalp, shoving his cowboy boot into the prisoner's upper back. The Wild Eight wolf couldn't arch his spine with the pull on his hair. The prisoner's scalp had to be burning at the roots from the pressure. Malcolm nodded toward Naomi. "You recognize that bitch over there?"

Within seconds, the crowd around Wes and Naomi thinned. Though Naomi stood behind Wes, it was no use. She was the only female within view. Out of the corner of his eye, Wes saw Maverick approaching. The packmaster couldn't have chosen a worse moment to make his arrival.

The Wild Eight wolf stared straight at Naomi. As if the pressure on his scalp hadn't been enough to make him say yes to end the pain, his eyes turned to Wes. The moonlight reflected back in the wolf's irises, illuminating a flicker of hatred that screamed at Wes loud and clear.

Judas.

Betrayer.

The young Wild Eight would stop at nothing to cause Wes pain. He held Wes's gaze.

"Yes, I recognize her," the Wild Eight wolf spat. "She works with us. She's a Wild Eight affiliate through and through. One of our most loyal."

With those words, something in the pack changed. Wolf eyes, sharp and piercing, turned toward Wes.

"No." Naomi was shaking her head. "No, he's lying!"

The scent of Naomi's fear flooded over Wes.

He didn't think. He brushed both arms behind him, shielding Naomi at his back as he crouched and prepared to shift. He bared his teeth, snarling. He didn't care who they were, Grey Wolf or Wild Eight…

He was ready for a fight.

Naomi didn't have to be a genius to recognize the sudden change in the air. Wes crouched in front of her, a deep, protective snarl ripping from his throat as Black Jack guarded her from behind. From the wild look in Wes's eyes, she had no doubt he would fight for her, but it would hardly be enough, considering half the pack appeared ready to pounce on her at a moment's notice.

Words failed her. The group that encircled them eased closer and closer. Her heart pounded in her chest. This was how she was going to die. Not at the hand of one mangy werewolf who'd been caught in her ranch trap but torn apart limb from limb by the jaws of many.

Her life should have been flashing before her eyes. Yet all she could think was not that she was too young or that it wasn't her time. Simply, what a horrific way it was to go. In the middle of the woods, surrounded by creatures who were either hateful or indifferent toward her.

All except one.

The one risking his life for hers.

But even *he* couldn't protect her.

And that's when she saw *him*.

She couldn't have mistaken him if she'd tried.

The Grey Wolf packmaster locked eyes with her, his entrancing emerald gaze searing into her. Maverick Grey towered over the crowd, only Wes equaling his impressive size. With broad, muscled shoulders and a lean, tapered waist with narrow hips, the two men were all muscle wrought from years of training and battle. At a quick glance, if not for the difference in coloring, she could have thought them brothers. The smooth midnight waves of Maverick's hair contrasted with Wes's wild blond locks. Searing emerald eyes battled against icy, piercing blue. But as she looked closer, it was more than their hair and coloring that differentiated them.

As Naomi stared into Maverick's eyes, she saw a man of immense power. Wes's gaze held that same strength. But in his eyes, she saw something wild, and from the way Maverick's eyes narrowed, he saw it, too.

Maverick lived beside his wolf.

But Wes *was* a wolf.

A wolf who refused to be tamed.

In an instant, she understood the underlying power struggle between the two. And she knew what she needed to do. Maverick answered to the will of the pack, but Wes answered to no one. Not even Maverick. If the wolves kept advancing, it wouldn't matter whether or not she was guilty, because Wes was prepared to defend her, even to his own death.

Which meant she had no other choice.

"I swear my loyalty," she said loud enough for the

pack to hear. "I swear on my life, on the blood of my ancestors, my people, that I have no connection to this man or these wolves."

The closing of the circle around them suddenly stopped, and silence spread through the crowd.

Stepping out from behind Wes's protection, Naomi stood before the Grey Wolf packmaster. "I swear my loyalty to you, Maverick Grey," she repeated, "leader of the Grey Wolves, and I ask that you allow me to join your pack."

Murmured whispers erupted among the Grey Wolves.

Examining her with careful eyes, Maverick crossed his massive arms over his chest. "Hold her," he ordered.

Within seconds, two guards seized her arms. Wes snarled, and Naomi was vaguely aware that it took several other wolves to restrain him. From the angry whinnies, Black Jack fought to save her, too. But her nerves drowned out the noise. The guards gripped her shoulders, forcing her onto her knees. Maverick stood over her. He drew his knife from the sheath at his belt and raised the blade.

Naomi's heart stopped as she waited for the lethal blow.

But it never came. Maverick staked his blade in the ground in front of her before he stepped back.

She looked up to meet his gaze. "I...I don't understand."

"Pack law dictates that those not born a Grey Wolf, those who are sworn to loyalty, are bound by another equally powerful force...by blood. You will live as one of us tonight, Naomi Evans. But only if the pack chooses. The decision doesn't lie with me. It's the choice of the last sworn member of this pack, who must vow on your behalf."

He might as well have uttered her death sentence. Which one of them would issue the decree? Malcolm, surely. Colt or Sierra might show her mercy. Maybe Austin? If it were one of them, maybe she might have a chance. Never, never in her life had she felt more alone.

Until Wes stepped in front of her.

As she took in the sight of him, that wry smile curled across his lips. Her eyes widened. He hadn't been born a Grey Wolf? He'd never said otherwise. She'd just assumed...

"Your choice, Wes?" Maverick asked.

Naomi already knew the answer.

"I vow on my life that Naomi Evans's intentions are true," Wes said. "She joins our pack this night."

At his words, the guards released her, and Maverick stepped back, casting a glance toward Wes. "The second time you've saved her life in only a handful of days."

"Third," Wes corrected. "But who's counting..."

She only counted two. The Wild Eight wolf in the clearing, and now.

Recognizing her confusion, Maverick answered for him. "Our pack law dictates that if our true nature is revealed to a human, the human must die to preserve the safety of our pack. When he brought you here, Wes risked his life to spare yours."

Naomi gaped at the packmaster, then at Wes. Wes shrugged a single shoulder, as if it was no big deal.

He'd been supposed to kill her that night. Not only had he protected her from the Wild Eight wolves in battle, but he'd risked his life for her, though she'd been a complete stranger.

Facing her fully, she watched as Wes bent and pulled

Maverick's blade from the ground. He straightened, and as he did so, his gaze seared into hers, so intense and intimate that she became painfully aware that the whole pack was watching, yet she couldn't bring herself to look away.

As Wes stepped forward, everyone else seemed to disappear, as if only the two of them stood there in the clearing. Momentarily, he broke eye contact with her as he slid the blade across his hand. At his hiss of pain, she stiffened with worry for him, but then his eyes locked with hers again, and her fear subsided.

He extended the hilt of the blade to her. "Barely a prick is all you need," he reassured her. "Not as much as mine."

"You do it." She extended her palm toward him, trusting him not to hurt her. She had no doubt in him.

He cradled her palm in his but hesitated.

"I'm not afraid," she said. "And you shouldn't be either."

At her words, Wes slowly eased the blade over her skin. She winced at the slight pain, and immediately, concern filled his eyes.

"I'm okay," she whispered. The wound stung, but the cut wasn't deep. He'd been careful with her. All traces of the minor wound would be gone in a day or two.

With both their sacrifices made, Wes stepped back, staking Maverick's blade in the ground between them again. He met her gaze, his golden wolf eyes catching in the moonlight as he extended his hand toward her. *Blood of my blood. Flesh of my flesh*, the searing heat in his eyes seemed to say. "I bind you to the Grey Wolves by my blood and my life, Naomi Evans."

Naomi clasped his injured hand with her own. As their palms made contact, a jolt of electric heat shot through her limbs. She felt the pulse and sensation of honest-to-goodness magic tingling on her skin. The soft autumn wind of the night air seemed to still.

She lifted her gaze to meet Wes's. She wasn't sure what she expected to see there. Maybe the heat that had been there moments before. Or relief, maybe even elation that following this, she would no longer be his problem. But when his eyes found hers, what she saw there tore any relief she felt in two and sent her blood running cold. Because for the first time since she'd met him, what she saw in Wes's wide, alarmed eyes was fear.

Chapter 11

A MIXTURE OF DREAD AND LONGING CONSUMED WES AS he stared down at his and Naomi's palms clutched together and felt the surge of power that passed between them in a way it never should have. The feeling shot through him as if he were being charged with a live wire, awakening every nerve, every sense, and then the scent of her hit him full force. The sweet smell of bitterroot flower that lingered on her skin heightened, twice as powerful as it had been only moments before, and twice as tantalizing.

His eyes widened. No, it wasn't possible. He shook his head. His mind was playing tricks on him. As he stared down at their clutched hands, the painful feeling of longing and need in his chest grew. Deep down, a part of him wanted exactly this, wanted *her*. But he couldn't allow himself this. His grief twisted and snarled like the beast inside him in an attempt to torture him. No. This wasn't real, and if it was, he refused to accept the reality. He would hurt her like the monster he truly was.

And that thought terrified him.

Wes snatched his hand away from hers. Her eyes widened, and he knew she'd felt what had passed between them as well. Tearing his gaze away, he looked toward Maverick. If the packmaster suspected anything, he didn't show it.

"The Grey Wolf Pack welcomes your fealty, Naomi Evans," Maverick said.

Cheers burst forth from his packmembers. Maverick stepped away from them, crossing the field back toward Wolf Pack Run with his guards carrying the Wild Eight prisoners in tow.

Wes couldn't shake the sneaking suspicion that Maverick knew exactly what he'd done. But how could he? She was human. This wasn't supposed to happen.

The mood in the pack became celebratory at the drop of a hat. Pack mentality at its finest. Wes should have been celebrating alongside them. He should have been glad that he was wrong, that she wasn't a liar, a Wild Eight associate, that his instincts had been right all along and now she was under the pack's protection. And while the doubts had niggled at him, it took hearing her strong, sure voice pronouncing her innocence and swearing her allegiance for all the suspicions to dissipate. He should've been glad, but the dread in his gut froze him in place.

Stunned and unmoving, Naomi stood across from him. Her eyes fell to her palm and then to him. She opened her mouth to speak. No. He wasn't having that conversation. Not now. Not ever.

He brushed past her, headed up the mountainside after Maverick. Within seconds, Naomi was trailing behind him.

"Will she be protected by the pack?" Wes asked Maverick.

"She'll have the Grey Wolves' full protection."

No. He knew what this meant.

"Does that mean I can go home?" Naomi chimed in. "Will I be protected there?"

Maverick faced Naomi. "You can either stay among

us or return home with the pack's protection. No vampires or Wild Eight have prowled your lands since we've been patrolling. It's your decision."

Wes wanted to tell her not to be angry with him. That he did want her. That his insistence on pushing her away had nothing to do with her. But he couldn't bring himself to form the words. She would choose to leave, and now as he'd only just discovered…

Without hesitation, Naomi nodded. "Yes, I want to go home. I need to get back to my ranch."

Wes's heart sank. He should have been happy. It was for her own good that she stayed away from him, but for her safety, he wanted her to stay. "So she's free to go?"

Maverick nodded. "Should she wish, yes."

Wes nodded toward Naomi, urging her to give him and the packmaster privacy. She must have sensed the urgency in his eyes because surprisingly, she listened, or maybe she was still stunned by the events of the evening. Hell, *he* was still stunned.

"You have to let me help stop the Wild Eight and the vampires. It's the only way to ensure her safety." Wes wasn't the kind of man to beg, and this was as close as he'd come to it. He'd wanted to stop the Wild Eight to protect his own life, but it was more than that now.

The packmaster didn't even stop to consider his proposal. "You should have thought of that *before* you brought her into this."

Black Jack trotted up beside them, seizing the moment to nip aggressively at Maverick's hand. Maverick pulled his hand back and grumbled at the horse. Black Jack might have been more of an ass than most donkeys, but he certainly had good timing.

Wes pressed further. "You know this isn't a long-term solution, and so do I. We can't keep troops on her land forever. When we need those men for battle, then what? How will we protect her? At the very least, let me head up the security of her ranch. I don't trust anyone else to do it. Not even Colt. I got her into this mess. Let me finish it."

Maverick growled. "No. I forbade you from involving yourself with anything concerning the Wild Eight, and my decision is final."

Maverick turned to leave, but Wes caught him by the shoulder.

"You did this on purpose," Wes snarled. "Forcing us together, making me care for her, and now ripping her away from me."

A hint of surprise flashed across Maverick's gaze. "I forced you to waste time protecting her no more than you wasted my time cleaning up your messes. As for caring for her, as you've proved with your actions time and time before, I have little control over you. Any feelings for her are your own. You know pack law forbids human-werewolf relations. Take her home and make your goodbyes worth it, because I expect you to return to Wolf Pack Run by tomorrow morn. And when you do, I forbid any further contact." He raked his gaze over Wes. "Consider it punishment for your disobedience."

~~~

The spell that the mountain air cast over them disappeared as soon as they left the clearing. After Austin had doctored Naomi's injuries, leaving her with several stitches in one arm, they'd returned to their horses and continued on their course without so much as a word between them. Wes's mind raced. The thought that he'd never smell her scent again haunted him, but somehow, it was unimportant now. A deeper hurt ailed him.

Ornery and stubborn as she was, he *liked* this woman.

Wes could only remember liking one other woman, one other innocent human, a woman he'd also had no business consorting with. Sure, he'd bedded plenty, and he felt amiable feelings toward the females at Wolf Pack Run for the kindnesses they'd shown him, but this was different. The more Naomi opened to him, the more he wanted to know about her. And that was more dangerous than any of the ways her scent called to his most primal urges.

As they reached the bottom of the mountainside, he saw her ranch off in the distance. A small, two-story house painted blue with white trim and white picket fences nestled into the mountain's lowlands, a wide spread of land stretching out before it. He allowed her to take the lead, and she led them to a gate in the fence. He followed her onto the ranch property.

Turn around now, his better judgment screamed at him. He'd fulfilled his duty in getting her home safely. He didn't need to ride beside her right up to her back door. He wasn't any kind of a gentleman, which was exactly why he needed to beat feet. He wasn't the kind of man to get tied up with a good girl like her. The last thing she needed was his dark, emotional baggage. Oh yeah, and then there was the whole matter of Maverick's decree...

When they reached the back of her house, they both dismounted, and she passed him Star's reins. He made quick work of tying the reins to Black Jack's saddle. Anything for the distraction.

"You don't have to worry about the Wild Eight and the vampires. Like Maverick said, we'll monitor your lands."

Her response wasn't what he anticipated. "Thank you for saving me."

He froze. She said it to his back, but still the words stunned him.

"You could have killed me right here in the pasture to save yourself, but you chose to risk your life for mine instead."

Slowly, he turned toward her. "It was selfish."

She opened her mouth as if she was going to protest but quickly closed it. The action drew his attention to her lips. The bottom one was plumper than the top. He wanted to suck it into his mouth, feel it between his teeth as he kissed her slowly and tenderly as he had that first night, see their actions through until this time, it wouldn't be his hand that caused her to reach climax. His cock immediately responded to the thought. He tipped his hat toward her with a curt nod. "I'm no kind of hero." As he started to walk away from her, he gripped Black Jack's reins until his knuckles turned white. One boot in front of the other. He was several steps farther away now. He could do this. He could walk away. He'd lived through far worse.

"Wes." Naomi's soft voice called to him.

Just keep walking. He urged his feet forward, but it suddenly felt as if his boots were glued to the ground. He couldn't do it. He looked over his shoulder toward her.

He never should have glanced back.

She stood on her back porch, arms crossed over

her chest as if she was trying to hold herself together and keep from crying. Her long, dark hair fell over her shoulders, brushing the tops of her breasts, and those warm brown eyes were staring right at him.

"I..." She struggled over her words.

The scent of bitterroot flower carried to him on the breeze. For a moment, she chewed on her bottom lip. The soft, pink flesh caught in her teeth before she released it, leaving it redder, plumper than it'd been only a moment before. "I'm glad I met you," she said.

A deep growl rumbled in Wes's chest, and he dropped Black Jack's reins. "Damn it, woman." He crossed the distance and was on her within seconds, his mouth claiming hers. Their tongues clashed together in a desperate dance, and he drank in the taste of her. She tasted just as sweet as she smelled. Of wildflower honey and clover and everything warm, earthy, delicious.

He sucked that sweet lower lip into his mouth and gently tugged it between his teeth. She let out a low moan that nearly undid him. He was fisting handfuls of her silky smooth hair, drawing her closer and closer to him. His cock pushed against the fly of his jeans, rubbing against the soft curve of her belly. His hand snaked down to her ass, intending to hike her up into his arms. It didn't matter that they were flush against each other. It would never be close enough. Not until he was inside her. He'd take her on the ground right here if he had to.

Her open-air porch would do.

They were all hands, removing each other's clothing in a fit of tugging and pulling as they stumbled onto the porch. The callused edges of Wes's fingers brushed against the smooth skin of her stomach as he tugged her

blouse over her head. When she finally lay bare before
him, his breath caught. Man, she was gorgeous. With
her dark skin bathed in pale morning light and the dark
strands of her hair cascading over her shoulders, she was
sin incarnate, and damn if he wasn't a devout sinner.

———

Wes claimed Naomi with a kiss so full of passion, it
was staggering. His tongue expertly parted the seam of
her mouth, making entry as his lips laid siege to hers.
His kiss was a taking, a claiming that delivered on the
dark promise in his eyes. His was the kind of kiss that
drove a woman ragged with need. The sweet burn of
bourbon coated her tongue. The instant their mouths had
collided, an amazing electric shock had pulsed through
Naomi, awakening parts of her she'd never known
existed, never known she should miss but now *did*.

Heat flooded her center, and she was ready for him,
for whatever he offered, no matter what the consequences. His kiss was part threat, part promise. Whether
for pain or pleasure, she wasn't entirely sure, nor did she
care. She wanted every part of him. Her head clouded
with the nearness of him, with the thick, masculine
scent of him so much that she couldn't think straight.
He smelled like the seasonal twig brooms she bought
to place around her house every October. Cinnamon,
clove, and warm spices, all things delicious and sexy.

Their tongues mingled, mixing in an erotic dance
before he drew back, his teeth grazing and tugging at
the sensitive skin of her lips.

His were a cowboy's hands. Rough and overworked.
She'd taken extra care over the years with nearly every

lotion on the market to ensure hers hadn't done the same, but on him, the signs of his hard labor made her hot with need and profound respect for the life he'd lived.

Her nipples hardened into taut peaks, and an aroused growl rumbled in his chest.

Breaking their kiss, Wes knelt before her, the early-morning sun glinting off the golden undertones of his hair. His chest was bare again, allowing her to admire the glorious sight of him in the early-morning light. He was still wearing his Stetson hat and his jeans as he gazed down at her, his eyes full of hunger at the sight of her naked. As if he recognized what she was thinking, he tossed the hat aside before he reached into the back pocket of his jeans, removing his flask and unscrewing the top.

He wanted a drink? Now?

"What are you doing?"

He didn't respond. She gasped as he carefully drizzled a small line of the whiskey over each of her breasts and down the length of her chest to her navel. The liquid that still burned hot in her throat left a cool trail in its wake, causing her back to writhe in anticipation as the liquid made its way down the line of her body.

"We both like the taste of whiskey, and I'm a man of my word," Wes whispered in a hungry promise. "When we were in the Grey Wolf stables, I warned you if you got any closer, I'd devour you." He bent over her, dipping his head just above the tip of one of her nipples. "I intend to keep that promise."

His mouth was on her, his tongue swirling and sucking her hardened nipple. The heat of his mouth mixed with the cool trail the liquor had left behind in a tantalizing swirl of fire and ice. She arched her back and cried out as he gently tugged the sensitive skin with his teeth. He made good on his promise—licking, sucking, teasing her flesh with his tongue and teeth, paying equal attention to both breasts before trailing down to her navel, ending only when the bristled hair of his beard brushed against the tender flesh of her thighs.

He nudged her legs open, spreading her wide for his pleasure. The growl that tore through him was pure wolf, and his eyes were just as animal. "You're glistening for me." He trailed a single finger over her wet folds before he suddenly dipped his finger inside.

A small gasp escaped her throat. With painstakingly slow movements, he pressed that single rough finger deep inside her, curling in a slight upward motion until he found a spot that made her moan and buck beneath him. It was a sweet, twisted torture, and that sexy smirk curled across his lips in response.

He eased two fingers inside her to that tantalizing spot deep within as the callused pad of his thumb grazed over her clit. Without warning, she shattered, falling apart in his hands. Her sudden orgasm rolled through her, making the tight walls of her pussy clench as a gush of wetness poured over his fingers. White heat filled her, and she let out a lengthy moan.

But she wanted—no, *needed*—more.

"Don't torture me," she panted. "I want you inside me. Now." She tried to sound demanding, full of every bit of sexual prowess a strong woman like herself could wield, but with her breath near gone from her cries, it sounded instead like a desperate plea. He hadn't even been inside her, and already he'd ruined her, reduced her to little more than a quivering mess of desire.

With rough hands, he hooked her legs over his shoulders, dropping his head until his mouth hovered over her wet slit. "Oh, Miss Kitty." He chuckled darkly, using that nickname he knew she hated to rile her with frustration while his tone stirred something deep between her legs. It was a dark sound that promised every bit of the destruction he'd spoken of in the stables. His delicious torture was hardly finished. "We're just getting started," he purred.

Wes ran his tongue up the length of her cleft, quickly locating that sweet bud between her legs. Man, she tasted divine. The flavor of her hot pussy mixed with the remaining whiskey was every bit as delicious as her scent suggested. She cried out again as his tongue circled her most sensitive flesh, prodding and teasing until she was bucking beneath him.

He gripped her ass cheeks, holding her still as his mouth ravaged her. He feasted on her in unrelenting, delectable torture, his mouth drawing her nearer, then releasing, nearer, then releasing until he felt the heat of her climax rising in her, his limbs tensing as each stroke of his tongue left her teetering on the precipice. Each moment of brief denial making her want all the more.

When he couldn't stand it a moment longer, he released her from his lips, drawing to his knees as he undid his belt buckle.

When his pants finally fell around his knees, his erection sprang forth, the hard, rigid length more than ready for her. Her mouth formed a slight O shape at the sight of him, but he didn't take the time to revel in her appreciation. He was too eager to be inside her.

Wes covered Naomi's body with his own, the combination of his kiss and the warmth of her skin heating him from the inside out, as if the electricity between them had sparked a fire they were both helpless to extinguish. And he'd be damned if he wanted to.

Easing himself outside her center, he rubbed the tip of his cock over her folds. He gripped her hips, holding her steady as he sheathed himself inside her. She cried out, her walls wrapping around him as if they were made for each other.

"Fuck," he groaned. She was tight and oh so sweet, and from the heat his tongue had created, she was dripping wet for him.

He thrust inside her, finding a steady, forceful rhythm that had her gripping the width of his shoulder blades, her nails digging into the skin.

"Wes," she panted.

The sounds of her quick breaths filled with pleasure drew him closer and closer. Her pussy closed around him. His balls tightened with each stroke. As they both inched nearer to the brink, he leaned down, kissing across the delicate skin of her throat, then up to her gorgeous lips. If he had his way, those lips would explore every inch of him by day's end.

"Come for me, Naomi," he hissed in her ear, addressing her by her true name.

She came hard and fast, her pussy wrapping him in sweet velvet heat as she shook beneath him until within a few more strokes, his own release quickly followed. He spilled himself inside her, pumping her full with his seed.

When they finished, they both lay there, shaking and gasping in each other's arms. As they stared up at the sky, reveling in their pleasure, both their bodies burning as bright and hot as the rising sun overhead, he found it hard to form sentences, words…hell, even coherent thought. There was only one thing Wes knew with all certainty: he wanted her again, and he wasn't certain any number of times he bedded her would ever satiate his craving. She'd woken something in him he'd long thought dead, leaving him feeling ragged and frayed around the edges in a way he couldn't wrap his head around.

He pushed onto his elbows beside her, propping himself up.

She broke the contact between them, a threat filling her voice. "If you leave now, don't ever come back here," she hissed.

He heard the hurt in her voice, felt it sharp and heavy in his chest.

She wasn't talking about Maverick's decree. He wasn't even sure she'd overheard that in the clearing. No, she was looking at him now, her threat leveled solely on him. Because as many times as he'd saved her from near-certain death, in these times, the most intimate ones, he was always the one to walk away. To leave her.

This is only temporary, he reminded himself. *Until she's safe.*

Until then, he'd have her as many times as he could before he reclaimed his logic, before reason told him he was digging himself into a deeper hole than he could never pull himself out of, until the dark shadow of his past consumed him again, and he realized the true extent of the damage he'd done.

If that meant only one day of true freedom, so be it. He would enjoy it to its fullest.

"Oh, I'm not leaving." He couldn't. Not now. Not after everything. Even if he had to risk his home among the Grey Wolves to do so, he would protect her. He knew he was only delaying the inevitable, but he didn't care. He wouldn't rest until she was safe. From the Wild Eight. From the vampires. And finally, from himself.

"I swore I would keep you safe until the threat against you and your flock had passed, and now isn't that time. I'll leave for good when I've secured your safety. In the meantime, I have a plan. But first…" He pulled Naomi toward him, slipping his cock between her legs as he teased her entrance.

She bit her lower lip as he ground against her. "Again?" She grinned, a hint of surprise in her voice.

The scent of her hair caught on the breeze, filling him with hunger.

"I told you we were just getting started."

He made certain neither of them slept until well past evening.

Chapter 12

"ONE MORE TIME, BUD, AND YOU'RE OUTTA HERE," Naomi grumbled.

She glared at Black Jack. She'd already spent far too long this morning attempting to get a saddle on him to no avail, and now she'd caught him in the act, red-handed—or hooved, as it were. Those black eyes stared back at her with all the innocent surprise of a small child with his fingers caught in the cookie jar, despite the fact that the horse was reared up on his hind legs in a clear attempt to mount and hump the filly she'd been riding only moments earlier. She'd managed to drop her herding stick, again thanks to Black Jack, and had to dismount, which she now recognized for the ploy that it was.

Apparently, the horse fancied himself as much of a stud as his cowboy wolf of a rider did.

When Wes had left this morning to enact his plan to ensure Naomi and her ranch's safety, he'd left the ornery beast in her care. After Black Jack had refused to take up residence in her stables, she'd had no choice but to bring him out along with one of her workhorses to round up the cattle. Thanks to her little rendezvous with Wes and the Grey Wolves, she was well behind on bringing the cattle in closer from out in the pastures. She needed to keep them close as their ship date to market drew nearer. The closer they were to plenty of feed and water, the less shrinkage when they were taken off their feed and water for a few hours to head to market. Too much excrement shrinkage led to a reduction in weight. Less weight, and her profits would see a significant drop—and the last thing this ranch needed was to lose any profit.

Black Jack lowered onto all fours again, trading his look of innocence for a pissed-off huff. The filly, unaware or maybe just unperturbed by Black Jack's advances, stood by idly, flicking her tail. Her ears pricked up in interest as she stared off into the distance.

From the look in the horse's eyes, Naomi knew there was a stranger on her ranch before he'd even called out her name.

"Naomi Evans?" a male voice called out.

She turned to find some young pretty boy with a clean-shaven face and a dress Stetson riding on one of the ranch's four-wheelers. Per her and Wes's plan, she'd been expecting him, and she'd instructed her ranch hands to send him out into the pasture where she was working.

The man dismounted the four-wheeler and sauntered toward her with an extended hand. "Quinn Harper."

She shook his hand, sizing him up. Quinn Harper. A man Wes told her was a hunter for the Execution Underground. As part of his plan to ensure her safety, Wes had instructed her to set up a meeting with Quinn. She knew that Quinn's group was hell-bent on protecting humanity against supernatural creatures at any cost. Supernatural creatures like Wes himself.

Black Jack snarled behind her, clearly displeased by the hunter's presence.

She ignored the horse and addressed Quinn. "Thanks for meeting with me on such short notice."

"So what led you to contact me, Ms. Evans?" Quinn

shoved his hands into his pockets and got straight to the point.

One of the nearby herd let out a long, drawn-out *moo*. The cows ambled around, confused, having been herded by her to this spot only moments earlier.

Naomi turned her attention from the herd back to Quinn. "Well, as I told you on my phone message, I have a vampire problem." She'd rehearsed this script well with Wes before his departure.

Quinn nodded. "I remember. They've been exsanguinating your flock, but that's not what I mean."

She grabbed her canteen of water from the filly's saddle and took a swig, something to distract herself. "And I'm not sure exactly what you do mean."

He pegged her with a hard stare that wasn't the least bit pretty boy. The look screamed accusation and suspicion. "I mean to say, how is it that a human rancher like yourself came into the knowledge that vampires exist?"

She turned away momentarily, eyeing the herd as if she were concerned they were going to make a break for it, which she wasn't. The question threw her for a loop.

The hunter continued. "It's my experience that unless you have a loved one who has been killed by a supernatural, my organization doesn't make a habit of sharing their secrets, let alone their contacts. I know that's not the case here. We don't have a file on you, which means someone had to spill to you. So was it another human or one of those monsters?"

Her mouth went dry. She'd never been a very good liar. She downed another sip of water, buying herself a moment of time. Finally, she cleared her throat. "I'm a resourceful rancher, Mr. Harper. When something's cutting into my profits, I'll stop at nothing to hunt that something down. I have my ways, and people talk." She took another long sip from her canteen, though she wasn't particularly thirsty.

"And who did you talk to, Ms. Evans?"

There was no fooling this guy. Instantly, she regretted having him come here. She knew it was all a part of Wes's plan. But with the way this hunter pried, if she didn't watch her words carefully, Quinn would find out everything he could about her, and likely Wes as well. Did the Execution Underground arrest humans for consorting with supernatural creatures? She cursed herself for not asking Wes before they'd parted ways.

Damn if she hadn't stepped boots deep in shit on this one.

All because she'd had to free that wolf from her trap.

The hunter's blue-green eyes stared at her, urging her with silent aggression to give up her source.

"I'd prefer not to say." No point in beating around the bush any longer.

In the background, Black Jack gave a rather satisfied whinny. How a horse could manage to look smug, she'd never know.

Quinn frowned. "A supernatural then."

She lifted one shoulder in a light shrug as she fiddled with the herding stick in her hands. It was the same shrug she'd given her brother when they were kids and he'd asked where she'd hidden one of his toys when he was being a nuisance, or nowadays when he was trying to run the family ranch his way.

"Suit yourself," Quinn drawled. "I would have pegged a ranching woman like you as more sensible, not the type to risk her life for some thrills and a quick bang with one of those monsters."

She stabbed her herding stick into the earth beneath her feet. That was it. "We're done here," she said. She turned and clicked her tongue, signaling her filly to come to her side. The horse followed her command. Wes could find another way to get to the Wild Eight that didn't include her standing in the middle of her pasture with some pretty-faced ass who felt entitled enough to insult her seconds after they'd met. "You don't know me, and I won't be insulted. This is my land. See yourself out."

She moved to mount the filly, but his hand grabbed her wrist. Within seconds, she had the blade stored in her hip holster in hand as she pushed the knife against his side. "If you value your life, you'll take your hands off me," she hissed.

His eyes widened. She'd underestimated him. From the strength in his grip, he was more than some pretty boy, but from the surprise on his face, the feeling was now mutual. He released her wrist. "I'm still interested in talking with you, Ms. Evans. Something tells me you have a very interesting story to tell."

She shook her head. "Don't patronize me."

"No offense meant, miss. I'd like to hear what you have to say."

She eyed him with suspicion.

"No sources necessary, Ms. Evans. Just tell me what's going on with this vampire problem of yours."

She did. Just as she and Wes had discussed, conveniently leaving out all the parts involving Wes and the Grey Wolves and how she'd been attacked by the Wild Eight. She highlighted how the vampires had been preying on her flock, as if that was the sole problem she faced.

He listened with keen attention, his eyes never leaving her face as she recounted her story. When she was finished, he stepped back and released a hefty sigh as he stared out over the vast land of her pasture. "Sounds like you have yourself a pest problem," he said.

She frowned. She didn't appreciate the casualness of his tone, as if vampires threatening her life and her livelihood were no big deal. As if he'd seen worse. He likely had, but that didn't matter. "I just want my land and my home back, Mr. Harper. I want to be safe as I sleep in my own bed at night."

He nodded. "Understood. We'll see what we can—"

"No," she said. "That's not good enough."

He crossed his arms over his chest. "Is there something you're not telling me, Ms. Evans? I can't help you unless you're truthful."

"I want the Execution Underground's full protection for my life and my ranch, and I'm willing to pay." She pulled the piece of paper from inside her coat pocket, as Wes had told her to do, and held it out in front of him. She felt like a traitorous woman in a mafioso movie, cutting a deal with the mob boss. "Inside you'll find the location of the Midnight Coyote Saloon. I'll take you there myself."

According to Wes, the Midnight Coyote Saloon was a western bar frequented by supernatural clientele only, including some of the worst supernatural baddies around these parts. No humans knew the location, and any human hunter in his right mind would go crazy to get his hands on the clientele in that place.

The cords of Quinn's throat strained as he swallowed, and his nose flared slightly on the intake of breath. His gaze fell to the paper and remained there. There was no doubt in her mind that he'd do anything for that information. He reached out his hand.

She pulled the paper back. "Not until you promise my protection. Not just against the vampires, but against any supernatural that may come toward me."

He looked up at her. For once, his eyes weren't judging. They were soft with human understanding as if he finally realized how serious her situation was. "You have a lot bigger problem than vampires, Ms. Evans." It was a statement, not a question.

She didn't confirm or deny it.

"They're not like you and me, you know. They may look human, sound like humans, but they're anything but. They're more aggressive and violent than you can imagine. Most of them don't have a shred of humanity in them." His face darkened, and suddenly, those eyes didn't seem so light and pretty.

She held little doubt he'd seen some horrible things.

When she didn't respond, he continued. "If I'm going to offer you all the Execution Underground's protective resources, I'm going to need something more from you."

She gripped the filly's reins, the sturdy strength of the leather offering her the support she needed. Suddenly, she was unsure of herself. Wes had insisted that the location of the Midnight Coyote would be more than enough. Depending on what this hunter asked of her, this could be a deal breaker, and then where would that leave her—and Wes, for that matter? He'd already drawn his last straw with Maverick by pursuing this when Maverick had told him to let it go. There was no going back to the Grey Wolves for him now. They were already in too deep.

Quinn returned to the four-wheeler to retrieve a briefcase he'd brought with him. She'd been so focused on the hunter himself that she'd failed to notice it before. He removed what looked like a plain manila envelope—some sort of file, if she wagered a guess. The manila folder stretched thick with paper, practically a book's worth.

He beckoned her over to the four-wheeler, and she followed, before he dropped the file onto the vehicle's seat between them. "I need you to look at a photo and tell me if you recognize this man. Share with me anything you know about him."

The tension inside her chest lifted. She could do that. How hard could it be? From the information she'd provided, he likely thought she was far more entrenched in the supernatural community than she actually was. The chances were high she wouldn't even know the individual. "Deal," she said.

Black Jack snarled. She shot him a disapproving look. The stubborn, ornery horse was far too well matched to his mangy wolf of an owner.

Quinn smiled. "Good. We have a deal then."

He reached across the off-roader, and they shook hands again. She passed the slip of paper she still held toward him. He stored it in the front pocket of his shirt and flipped open the file on the four-wheeler's seat. The first image immediately caught her interest.

She didn't hesitate to point to the image. "He's been to my ranch before. He told me he was an investor."

Quinn shook his head. "Criminal is more like it. That's Donnie White. Werewolf and current packmaster of the Wild Eight."

A lump lodged itself in her heart. Wes had suspected her of consorting with the Wild Eight when they'd only been desecrating her lands. If he found out she'd nearly done business with their packmaster, she feared he'd turn tail and run in the other direction. To think she'd been standing across from her enemy—an animal—and she'd never had a clue.

Quinn cued up a second photo, and Naomi gasped. Her hands flew to her mouth in an attempt to cover up the sound, but he'd heard it.

"Do you know him?" Quinn leaned halfway across the ATV now, shoving an excited finger toward the image in the file.

Naomi's heart leaped inside her chest, thumping in a rhythm that echoed in her temple. For a long moment, she couldn't breathe. She shook her head. "No, I don't know him," she lied.

Inside the file, a photo of Wes, blood dripping from his mouth, wolf eyes full of rage, stared back at her. He looked feral, monstrous, inhuman. Everything this hunter thought him to be, and everything she had thought he wasn't.

"I know. It's shocking if you've never seen them like that before." Quinn eyed her reaction, gauging her every move.

Slowly, she lowered her hands from her mouth, her eyes still fixed on the image. She had to play dumb. Had to make it look like she had no clue who he was. "Who is he?" she asked.

"Meet Wes Calhoun, former packmaster of the Wild Eight."

Naomi's heart stopped. *Former packmaster?*

"He disappeared three years ago after one god-awful bloody night in which he left the bodies of an innocent human woman and his monster of a predecessor—his father, Nolan Calhoun—in his wake."

Naomi was shaking her head. No, this couldn't be true. It couldn't. It had to be some sort of cruel trick. This wasn't the Wes she knew. Not the man who'd risked his life to protect hers on countless occasions, even when she'd been a total stranger, who'd fought the very wolves Quinn reported had once been his brothers to save her life.

He removed the top photo to reveal another. Naomi gasped again, not bothering to hide it. The photo depicted the corpse of a woman in a white linen bed. Blood poured from her neck, which appeared to have been mauled, torn to pieces by an animal.

By a wolf…

Hot tears stung Naomi's eyes, and her hands shook. She tucked them into her coat pockets, where Quinn couldn't see. Wes was the newest member of the Grey Wolf Pack and clearly had a bone to pick with Maverick, for reasons she hadn't even begun to fathom…

The realization that the information might be true, that it fit every missing puzzle piece, dawned on her.

"Calhoun's a monster. A murderer. We've been trying to find him, but he's been off the grid. We have reason to believe the Wild Eight are resurging in membership, and we're eager to find out if that means this bastard is back in the game."

Naomi continued to shake her head. Though she couldn't deny the validity of the information, there had to be some reason for his past actions, something the hunters were missing. She had to believe that no matter how rough around the edges he might be, the man who'd saved her life, the same man whose kiss twisted her insides and haunted her dreams, the man who had given her her first small taste of freedom couldn't be a cold-blooded, malicious beast.

She refused to believe it. Not until she heard it from his lips. She'd sworn fealty to the Grey Wolves, and though it'd been no more than a means to an end at the time, she was a woman of her word. And the Grey Wolves included Wes. What would it say of her if she was so quick to believe the worst of him? A tear slipped down her cheeks, pooling on the black plastic seat of the ATV.

"It's horrifying. I know." Quinn must have interpreted her horror as a sign that she didn't know the man in the photograph, because he didn't press her further.

Naomi nodded and swiped at her tears with the back of her hand. Collecting herself, she searched for something to say. "Three years. Wouldn't that be a cold case?"

"It *is* a cold case, but I have a personal interest in it."

"Personal?" Naomi raised an eyebrow.

Quinn nodded. "She was a fellow hunter. She was undercover working alongside that monster when he killed her." Quinn closed the file. He tucked it back into his briefcase. The locks clicked closed, and he turned back toward her. "And she was my wife."

He was a glutton for punishment.

Wes decided this as he stood in the middle of a godfor-saken alley in downtown Billings and pounded his fist on the steel door to the Midnight Coyote Saloon. Adrenaline buzzed beneath his skin. A cold gust of early November air whipped through the alley, sending a chill down his spine. In the past, he'd longed to come here countless times. Coyote's had once been his home away from home, but after his betrayal, he might as well have been stepping into a pit of vipers. The Midnight Coyote resided firmly in Wild Eight territory, run by a warlock known only as Boss, who, though not exactly affiliated with the Wild Eight, was far from averse to serving them. Wes showing his face here was tantamount to a death wish.

The door to Coyote's swung open.

The bouncer took one good look at Wes and swore. He turned his head over his shoulder and bellowed, "Boss! Get your ass out here." Then he turned back to Wes. "My night just got a whole helluva a lot harder." His Jersey accent still sounded out of place so far out west.

Wes smiled. "Nice to see you, too, Frank." He pushed past the man and stepped inside.

Dim lighting barely illuminated the back-hall entrance, but Wes's nocturnal retinas instantly adjusted.

The large bouncer was shaking his head as if he couldn't believe his eyes. "You're asking for trouble coming here, Wes."

Wes knew that, but apparently, he was desperate enough not to give a shit. He ignored Frank's comment. "How's the wife?"

Frank lifted his large shoulders in a shrug. "She's good, real good, but you didn't come here to talk about Nic."

The two men lingered in the doorframe.

Footsteps echoed down the short hallway. Wes turned to find himself face-to-face with the bar owner himself.

"You shouldn't have come here, Wes." The words dripped with warning, but Boss's low voice wrapped around them like smooth velvet. The dark-skinned cowboy peered through the darkness at Wes. Beneath the rim of his hat, one brown eye and one green narrowed in an unsettling stare.

"You kicking me out?" Wes knew the answer before he asked. Boss never denied anyone entry. Wild Eight or otherwise. As long as they checked all their baggage at the door.

Rules or no, that didn't stop a fair number of fights from breaking out at the bar. Considering the supernatural types who frequented the establishment—and it was well known that the Wild Eight were frequent and valued patrons here—those fights quickly turned into spilled blood and frequent death. But that didn't even begin to speak to what lay in the Coyote Saloon's basement.

Boss shook his head. "I like you enough to prefer not to see you killed, and I won't offer you protection from them."

Wes's eyes flashed to his wolf's. "I wasn't asking for it."

Boss clapped him on the shoulder. With that, he nodded toward the door leading to his office, beckoning Frank to follow him. As the bouncer and the warlock stepped inside, Boss shot a glance over his shoulder. "When you disappeared, some thought you were dead. I'm glad that wasn't the case." With that, Boss closed the door to his office, leaving Wes alone.

Bracing himself for what lay ahead, Wes inhaled a sharp breath and sauntered down the hallway toward the main room. Stepping through a cloud of smoke, Wes prowled toward the far side of the bar top, his boots creating an awful crunch with each step. Country music blared through nearby speakers, and the bar reeked of whiskey and peanuts. What was it with western bars and the need to drop peanut shells all over the goddamn floor?

Wes sauntered up to the bar top and took a seat. The bartender had her back turned, polishing a beer mug.

"Trixie," Wes greeted her.

She spun to face him, and her eyes grew wide. The bar towel slipped from her hands. She quickly snatched it up off the garnish tray and let out a low whistle. "Well, I'll be damned. If it ain't Wes Calhoun in the flesh."

"Say that a little louder, and you're likely to start a brawl."

She grinned. "Well, ain't that what you're here for, darlin'? You didn't come in here looking for a good time." She winked at him.

Wes smirked. Back in his Wild Eight days, Trixie had offered him plenty more than a good time on multiple occasions over the years, but he'd never accepted, and he had no plans of starting now.

Though maybe the barmaid would serve to get someone else out of his mind. He scanned Trixie as she shelved the beer mug she'd been cleaning, but his cock didn't so much as stir. The image of Naomi splayed open before him on her porch seared into his mind, and then his dick was doing far more than stirring. Apparently, his body had decided there was no other woman for him. Wes tried not to think about the implications of that.

Trixie poured a glass and clapped it onto the bar top in front of him. Maker's Mark bourbon. Four fingers worth. Enough to work through his alpha-wolf metabolism.

"You know me well."

"I drowned you in enough of these bottles over the years to know old troubles die hard." She grabbed a lemon from the fridge and a nearby knife and started chopping some garnishes. Trixie always kept the bar fully stocked for mixed drinks, though Wes had never seen anyone order anything other than beer or straight liquor.

Her eyes darted over Wes's shoulder. "Speaking of which, old trouble is headed straight toward you."

He turned to find two Wild Eight members prowling in his direction. That hadn't taken long. He hadn't even started his drink. He only recognized one of the two men. Years ago, he'd known every member of the Wild Eight, which meant the one to his left was yet another new recruit. Of course, Donnie wouldn't think twice about increasing the pack's numbers indiscriminately. He wouldn't think about the long-term consequences, wouldn't care whether he'd be able to control that many young, reckless wolves, whether he'd devalued the pack with subpar members.

"You've got a lot of nerve coming here." The new wolf's hands clenched into fists.

Wes took a calm swig of his drink as if he had not a care in the world. The liquid burned down his throat. "I've been coming here since you were a pup." He shot a glare to his right. "Since both of you were pups." Wes's gaze finally fell on the new wolf's companion. "Finally swore in, I see…"

Gabe stood in the shadow of his overly confident

friend. The years had made a lifetime of difference. The young wolf had filled out his lanky limbs, coming into the width of his shoulders and starting to look like a man instead of a boy. Gabe glared at Wes with anger in his eyes. There had been a time when Gabe's gaze had been nothing but pure admiration and respect when he looked at Wes. Neither of which Wes had earned or deserved.

But Gabe had been hell-bent on becoming a Wild Eight, and at the time, Wes had been packmaster. He'd thought the wolf too young for the life they lived.

"No thanks to you." The hatred in Gabe's eyes seared into Wes. "Newly joined."

"And did it work?" Wes asked. He took another cool sip of his whiskey.

Gabe's features twisted in confusion.

"Did it make you feel like a man? Like your balls finally dropped?" Wes intended for the words to sting, to make the young wolf see that he was no more fulfilled by this life than he'd been in the years Wes had known him. If Gabe had just been sworn in, he was still green enough to save.

Gabe's face flushed red with a mixture of anger and embarrassment. "You'll be eating those words inside the ring, Wes."

And there it was. Exactly what he'd come here for. While the upstairs of the Midnight Coyote Saloon remained neutral, what lay beneath the floorboards was anything but. The downstairs boasted a supernatural fighting ring, the level of fighting rivaled only by those used by professional MMA fighters. Two in the ring. No seconds to tap out. The wager: whatever the opponents agreed to, sworn and bound by the Boss's magic. And the only rules in the ring were that no one stopped until someone hit the floor. More often than not, that someone never got up again.

Call it barbaric or animalistic, but for an elite fighter, it was a helluva way to get information or favors they wouldn't come by otherwise, and that's exactly what Wes intended to do.

"You challenging me to the ring, Gabe?" Wes was prepared to fight the young wolf if he had to. A match between them would present barely any challenge. It might as well have been a fight between a pit bull and a Chihuahua. The Chihuahua might have heart, but the pit bull's jaws would snap him in two every time.

A smug grin crossed Gabe's lips, and for a second, Wes almost thought the young wolf was stupid enough to accept the challenge. Gabe shook his head. "No. Not me. But I'll wager a bet that Ethan will."

That's when Wes saw him. Prowling across the bar toward them was Ethan Lawrence.

A deep growl tore from Wes's throat. That was no worse outcome than if Wes had been forced to fight Donnie himself. Ethan came to stand in front of the group, crossing his powerful arms over his chest. Immediately, Gabe and the new recruit stepped behind him, flanking his back and falling into line to show their deference like the errand boys they were.

"Wes," Ethan greeted him.

Wes didn't bother to respond with the bastard's name.

"You came here for a fight."

"I came here for retribution."

"Then lead the way, Packmaster." The moniker was intended to taunt.

The words stung exactly as Ethan had intended, but Wes's expression betrayed nothing. He cradled the rage deep inside him, prepared to release it when they were in the ring. "Boss," Wes hollered.

The warlock appeared from the hall where Wes had entered moments earlier. He didn't even need to say the word. Boss simply shook his head and beckoned the group of werewolves down the nearby stairs. At the sight of the group of wolves descending the staircase, a collective whoop erupted among the bar patrons, who quickly downed their drinks and followed.

Patrons hungry for violence formed a ring around Wes and Ethan.

Boss stood at the center with them, his dark features indifferent. "The terms?"

Ethan pointed one large thumb toward his chest. "If I win, I take him bound and tied back to the Wild Eight clubhouse. Serve him up to Donnie on a platter."

The crowd's eyes turned toward Wes. "If I win, you tell me why the Wild Eight is now involved with vampires and what Naomi Evans has to do with it."

Boss gestured them both forward. "Shake on it."

Wes's hand collided with Ethan's in a shake that could only be described as pure aggression. Boss's hands hovered above theirs. Purple light coiled around Wes's and Ethan's wrists like a snake, twisting and turning until the bond seared into their skin. They were bound to their word now. Short of death, Boss's curse was unbreakable. If honor didn't compel them to keep their word, the curse and the pain it inflicted would.

When Boss lowered his hands and stepped back, Wes and Ethan released each other's grip and fell into fighting stance. The walls echoed with jeering shouts, egging them on.

Wes waited, shifting on the balls of his feet. In his Wild Eight days, he had fought and struck in blind fury. Little plan. Little strategy. Nothing but flying fists and rage. At times when he thought back to then, he realized he had been asking to die. Not because his life, his position, required it, but because he'd longed to feel. Pain. Pleasure. Anything. Anything that would take the numb edge off.

Then in the span of a night, his life had crumbled to pieces, and suddenly, he'd felt everything too much. The pain. The guilt. The betrayal. He'd felt them so acutely that he'd run.

But he wasn't running now, and this time, he didn't intend to gamble with his life. He would harness his rage, fuel his hate with strategy. And he would win.

Ethan hovered, waiting for Wes to take the first punch as he would have in the old days.

"Come on, Wes. You scared to throw the first punch?" Ethan taunted.

"I could say the same to you."

Ethan charged, his pride getting the better of him. He raised his fist, lunging toward Wes. The move was sloppy, dramatic, and easy to dodge. Wes countered with a jab of his own, landing a blow in Ethan's solar plexus. Ethan sputtered for air, and then Wes was on him. He punched the other man in the jaw, his fist connecting with bone. Ethan's whole body twisted from the weight of the blow. But he harnessed the momentum, circling around with a punch of his own. The large man's fist collided with Wes's eye. Wes's head snapped back, causing him to stumble. Pain seared through his

cheekbone and eye socket, throbbing with the beat of
his pulse. A groan sounded from the crowd. He'd sport
a shiner for certain.

Ethan dove for Wes's legs, and the two men crashed
to the floor in a heap of tangled limbs. Ethan had the
upper hand in weight and size, but Wes was faster, and
he would use that speed to his advantage. Before Ethan
could pin him, Wes rolled and jumped to a crouching
position. Ethan turned his head toward him, wolf eyes
blazing and canines bared.

Wes lunged, leaping onto the other man's back. He
wrapped both arms around Ethan's neck, pulling the
bastard into a choke hold. Ethan clawed at Wes's grip as
he struggled for air. Using all his strength, Ethan pushed
himself up from the floor, Wes still clinging to his back.
With slow, pained movements, he rose to his full height.
Damn it. Wes pressed harder against Ethan's throat. The
bastard had to be close to passing out. *Shit.*

Ethan threw himself backward, body slamming Wes
to the floor. Rage coursed through him.

Before Wes could scramble to his feet, Ethan shifted
into his wolf. It was an unfair move, shifting when Wes
was down. It changed the playing field completely. But
there were no rules in Boss's ring, which meant Ethan
could fight as dirty as he pleased. His paws hit Wes
straight in the chest, pinning him to the ground. Sharp
canine fangs sank into Wes's shoulder, tearing at flesh
and muscle. A garbled roar of pain ripped from Wes's
throat. The Wild Eight members of the crowd released
a victorious roar.

Ethan shook his head back and forth, ripping into
Wes as if he were a particularly juicy steak. Wes's

vision blurred. Cold. He was so damn cold. He could feel the blood draining from his face.

He was losing blood fast. He had no choice but to shift as soon as possible. He would heal faster in wolf form. But he couldn't focus through the pain in order to shift.

Until he heard them laugh.

They fucking laughed.

The sound of their amusement rang in Wes's ears, filling him with rage and a newfound vigor to fight. He had been their packmaster. He had created them, and now he would destroy them.

Ethan pulled back to strike a second blow. Snarling teeth plunged toward Wes's throat. Wes didn't think through the pain. He acted on pure instinct alone. He punched the wolf straight in the neck with his functioning arm and the full weight of his strength. The blow made Ethan pause enough that Wes could lodge his knee between them, kicking the wolf square in the chest. The beast was off him.

Muscle and sinew shifted as Wes's wolf burst from beneath his skin. In wolf form, the injuries to his head and shoulder were no more than what he'd sustain in any pack brawl or fight, nowhere near the maiming injuries to his human form. A snarl tore from his lips as he lunged toward Ethan, not an ounce of remorse or mercy in him.

Ethan met him head-on, and the two wolves clashed in a battle of teeth. Head reared back, Wes aimed his next bite at Ethan's throat.

He had the bastard on the ground. Just a few more blows, and he'd have all the information he needed handed to him courtesy of Boss's curse.

It was almost too easy. Too simple. Ethan had been Wes's high commander. Next to Donnie, he was the best fighter the Wild Eight had. In some ways, maybe even better than Donnie. What he lacked in agility and speed, Ethan made up for in brute force and strategy. Wes had anticipated that any fight against the other werewolf would leave him bloody and broken. He had counted on winning, but Wes wasn't stupid. He had known that even a win against Ethan would be hard fought.

And this wasn't.

Wes drew back his fist and paused. It was too easy.

But he wouldn't allow the fight to be for nothing.

"Boss, call it!" Wes barked.

He turned his gaze toward the crowd. Gabe and several other Wild Eight stood there, seemingly oblivious to everything but him on top of their fellow packmember. Gabe pounded his fist into his palm, his eyes flashing into his wolf's.

Wes knew what would come next. They far outnumbered him.

A loud bang sounded from upstairs, like a door being blown off its hinges with dynamite.

Screams erupted, silencing the crowd below. Wes's gaze shot toward Boss. The warlock trained his eyes on the ceiling.

The door to the basement burst open, and Frank's voice boomed down the staircase. "We're being raided!"

The crowd scattered like mice. The sounds of flesh hitting flesh were instantly drowned out by gunfire and shouts. Wes remained on top of a barely conscious Ethan. *No, goddamn it.* He needed Boss to call the match, or all of this would have been for nothing.

Rage twisted over Boss's face, his eyes gleaming with violence. "Humans."

"Boss!" Wes roared.

But it was too late. The warlock charged up the stairs, taking his magic with him, just as six Wild Eight members headed straight toward Wes. He was outnumbered and surrounded.

Wes rose to his feet. Aside from a full-out attack from the Grey Wolves, there was only one group that would warrant the Wild Eight's rage enough to distract them from killing Wes, earning him enough time so he could escape with his life. And Wes had bet his very life on it.

The Execution Underground had organized a helluva lot faster than Wes had anticipated.

And now he had two sets of enemies to confront.

Chapter 13

"STAY IN THE VAN." THE HUNTER'S WORDS CAME ON A growl nearly as menacing as if they had come from Wes. "There's a gun in the center console, but only use it in case of emergency. And whatever you do, stay in the van," he repeated.

"Yes, sir," Naomi replied. She crossed her arms over her chest and frowned.

She'd been sitting in the back of a utility van— property of the Billings division of the Execution Underground—for the better part of two hours, listening to the intricate raid plans. She and Wes had anticipated that the Billings division would raid the Midnight Coyote as soon as they gathered the manpower, a plan that would allow Wes to escape the Wild Eight amid the melee. What they didn't anticipate was Naomi being held hostage by the Execution Underground leading up to the raid. The plan had been for her to lead Quinn to the Midnight Coyote and then get the hell outta Dodge and back to the safety of her ranch. So much for that.

With one more stay-put-or-else glare, Quinn slammed the door behind him, leaving Naomi alone. She climbed into the front seat and saw the crew of ten heavily armed men barrel down the alleyway.

The small explosion that busted the door in echoed down the alleyway. Smoke billowed from the explosion as the hunters flooded inside. The sounds of shouting followed. For a moment, Naomi half considered staying with the Execution Underground, fellow humans who would protect her, her flock, and everything that mattered.

But then she would never see Wes again. A sharp ache pierced through her chest.

She shook her head. It didn't matter. Her flock, her livelihood, and her own protection mattered more. Even Wes would tell her that. The allegiance she'd sworn had been false, and the heat that had passed between her and Wes was nothing more than sexual attraction. It would never be more than sexual attraction. He may have saved her life, but she didn't owe him anything. Though she hadn't heard Wes's side of the story, hadn't Quinn, a fellow human, just outlined all Wes's horrible misdeeds?

It didn't matter that Quinn, a man who claimed Wes had killed his wife, was in there. Ready to extract his revenge. Wes himself had told her to leave, to forget about him and everything she knew about the Wild Eight. She wouldn't need the long-term protection of the Grey Wolves or the Execution Underground if all went according to plan.

She would stay in the van as she'd been told. Any sane person would.

Her gaze darted back toward the blown-apart doorway, to Wes inside with ten hunters, and him, the man who'd saved her life, a wanted man at the top of their target list...

Apparently, she'd lost her marbles long ago.

She snatched the gun from the center console, tucking it into the back of her pants in case she needed backup. Like hell she was staying in the van.

Naomi threw open the sliding door and made a beeline down the alleyway. She ran as fast as she could, her boots pounding against the concrete. She tore her knife from its holster on her belt, ready and prepared should she need it. The smell of smoke from the explosion filled her lungs as she rushed inside the Midnight Coyote. The hall was so dark, she could barely see a thing.

When she rounded the corner into the main bar area, she saw the hunters in hand-to-hand combat with the supernaturals. For a moment, she stood frozen, her eyes scanning over the violence. In the midst of the melee, she counted all ten hunters here, fighting.

But no Wes.

He wasn't here?

Maybe he had changed plans. He had told her to forget about him. Before she could spend another moment contemplating this, a hand slipped out of the darkness and wrapped over her mouth. Someone dragged her back into the shadows, through a door to her left. The door snicked shut behind them, and the hand released her. She spun around, knife raised at the ready, prepared to lunge at her attacker.

A blond woman with amber eyes stared back at her, her hands lifted in surrender. From the all-black outfit she was wearing and the bar rags hanging from her belt loops, Naomi guessed she was a bartender. They were standing at the top of a staircase that appeared to lead down to the basement.

Naomi opened her mouth to speak, but the woman laid a single finger to her own lips, silencing Naomi immediately. She pointed down the staircase. Descending several steps, she beckoned Naomi to follow her. Together, they crouched at the top of the staircase, peering down into the basement below.

Naomi choked back a gasp.

Three werewolves in human form held Wes. They had to be Wild Eight. From the looks of it, he'd taken out two in a group of six, but he'd been too far outnumbered. The fourth werewolf, the ringleader of the group, held a knife to Wes's throat. Though Wes's arms were behind his back, the three men barely contained him as he writhed and struggled against them.

Naomi leaned over to the woman at her side. She whispered directly into the woman's ear. "You any good with a knife?" She held out her blade to the woman.

Her companion shook her head. She mimicked Naomi's gesture, leaning in to whisper in her ear. "I'm better with magic." She lifted a hand that suddenly radiated a hot shade of glowing pink.

Naomi nodded. She holstered her knife and drew the standard nine-millimeter from the back of her pants. As she locked eyes with her companion, they shared a moment of understanding.

It was now or never.

Gun trained at the ready, exactly as her Marine brother had taught her, Naomi charged down the stairs, the other woman at her back. She might have been nothing more than a cowgirl, but she sure as hell knew how to put a wild animal down when needed.

"Drop the knife, or I shoot," she said as she reached the bottom of the stairs.

All eyes turned toward her and her companion.

The ringleader shot her a glare. "Who do you think you are, bitch?"

At the sight of her, Wes fought even harder against the wolves' hold. "What are you doing here?" His voice was laced with fear for her safety.

"Saving your ungrateful ass," she shot back. She aimed the gun toward the ringleader. "I said drop the knife, asshole."

The ringleader laughed, spreading his arms wide. "Go ahead, sweetheart. I've taken plenty of bullets before."

"Likely not a silver bullet." She'd heard the Execution Underground hunters talking about it during the van ride over. Silver was like kryptonite to all shifters. From the hunters' private conversations, she'd gathered more than enough information to know a werewolf's weaknesses—or at least enough to bluff her way through this. She brandished the gun again. "I said, put it down."

Wes's eyes were pleading with her to leave, to save herself. She tore her gaze away.

Seemingly ignoring her as if she were no more than a pesky fly, the ringleader shifted his attention to her companion, whose hands pulsed and glowed with magic. Naomi had no clue what the witch threatened, but she'd wager no one wanted to be on the receiving end of it— Barbie pink or not.

"What happened to valuing my patronage, Trixie?" the leader growled. "You'll lose your job for this."

"Desperate times and all." She shrugged. "Plus, you're a shitty tipper, Gabe."

Gabe scowled.

Naomi stepped forward. "I said drop the knife."

A smile curled over his lips. "Go ahead. Shoot. My friends here will snap you little bitches in two, and I'll still kill this Grey Wolf piece of shit." He spat the words at Wes.

Naomi shook her head. "If I pull this trigger, ten Execution Underground hunters come running. Don't make me repeat myself."

Gabe held her gaze, locking eyes with her in a head-to-head challenge. Wes snarled, but Naomi refused to look away. Gabe's snarky grin grew even wider. He lifted the knife into the air, waving the blade as if in a show of surrender. Slowly, he crouched as if he was about to place the knife on the ground.

And then he lunged.

Naomi pulled the trigger. Chaos broke loose. The kickback from the gun jolted up her arm and through her shoulder. A sharp ringing filled her ears. The sound of the gunfire rattled the concrete walls of the basement as several things happened at once, and before she knew what was happening, she was on the ground. Gabe was on top of her, his hands at her throat, despite his shoulder sizzling as if the bullet inside it had burned him from the inside out.

She tried to breathe, but Gabe's hand constricted her windpipe. Heat burned through her cheeks as she struggled to draw breath. She beat the butt of the gun against Gabe's wrists, but it was no use. *Air. Air.* She needed air. Her lungs screamed in pain, her chest constricting.

And then she heard it.

A resounding roar tore through the basement, seeming to echo louder than the gunshot itself. The noise sounded as if it belonged to a lion. But Naomi knew better. She'd heard it once before. Suddenly, Gabe's weight was lifted off her. She sucked in a massive breath. Wes didn't hesitate. Having torn apart the other wolves holding him with no remorse, he snapped Gabe's neck as if he were nothing more than an insignificant twig.

He turned his bloodied and bruised face toward her as she struggled to draw breath. What Quinn had told her was the truth. She could see it, all of it, reflected in the golden depths of his eyes. The man, the wolf, the human, the monster. All of him.

He was beautiful and horrifying, Wes Calhoun, nefarious former packmaster of the Wild Eight. A ruthless, fearless murderer who'd sought solace among his worst enemies.

The man who'd risked his life for her.

She should have been terrified. But she wasn't. She couldn't find it in herself to be scared. Instead, as he stared down at her, his wolf eyes blazing with unchecked aggression, a steady stream of power coursed through her, a sense of security and protection.

Because the look in those eyes said he'd tear out the throat of any man who dared lay a hand on her…

———

The door to the basement rattled on its hinges, signaling the Execution Underground's discovery of the locked basement door.

"Wes!" Trixie shouted. She beckoned to them, then disappeared behind a bronze hot-water tank. Wes yanked Naomi to her feet, and they darted toward the bartender. Behind the water tank, Trixie pulled open what appeared to be an air vent, revealing a small tunnel. She climbed inside. Wes and Naomi quickly followed suit.

Just as the door to the basement broke open, Wes

pulled the air vent back into place. He could see the out-line of the hunters' boots at the bottom of the stairs, but he didn't dare linger. A short crawl through the tunnel, and Wes found himself encircled by darkness. The steady sound of water dripping in the distance echoed through the space. Even with the eyes of his wolf, he had trouble seeing.

Suddenly, blue-tinged light illuminated from the flash-light on Trixie's phone. The electronic lighting revealed the three of them standing somewhere dark and dank. From the looks of it, they had to be in the Billings sewers.

"Boss has secret exits out of the saloon in case of emergency," Trixie whispered. She waved for them to follow her. With quiet footfalls, Wes and Naomi jogged behind her down several passages before they finally reached one that led in two separate directions.

Trixie pointed to the left. "That leads east." She mimicked the gesture to her right. "And that leads west. When you hit either dead end, there's a ladder to climb out. You just have to lift the sewer grate."

"Thanks, Trixie."

"Anything for you, darlin.' But whatever fool's errand you were pulling at Coyote's tonight, you'd best not repeat it."

Naomi quickly interjected, defending him. "He was trying to find out why the Wild Eight are involved with the vampires, and why they're targeting my ranch. He did it to save me."

And for his own interests in destroying the Wild Eight. But he didn't bother to correct her.

Trixie clasped her hands together in a look that was all Southern sorority girl. "Oh, how heroic," she cooed.

She slapped playfully at Wes's arm. "Who knew you had it in you, you big brute."

Wes shook his head. "I'm no hero." He meant the comment both in general and to highlight his failed plans.

Even in the darkness of the sewers, he saw Naomi's eyes widen in horror. "You did get the information, didn't you?"

He shook his head.

Naomi released her breath on a sharp hiss.

Trixie placed a hand on one rounded hip. "Well, that ain't neither here nor there. The Wild Eight are partnered with the vamps to destroy the Grey Wolves and take back their territory, all the same jazz they're always spoutin'. Only difference is, this time, the vampires aren't right."

Wes raised a brow. "What do you mean, not right?"

Trixie gave a small shrug. "He didn't say. Just that it was going to get real nasty, real fast."

"And how do you know this?" Naomi took a step back, as if suddenly wary that Trixie herself might be Wild Eight.

Flashing Naomi a tender smile, Trixie met Wes's gaze. "When I can't have what I really want, I make do." She gave Wes the once-over before her eyes flicked to Naomi. Wes grumbled, and Trixie grinned, her eyes sparkling. "I guessed as much," she muttered to him. She directed her next comment at both of them. "Though I suppose I'll have to find a new toy, considering you just beat the man's face to a pulp."

Wes chuckled. Trixie and Ethan. He shouldn't have been surprised. The feisty little bartender had always had a penchant for bad boys, and she was in no short supply working at the Midnight Coyote.

"And my ranch? Do you know anything about that?" Naomi asked.

Trixie shook her head. "Sorry, darlin'. That I don't have the answer to." She turned on one high-heeled cowgirl boot and shot Wes a knowing look. "If it don't work out, you know where to find me."

"Wait!"

Trixie turned back at the sound of Naomi's voice, one eyebrow cocked.

"How did you know I was with Wes?"

Trixie laughed. "Oh, honey, in my line of work, you learn fast that when there's trouble in a man's eyes as he's sitting at the bar top, it's always of the female kind." With that, she sauntered off into the darkness, that Georgia peach ass that somehow no longer did a damn thing for him bobbing with each high-heeled step.

And then they were alone in the darkness.

Naomi grabbed hold of Wes's hand and squeezed. "I can't see a thing now," she said.

Metal rattled off in the distance, coming from the direction of where they'd been. Someone removing the air vent.

Wes squeezed Naomi's hand. "Let's go." He led her through the darkness.

Before her meeting with Quinn, they had gone to check Wes into a hotel room on the other side of the city. Wes had thought he would need somewhere close to Coyote's to lie low after the run-in with the Wild Eight and once the Execution Underground had taken Naomi under their protection. They made their way from the tunnel to the hotel. Wes didn't release her hand until the dead bolt on their room was safely locked behind them. They couldn't go back to her ranch. The Execution Underground might follow them there and find him.

"I told you to hightail it out of there. You could have been killed." He spoke the words toward the closed door in front of him. He couldn't turn and look at her. Not now. Not when he was so full of anger and simultaneous relief. He'd thought he would never see her again, hoped he wouldn't. It was the darker side of him that wished otherwise, that wanted to keep her here for himself, that willed him to slam her onto the bed and claim her as if she was his, consequences be damned.

But he'd played this game before, and he knew how it ended.

She wasn't having any of it. "What was I supposed to do? Just sit there? They were storming in early. I knew you'd still be in inside. I kept thinking if I didn't get there in time, then…" The fighting spirit in her voice that he'd grown so accustomed to melted away.

Instinctively, he moved toward her. That was his first mistake.

She stood before him, tears running down her cheeks as she wrung her delicate hands together. The sassy, stubborn cowgirl he'd come to know disappeared, her guard falling completely. "…t-then I would lose you," she finished. She drew her eyes up to him. Thick, dark lashes sparkled with the evidence of her tears in the dim light of the hotel room. Her irises were such a deep shade of warm brown that they were nearly black. He wanted to fall into their deep abyss and lose himself. But the pain he saw there tore his heart open, the pain as acute and fierce as if it were his own.

She wasn't crying *because* of him. She was crying *for* him.

For the fear of losing him. Him. Wes Calhoun. Monstrous brute of a man that he was.

No. No. She shouldn't care for him, couldn't care for him. He didn't deserve her tears, her tenderness. He'd made a grave mistake in bedding her. He should have realized he wasn't the only one whose emotions could be wrapped up in the senseless passion between them. It was past time he ended this. For both their sakes.

"Save your tears, Miss Kitty. They're wasted on me." He moved to push past her, but she caught his hand in hers.

———⁂———

Naomi wasn't letting him off that easily. Not this time.

Not when she'd been forced to watch him nearly killed, all to save and protect her. He could try to push her away all he wanted, but she knew the truth. Dark past or not, he didn't keep putting his life on the line for her because of some ridiculous sense of duty or care for humanity. No, he cared for her. He might have been a reckless, stubborn, wild wolf of a man, but she wouldn't allow him to deny there was something growing between them. The initial spark she'd felt the first night he'd held her in his arms had stoked into steadily burning embers. Given time, she knew those embers would rise into a roaring, burning flame, and she'd be damned if she'd allow him to stomp out those fragile embers before they even truly began to grow.

"You could have stayed with the Execution Underground, protected yourself, your ranch from all this, but instead you—"

Risked everything for you, she thought, finishing his sentence.

She gripped his hand, refusing to let go. "You can't tell me how to feel, Wes. It's my heart. I get to choose who's a part of it."

"If it's me you choose, then you're a fool," he said.

His words stung. But there was a softness, a tenderness under his hard exterior. She'd seen it. Let him growl. Let him snarl and bare his teeth as he fought against her. She'd come to this fight prepared to tame the beast in him with an arsenal of her own.

"I'd rather be a fool than a coward."

A snarl tore through him, feral and terrifying. "You have no idea who you're dealing with," he warned.

Instead of drawing back, she stepped closer, challenging him. "Then show me. You want to scare me and drive me away, then so be it. But we've been together for days, and I've yet to see this monster of a man you speak of."

Silence hung between them as his eyes flashed to his wolf's and his grip on her hand tightened. When he stepped toward her, golden wolf eyes ablaze with hunger, a rush of heat flooded her core.

"Wes," she breathed.

And then his mouth was on her. His tongue parted her mouth as she melted into his kiss. Her nipples tightened. As she drew her hands up the length of his chest to wrap her arms around him, his hands were on her waist. Before she realized what he was doing, he stood behind her, nudging her down until she was bent over the hotel bed as he unclasped her jeans. His movements were firm and commanding.

She bit her lower lip in anticipation. "What are you doing?" she murmured. Did he plan to take her from behind?

Tugging open the fly of her pants, he ripped her jeans down and over her hips, exposing the lacy purple material of her panties. Her ass spread wide in offering before him, and her underwear was gone moments later, the rough pad of his thumb teasing over her clit. She moaned in response. Yes, his intentions were clear.

"What do you think I'm doing?" He bent over her. The weight of his muscled torso pinned her to the bed. The hand between her legs trailed down the length of her slit, and he drove his fingers into her as he growled in her ear, "Claiming what's mine."

She was instantly wet for him.

The sound of his belt dropping to the floor was followed by his pants soon after. "Naomi."

The use of her given name startled her. She'd become so accustomed to that awful nickname that a wave of desire burned her skin. The length of him pressed between her ass cheeks, rubbing across the wet opening of her pussy with teasing, calculated movements. Her head was so clouded with the feel of his cock massaging over that sweet bead between her legs that she failed to think straight.

"What if I told you I was once Wild Eight?" he confessed. His large hand gripped her ass. His palm drew circles over the bare skin, gentle but filled with a dark promise. At any moment, he could spank her, if he so chose, leaving her skin glowing pink. The thought both thrilled her and intimidated her.

She struggled to speak. "I'd say the past is behind you."

He chuckled darkly. "It's *me* who's behind *you*." Leaning over her again, he ran his free hand up her side until it cupped the plump weight of her breast, squeezing and kneading until her nipples tingled. "Do you want me, Naomi?"

When she didn't immediately respond, he pushed against her, the tip of his head parting her wet folds until she was aching, throbbing with need and want for him. "Answer me, Naomi."

"Yes." It was as much a plea for him to be inside her as it was an admission.

At that one word, he thrust inside her, causing her to brace her weight across the mattress with her elbows as her hands balled into fists among the sheets. She cried out in pleasure. In fast, fierce strokes, he drove into her, stretching her to the max as he pushed deeper and deeper.

Pressure built inside her with every thrust. By the time they both reached their climax, Wes spilling himself inside her as she came apart beneath him, they both glistened. Beads of sweat rolled down their bodies, and they both shook with the intensity of their connection. Collapsing on top of her, Wes rolled onto his back and pulled her into his arms, tucking her against him as the last waves of her orgasm continued to pulse through her. She folded into him, burying her cheek in the crook of his neck.

Despite the gritty intensity of their lovemaking and his confession, she felt safe here, protected. Slowly, her eyes fluttered closed, and she would have drifted into a peaceful sleep had his next confession not torn her to pieces.

"I'm a monster, Miss Kitty," he whispered against the crown of her hair, "and I don't deserve you."

She felt the weight of his pain in her chest, reopening wounds that had barely begun to heal.

"I wasn't just one of them," he whispered. "I *am* them. Their hate is born of me, of my leadership, of my family bloodline. If it weren't for the Calhouns, for me and my family, they'd never be able to kill as indiscriminately as they do. They would be nothing, no one without us." His confession came hot and searing against her ear. "I was their packmaster, their leader."

"You're a good man," she whispered back. Despite his past, she believed it. She had to, needed to believe it. There was no alternative. She'd struggled to find the truth in the question of his goodness since the moment she'd met him and only tried harder since she'd learned the truth. The man she'd experienced these past few days was good, pure of heart, but did she really know him? Did she dare trust her heart to him despite the horrifying reality of his past? Was she glossing over his misdeeds in favor of his kindnesses out of truth or mere delusion because she wasn't sure if she could handle the alternative?

As if he heard the questions racing through her mind, he chose that moment to say, "Every good deed I've done since I've been with you hasn't been out of the kindness of my heart. It's been in penance." Wes's gaze seared into hers. "And you expect me to believe you're okay with that?"

"I want you," she whispered as she leaned in to him. "All of you."

Wes's pain hurt because it was all too real, and because in caring for him, she'd realized it wasn't true. He might believe he was a monster, but she saw the real him. She could see that love was now Wes's guiding principle. She'd seen it in every sacrifice he'd made. Her only hope for him, as she lay there wrapped in his arms, was that someday, he would see it for himself.

Chapter 14

AN INCESSANT JINGLING RANG THROUGH THE MOTEL room like wind chimes, sharp and staccato. Wes was stretched across the bed, half-asleep with his limbs twisted in the sheets. He and Naomi had taken their pleasure multiple times since his confession. He couldn't seem to get enough, and from the sounds she'd been making, neither could she. The door to the hotel bathroom opening and the sound of the hot shower running had filled the room only moments earlier. Wes had been contemplating whether to unlock the door and sneak into the steamy heat after her or to finally succumb to the dreamy haze of after-sex sleep when the electronic dinging had started.

Leaning over the edge of the bed, he removed the device from the pocket of Naomi's discarded jeans and glanced at the screen. As he stared at the unidentified number flashing across the screen, the fine hairs on the nape of his neck raised on end. Something wasn't right.

Wes realized his error as he stared at the cell phone as if it were a ticking time bomb. She had spent several hours with the Execution Underground, and amid the chaos of escaping the Midnight Coyote, he'd neglected to check her over for bugs. The clandestine human organization was into Area 51–level security bullshit, extreme hacking, wiretapping, whatever the hell it took, as long as they killed a monster like him…

And to them, he was a wanted man.

Wes swiped the screen and pressed the receiver to his ear. His instincts never failed him.

"There are three things you should know. I've killed before. I won't hesitate to do it again, and I have nothing to lose. If I decide to hunt you down, I'll find you. Make no mistake." He pushed to standing and crossed the room to the window, peering through the curtains and down into the empty parking lot. "Give me one reason not to start right now."

A ragged intake of breath crackled from the other end of the line. It was rare anything intimidated Wes, but the response that followed the long pause chilled him to the bone.

"You may not value your life, but you value hers." A gruff male voice sounded from the other end of the receiver, garbled through the sound of a voice distorter as if the speaker had swallowed burning-hot coals. "Meet me in an hour. Both of you. I'll send the location."

The phone beeped, indicating the caller had hung up, and the ominous silence rang in Wes's ear with all the force of a gunshot.

An hour later, Wes and Naomi approached the designated intersection. Wes was already armed to the teeth from his stint at the Midnight Coyote, and though Naomi still had her knife and the handgun she'd stolen. Wes slipped into the alley, Naomi following, closely mirroring his every step. His heart pumped with adrenaline, and his muscles were primed for a fight.

He'd hated bringing her with him like this, putting her in danger, but considering the caller's instructions and knowledge of their whereabouts, and Naomi's bad habit of falling constantly into trouble—no doubt due to keeping company with a man like him—he wasn't certain if the hotel room was safe either. Now that he'd brought her with him, he was so painfully aware of her presence, so hyperfocused on protecting her that he didn't hear their cryptic caller sneak up behind them.

"You couldn't have listened to me, could you?" The deep, gravelly voice that came from the darkness needed no distorter to intimidate.

Wes spun toward the deep voice behind him as Naomi let out a terrified and not-so-stealthy shriek. A pair of steely-grey eyes stared back at him.

"Colt?" Wes lowered his knife, staring at his friend and packmate in alarm. "What the hell are you doing here?"

Naomi seemed as surprised as Wes.

"All that work to be a Grey Wolf, and you throw it away at the drop of a hat." The massive Grey Wolf commander stepped forward, crossing his arms over the expanse of his chest. "If you had listened to me that night with Kyle, you wouldn't be in this position. If you had listened to Maverick this last time...and one of a hundred times."

Wes understood the implication in the tight line of Colt's jaw. He'd stepped over the line Maverick had drawn in the sand one too many times, and if he returned to Wolf Pack Run, he'd need to pay the price. He'd figured as much.

"He's not very good at listening," Naomi chimed in from beside him.

Wes frowned. "Neither are you," he shot back.

Colt nodded, the warrior's stare seeming to see straight through both of them. "I'm aware."

"You're here to drag me back?"

"No." The answer caught Wes off guard. Colt didn't do anything without Maverick's approval. It was common knowledge among the Grey Wolves. He was the perfect soldier. Loyal to a fault.

If Colt noticed Wes's surprise, he didn't show it. "While you were off gallivanting with the Wild Eight, I was doing the real work to get you back into Maverick's good graces. Maverick is a reasonable packmaster, but his sense of reason is selective when it comes you. While he was keeping you busy watching Naomi, we were using our contacts to gather intel on the Wild Eight and their partnering with the vamps. Maverick's already seen this, but we need proof before we can act…" He shot Wes a pointed look. "You're a hard man to track. It took me all night, and I only found you because I know your habits."

Wes grumbled. "There's a reason for that."

"I'm aware," Colt repeated. He retrieved something from the shadows and extended it toward Wes, revealing a tablet. A video waited to be played on the screen.

Wes took the device and pressed Play without question. If Colt was risking himself for this, whatever it was, it was worth watching. Instantly, the blue light from the screen illuminated the alley. Wes's eyes fell to the video before him. Naomi peeked around his shoulder. The camera used to film the video shook with an unsteady hand. That, coupled with the low resolution, made clear the scene had been recorded on a cell phone or some similar device.

The camera faced a brick wall. Through the speakers, the cameraman's heavy breathing sounded ragged and rushed. Slowly, the shaking camera extended around a corner, revealing an alleyway much like the one they were in. At the mouth of the alley lay two men, seemingly in a lover's embrace.

"What is this?" Wes asked.

"Keep watching," Colt urged.

Wes returned his eyes to the screen, and his pulse quickened. The bent figure lurched backward. The man wasn't a lover at all, nor was he a man.

The vampire slowly rose to its feet, revealing its victim.

"Shit," Wes swore. Naomi covered her eyes and looked away.

This was no normal vampire bite. The vampire had mauled its victim's throat. Then the video ended, and Wes could only hope that the cameraman had gotten away.

In all his years, he'd never seen a vampire tear into its victim that way. The vamp had taken a chunk out of that human as if it were some kind of undead cannibal.

Wes passed the tablet back to Colt. "Damn bloodsuckers," he swore again. He loathed *all* vampires, but something about the one in the video, its eyes, its mannerisms… "What the hell was wrong with that thing?"

"It's half-turned," Colt replied.

Wes raised a brow. "Half-turned?"

"They're not like other vampires. It's some kind of deformity in their initial transformation. It leaves them still half-human, so they become deranged. They're savage, unpredictable, and insanely strong. They're slaves to their bloodthirst, only their master vampire can control them, and they turn all their victims."

Wes's eyes widened. "What did you say?" Wes felt certain he'd heard Colt correctly, but the reality was ludicrous at best, terrifying at worst.

"If they don't drain their victim entirely, the change

happens within minutes, creating another half-turned, deranged bloodsucker."

For a moment, Wes forgot to breathe.

He swore again. This was bad, so bad. For the Grey Wolves, for humanity...

His thoughts turned to Naomi. Those monsters roamed her property.

Traditional vampires only ever turned a human intentionally, as the process involved sharing their blood, then burying the "human" for three days before it rose again, a time-consuming process the fangers rarely bothered with. It was advantageous to keep their numbers down. The smaller their covens, the more human resources were available to them.

But this could change all that.

"The Wild Eight is allowing the master vampires to unleash the half-turned among them in their territory, testing them out on livestock"—Colt eyed Naomi knowingly—"before they turn their sights toward the real target. All the master vamps have to do is give the orders, and these monsters do their bidding like damn trained dogs, even from a distance. The Wild Eight is building numbers to team up against the Grey Wolves, just as Kyle told you. It's their intention to partner with the vampires to take out the Grey Wolf Pack." Colt pointed to the screen. "And these half-turned vampires are their surprise weapon."

"What about me?" Naomi asked. "How do I fit into this?"

Colt shrugged. "We don't know. Other than that your lands lead directly into ours. It would be a strategic advantage in an attack."

"And what about them wanting Wes's life?" Naomi asked.

Colt shook his head. "Wes is a bonus. Not the end goal."

Wes fought back another string of profanities. It had been bad enough that the Wild Eight had betrayed their kind and partnered with the vampires, but now this? Without the Grey Wolves supporting the Seven Range Pact and the Execution Underground's sanctions, the vampires and the Wild Eight would run rampant. That would create an all-out war with mankind.

And now he'd managed to get himself cast out of the Grey Wolf Pack. He must really have a death wish, the way he'd been disobeying Maverick recently. There was no way his alpha would be able to spare him *again*, so even if he held up his vow to keep Naomi safe, there would still be a reckoning. Yet there was no other way to ensure her protection. He'd need to provide Maverick with the proof he sought to have even a chance of returning to the Grey Wolves. Even then, it might not be enough.

Wes's brows drew tight as he stared at Colt's darkened silhouette beside him. "No one does anything for free. What's your role in this?"

"You may be disobedient, but you're loyal to the Grey Wolves. We know the Wild Eight are housing some of the half-turned vamps, but we don't know where. Bring Maverick proof of the threat, and restore yourself to the Grey Wolves in time for battle. Who better than a former enemy to tell us how his old packmates will strike? I won't lose troops for Maverick's pride. I trust you'll do the work necessary."

So it was a strategy game. A *major* strategic move.

One worthy of a cunning high commander and warrior, born and bred. Colt lived up to every bit of his title.

"And if you ever speak a word of this to Maverick, to anyone"—Colt stepped closer, something cold and calculating flashing in the wolf's golden eyes—"I'll kill you myself."

Wes would stay silent, but he dared the commander to try.

With nothing left to say, Colt slipped down the alley, heading back in the direction from which he'd come.

"Colt," Wes called after him.

He paused, glancing back over his shoulder.

"I never would have thought you'd disobey Maverick."

Colt's lips drew into a thin line, not a smile but a look of amusement for the otherwise stern commander. "I admire Maverick. But my loyalty to the Grey Wolves extends beyond him as packmaster."

Having had the last word, the Grey Wolf high commander turned and left, leaving Wes and Naomi just as stunned as the moment he'd arrived.

"All I have to do is hold the flashlight." Naomi repeated the words to herself on a whisper as if they were a mantra, trying to keep her hands from shaking. She stood behind Wes outside the Wild Eight warehouse, holding up the Maglite so Wes could pick the lock. She braced her elbows to hold the light steadier. "Don't you have night vision?" she whispered.

He shook his head. "Not enough to pick a lock this small when I'm in human form."

She clamped her lips shut and waited. A moment later, a small click indicated Wes had jimmied the lock open. He quietly placed the metal lock on the ground, pulled the door open, then signaled for Naomi to turn off the light. She clicked it off, and they slipped into the darkness of the building.

Wes's hand brushed against hers, gripping her palm to lead her deeper into the building. Even with the adrenaline of their break-in pumping through her veins, somehow, the touch felt intimate in a way it wouldn't have days earlier. The memory of those hands caressing her most intimate skin was still burned into her.

Wes led her down several hallways, treading lightly. The hairs on the back of Naomi's neck stood on end, and sudden uneasiness bubbled in her stomach. She trusted her instincts implicitly. Something wasn't right.

After one more turn, Naomi tugged on Wes's hand. He stopped and leaned toward her.

"Where are the guards?" she whispered into his ear.

Wes didn't respond, but she felt the gentle lift and drop of his shoulder. He'd told her the place was likely to be heavily guarded, yet so far, they hadn't seen even one guard.

When they reached the large, open floor of the storage warehouse and were still in the clear, Wes nudged her. "Turn on the flashlight until I can find the light switch. Don't be scared."

She clicked on the flashlight, and a catlike hiss sounded from the far side of the room.

"They'll have it chained up. Don't worry," Wes grumbled. He seemed too focused on finding the light switch to pay much mind to the vampire.

As Naomi pointed her light in the direction of the noise, a sharp gasp tore from her throat. She stumbled back against the far wall, nearly dropping the flashlight as she went. Red eyes glared at her in the glare of the flashlight. She'd known they were coming to gather evidence that such a creature existed, yet the reality shocked her.

"I can't find the damn light."

Gathering her wits about her, she repositioned the flashlight, intending to point it toward where Wes was searching the wall. As the path of the light crossed the half-turned vampire, she paused. The monster hissed again, shielding its red eyes with its hands.

"Wes." Naomi barely managed to choke his name out, horror gripping her voice.

A second later, Wes found the light switch. Fluorescent lighting flickered on throughout the room, illuminating the unleashed, untethered vampire.

Naomi screamed as Wes charged the beast head-on, meeting it midleap. What the vampire possessed in strength and speed, it lacked in technique and strategy. It was a bloodthirsty killing machine, but Wes was an elite fighter.

Naomi's breath stopped short as the monster over-powered Wes, pinning him to the brick wall. She didn't think. Acting on pure instinct, she drew her blade from its sheath, aimed just as her brother had taught her a thousand times, and threw. The knife catapulted across the room, piercing straight into the vampire's shoulder. The vampire reared back with a hiss.

It was the momentary break Wes needed.

"Turn away," he yelled.

For once, Naomi complied.

She grimaced and flinched with each sound of her blade slicing into the vampire and its accompanying screeches until Wes finished the monster off and the screeching stopped.

Naomi kept her eyes squeezed shut as she struggled to regain the breath she hadn't realized she'd been holding and released a deep sigh, completing the sentence she'd failed to say earlier. "That's why there were no guards."

Chapter 15

IT WOULD BE A SWIFT AND JUST DEATH. THAT WAS all Maverick had ever promised him, and Wes trusted the packmaster to make it so.

"Are you certain about this?" Naomi's question hung heavy in the early-morning air between them.

He sat mounted in Black Jack's saddle on the edge of the ridge, Naomi beside him on Star. Wolf Pack Run glittered in the distance. Wes nodded without hesitation. He had made the decision as soon as Colt had delivered the news about the half-turned. He knew Maverick well enough to know the packmaster would settle for nothing less. The severed vampire head inside the duffel on Black Jack's saddlebag would prove enough.

Among the Grey Wolves, only Maverick rivaled Wes in a fight, but inside the Wild Eight warehouse, had it not been for Naomi's aid, Wes would have fallen prey to the unfettered strength and speed of the bloodthirsty vampire. Now he held the key to protecting the Grey Wolves. His proof would cement the votes they needed for the Seven Range Pact and their fellow shifters to go to war.

Even if the Grey Wolves were able to win the impending battle with the Wild Eight and the vampires, any such fight would cause casualties the likes of which the Grey Wolf Pack had not seen in centuries. Though Wes had been their enemy, Maverick had spared his life for no reason other than to give him a second chance.

The Grey Wolves had taken him in, showing him hospitality and loyalty in ways his own pack by birthright never had. Even if it didn't buy him his way back into the pack, giving Maverick the proof he needed was the right thing to do. He owed the packmaster that much.

Even if it cost Wes his life.

Part of him accepted his fate. Hell, every day these past few years had been an extension on what he'd already deemed a death sentence. Now Maverick would finish it. Wes only hoped the reckoning would come *after* the war. In the battles to come, they would need every wolf.

"Are you certain about this?" Naomi asked again.

The only thing Wes was certain about was his need to keep her safe. She'd sworn fealty. Returning her to Wolf Pack Run would bring her back under the protection of the Grey Wolves.

"There's no other choice."

Wes nudged Black Jack with the heel of his boot. The horse gave a responsive grunt, turned around, and ambled in the wrong direction—on purpose. Wes spent the next several moments struggling to get the horse to move in the right direction until finally Black Jack obeyed with an annoyed huff as if to say *suit yourself*. When the horse's hooves finally came to rest on the shriveling late-autumn grass, several of the Grey Wolf guards already stood at their sides, pulling Wes and Naomi down from the horses with rough hands.

"Hey! Get your filthy paws off me," Naomi snapped. She slapped and kicked at the Grey Wolves tugging her from Star's saddle.

Wes didn't resist. He dismounted and placed his

hands behind his back. The silver handcuffs around his wrists seared with a burning hiss.

"Let go of me!" Naomi shrieked. "We didn't do anything!"

"Release her." Maverick echoed her words. "She's no concern of mine, and she's under pack protection."

The grip the guards held on Wes's arm tightened as Maverick's dark gaze turned toward him. The guards released Naomi. Gathering her wits about her, she stared at Maverick, then Wes, as she waited for Maverick to release him. Slowly, a dark realization crossed her face, her eyes growing wide.

"You lied to me." Her words escaped on a whisper, full of pain and hurt.

The betrayal that clung to her words hurt Wes more than the silver at his wrists ever could. He wanted to say he'd done it for her, to protect her in the only way he could, but it would have been a lie. He had done it for her for all those reasons, but it had been for himself as well. His conscience would accept nothing less. He couldn't be that monster again, not for her, not for anyone. Wes met Naomi's gaze, trying to convey everything he struggled to say in a single look, but she was having none of it. She turned her wrath and hurt toward Maverick.

"And you," she hissed. "He's one of your pack. He gave up everything for you, so you could teach him to be a better man, and this is how you treat him!"

"Disobedience will never be tolerated among the Grey Wolves," Maverick shot back. "Take him away," he ordered the guards.

A rough tug pulled on the cuffs at Wes's wrists.

Though the pain of the silver seared through him, he didn't fight their lead.

"No!" Naomi shouted. She rounded on Maverick, stepping forward until she was jabbing an accusatory finger into the werewolf packmaster's chest, not an ounce of fear in her eyes. "He may have lied to me, but I'll be damned if I'll let you lock him up without hearing him out! Not after everything we've been through."

"I've changed my mind. Take her with him. You can release her when she's blown off some steam." Without another word, Maverick turned and stalked back toward the compound.

The guards reached for Naomi, grabbing at her arms even as she slapped them away, charging after Maverick. To their credit, they didn't hurt her.

"No, you have to listen! Listen to me," she called after Maverick. Within seconds, the guards held her, pulling her toward the dungeon. She fought against them until Wes shot her a warning gaze that caused her to still. She calmed but still said loudly, "I can walk there myself, damn it."

The guards marched them toward the compound and down into the depths of the Grey Wolves' cellar, where an old dungeon remained, preserved from a time in their early history when the Grey Wolves had battled vampires and other shifters—before the Seven Range Pact, before peace, before their only problem was the challenge of the Wild Eight. As the guards threw Wes into a holding cell, slamming the silver doors shut behind him with a resounding bang, it occurred to him that their history was more relevant now than it had been in centuries.

They threw Naomi into the same cell with him. He

supposed it was too much to ask of his luck that they'd put her in a separate cell. At least Maverick hadn't chosen to kill him on sight. As the door slammed shut behind them and the guards disappeared, Naomi rounded on Wes, her anger radiating with all the heat of a blazing fire.

"You lied to me," she accused him again.

He said the only words that were the truth. "I had to."

"Horseshit. There was no 'had to' about it—" She opened her mouth as if she had more to say, but he cut her off.

"Would you have come here if I'd told you otherwise?"

The question caught her off guard. She gaped at him, struggling for a response.

"Where would that have left you?" he continued. "In the protection of the Execution Underground? Because last time I checked, you had blown that plan out of the water, and we both know that as much as you want to return to your ranch, it's not as safe as Wolf Pack Run."

If he thought she'd been angry before, it was nothing compared to the rage that flared in her eyes now. "Don't you dare put this on me. You've been all too eager to place your life on the line since the moment you stepped foot on my ranch."

"What's that supposed to mean?"

"It means that you're so desperate to prove yourself the hero that you couldn't give two shits about your life." The words hit him like a blow straight to the heart. "Hardly a sacrifice when you're so eager to give it up."

The truth in her words pierced through him, shattering any hint of self-control or resolve he had. Because she was right. Because it was true. Because as much as he wanted to redeem himself, even his life would never be enough. His life was worth nothing. He was a monster, and he deserved every bit of pain he received. No matter how it came, his death would be just and warranted. From the day he had knelt at Maverick's feet, expecting death to come swift and true, he had accepted that reality without fear. No sacrifice, no matter how final, would change that.

"You're right," he muttered before he realized the thought had fully formed in his mind.

Again, he caught her off guard. Naomi's eyes widened, and she dropped that damn accusatory finger of hers. "What?" she whispered.

Wes repeated the words. "You're right. Since the day I became a Grey Wolf, I've been on a quest for redemption I'll never earn and forgiveness I'll never deserve."

"Wes—" Naomi's voice softened, and she reached toward him. "That's not what I "

"No." He stepped back, avoiding the gentle caress of her touch. "It's the truth, and it needed to be said." To remind him, to force him to remember exactly how undeserving he was.

"Wes, I can't imagine—"

"No, you can't." He tore his gaze away from hers and turned to face the metal bars of the cage. He was a wild animal, more wolf than man. Hadn't that always been what he needed? Not the freedom he'd fought for with the Wild Eight, but a cage to protect him from the darkness that lurked inside his own heart.

"You're right, I can't." Naomi's voice rang confident and true. "I'll never begin to understand why you're this way or the choices you've made that have allowed this darkness to consume you…"

The affirmation that she understood should have been a relief. Hadn't he wanted her to see the monster he truly was all along? To protect her from him? To push her away in a way he had never wanted to and never would? He had longed for his past to do what he couldn't, what he was too weak, too selfish to do. Yet somehow, her agreement sliced through him.

"…not unless you show me."

The invitation shook him to his core. He should have refused. She already saw the darkness in him. She didn't need the images of his darkened past burned into her memory as well. But somehow, knowing he was on the eve of his death, knowing that this was some of the last time he'd spend with her, and seeing the metal bars around him caging him in, he couldn't escape the past any longer. Even as he'd confronted the Wild Eight, he had kept the memories at arm's length. Now they all flooded back to him in vivid detail, a reminder of how truly unworthy he was.

He sat down on the thin, wooden bench inside the cell. He allowed the rim of his Stetson to dip over his eyes as he leaned his weight into the concrete wall behind him. "Her name was Delilah. I met her in a bar." Wasn't that how all the best trouble started? With a man's mistakes and foolishness in the face of a beautiful woman. It was easier to begin than he'd thought it would be. He released the memories—maybe if he spoke the words aloud, their reality would finally sink in.

"I had been packmaster for several years, but the weight of the role was finally beginning to sink into me. I'd had enough of the violence, of the fighting, of that way of life. I'd been born and raised in the Wild Eight, groomed to live, eat, and breathe everything that was that pack, but deep down, I wanted something different, a legacy to call my own that didn't reek of blood and violence. I was searching for something good, something pure, the freedom I had realized the Wild Eight would never truly taste. I found that in her…"

He paused, his gaze flickering toward Naomi. Considering the passion that had passed between them, he half expected to see a hint of jealousy on her face, but she was too good for it, too beyond the pettiness of woman-versus-woman competitiveness. Instead, there was nothing but understanding. He tore his gaze away and refocused on the floor.

He couldn't look at her. Not now. Not as he lay bare and naked and raw in front of her as he'd never shown himself to any other.

He continued. "She was mild-mannered, sweet, amiable. I was drawn to her because she was everything I wasn't, everything I could never be. She was human, and I fell in love with her."

"There's nothing wrong with falling in love with a human…" Naomi whispered. Somehow, he knew she wasn't talking about Delilah. But he couldn't begin to think about that, not as he faced certain death at the hands of a man who was both his friend and his enemy.

"She betrayed me." The phrase hung heavy in the space between them.

"Oh, Wes…" Naomi sighed.

He raised a hand. "No. Spare me your pity." He dropped his hand back to his side with a small shake of his head. "She was a hunter, somehow affiliated with the Execution Underground. By the time I found out, she'd already gained access to some of the most intimate parts of my life and the pack's innermost secrets. There's nothing worse to a Wild Eight than betrayal, and they wanted her life for it." He continued to shake his head.

"But I wouldn't let them. No matter how much it hurt, she filled a void in me I thought could never be filled. I had killed hundreds of times before, mainly other wolves, the occasional vampire or other supernatural, but never a human, and no matter what she did to me, I couldn't turn off caring for her. I couldn't stop myself." He drew up his knee and rested his hands on the worn knees of his jeans. "The Wild Eight viewed that as a sign of weakness…my father, the former packmaster, in particular. Even in his old age, he thought I was going soft, and there was nothing worse than that in the eyes of Nolan Calhoun." He shrugged a single shoulder. "Maybe I was. In any case, they decided to take matters into their own hands.

"Nolan and Donnie gave me an address, intel they had gathered on the location of one of our long-time enemies." He released a long sigh through his nose. "I led a small pack of our men there in the dead of night, Donnie included, with the goal of killing our enemy."

From the corner of his eye, he saw Naomi lift her hands to her face, covering her mouth as if she dreaded the words that came next. "It was dark in the room when I entered. All I could see was a still body lying asleep in the bedroom inside the cabin. My only thought was of destroying our enemy."

He paused, the memory nearly choking him into silence.

"I knew something was wrong before I even thought

to shift. The room was too still, the wolves—my packmates—too anxious. I knew something was wrong. She… Her body… It was already cold. Donnie and Nolan had killed her. But they wanted me to see what they'd done and to know she was dead *because* of me."

Naomi gasped. It was a sound as full of every bit of shock and horror as it should have been, enough to scare her away from him for a lifetime. Maybe then she wouldn't mourn his death, wouldn't wonder what could have been.

"I didn't kill her, though I may as well have. Her blood is on my hands. I was their packmaster. When I realized what they'd done, how they had tricked me, I still didn't stop the violence. I killed my father to take my vengeance. I should have killed Donnie too, but the other pack members whisked him away into hiding. I couldn't have continued as packmaster after that betrayal, even if I'd wanted to."

He removed his Stetson, lowering it into his lap. "I betrayed them in the same way they betrayed me, and you're right, when I handed myself over to Maverick, I expected… Hell no, I welcomed death. His greatest act of kindness, and the worst punishment he ever could have given me, was allowing me to live."

As he finished relaying the memory, Wes set his Stetson on the bench beside him. He leaned forward, perching the weight of his upper body on his knees as he hung his head in shame.

"I don't deserve an ounce of pity. I killed the woman I loved in cold blood as surely as if I'd done it with my own two hands."

The silence that hung between them was deafening.

They lingered that way for a long time, Wes both hoping and dreading her response.

When it finally came, she whispered it so softly that the sound brushed against him as gently as a caress. "I forgive you."

His breath caught, his chest constricting so tight that breathing seemed impossible. "What did you say?" He exhaled. He lifted his gaze toward her and regretted it instantly.

Naomi stood across the cell, inside the cage with him, a hand wrapped around one of the silver bars as she clutched it against her, as if she relied on the metal instead of her legs for support. Her dark locks fell over her shoulders in windblown waves, cascading down the length of her arms and contrasting against the light-golden suede of her jacket.

"You weren't the one to kill her, Wes, and I know I'm not her," she said. "I know I'll never be her. Lord knows you've tried to push me away from the start for that exact reason. But I'm grateful that I'm not her. You know why? Because I would never betray you or hurt your trust the way she did. She didn't deserve what the Wild Eight did, but you weren't the monster she thought you to be as she tricked and hunted you, not until they made you that way."

He wanted to tell her that wasn't the truth, that he had always been that monster, that he had been born into that destiny no matter how he had tried to escape it, but he was too consumed by her whispered promises to stop her.

"I'm not her," she whispered again. "But I'm just as human…" Her grip on the bar tightened. "And I forgive you, Wes Calhoun."

Her words broke him into a million pieces as if he hadn't been born and forged from steel, hadn't lived a life that had hardened him so completely that he had only his enemies to call friends, nothing but hurt and betrayal and blood and death to his name.

Nothing but hurt.

And her...

She shattered him completely, and with that shattering, he lost any sense of resolve he possessed. There, in the cage he deserved to be in, he found freedom in the forgiveness in her dark eyes.

And he lost himself in it.

He was on her before he'd even made the decision to move. He gripped her by the base of her neck, pulling her into his arms. His lips crashed into hers, wanting, needing to draw the sweet words she'd whispered to him inside him, where he could capture the way they made him feel and never let her go. He ran his tongue along the seam of her lips, and she opened her mouth to him. His tongue dipped inside, swirling against hers.

She undid him completely, even as she pulled him back together again. He wouldn't have blamed her if she pushed him away. With all he had revealed, with all the darkness and destruction that lay in his wake, her disgust would have been more than warranted. But she didn't. Instead, she melted into his arms, into his kiss, trusting him not to hurt her. As if he deserved her forgiveness, her trust, her love.

As if he deserved her.

His whole life he'd searched, fought, and wrought violence in want of true freedom, the feeling that he was fully alive, but never once had he come near tasting it.

He'd been too consumed by the past ever to come close. But if just for the moment, he allowed himself to believe he deserved her, to lose himself in a kiss that seemed to consume them both, as if a force greater than themselves had pushed them together. Their kiss was electric fire, pure spark and heat and raw trust. In that dark, damp cellar, in a silver-barred cage under lock and key, he found freedom in the feel of her soft curves beneath him. And for once in his life, Wes felt alive.

Chapter 16

WES HAD KISSED HER BEFORE, BUT NOT LIKE THIS. Every kiss before had been pure heat. This time, as his lips claimed hers, there was something deeper. A desperation she'd never felt before flooded their kiss, as if he not only wanted her, he *needed* her. Naomi poured herself into him, her body bending and molding to his as if somehow, her touch could make him whole, as if she had a choice in the matter. Somehow, she knew they'd been careening toward this from the moment their lips had touched that first night in the forest. His kiss stole her breath away. She couldn't have stopped the fire between them even if she wanted to. Not even at the start.

With a gentle trail of fingers, his hand brushed through her hair all the way down to her lower back, leaving a delicious shiver down her spine. He palmed her ass, hard and forceful in a way that made her weak in the knees. Lifting her into his arms, he laid her out on the cellar floor beneath him.

"Wes," she murmured against his lips.

He took that moment to nibble on her lower lip, tugging the soft flesh between the sharp ridges of his canines until she gasped in pleasure.

His hands tugged at her blouse, slipping the material down over her shoulders and stomach. The front clasp of her bra didn't stand a chance against his powerful hands.

Within seconds, the cold, damp cellar air hit her nipples, tightening the dark-brown flesh.

He captured one of her breasts with his mouth, his hand claiming the other. A throaty moan tore from her lips. His tongue swirled over the taut peak, suckling one breast as his fingers gently tugged and kneaded the other.

"Wes," she whispered. "Wes?"

He released her breast only long enough to mutter, "Yes?" Then his mouth was on her again, his teeth grazing the sensitive skin.

"The guards could come back," she panted.

His gaze swept over her, burning a trail of heat. His wolf eyes flashed. "Let them."

The words sent a shot of excitement through her.

He dipped his head to her breast again. His teeth tugged on her nipple while he slipped open the fly of her jeans. She arched into his bite, another gasp tearing from her lips. It was an intoxicating mixture of pleasure and a hint of pain.

As he released her, he stripped her of her pants and the remnants of her blouse. She lay bare before him.

Hands on her thighs, he spread her wide before him. She braced herself for the heat of his mouth.

His lips drew lower, peppering kisses over her stomach and blazing a trail of heat downward. Slowly, he ran a finger up and down her cleft, the rough callus of his thumb nearing but never touching the sweet bead between her legs in a torturous, intimate dance.

"Fuck, you're so wet," he whispered. "I can already taste you on my tongue." He nudged her legs further open with his face. The stubble of his beard bristled across her sensitive skin. And then his mouth was on her, his tongue circling her clit in a sweet, steady rhythm. She opened to him, easing back onto the silver bars behind her for support. Already she could feel the thrum of pleasure building. She buried her hands in his hair as her pleasure heightened with each stroke.

He licked her, sucked her, tormented her, the pressure inside her growing until she'd nearly reached her breaking point. Just when she thought she could bear no more, he pulled back. His tongue broke its rhythm, parting her folds as he released her. The wetness of her pussy drenched the coarse hair of his beard.

He ran his tongue through it, tasting what remained of her on his chin. "You'll come for me, Naomi." That delicious smirk curled over his lips, still wet from the slickness of her. "But not yet."

As he lifted his head from between her legs, his eyes bore into her, never leaving hers. He gripped his shirt hem and stripped the shirt from his back, then turned to unbuckling his pants. The jeans hung loose on his narrow hips, and they were off within seconds. He wore no underwear, and his erection sprang forth, rock hard and virile. In the flickering yellow light of the cellar lanterns, she admired the curve of his chest, his abs, the muscles of his hips that led to his long, hard cock. A glistening bead of moisture clung to the tip of the head.

Her breath stopped short. He was beautiful. Rough, terrifying, scarred, wild, and gorgeous, like a coiled viper right before it struck to kill. The length of him rubbed between her legs as he positioned himself outside her center. Then he sheathed himself inside her.

"Wes!" she cried out.

His lips found hers, silencing her cries of pleasure.

The length of him filled her, stretching and surprising her with a sweet, burning ache. She took every inch he gave. Slowly, he allowed her to adjust to his width, and then he was moving, first a gentle rocking that warmed her from the inside out, building steadily until he thrust into her.

His strength was unparalleled. She gripped the silver bars behind her, bracing herself against the intensity until she lost herself in him.

———

Naomi couldn't sit idly and allow him to die. Not now. Not ever.

She lay awake in Wes's arms, her thoughts churning. The sounds of his sleep-laden breathing tickled her ear as her head rested in the crook of his shoulder. Rolling onto her side, she snuggled against his muscular chest, tracing her fingers idly over the bare skin. He let out a wolfish grumble before he settled into sleep again beneath her touch. Her forefinger traced the outline of one puckered, silvery scar. She'd never found scars attractive before, but somehow, he made them that way. No boyish face could compare to Wes's brand of rugged masculinity. Somehow, his scars, his battle wounds, only made him more complex, his beauty dark and hard to come by.

It was like the difference between a bottle of cabernet from the local grocery store and drinking a glass on the hills of Florence while overlooking the vineyard, where the smell and taste of the earth the grapes were grown in danced across the palate. The latter experience was something rare and truly exquisite. Wes was just as rare.

Naomi's thoughts returned to the issue at hand. Several months earlier, she'd lost her father, one of the greatest loves of her life. She wasn't about to go through such grief again, when she'd finally found someone who helped make her feel whole. But locked in a cell, there was little she could do about it.

Out of the corner of her eye, she saw movement in the shadows of the hall that led to the end of the cellblock. Careful not to disturb Wes, she pushed herself into a sitting position and focused on the darkness. Again, she sensed movement.

"Hey. Hey, you," she whispered, hoping she wasn't talking to a figment of her imagination. Wasn't running around with werewolves and slaying vampires enough crazy for one human?

Hope sparked as a young guard shifted into the light.

"Hey. Hi," she said. "Come over here." She beckoned him out of the darkness.

He emerged from the shadows and stepped closer.

"How long have you been there?" she asked, though she wasn't sure she wanted to know the answer.

The guard shrugged. "Long enough."

Heat flamed across her cheeks.

"I didn't see anything. I took my lunch break outside the cellar doors. I promise."

The thought seemed to embarrass him as much as it did her.

She nodded. "That was kind of you." She glanced over her shoulder toward Wes. "You realize I care about him then?"

The guard nodded in return. "I gathered that much."

"Then you have to help me."

He was shaking his head as soon as the words had escaped her lips. "I can't do that. I—"

"I'm not asking you to let him out," she interrupted. "I'm asking you to let *me* out."

From the look on his face, he didn't seem to understand the distinction.

"Maverick threw me in here to blow off some steam…nothing more. He didn't want to hear what I had to say, but it's important. The safety of the Grey Wolves depends upon it."

The guard eyed her with skepticism. The quirk of his brow said he didn't believe her for a second.

"I've sworn fealty to the Grey Wolf Pack," she continued. "I have no qualms with Maverick." Other than his decision surrounding Wes, though she wasn't about to say as much. "But this is time-sensitive. If Maverick doesn't hear this soon, it could be too late."

Still, the guard hesitated.

"Please," she pleaded. "You can cuff me and everything. Just let me see Maverick."

Eyeing her suspiciously, the guard looked her up and down, as if sizing up her strength. He must have decided she wasn't worth the fight, because he drew his keys from his pocket. "Fine," he said. "But if I find out you're lying, I throw you in a separate cell without him," he warned.

"Done."

The keys jingled in a merry chorus as he unlocked the padlock. The door to the cell swung open and she stepped out, glancing behind her as she did so. Wes didn't so much as stir. The door to the cell clicked shut behind her, and she extended her wrists toward the guard.

He shook his head. "I don't need to cuff you." His eyes darted toward Wes. "Any woman who could melt that cold bastard's heart must be made of pure sugar…"

Or stronger stuff than most, but she held her tongue.

"Besides, I could break you in two."

Naomi sized him up in a glance. Considering his role as a guard, she was betting he was a beta, and he wasn't nearly half the size of the alpha wolf she'd taken down in the mess hall. But again, she didn't say as much. She really did intend to talk to Maverick and nothing more—if giving the packmaster the knocking down to size he deserved could be called a "talk."

The guard led her out of the cellar and onto the route to the main compound of Wolf Pack Run and toward Maverick's office. By now, she knew the way. When they reached Maverick's office, the guard knocked on the door.

"Come in," Maverick called.

When they stepped inside, the packmaster rose to his feet. The guard started to explain, but Maverick waved him away. "Leave us."

The guard scurried from the room, shutting the door behind him with a sharp click.

It was Naomi who spoke first. "You need to make an exception."

"Perhaps you don't understand that in our pack—"

"No, *you* don't understand."

Maverick raised a single eyebrow, as if her daring to interrupt him was something he didn't experience often. Boy, was he in for a wake-up call. She was just getting started. For the past year, she'd spent the better part of her time among a group of good ol' boys, and she was decidedly not old or a man, nor was she—at least by their standards—good enough. She knew firsthand what it was like to be ignored by powerful men, and she'd be damned if she was about to get the same from Maverick. Werewolf packmaster or not.

Not when Wes's life was on the line.

Now that she had Maverick's full attention, she continued. "Wes put his life on the line to save me." Maverick opened his mouth again, but she raised a hand to silence him. "Heck, I've lost track of how many times!"

That seemed to shut him up.

"If he hadn't defied your order, I would have died at the hands of the Wild Eight. Considering I swore fealty to the Grey Wolf Pack, you could consider his actions a part of protecting the Grey Wolves' better interests. Then he risked his life at the Midnight Coyote Saloon, fighting the Wild Eight again, just so he could find out what they and the vampires are up to. If it hadn't been for the Execution Underground arriving too early, he would have been dead."

Maverick's eyes widened, but she ignored his reaction, continuing on.

"As if that wasn't enough, he risked his freedom *again* to gather still more information to protect the Grey Wolves. Not only have the Wild Eight partnered with the vampires, but they also have half-turned vampires on their side that are bigger, faster, stronger even than Wes. To prove it all to you, he fought one of those vampires and brought you its head in a damn duffel bag, even though he knew you would kill him upon his return for his disobedience…all because he's grateful to you and the Grey Wolves, because he thinks you made him a better man. But what you don't realize is that he was already a good man when you took him in. Why else would he leave everything in his life and throw himself into the hands of his enemy, all with the hope that you could end the cycle of violence he'd been born into?"

At this point, Maverick's mouth hung open, as if the packmaster was completely flabbergasted. Naomi stepped forward, her finger jabbing in the air as she drove the point home.

"So if you're even half the man that he thinks you are, you'll realize that his disobedience means nothing. Everything he is, everything he's done has been for the Grey Wolves, for *you*. And if you don't see that, you're not even a smidgen of the packmaster he would be."

Maverick's lips curled into an uncertain smile. "A smidgen?"

She blushed but ignored the comment. "Obedience isn't everything. Truly great men aren't made for it, not when someone's life is on the line. Not when disobedience is the right thing to do."

Maverick watched her with guarded eyes. "Be that as it may, it doesn't change who he is." He turned away from her as if he was done with their conversation.

But she wasn't through. "And what exactly would that be?"

Maverick twisted back toward her, only enough for her to see his face. Annoyance tightened his features. "He's a murderer," he hissed. "What do you think landed him here in the first place? The man killed his own father. He couldn't control his rage…"

Naomi's frustration flamed. He made it sound so black and white, but as far as she was concerned, it wasn't. Sure, Wes wasn't innocent, but he wasn't the big bad wolf either. He was no monster. He existed in an area of grey. His past and his actions weren't good, nor were they evil. Intention mattered, damn it. Why couldn't Maverick see that?

"And you haven't killed before?" she accused.

Maverick stilled. His whole body stiffened as if she'd thrown one of her knives straight into his back.

Slowly, he turned back toward her. His wolf eyes blazed with fiery rage. "This isn't about me."

Naomi shook her head. "But it is. With all due respect, Packmaster, this is about you as much as it is about him."

"I never killed my father or an innocent woman," Maverick growled.

"You would have killed Nolan Calhoun if you had the chance. From the sound of it, he was as awful as they come. A horrible tyrant and abuser who'd taken a young, impressionable child who'd lost his mother and molded him into the monster you think he is. Nolan deserved to die." She said this with absolute conviction. "And as for the woman, you could hardly call her innocent, and Wes didn't kill her. His packmembers did. But it wasn't enough just to kill her. They set it up so he'd be the one to discover her body. He was betrayed by his father, his brethren, the woman he'd loved. Every single person dear to him."

Something flickered in Maverick's eyes. A deep emotion he fought not to reveal. She would have said it was a hint of confusion if she didn't know better. At that moment, realization gripped her, and her breath caught.

"Did you know he didn't kill her?" The question fell from her lips before she could stop herself.

Maverick turned away from her again, but she grabbed his wrist as he did so, forcing him to turn back toward her. She saw it then in his eyes, ignorance and confusion.

He hadn't known. He had no idea.

When he didn't answer, she questioned him again. "Do you know he didn't kill her? That he was framed? Did you know that's why he killed his father?"

Maverick tore his wrist away from hers. His silence said enough.

Naomi's jaw dropped open. "You never bothered to ask him what his motivations were or if he actually did it?"

"His motivations are of little consequence to me."

Naomi wasn't buying that for a second. She knew enough about the opposite sex to know that men like Wes and Maverick, warriors forged hard as steel, rarely communicated thoroughly.

"Horseshit," she swore. "Motivation, intent, it means something. In the human world, that's the difference between a manslaughter conviction and cold-blooded first-degree murder."

"This isn't your world," Maverick was quick to remind her.

She attempted a different approach. "You aren't the least bit curious?" She had him then. She'd seen the hint of curiosity in his eyes.

He didn't deny it. Instead, he busied himself with a stack of papers on his desk, as if he couldn't care less.

"She was a hunter, you know. For the Execution Underground."

Maverick shook his head. "The Execution Underground has never allowed female hunters."

"Maybe not officially, but her husband, Quinn Harper, was official enough."

At the name, Maverick's head flew up from his papers, his eyes wide. She had his attention again.

"She went undercover with the intention of capturing Wes, tricked him into caring for her under false pretenses. I heard as much from Quinn himself."

"If he cared for her, all the more reason he would—"

"They framed him. Nolan, Donnie, and the Wild Eight. They told him it was his enemy lying in that room, and instead, it was her."

Maverick swore.

"You would have killed Nolan, too, if he'd framed you that way."

Maverick was shaking his head as if he couldn't believe what she was telling him.

He gave a deep grumble of acknowledgment that somehow spoke volumes.

"I'm not saying Wes is innocent." She shook her head. "Far from it. But he admires you more than you know, more than he would ever let on, and though he doesn't show it in the conventional way, he's loyal to you, almost to a fault. He may not be perfect, but he deserves your consideration. At least give him that much." She turned to leave, to head back to Wes.

As her hand touched the door handle, Maverick called after her, "Naomi."

She glanced back toward him.

"The half-turned vampires. You say he has proof?"

She fought the smile tugging at her lips. At the very least, she'd piqued Maverick's interest. Even if he still sentenced Wes to death, at least that death wouldn't be in vain. Wes would still have protected the Grey Wolves as he'd intended.

"Check the duffel bag the guards took from him when we arrived. You'll find one of the half-turned's heads in there. The Wild Eight is planning to attack the Grey Wolves...and soon. The vampires are their secret weapon."

With that, she twisted the door handle and walked out of Maverick's office, leaving the hardened packmaster speechless.

Chapter 17

THEIR BLOOD WOULD FLOW IN RIVERS DOWN THE mountainside. Loyalty to the pack be damned. Wes paced the length of his cell for what must have been the hundredth time in only a few minutes. When he'd awakened, he expected to find Naomi lying in his arms. Instead, she was nowhere to be seen, and all the guards were equally absent.

If they hurt her, he would murder every single one of them.

Slowly.

Just as he was preparing to launch an all-out assault on the cell lock in an attempt to break it, footsteps echoed from the darkened hall.

"Where is she?"

The guard, a young wolf named Kieran, approached.

Kieran lowered his voice to a whisper. "She's safe. Unharmed. That's all I can say for now."

His words came to an abrupt halt as Colt and several other guards entered the hallway. As high commander of the Grey Wolf armies, Colt stood in front, the other guards falling behind him in deference. Colt crossed his arms over the large expanse of his chest. He was shaking his head. "I warned you not to defy Maverick." Colt played his part, as if he hadn't played a key role in Wes's return himself.

"You did." Wes nodded. "That doesn't mean you were right."

Colt crossed over to the cell. One of the nearby guards passed him the keys. "Do I need to cuff you?"

"That would be wise." Considering they meant to lead Wes to his death, Colt was a fool to think he'd go without a struggle.

Colt shook his head again, as if he was somehow both pleased and disappointed. "You're the most stubborn wolf I've ever met."

Wes smirked. "And you're the most arrogant."

Colt jammed the key into the lock. "For what it's worth, I'll miss that hideous scowl of yours."

Wes lifted a shoulder in a shrug. "Naomi calls it a smirk."

The sound of Colt's keys jingling in the lock echoed throughout the cellar. "It's a shame she has such poor vision."

Wes snorted a laugh. "You'd be a lucky man to find the same in a woman someday. God willing, she'd put up with your ego after Maverick names you second."

"Or maybe I'll just strike up your girl, seeing as how she's a packmember now." Colt smiled. From anyone else, it would've been a taunt. But Wes grasped what Colt was saying: Naomi was safe, even in Wes's absence. And for that, he owed the commander his thanks.

He breathed a sigh of relief. There was sorrow, yes, for what he'd leave behind, but he took solace in knowing that Naomi was safe.

Colt gave the key one last turn, and the lock clicked open. A dark look sparked in the wolf's steely-grey eyes, but Wes wasn't certain what it meant. "Goodbye, Wes."

Wes stepped out of the cell, extending his wrists for Colt to cuff. "Goodbye, Colt."

Colt cleared his throat and turned toward the waiting guards. "Get him out of here!" he ordered. The other guards wrestled Wes from the cellar. He fought them every step of the way. He might have surrendered himself. His own life mattered little, but he would fight to the death on Naomi's behalf.

The guards escorted him out into the cold night air and into the woods. The smell of the pine trees filled his nostrils, calming and soothing. When they finally reached the clearing, he stilled. This was the same clearing where Maverick had spared Wes several years earlier, where tonight, he would condemn him.

The warm light of torches flooded the large clearing and cast a burning glow. Colt took his place next to Maverick as the guards led Wes up to them, tossing him to his knees. His jeans ground into the cold dirt as he knelt before the packmaster, who held ultimate power and sway within the pack. In the distance, the rustle of branches and leaves indicated the Grey Wolf packmembers hidden within the brush, welcome to watch the proceedings without intervening. For something of this magnitude, the whole pack would be in attendance.

Maverick raised a hand to silence the movement of the packmembers among the trees. When nothing but the whistle of the wind answered back, the proceedings began.

Maverick raised his voice, projecting to all in attendance. "Wes Calhoun, fellow Grey Wolf and former packmaster of the Wild Eight, you have been charged with failure to obey your pack leaders, insolence, and exposing our pack to human eyes. You are a wild, disobedient wolf with little respect for authority and the leadership of this pack. Through your disregard and betrayal, you have endangered your own life as well as the lives of every other wolf here. On the charges set forth, do you claim innocence?"

The gazes on Wes's shoulders intensified, weighing him down as if he were the only wolf, the only man in the world. He met Maverick's stare. Some deep emotion reflected in the light of the packmaster's eyes, almost as if he was urging Wes to defend himself. Wes laughed, deep and throaty.

No, he would never make it that easy on Maverick. The packmaster had made his choice. He hadn't given Wes a chance, had never taken Wes's motivations into consideration. When they examined the half-turned vampire head in the duffel bag they had confiscated from him, they would find out the truth, the warning he'd brought with him. He'd made his peace. He and Maverick had both made their beds. Now it was time for them to lie in them.

The Grey Wolves wouldn't believe the truth anyway.

"No." He said the word every packmember wanted to hear, reinforcing what they all thought of him, what they expected of the nefarious Wes Calhoun, former packmaster of the Wild Eight, their former enemy, and a known murderer of werewolves and men alike. The word he deserved. The deep sound of his voice fell flat among the mountain pines, dying nearly as soon as it had left his throat.

"Such a charge warrants death as our laws call for." A grim expression darkened Maverick's face.

A burst of murmurs sounded from around the clearing. Though Wes had never doubted the outcome, somehow, the finality of it hit him. Even faced with his own mortality head-on, he didn't mourn his death. No, this was a worthy death, a death on behalf of the pack he had grown to love even as they condemned him for his disloyalty. The pack that had changed him, made him into a better man. He was still a monster, but at least now he could die knowing he hadn't succumbed to his fate without a fight.

His only regret was the thought that he would never get to kiss Naomi goodbye, never get to tell her how he felt about her.

Because he loved her…

He realized it then from the deep and burning ache in his chest. Though their time together had been brief, he needed her like he needed air, and his feelings for her only grew deeper with each passing day. She was brave, strong, resilient, passionate, and fierce. Everything he could ever want and more.

And soon, when the Grey Wolves defeated the Wild Eight, she would no longer need him, need his protection, and she would return to her life in the human world, the life and legacy she wanted on the ranch.

Not to a life with him.

That made his death just as well. The thought of being forced to live without her cut deeper than any wound. As if to prove him correct, Malcolm's executioner blade pressed against the skin of Wes's throat, drawing him to his feet.

He stared into Maverick's eyes, holding his gaze with unflinching resolve. If he was going to die at the orders of the man who was once his enemy, he would look him in the eye as the deed was done.

"Wes Calhoun," Malcolm growled. "Any last words?"

Something flickered in Maverick's gaze.

"I promised you my loyalty, not my obedience. I've kept that promise."

With Wes's final words, Malcolm drew back his blade, prepared to slice.

"Wait!" The shout rang out through the clearing.

But not from anyone whom Wes would have expected to dissent.

No, the yell that had pierced the night, that had stopped his execution, came from the man who had condemned him. Suddenly, Maverick stood in front of Wes, tearing the blade from Malcolm's hand.

Apparently, the bastard had a sick streak after all. He wanted Wes's death for himself.

Or so Wes thought.

Maverick dropped the blade into the dead grass beneath his feet. He held Wes's gaze as he spoke. "No," he said. "This would be a gross miscarriage of justice. I've made a mistake. I've made several mistakes, and packmaster or not, I'm man enough to admit them."

Wes stared at Maverick in confusion.

"You did what you did to protect the Grey Wolves, to force me to see reason when I wouldn't see it. You disobeyed me in service to this pack. A service I intend to repay, not punish."

"What's going on?" Blaze and several others raised their voices in a chorus of shouts, demanding explanation.

"There will be no blood spilled here tonight," Maverick announced. "Wes Calhoun is guilty as charged, but he has also done a great service to this pack."

Malcolm stepped forward then. "Maverick, what are you talking about?"

"The Wild Eight have partnered with the vampires. They plan to attack us, and soon."

"Then we'll defeat them as we always have." Travis, tried-and-true warrior that he was, lifted his fist into the air, and his sentiment was echoed by a chorus of shouts and battle cries from the surrounding woods.

Maverick shook his head. "Not this time. The vampires are half-turned. They're stronger than ever, and they're changing faster. They'll outnumber us. We must prepare."

Colt stood still, a ghost of a smile tugging at his face as his alpha rallied. Wes had to wonder if this had been his plan from the start.

Austin cleared his throat. "Maverick, how do you know this?"

"Because Wes brought proof. That's why he defied me. He tried to tell me, but I refused to listen. He did what he did to protect this pack. We must call a meeting of the Seven Range Pact at once if we expect to survive. This will mean war."

Another round of hushed murmurs ignited through the crowd.

Maverick turned back toward Wes, a meaningful glint in his eye. "Someone wiser than me once told me that obedience isn't everything. That great men will be disobedient when it's the right thing to do. You are a great man, Wes Calhoun, whether you see it in yourself or not. You challenged me when I was wrong, put your life on the line for me, for this pack. I'm sorry I didn't see it sooner, and for that, I owe you a great debt." Maverick dropped to his knee in a bow that silenced every sound within and surrounding the clearing. "I would be honored to have a wolf like you serve at my side." He lowered his head in submission as he said, "As my second-in-command."

There were few times in his life when Wes had considered himself at a loss for words. Seeing Maverick on bent knee, bowed before him, made this one of them. One by one, the members of the tribunal dropped on bended knee. When Wes's eyes sought Colt to protest, to apologize, the noble wolf was gone. Slowly, the packmembers emerged from the trees, falling to their knees. Wes stood there in the middle of the clearing—where twice, Maverick, once his sworn enemy, could have taken his life—with the entire Grey Wolf Pack bowed before him.

In the distance, his eyes found Naomi standing among the trees. Though she didn't kneel, she tipped her head toward him. A smile glinted on her lips, as if to say she'd seen all along the great man that he was.

"Do you accept the position?" Maverick asked, rising to stand before him.

Wes nodded, his eyes never leaving Naomi's. "I accept."

With that, a massive cheer rattled the mountains, the energy of the Grey Wolf Pack shifting at once from eagerness for Wes's death to celebration of his victory. Werewolves were an unpredictable bunch, quick to anger and easy to sway.

Maverick lowered his voice so only Wes could hear. "We need to call a meeting of the Seven Range Pact at once." Maverick's gaze followed Wes's over to Naomi. "You have it bad," he said to Wes quietly. "Don't let it become a problem. You know pack law."

Wes did, but much as he wanted it, Naomi couldn't

be his. He'd known this all along of course, pack laws or not. As soon as this was over, she would return to her normal life, to her ranch. He'd be little more than a distant memory, perhaps a dream she relived fondly. A great love story to share with her children, her grandchildren.

Human children that would never be his.

He wasn't entirely certain how he had existed prior to her, to her touch and forgiveness. He'd been a shell of a man. He knew that now, and that's why he had accepted his death—because he knew if he continued to live, he would face a far graver fate…

Life after her.

"I know what it's like." Maverick placed a hand on Wes's shoulder. His tone softened and a hint of longing filled the packmaster's eyes. He spoke of his mate loved and lost. "It's all consuming and temporary, even when it isn't supposed to be. Make the most of it, because it will have to end." He cleared his throat. "But for tonight…"

Wes tore away from Maverick's hold before the packmaster had even finished his sentence. This was one order that Wes didn't need to be told twice.

—⁂—

Wes's hand cupped Naomi's as he tugged her into the darkness of the woods. The cold night wind blew on her face, chilling her to the bone, but with the warmth that radiated at the center of her chest, she failed to care.

A wave of relief washed through her as they walked hand in hand through the woods. Yet her heart pounded in her chest, still racing from the scare. Wes had escaped the executioner's blade. The thought alone was enough to make her stomach churn. She paled to think what would have happened if Maverick hadn't changed his mind. She'd never felt so helpless, so scared as when she had stood among the Grey Wolves, sworn to silence and immobility. The pain was so sharp and fierce that it felt like losing her father all over again.

After several minutes of hiking, they reached a small clearing where one of the remaining patches of long grass had been left unclaimed by the autumn winds. One final tug of her hand, and Wes caught her in his arms, claiming her lips on a low growl that only served to warm her insides further.

"You had something to do with this," he grumbled as he teased her mouth. He nipped at her lower lip and then swept his tongue over the seam of her lips until she allowed him entry. He tasted of all things male and delicious.

She broke the contact between them long enough to whisper, "I let your actions speak for you."

Wes chuckled, the closest Naomi had heard him come to a laugh. Sweeping her into his arms, he cupped her behind as she wrapped her legs around his waist.

"Don't lie to me, Miss Kitty," he whispered against her lips.

The nickname from when they had been no more than enemies sent a wave of heat straight to her core. Even as enemies, the fire between them had crackled.

"This has you written all over it," he said.

She wrapped her arms around his neck and shrugged a single shoulder. "I just gave Maverick the dressing-down he deserved."

Even in the dim light of the moon, she watched his eyebrow quirk. "Dressing-down?"

"I told him why you disobeyed him and then informed him that if he was half the man you were, he'd spare you."

Wes shook his head. "I've said it once, and I'll say it again. You're a recipe for trouble."

"I'm rather pleased with the results of this particular recipe," she said.

That familiar smirk crossed his lips. "Me too."

"I can't even begin to think what would have happened if—"

Tears poured down her cheeks, icy cold against the night air. They were tears of joy, of relief, of fear for the fate he'd narrowly avoided, for the trials they still had ahead of them.

"Shhh." Wes swiped away her tears. "Don't cry." The words were tender in a way she'd never heard from him before.

Lowering them both to the ground, he lay beside her in the cold grass, pulling her in to him. She rested her head on the hard expanse of his chest, curling into him as they both stared up at the night sky. Stars peppered its vast expanse, white bursts swirling against the deep, dark blue. It was as if the sky stretched on forever. Naomi wrapped her hand around Wes's and squeezed.

The tears welled anew. She wanted to tell him that he'd never have to lose her, that she would be right here by his side forever if he'd have her, because she loved him, but with the emotions of the evening still running high, now didn't seem the time. Or maybe she was scared. Scared of what he would say in return.

"And what will happen when…?" Her voice trailed off. *When all this is over…*

She couldn't force the words across her lips. What about them? What about her? Would he forget her?

"Shhh." He hushed her again. His thumb traced the curve of her cheekbone. He wiped away tears she hadn't even realized she'd been crying. Tears for him, for what could be. For what she feared would never be.

They lived in separate worlds, light-years apart. The chances of their worlds colliding again once all was said and done seemed more far-fetched than the distance to the heavens sprawled above them, so close that she felt she could touch them, yet never farther from reach.

Nudging her chin toward him, he rested his forehead on hers, their noses brushing together.

"Don't think," he whispered. "Don't think of anything but tonight."

Gently, she nodded. "Tonight," she whispered back.

Pulling her deeper into his arms, he kissed her there beneath the stars with every bit of that wild abandon that captured her, thrilled her, his intent to make love to her right there in the cold autumn grass as clear as the night sky. The passion in his kiss billowed through her until it swept her heart away with all the force of the wind in her hair as she rode across the mountainside—strong, exhilarating, but fleeting.

But for tonight…

Chapter 18

IF WES HAD EXPECTED ACCEPTANCE UPON Maverick's announcement, he'd been sorely mistaken. The following morning, he sat in the Grey Wolf conference room beneath the alarmed gazes of the leaders of the Seven Range Shifter clans, feeling every bit the monster he'd always known himself to be. Grey Wolf, Grizzly Bear, Black Bear, Bobcat, Canadian Lynx, Coyote, and Mountain Lion shifters alike were represented at the table. One clan for each of the seven mountain ranges surrounding Billings, and displeasure twisted every one of the shifters' faces. As if the battle they were about to propose wasn't enough to stop the hearts of the elder members among the clans—a battle with the potential to escalate to full-blown war, the first of its kind in nearly a century—announcing that the nefarious Wes Calhoun, former packmaster of the Wild Eight, was now the Grey Wolf second-in-command hadn't gone entirely as Maverick had planned.

"Maverick, are you sure about this?" The question came from Wayne, the leader of the Grizzly Bears, as if Wes wasn't sitting only a few feet across the table from him. By shifter standards, the old bear was ancient, having lived to the ripe old age of one hundred and sixty, but in human form, he appeared only a few years past prime, in the peak of his fifties. If you asked Wes, it was well past time for Wayne to cede power to Butch, his second-in-command, a much younger, more virile bear who wasn't so steeped in tradition.

"Do you question my judgment?" A hint of a challenge entered Maverick's tone.

Butch cleared his throat. "I think what Wayne means to say is it's…" He searched for the right word.

Insane, outrageous, ludicrous: Wes read the thoughts clearly painted across Wayne's face.

Butch finally settled on "…unprecedented."

More diplomatic, but just as disapproving.

Butch continued on, "It's unheard of to have a non–Grey Wolf as second in line for the Grey Wolf pack leadership…"

Non–Grey Wolf? Wes fought back a snort. The Calhoun bloodline had been a part of the original Grey Wolves, which meant in terms of blood alone, he was as Grey Wolf as Maverick himself. His bloodline wasn't the issue. *He* was the issue.

"Especially considering the recent turn of events," Amos, the leader of the Black Bear shifters, chimed in. Never mind that Amos had considered collaboration with the Wild Eight at one point while Wes had been leader—going behind the Grey Wolves' backs to do so. He and Wes had built a personal working relationship, but the deal had fallen through. The bear was lucky Wes didn't intend to reveal that inclination before all the Pact leaders and Maverick himself. Business was business, and the two bear shifter packs always aligned with each other. Shared-species-loyalty bullshit that it was.

If Maverick got killed in battle, the Seven Range Shifter packs would be stuck with Wes as their de facto leader. Though each of the shifter clans held their own territories and had complete control within their individual packs, the Grey Wolves maintained unfettered leadership. The Grey Wolves were the farthest east and the only pack with a foothold in Billings and the eastern regions of the state. As the purest blooded among their kind, they guarded the entryway into the western mountain ranges containing dozens of smaller wolf packs. They were one of many, and if the bear shifters thought their species loyalty tied them together, they had yet to experience the pack mentality of wolves. Threatening one wolf pack threatened them all.

Maverick bristled at Amos's words. "What I choose to do within my pack is no one's concern but my own."

"Which is why we need to focus on the issue at hand." Clementine's quiet feminine tone worked as the voice of reason.

At the far end of the table from Wes, the leader of the Bobcat shifters sat beside her cousin, Josephine, the leader of their sister clan, a small pride of Canadian lynx. As the larger apex predator of the two small groups, Clementine often spoke on behalf of both species.

With a voice and name that belonged more to a wood nymph than a small predatory cat, Clementine should have been the least threatening among them, even in shifter form, but since the shifter gene carried solely among the females of the sister Lynx clans, the women had trained themselves to be strong, fierce warriors. In human form, they were as formidable as any other shifter at the table, perhaps more so considering how they had had to fight and earn their place in the male-dominated shifter hierarchy.

From outside their shifter clans, they appeared to have

no problem doing so. It was Wes's understanding that the males among their species did not shift and were used for mating purposes only, leaving the lion's share—or lynx's share, as it were—to the females, who ruled their packs with an iron fist. Size of the shifter be damned.

"We're still left with the question of what to do regarding the threat of the Wild Eight." Clementine's long lashes fell on Wes, as if he somehow still represented the eighth and only illegitimate shifter pack. Once upon a lifetime ago…

Clay, the leader of the Mountain Lion pride, sat forward in his chair. He crossed his arms over the expanse of his wide chest and scowled. Until then, he'd been silent throughout the meeting. "I've said it once, and I'll say it again. The Wild Eight are the Grey Wolves' problem and their problem alone."

For the first time during the meeting, Wes couldn't hold his tongue. "When they unleash an army of half-turned vampires and obliterate the shifter population, they'll be your problem," he snapped.

The conference room fell so silent that Wes could have heard a pin drop…on the carpeting.

"Vampires?" Clementine squeaked.

"Half-turned?" Josephine echoed.

"What the hell is he talking about, Maverick?" Logan, the Coyote packmaster, growled.

Wes's eyes shot to Maverick beside him, who murmured out of the corner of his mouth, "I hadn't sprung that gem on them just yet."

Of course he hadn't, because Maverick knew the art of restraint, something Wes had never mastered—and didn't really care to. He shook his head. When he'd been the Wild Eight's packmaster, pack politics had never been the name of the game. He'd answered to no one and cooperated with no one—at least no one who didn't serve his purpose. He'd warned Maverick this morning that he wasn't cut out for this side of being the Grey Wolf second-in-command.

As Maverick launched into an immediate explanation interlaced with damage control, Wes sat back in his chair. From the corner of his eye, he watched the Mountain Lion packmaster. If the dark expression and the tense line of the cougar's shoulders provided any indication, Wes expected the mountain lions to vote no against the Seven Range Pact involving themselves in the battle. Such a vote would leave the Grey Wolves' already strained relationship with them tenuous at best.

At this point, Maverick was finishing his explanation with, "You can see why Wes is naturally the best choice to help lead our armies against the Wild Eight. He will be able to anticipate their movements and actions better than anyone."

Amos was shaking his head. "Why can't the Grey Wolves call in reinforcements from the other wolf packs from the west for this, Maverick?"

A feral snarl sounded from the other side of the table. Logan. "This is your problem, too, bear."

The coyote often aligned his pack with the Grey Wolves, if for no other reason than to keep the peace, as his pack was the farthest north of its kind, far removed from their central leaders in Texas.

Maverick nodded. "As Logan mentioned, this affects all of us, and we don't have much time. The intel our technician, Blaze, gathered anticipates the Wild Eight launching their attack within the next seventy-two hours. The western packs will be waiting in the wings as backup. They're on alert. I can't relocate eleven other packs for a problem that can easily be solved within the east if we band together as the Pact calls for."

Wayne shifted in his chair as if the seat were making him uncomfortable. "I call for a vote then."

Maverick cast a troubled glance at Wes. Given time, he'd been hoping for the opportunity to whip votes in the Grey Wolves' favor. A call for a vote so soon negated that possibility. Pact law dictated that the majority vote applied to all shifter packs as long as they chose to continue their participation within the Pact, and doing otherwise was tantamount to declaring war against them all. Which meant that it was all or nothing. A no vote from the Seven Range Shifter Pact would leave the Grey Wolves to face the Wild Eight and the vampires alone.

The air in the room thickened with tension. With no other choice, Maverick sat forward. "With such a grave situation before us, let us begin." His words set the tone for the votes. Turning toward the Grizzlies, Maverick stared them down with obvious expectation.

But Wayne, old bear that he was, crossed his arms over his chest in stubborn dissent. "The grizzlies vote nay."

Butch cringed beside him in obvious disagreement with his leader.

"Nay for the Black Bears," Amos said, echoing the bear consensus. No surprise there.

Maverick faced Clementine and Josephine across the table. The warrior women exchanged a quick look of agreement before saying in unison, "Yea."

Logan nodded. "It's a yea for the Coyotes. We stand with the Grey Wolves as always."

Which left only the Mountain Lions.

Clay shook his head. "Nay for the Mountain Lions."

Which left the vote an even three to three, meaning the deciding vote, the tiebreaker, fell to the Grey Wolves. A satisfied grin spread across Wes's face as he locked eyes with the Mountain Lion leader. He wasn't sure why, but he didn't care for the bastard one bit, little as he'd said throughout the whole meeting.

"The Grey Wolves vote yea with all due haste," Maverick said. "We'll begin battle preparation immediately once all your generals arrive."

With the meeting temporarily adjourned while the other packs sent for their commanders and warriors from their respective territories, Maverick stood and Wes followed. As they approached the door of the conference room, Clay reached for Maverick's shoulder with Maverick's back turned. Wes stepped in his path, blocking the mountain lion's outreached hand with a menacing growl. Maverick was more than capable of holding his own, but Wes was eager to put the mountain lion in his place. Instinct told him he would soon have the opportunity.

"You're making a mistake, Maverick." Clay spoke around him as if Wes wasn't even there, but from the way he inched backward, he was well aware of the threat Wes posed.

Maverick turned toward Clay. "The Pact has made its choice, Clay. We all play by the same rules." With that, they turned and left the conference room, leaving the pissed-off mountain lion prowling away in their wake.

Blaze waited for them in the hall outside the conference room, a tablet clutched in his hands. "There's something you need to see," he said to Maverick.

When Wes continued walking, Blaze cleared his throat. "Both of you."

Ushering them into the security office, Blaze closed the door behind them and clicked the lock into place. Wes's brows drew together as he and Maverick stepped closer to the massive wall of Blaze's many monitor screens.

Blaze bent over the desk, forgoing his desk chair. His fingers tapped across the keyboard in a flurry of code. "As soon as I saw this, I knew you'd need to see it immediately." Though his words should have been directed at Maverick, Blaze shot a grave glance at Wes. "I've been trying to hack into the Execution Underground's files to see what they have on the Wild Eight and the upcoming attack, and as I was going through the files, I stumbled upon this." Blaze jabbed his finger onto the enter key.

The image that consumed the screen caused Wes's breath to stop short. Wes shook his head. No, it couldn't be true. It couldn't.

On the screen, an image of Naomi on her ranchland, smiling and shaking hands with Donnie, stared back at him. All sound, all thoughts ceased. Wes stepped forward, his nose mere inches from the screen. He stared at the image of his reflection transposed over the photo, the twitch of his eye, the pained curl of his upper lip. A part of him wanted to reach out and touch it, as if running his hand over the screen—realizing it was nothing more than colorful pixels, nothing tangible, nothing he could hold—would somehow make the dark hole growing inside his chest easier to handle. But it didn't. He was paralyzed as the burning sting of betrayal tickled his throat. He'd thought she was different. That he was different because of her. Worthy of love and acceptance, of being more than an instrument of violence. That his love was more to her than a weapon of war meant to be used against him.

But it had all been a bold-faced lie.

Not again…

Wes tore from the room, ignoring Maverick and Blaze who shouted after him in favor of the ringing that filled his ears and of the way Naomi's photogenic smile seared into his retinas.

———

She was in for it now. Naomi stood at the edge of the forest surrounding Wolf Pack Run, hand posed on an aging pine as she watched Wes close the gap between them. She'd been watching the pack's calculated preparations for war. Their warriors had already headed off into the woods, weapons in hand, and from what she'd observed, the women and children, cherished as they were among the pack, intended to remain at Wolf Pack Run, the center and most guarded part of their inner territory, far from where the front lines were sure to be at the edges of their lands and surrounded by a guard of warriors. She'd searched for Sierra in the fray but had seen no sign of the warrior she-wolf. For the better part of the afternoon, Naomi had been watching a steady stream of women, some mothers with their children, heading into what appeared to be an underground bunker.

The sight had pulled at her heartstrings until Wes had caught her attention.

He prowled across the open terrain toward her, his lithe body all predatory rage and languid movement. When she hadn't listened and stayed in his apartment during his meeting with the Seven Range Shifter clans as she'd promised, she had expected him to be annoyed, maybe even peeved, for the sake of her safety. But not this.

This was overkill. She knew that even from a distance.

The anger flying off him was barely contained, a mixture of territorial challenge, protective instinct, and some other alpha male behavior she couldn't quite place her finger on. Sure, he was still concerned another wolf might attack her as Malcolm had. Never mind that she'd put Malcolm in his place and she'd do the same to any other. What exactly had Wes expected? It had been hours since he'd told her he would be back, and he didn't even have cable, let alone any books to read.

He drew closer. The space between them grew ever smaller. It was as if he was going to barrel over her. His pace never slowed.

She took a cautious step back. "Wes..." she warned.

Before she uttered another syllable, her back pushed against the trunk of the tree as she stumbled over the tree roots. Wes was on top of her, his hands on either side of her head with his lips not claiming her but kissing her with such ferocity, it was as if he waged war against her mouth, against her. His tongue demanded entry, and the deep flavor of whiskey on him disarmed her. She melted into him in total surrender, wanting, needing. She stuck out her lower lip, anticipating the gentle tug of teeth, but he bit down hard but without hurting her, enough to cause her to moan. Heat flooded her core in response.

This kiss was a fierce clash of wills, a battle that she could never win.

When he released her, she gasped for air and struggled to regain her footing among the tree's gnarled roots. She reached out a hand, expecting him to grab her and draw her into his arms, but he didn't.

"I can taste it on you." He turned away.

Something was wrong. She wiped his kiss from her lips in a way she'd never felt she had to before. It was as if his lips had burned into her, branding her—and with a kiss, no less. She marveled at the power of it, at the dark passion that had been there, that made her want more.

Leaning against the large adjacent pine, his arms crossed over the massive expanse of his chest, he stared at her without speaking. He didn't yell or scream, but she could see the anger in the lines of his body, the tightness of his jaw, the white knuckles of his clenched fists. His body language seethed of rage…and hurt, a painful, sad hurt.

"Wes…" she whispered again. When he didn't respond, she reached out to touch him, to calm the tempest storming inside him. "Are you okay?"

He yanked away from her as if she'd scalded him.

Suddenly, she was against the tree again. His hand plunged between her legs, down the front of her jeans. He cupped the heat of her in his hand, his thumb locating the sweet bead between her legs within seconds. She cried out, pushing closer toward him, the pressure of his callused thumb both wondrous and jarring, like the first touch after an orgasm. Immediately, she slickened for him, and from the dark satisfied smirk on his lips, he felt it.

"Did you do the same for him? For Donnie?"

For Donnie? The Wild Eight packmaster? The question stunned her into silence. For a moment, she stood immobile, his fingers buried deep inside her with the promise of more to come. Her body longed for what he offered. Not making love but fucking, pure and raw. It would be as glorious as it was hideous, and she would come hard and fast. She wanted him unrestrained, with every bit of the strength in his touch unleashed. Nothing held back.

But not like this.

She shoved him square in the shoulders, but all of her strength didn't even nudge him. Her attack didn't faze him. Still, he loomed over her, dark and menacing. The coiled viper. Of his own volition, he released her from the cage his arms had created around her, stepping away from her.

Yes, something was wrong. Horribly wrong. There had been a shift in the electricity between them. The change in his touch left her heart feeling like she'd been cut open and empty, yet she had no idea what had caused this. This was not Wes, the man and werewolf she loved, a man with deep darkness in his past, a man who was good even if he didn't recognize it beneath his flaws. No, this version of him lived hand in hand with that darkness, as if the past had come back and devoured him and he intended to use it to maim, to punish. Somehow, that hurt her more than any wound at the hands of the Wild Eight ever could.

Once he stood a safe distance away, far enough that he couldn't persuade her with that angry heat in his touch, she launched her counterattack. "What the hell are you talking about?" She gestured back and forth between them.

"Don't pretend you didn't enjoy it."

The fact that she *had* enjoyed it in all its dark glory enraged her even more. It had killed her to stop. Angry sex with Wes would be like a wild ride she could never dream of controlling, but she could lose herself in the submission of it, in the command of his hands. But she would never admit as much.

"I spent most of my life inside that clubhouse," he continued. "You think I don't know exactly what he's done to you there, how he's handled you?"

Donnie again? Rage filled her. "I have no idea what you're talking about. We've been through this. I've never had anything to do with the Wild Eight. Not before you. I—"

"Don't lie to me," he roared. "Not anymore."

Bile rose in her throat. She knew then that she'd lost him, as swiftly as if Malcolm had stood behind him again with his executioner's blade.

Wes stepped closer to her, his words dripping with venom. "I know everything," he hissed.

She shook her head. "Wes, I can explain."

He turned his back on her, stepping back toward Wolf Pack Run. She grabbed his wrist, but he tore away from her.

"Wes, you don't understand," she pleaded. "I didn't know. He pretended to be an investor for the ranch. By the time I learned who he was, if I had told you, you would have—"

He whipped toward her. "You lied."

The accusation hung in the air between them, sharp as a blade, and she stood defenseless against it. Because it was true. She *had* lied. To protect herself, and then, when she'd learned the truth, to protect him. She'd cupped the small spark between them in her hands, sheltering it from the cold autumn winds of circumstance that threatened to extinguish it. What she hadn't realized, what she knew now, was that she had done nothing but ensure its destruction from the start.

The glare in his eyes was tinged with what she thought might be hate, even though only hours earlier, she'd thought she'd seen love there. She wanted to fight him, to tell him they still had a chance. But through the pain she'd caused, he couldn't see her. She could see in his eyes that he'd been drawn back there again, to three years earlier when another woman he'd loved had betrayed him.

The only difference was that Naomi had never meant to hurt him. Not like she had.

"Please don't hate me," she pleaded. "I'm not her." She reached toward him again. This time, he allowed her to touch him, to trace her fingers over the muscles of his chest. "I never meant to—"

"But you did." The pain in those three words pierced her heart.

She had three words of her own, the only three in her arsenal. "I love you." She said it before she realized it had slipped from her lips. It was the truth. Perhaps the first real, full truth she'd shared with him since they met, now that everything between them was out in the open, exposed and raw to the cold, cruel mountain air.

And it was the only weapon she had left in this battle between them.

Even in the volatile mess of the moment, she ached with hope that her words reached him, prayed that they would break through the walls he had erected to keep her out, that he would say the same back.

His hand clutched hers, stopping her touch in its tracks. "Leave."

Naomi's heart stopped. She struggled to form words. "Wes, I—"

"Leave," he repeated.

"I love you," she said again. Tears clouded her vision. A damn shame, because she had a feeling this was the last time she'd ever see his rugged, handsome face. She fought to memorize the color of his eyes, the way grey starbursts surrounded his pupils, interlaced with the icy blue that was fringed with long, blond lashes. The sharp lines of his cheekbones, the bristled texture of his beard, the jagged curve of his nose, the plump slash of his lips. She would have given anything to see that damn smirk, to see anything but the pain etched in his features.

He dropped her hand, tossing it to the side as if it meant nothing to him, as if she meant nothing to him. "Save your love for someone worthy."

You're worthy. She wanted to scream it, but she knew that if she said as much right now, he'd never believe her. To him, it would be another lie on her lips.

"I'm not capable of love."

The words pierced through her heart. So he didn't feel the same.

Turning away from her, he shifted and tore into the woods. And then he was gone, torn from her life as quickly as he'd charged into it.

"Wes!" she shouted after him, but her cry fell on deaf ears.

She struggled to breathe. It felt as if her heart had been

gutted from her chest. Clutching at her throat, she turned her gaze toward Wolf Pack Run. Someone, someone had to believe her. To help her get through to Wes. To make him realize she'd never meant to hurt him.

In the distance, three guards headed straight toward her. Their intentions were clear. If Wes thought she was Wild Eight, they likely did, too.

No. No. Any remaining chance to win him back crashed and burned as the guards advanced toward her. Wes didn't believe her. Maverick didn't believe her. No one would.

With no other choice left, she heeded Wes's words. She mounted Star, kicking the horse into full speed until she tore into the trees and headed down the mountainside in the direction of her ranch, her home.

Several days ago, she'd wanted nothing more than to make this very trip, to leave Wolf Pack Run, to return to her normal life and never come back. But now that the decision had been made for her, she wanted nothing more than to stay here in this place, in the arms of the man, the werewolf she loved. Because he was more than worthy of her love. She could see that.

She wished he could see the same.

Chapter 19

WES RAN THROUGH THE FOREST, HIS LEGS PROPELLING him forward with increasing speed. His pulse pounded in his ears, a steady thrum highlighting the singular thought that echoed through his head: it was too good to be true. He had known that from the start, of course. But somehow along the way, he'd forgotten that reality. Naomi had brought him to life, resurrected a part of him he'd thought long dead. Only to bury him six feet under once again. With three beautiful, terrible, destructive words, she'd ruined him for all others before and after her.

There would never be anyone but her…

And her betrayal…

So he ran.

Even when all four legs burned with the ache of the distance, Wes allowed the depth of his pain to act as fuel. The heat of his muscles tearing seared through his legs with every leap and bound, yet he didn't stop until he reached the edge of the mountainside, until the crevice in the landscape unfolded beneath him, leaving nowhere left to turn except to fall into its depths. The earth opened herself to him, offering to swallow his misery. He threw back his head and let loose a long, pained howl.

He stood at the edge of the cliffside, staring down into the abyss. Miles below, a river ran through the craggy rock. The orange and blue hues of the early evening sky reflected back on its surface. In the distance, an eagle perched in its nest, prepared to take flight. The mighty bird swooped down into the chasm with a harsh screech, flying away and leaving its nest, everything, behind in its wake. True freedom.

If only…

Wes would never be that free, and the events of the day had only served to remind him of that. He'd always known that whatever had passed between him and Naomi wouldn't end well. He'd said as much from the beginning when Maverick had first tasked him with protecting her. But for a moment, he'd lost himself in her lips, in her touch, in her forgiveness, and allowed himself to believe it. Believe they could somehow be together even though they lived in separate worlds, believed that she could love him. Believed he could escape his haunting past. Even now, in the wake of her betrayal, something inside him whispered that maybe it was true.

He desperately wanted—hell, needed—to believe it was true.

But it was a lie. A beautiful lie. The past history he'd fought so hard to outrun dictated that, no matter how much he wanted otherwise. His past had caught up to him, no matter how far or hard he ran.

He realized now the effort had been futile. He would never outrun his past. He had never even stood a chance. He would always be a Calhoun, born and bred. A monster, an outlaw, a murderer. A man who trusted no one, whose friends were his enemies, whose lovers were his betrayers. No love could wipe his sins clean. He was destined to this life, even as it destroyed him.

But he couldn't allow it to destroy him, at least not

yet. He steeled himself. Pushing down the emotions, the loss of her, into the deep, dark part of himself that housed his most damaged pieces, the part of himself where he'd lived for the better part of three years before she'd burst into his life, tugging him out of the darkness with all the strength of a force of nature. It was the only way he could survive her loss. He couldn't live without her, but he could exist, go through the motions. And he would do just that, because there was one emotion he could keep.

His anger. His drive for revenge flaming anew. For everything the Wild Eight had ever taken from him. His childhood, his innocence, his life, his love. And now, Naomi. They'd taken everything from him, and they would pay.

The eagle reappeared and flew back into the chasm, skimming the waters below with the wide expanse of its wings. It snatched a fish in the sharp clutches of its talons. Soaring through the air, it carried the live, flopping morsel in its hooked beak to its nest. In several quick chomps, it devoured the salmon before it nestled into its perch, fed and sated.

Maverick and the other Seven Range Pact members would be waiting for him to consult on their battle strategy. With one last look at the cliffs, he turned back toward the forest. This time, he ran with purpose, with intent.

Somewhere halfway back to Wolf Pack Run, the scent of another shifter caught on the breeze. Not Grey Wolf or Wild Eight but familiar, and the track was fresh. Wes slowed his pace and drew closer to the scent, each step intensifying it on the trail as he headed east. Crouching low among the bushes and bramble, he slunk through the underbrush. Through the leafy growth, he spotted two mountain lions ahead. He remained hidden and watched as the pair shifted, revealing themselves as Clay, the mountain lion pride leader, and Jonathan, his second.

Jonathan paced among the trees. "I knew that bastard Grey Wolf Maverick was holding something back as soon as he called us here, and now they expect us to fight a war on their behalf."

Clay stood before him, a calm pillar among the gentle swaying of the breeze-blown trees. "We won't be fighting. Not this time."

Jonathan stopped in his tracks. His eyes narrowed in skepticism. "But the Seven Range Pact states…"

Clay shook his head. "I don't care what the Pact says. I will not risk our pride members' lives on petty, inbred fighting. If the Grey Wolves need to battle their own kind for control, they can do so without us. We will put on the necessary face, play by the rules as long as needed to gain the necessary information and advantage, but when it comes down to it, we will not take part in this fight."

Wes's blood ran cold. They were planning to hang the Grey Wolves and the other shifter clans out to dry when the others needed them most. It wasn't a death sentence for the Grey Wolves, but it was one more disadvantage they didn't need in a fight that was already certain to cost lives. Such a decision amounted to little less than a declaration of war against both the Grey Wolves and the other shifter clans of the Seven Range Pact.

Sure, at a time like this, it was unlikely to result in Maverick ordering a direct attack against the Mountain

Lions, particularly when they had the Wild Eight and their vampire allies to contend with, but the relationship between the two packs would remain in shambles long after this battle was over.

And what Wes knew that the cougar leader failed to realize was that this first battle was just the beginning.

"At what cost? We will lose the protection of the Seven Range Pact, and if the Grey Wolves are right about the vampires, we will need the strength of the Pact for protection. This decision would make the Grey Wolves our enemies."

Clay rounded on Jonathan. "Are you suggesting that some outdated Pact is worth more than the lives of our people?"

"I am suggesting equal lives will be lost, should we choose to double-cross our allies. It's a poor decision made only for the sake of your pride."

"Hold your tongue," Clay hissed, stepping forward in a clear attempt to assert his dominance over the other man. But Jonathan wasn't having it. He stepped forward with equal vigor, drawing his shoulders wide. The two cougars stood nose to nose, the challenges in each of their stares clear. For a moment, something flickered in Jonathan's eyes; then, after a long beat, he lowered his gaze.

Clay smiled a smug grin. "It is a good thing that the lives of our people do not depend upon your decision, Jonathan. Let me remind you that your place as second does not warrant your disobedience," he said. With his point made clear, the pride leader turned his back, shifting back into his beast as he prowled eastward from the clearing toward Wolf Pack Run.

Wes lingered there among the bushes, watching

Jonathan with careful movements. Jonathan glared after his pride leader. Rage and frustration twisted Jonathan's face into a silent snarl. The intensity of his gaze spoke volumes about the relationship between the two men. It was commonplace, even expected, for a second to challenge his leader, but this was different. Wes had seen that look reflected in Donnie's eyes. What he assumed then to be fleeting anger had actually grown into greater discord with time, perhaps leading to Donnie's betrayal and his following indirect coup.

To this day, there was still no one who wanted Wes dead more than Donnie, and considering Jonathan's expression and what Wes had overheard about the mountain lion leader's plan to double-cross the Grey Wolves and the Seven Range Pact, Clay would do well to guard his back.

Chapter 20

WHEN HALF A BOTTLE OF ROSÉ AND SEVERAL LONG bubble baths failed to do the trick, sometimes a woman's best course of action was to stop moping and get even. Naomi wore dress boots for the occasion—to make it convincing. Though she'd checked herself into a hotel upon her return, still uncertain if her property was truly safe, she'd returned home briefly to gather her best clothes in preparation for what she was about to do, the aforementioned dress boots included. She paired them with her best unscuffed jeans and a black blouse and overlaid the ensemble with a simple jean jacket, turquoise earrings, and a matching turquoise belt buckle. With her hair pulled up in a loose, gentle twist and a bit of rouge on her cheeks, she looked more put together than she had in months.

She was a new woman. A dangerous one, as it were.

Her hand slid inside the pocket of her jean jacket, running over the hilt of her blade. Backup, if she needed it. She had never killed a man before, but somehow, she knew in this case, she wouldn't hesitate if it came down to it. Broken heart or not, she wasn't the type of woman to disappear quietly into the night, and Donnie had another think coming if he thought as much.

She was no fool. She knew some of the fault in her and Wes's rough parting had been her own. She should have trusted him and told him the truth the moment she'd realized that the Wild Eight had been the "investors" after her land. He'd never given her reason not to trust him. But in her defense, she'd been scared and afraid, uncertain at that point whether he had been an enemy or ally. By the time she'd realized Wes was more to her than she ever could have fathomed, it was too late to reveal the truth. She realized now that had only made the situation worse.

I'm not capable of love. The sting of his response to her confession still burned fresh and raw in her chest. She'd ached for him in that moment, for everything she realized now she couldn't have. Though she knew the feeling would lessen in intensity over time, she doubted it would ever really disappear. But it didn't matter that he didn't love her like she loved him, that he couldn't love her. She'd known from the moment she'd said the words that she was casting her bets on a man who'd never known true love, who anticipated—no, expected—to have those closest to him be the ones to destroy him.

Considering his past history, she understood why he could think the worst of her. In the heat of their argument, she'd wanted him to hear that the Wild Eight had been gunning for her lands from the start, lying and using her just as they'd done to him. That made them one and the same, not enemies. But he had refused to listen. Stubborn, hardheaded, wonderful wolf that he was.

So she would make him listen with her actions.

Though she knew he'd never love her, she refused to add to his destruction. She would prove her innocence to Wes. She was certain of it.

The previous time she had met with Donnie, it had been on her ranch. Her home turf. Though she knew now that the Wild Eight had prowled through her land enough that meeting there didn't provide her with any hint of tactical advantage. This time, she had invited him to meet her on neutral territory, out in a secluded section of the rimrocks, to talk, to turn down the deal.

Not without backup waiting in the wings, of course.

Because if she refused to sell the ranch, then maybe Wes would see the truth. She had been a pawn in the Wild Eight's game all along, and she had no desire to be indebted to the likes of those monsters, impressive investors or not. If that meant blowing this shot, then so be it. She would find another way to save the ranch. If she gave herself the freedom of honesty, something Wes had taught her, she had never wanted investors anyway. She had been too easily influenced by the will of others. In her last-ditch effort, it was time she trusted her own instincts. Risks be damned. It was the only way to real freedom.

The thought of such a loss sent an ache through her chest. Aside from her memories, the ranch was the last tangible bit of her father she had left. She still feared that loss, but not as she had before. She realized now the loss of the ranch would be devastating, maybe even like losing her father all over again, but it wouldn't destroy her.

Not like losing Wes would.

She had already lost one great love of her life. She couldn't stand to lose another, at least not without a fight. No piece of land, no memory, no legacy was worth it.

The image of her father's smiling face came to mind. The old cowboy mounted on top of his horse as he rode up to the back of the house at the sound of her mother's dinner bell. Though she had only been a child, she recalled in vivid detail the warmth and love evidenced by the crow's feet lines at the edge of his eyes when he smiled. Her father had thought the sun rose and set in her mother's eyes. The loss of her, of her love, had nearly killed him. Richard Evans would never wish the same for his only daughter.

And she would never forgive herself if she didn't try to earn Wes's forgiveness. And if she failed, if Wes refused to see her for the woman she truly was, she would fall to pieces, but she would survive. Like a phoenix, she would rise from the ashes no matter how hot they burned. She was the master of her own destiny and made from far tougher stuff than she'd ever imagined. She wouldn't allow life, or death, to break her again.

As she waited, her pulse thrummed in a quick rhythm, filling her with anticipation. The early evening sky cast shades of navy blue and cerulean across the mountain peaks. The glowing lights of downtown Billings glittered below. Despite what she was about to do, she felt calmer, steadier on her own two feet than she had in months.

The sound of tires crunching over dirt, gravel, and rock broke through the whipping silence of the wind. She turned toward the noise. An old beater truck— the kind driven by cowboys, ranchers, and rednecks alike—pulled to a stop several yards away from her. The driver's side door opened, and Donnie eased out of the vehicle. The passenger doors also opened, revealing two other men. Despite the suits they wore, they couldn't be anything other than Wild Eight. It was like putting a Hells Angel in a bow tie.

She had been too blind, too desperate for any financial help she could get to see that before.

At the sight of them, Naomi frowned. "I thought this was a private meeting."

"These are my associates."

"Associates or not, four is a crowd," she countered.

"With all due respect, a last-minute meeting out in the middle of nowhere is not what I would call a formal business meeting."

"Clearly, you don't do as much business with ranchers as you'd boasted. We're an outdoorsy group."

Donnie returned her frown with a scowl of his own. "If it's more money you want, I don't have time to play games. Name your price."

She shook her head. "I don't need your money."

Donnie's eyes darkened. "I've seen your financial books. You need our money."

"That's my call to make." She crossed her arms over her chest, slipping her right hand into her coat pocket to finger the hilt of the knife. "Other opportunities have come to light."

"With no chance to counteroffer?"

She shrugged. "No, unfortunately, I'm sold."

His eyes narrowed. "Sold to the Grey Wolves..."

The words caught her off guard. She hadn't expected him to openly admit anything. When they'd met previously, he'd kept to his script, pretending to be nothing more than a human businessman. If it hadn't been for the Grey Wolves, she never would have known who he was.

She tried to keep her face straight, but she'd never had much in the way of a poker face. They'd told her to keep him talking while they arranged the best tactical entrance. She raised an eyebrow. "Excuse me?"

Donnie shook his head. "Wes put you up to this."

Naomi took a step back. "I don't know what you're talking about."

"Don't play dumb with me, bitch." Donnie stepped forward. "You either cooperate and let us buy your land, a win-win situation for us both, or this doesn't end well for you."

"What do you want with my land anyway?" she snapped.

"It's prime entrance into Grey Wolf territory. Owning the rights to that land will make it that much easier to wage our war."

"With your half-turned vampires."

"The Grey Wolves know then." A satisfied smirk spread across his face. "It's no matter. There's no way for them to prepare for this. They don't stand a chance."

She shook her head. She had to keep him talking, just a few moments longer. From the corner of her eye, she spotted one of the men taking position. "Why not just take my lands? If you're so powerful, why not just force me to hand the land over?"

Donnie chuckled. "Even the Wild Eight have to play by the Execution Underground's rules in order to fly beneath their radar. Humans are strictly off limits." That smirk returned, twisting into something darker and more sinister. "But since you've put in the request, in this case, I think we can make the exception." He stepped toward her.

She drew her knife. "I'm not so easy to kill," she said, stopping him in tracks. "Being a human around these parts has its advantages."

Donnie quirked a brow.

Naomi flashed him a smile of her own as she gave a small shrug. "It means I have friends."

At that moment, the barrel of Quinn's gun pushed against the back of Donnie's skull. "Move another muscle, and I'll blow your goddamn head off, wolf."

"You bitch," Donnie growled as several more Execution Underground hunters emerged, armed and prepared to take on the Wild Eight wolves.

"The plan was mine." Naomi smiled. "But you can thank Wes for introducing us."

The rage in Donnie's eyes flared.

"Cuff them and throw them in the van," Quinn ordered his fellow hunters.

Satisfaction filled Naomi as she watched the Execution Underground hunters load Donnie and the other Wild Eight wolves, wrists bound with silver handcuffs, into their van. It wasn't until Quinn had safely slammed the door shut behind them that she breathed a sigh of relief.

The hunter turned to face her, his Stetson falling low over his handsome eyes. "You're sure I can't convince you to hand in that son of a bitch Wes Calhoun while I'm at it?" He asked the question with a small grin on his lips, but she detected the hint of fire in his eyes.

"No, that wasn't part of our agreement," she reminded him.

Quinn nodded. A strange sort of peace had settled over the hunter since they'd first met that morning. It seemed as if having Donnie's head was enough to appease his drive for revenge, at least for now. Though she still held the distinct impression that if she'd hadn't been human, Quinn wouldn't have been so understanding of her silence.

She and Quinn had gone round after round in a verbal sparring match for the better part of the morning, with the hunter trying to convince her to turn Wes in. She'd simply told Quinn no dice, or her offer was off the table. But when she'd told him she would give him the wolf actually responsible for Delilah's death, his interest was piqued. She'd explained to Quinn that Delilah's death had been the result of Donnie's setup and that Wes had been framed. It hadn't lessened the hunter's desire for Wes's wolf hide lying skinned and tanned across his living room floor, but it had helped them strike a temporary truce.

With the agreement that she wouldn't have to disclose anything about Wes or the Grey Wolves, she and Quinn had struck a deal. The Execution Underground's manpower against the Wild Eight in trade for her provided location and cooperation. It was a win-win situation.

Quinn crossed his arms over his chest. "Well, if you change your mind, you know where to find me. In any case, I'm going to need you to ride along back to headquarters for questioning."

"Well, since you were my ride here, I guess I don't have much of a choice." She'd anticipated as much. Pointing toward the back of the van, she raised a brow. "You don't expect me to ride in the back, do you?"

The hunter slapped a hand on the side of the cab. "No, you can ride up front with me. They're a dangerous breed. Leave the wolves to us professionals." His eyes darkened. It was a mixture of warning and, from the playful gleam in his eye, maybe even a hint of suggestion.

She didn't have the heart to tell him it was too late. Though she'd thought the hunter brash and asinine on initial impression, she realized now the man had little tolerance for the runaround and games, which is exactly what she'd been doing at their first meeting. Over the past few hours, he had grown on her. In his Stetson and well-fitting blue jeans, Quinn proved a very handsome, very human specimen, but she'd already been ruined for any other.

"That won't get me to spill the beans on Wes." The words came out with slightly more bite than she intended. "I'm not so easily persuaded."

Quinn's smile faded. "Pity."

They climbed into the cab of the Execution Underground's van. The engine rumbled to life as Quinn twisted the key in the ignition. They pulled onto the road, headed away from the rimrocks and toward the nearby highway. Naomi fought not to glance over her shoulder. Nothing but the seat where she sat separated her from Donnie and the other Wild Eight members. Though two other hunters sat in the back, armed and ready. The Execution Underground's van seemed somewhat poorly equipped for transport. She had expected something more along the lines of a police vehicle with a cage separating the driver from the prisoners.

When she said as much, Quinn responded with a huff, "Tell that to headquarters."

A deep snarl tore from the back of the van in response.

"Cut the growls before I shut you up permanently, wolf," Quinn barked over his shoulder into the back seat. As he turned back toward the road, he glanced in Naomi's direction. "Don't forget your seat belt."

She reached over her right shoulder and pulled the strap down across her body. Twisting to buckle it in, over her shoulder, she spotted Donnie. Though his hands were bound, his eyes remained trained on Quinn, unmoving and feral. She'd seen that look before. In Wes's eyes just before he...

"Quinn!" she shrieked.

But it was too late.

Donnie lunged, launching himself into the front seat before either hunter guarding him had so much as a chance to stop him. The van swerved. The tires screeched as the massive vehicle skidded. The smell of burning rubber filled the air, and then an unknown force lifted Naomi from her seat. She was falling, tumbling over and over again. She felt weightless as shards of glass and debris flew past her face, a stream of constant motion she couldn't stop or control. The seat belt jolted her into place, knocking the wind out of her even as it saved her from flying from the vehicle. Still, her head bashed against the side panel of the vehicle. Pain seared through her, sharp and fierce.

Then everything went black.

She had no idea how long she was out. When Naomi regained consciousness, she hung upside down from the front seat of the vehicle, the seat belt alone having kept her from having been thrown from her seat during the accident. Her vision remained fuzzy, and her head pounded with clouding pain. Someone tugged at her, unlatching the seat belt and pulling her from the vehicle. Though her battered body didn't have the energy to fight, she relaxed into the touch. It was warm, heat embodied, so distant, yet so familiar.

Wes, her muddled thoughts cried. She searched for him, weak hands reaching out to clutch his warm shoulders, to stare into those blue eyes, so cold at first but that warmed over time. But when her muddled vision focused on the face of her rescuer, a sharp chill of ice shot through her. Because the bloodied, warm hands that had pulled her from the wreckage weren't Wes's at all.

Donnie's dark features stared back at her, having survived the wreck with minimal injuries. It all rushed back to her. Of course Donnie would have survived the wreck. The beating and battering of a car crash would be barely more than a scratch to a werewolf with unlimited healing resources.

But to a human...

"Quinn," Naomi tried to scream, but the hunter's name came out as barely more than a whisper rasped from her throat. She still struggled to breath from where the seat belt had constricted and saved her.

Donnie smiled through blood-stained teeth. "No humans to save you now, bitch."

<div style="text-align:center">~~~</div>

No. Wes refused to bear the weight of it. His muscles tensed, and his lips curled into a deep scowl. He could handle Maverick's rage, his anger, his censure, but never his pity. That was the emotion etched across the packmaster's features as Wes strode, unannounced, into Maverick's office the following morning. But Wes wouldn't allow Maverick to pity him. Not for another damn second. He didn't deserve pity, and he didn't deserve her, betrayal or not.

"The cougars plan to break the alliance."

Maverick's pity melted away, turning instead to stern calculation. "How do you know this?"

"I overheard them in the woods. Clay and Jonathan. They plan to slip away before the fight, only staying until then so they can gather information. With your attention divided, Clay thinks he'll avoid your wrath, at least until the battle with the Wild Eight is over."

Maverick stilled, though from the cinch in his jaw, it was clear his anger simmered beneath the surface. "And you're certain?"

Wes nodded. "Jonathan disagreed, but Clay wouldn't hear otherwise."

And their sources had told them the Wild Eight would attack tomorrow.

Maverick slammed his fist onto his desk. He perched both his hands on the carved wood, fingers splayed wide as he hung his head in thought. His dark-brown hair fell into his face, shrouding his expression. After a long beat, he mumbled, "The lives that will be lost…"

Wes didn't envy Maverick, not even for a moment. In a battle of this caliber, there would be death. That was certain. The lives lost would lie on Maverick's shoulders, as the lives of the Wild Eight had once rested on his. How the tables had turned…

"We will win this battle." Wes said it as much for himself as for Maverick. He needed to believe that to be true, because the thought of any other outcome was unacceptable. The Wild Eight would pay. For stealing his life from him, for Delilah, for Naomi. Everything they'd taken from him.

Maverick lifted his head. "I can't say I'm surprised. Clay has long thought the Seven Range Pact is beneath

him, except when it benefits him, of course." He stood
to his full height. "What would you do in response to
the cougars?"

The question struck Wes, catching him off guard. A
week ago, Maverick never would have bothered with
Wes's opinion. Now, the wolf asked it of him as if they
were old friends.

"We sit back and let them do the work for us."

Maverick stepped from behind his desk. "What
exactly are you suggesting?"

"Jonathan isn't pleased. We offer the resources to
stage a coup, then sit back and watch."

Maverick crossed his arms over the large expanse
of his chest. "There's Wes Calhoun, packleader of the
Wild Eight, the only enemy whose absence I've ever
missed." A small grin crossed Maverick's lips, and a
fiery spark lit in his eye. "I was a better wolf, a better
packmaster when I fought you. Tell me more."

"On that course, we may not have the cougars' help
for this battle, but we'll have it as the war continues.
We both know this is only the first battle of many. Even
if we wipe out the Wild Eight and the half-turned vampires, the vampire overlords will retaliate."

Maverick cupped his chin in thought, turning away
and giving Wes his back. Years ago, Wes wouldn't have
hesitated to use such a shot to his advantage.

"I'm still the same wolf," Wes reminded him.

Maverick's shoulders tensed before he twisted back
toward him. "Not according to your human female."

At the mention of Naomi, a snarl tore from Wes's
lips. "She's not mine." And she never was, never had
been. Not as he'd hoped, not as he desperately wanted.

"And she's wrong." She'd always been wrong, even as he'd wanted to believe it himself.

He couldn't even bring himself to say her name. The pain in his chest burned so raw and fresh. He didn't know what she had told Maverick about him to make the packmaster trust him enough to spare his life, enough to make him second, but clearly, she'd spoken well of him. But to what end? If she meant to betray him, if she was Wild Eight, why sing his praises? Why not turn the Grey Wolf packmaster against him instead? The questions plagued him, but Maverick quickly brought him back to the moment.

"Perhaps." Maverick scanned Wes as if trying to detect evidence to the contrary. His eyes narrowed, assessing. "Or maybe she isn't. Maybe you have changed. If you were given the chance, would you do the same? What Jonathan will do to Clay?"

Wes stiffened. "I have no desire to be Grey Wolf packmaster."

Maverick shook his head. "That's not what I asked."

"If you question my loyalty, Colt is more deserving."

"Of course he is. Blind loyalty being the problem. He's loyal to a fault, which is exactly why I didn't choose him. Colt would never have challenged a word I said, even if I was wrong."

That was debatable. And Maverick deserved to know that Colt had indeed moved heaven and earth to see that Maverick reached the conclusions he needed to. Wes had never given Colt the credit he was due, and looking back, he regretted it. He'd carried a chip on his shoulder for years at being judged at face value, yet he'd done the same damn thing to Colt. He really should set Maverick

straight on his high commander, but something stilled
his tongue.

"Let's get back to my original question."

"Oh?" Wes played dumb.

"Would you usurp me?"

Wes glared at the packmaster. He'd been intentionally avoiding it. "If you thought that to be true, I
wouldn't be standing here."

"Or maybe you would." Maverick pinned Wes with
a harsh stare. "As I get older, I find I'm a bit of a mas-
ochist, and as they say, keep your friends close…"

But your enemies closer.

Wes was more than familiar with the phrase. In
the past, he'd often applied such words to Maverick
himself.

Maverick grabbed a stack of papers off his desk
and shuffled them together. "The cougars exit plan
will weaken our army. We need to reassess, and fast.
Our sources say the Wild Eight may attack as soon as
tomorrow. We'll go with your plan for the cougars. I'll
find a way to discreetly offer Jonathan resources. In the
meantime, I'll task Colt with reconfiguring our battle
strategy in light of this information."

Viewing this as enough of a dismissal and glad
to know that Colt had returned—not that he'd ever
doubted the wolf's dedication amid this all-out war—
Wes intended to get the hell out of Maverick's office.
Turning toward the door, he'd placed his hand on the
handle when Maverick stopped him short.

"Wes?"

Wes paused. Without turning his back, he waited for
the packmaster's next words. He noted that apparently

Maverick wasn't the only one who'd gotten sloppy in their trust of one another.

Maverick cleared his throat. "Would you use a blade or a gun?"

Wes's hand lingered over the door handle. "If I don't die in this battle, neither."

Maverick grinned. "Yet you say you haven't changed, that you're not a better man."

He hadn't changed. He was aware of that now more than ever as the feelings of losing Naomi scorched through him, destroying him slowly from the inside out. She and Maverick were wrong. The rage that lived inside him still burned. He'd simply learned over the years how to suppress it.

A spark ignited inside Wes's chest. "I said neither blade or gun. I didn't say I wouldn't kill you." Wes cast a glance over his shoulder. "For you, only my bare hands would do."

Any remainder of Maverick's pity disappeared, twisting instead to a look of dark consideration. "Someday, we'll see…" With those words, some hint of dark macabre humor pulled at Maverick's lips, as if he somehow failed to take Wes at his word. Or maybe he dared Wes to try.

With that, Wes turned and left, leaving the packmaster chuckling in his wake.

Chapter 21

WES WAS ONLY HALFWAY DOWN THE HALL FROM Maverick's office when the adjoining door to the control room swung open. If not for his quick reflexes, it would have hit him. His hand slammed into the door, stopping it on its hinges. Blaze stood in the doorway, his eyes wide and stricken. "Where's Maverick?" he demanded.

Wes didn't have a chance to answer.

At the commotion, Maverick stuck his head out of his office door. Blaze's eyes darted back and forth between the two men. "The Wild Eight just entered our packlands."

Wes and Maverick swore in unison.

Based on their intel, they hadn't expected the Wild Eight to attack for at least another twenty-four hours, if not longer. With the news of the cougars abandoning the Seven Range Pact and no time to prepare, that left them severely disadvantaged.

Maverick stepped forward. Though he'd been laughing moments before, his expression was all business, fierce and focused, the face of a true warrior. "How long do we have to prepare the troops before they reach Wolf Pack Run?"

"Two hours at most." Blaze shook his head. "And there's something else."

Wes barely heard Blaze. The words failed to register. Instead, his eyes focused on the massive monitor over Blaze's shoulder. Pushing past Blaze and into the control room, Wes scanned the timeline. *No. No.* It couldn't be true. A dozen images lined the screen, telling a story in sharp, pixelated color. Naomi meeting with Quinn, then meeting with Donnie, Quinn leading a handcuffed Donnie to a van, and then photos of that same van smashed to pieces, overturned in the mountain dirt.

Maverick and Blaze came to stand behind him.

Blaze's voice easily filled the small room. "I was checking again for any updates the Execution Underground might have on the Wild Eight's movement when I found this. From what I can tell, she contacted the Execution Underground and then set up a meeting with the Wild Eight. She aided the Execution Underground in capturing him, but then clearly, something went wrong in transport."

Wes's heart stopped. The reality that she had been innocent from the start slammed into him. The proof stared back at him from the screen, clear as day. Why would she use the Execution Underground to go after the Wild Eight if not to prove her innocence? She was no hunter. Yet he'd refused to believe in her, in the good, pure woman who had been standing right in front of him. A woman who when she said she loved him, the emotion touched him so deep, his chest ached.

And then he'd told her he could never love her.

What a lie. He'd regretted the words the moment they'd left his mouth. Even in the face of what he thought was her betrayal, he loved her. He still loved her. He would never stop loving her, but now…

His eyes scanned over the last image. The vehicle had overturned several times, the smashed metal landing supine in a ditch along the rimrocks. Shards of glass littered the surrounding ground. Wes envisioned the smooth lines of Naomi's face, the deep tones of her skin, strong yet so fragile, so human. A werewolf would survive such a crash, but a human? He opened his mouth, but drawing breath proved impossible. He'd couldn't even think the words, let alone form them into speech.

"Is she…?" Maverick asked the question that was lodged in Wes's throat.

Wes tensed.

"No," Blaze answered.

The tension in Wes's muscles released. She was alive. He wanted to collapse to his knees, praising every deity in existence, thanking the universe…

"She wasn't among the bodies at the accident," Blaze continued. He paused, clearly uncertain how to present his next phrase. "And neither was Donnie."

Wes froze.

The bastard had her.

First, Donnie had betrayed Wes, then stolen his life, his position, and now he threatened the woman Wes loved. Wes didn't deserve her in the slightest, but he was too damn selfish to care. He wanted her, and she wanted him. That was all that mattered. He saw that now. And he would fight for her to the death, until the last drop of his life's blood poured from his veins. The need for revenge boiling in his blood confirmed what he'd known all along.

Wes Calhoun, nefarious packmaster of the Wild Eight, wasn't a changed man. He'd been alive and well, lying dormant, waiting for the right moment to rise again. He would spill his enemies' blood without remorse just as he always had.

Except this time, he fought for the right side.

Naomi faded in and out of consciousness, only vaguely aware of the sway of someone's arms—or maybe it was a horse again—carrying her up the mountainside. Somehow, deep in the recesses of her mind, she knew wherever she was headed, it wasn't somewhere she wanted to be.

Her eyes flickered open, and she stared at the dark sky overhead. She'd been dreaming of Wes, of the smile on his face the day he'd led her across the canyon, how the lantern light of the stable had lit him from within, highlighting the golden undertones of his tanned skin as he'd held her in his arms. She wanted nothing more than to stay in that dream, to lose herself in it. Yet her instincts drew her awake as if her body intrinsically knew that her unconsciousness made her all the more vulnerable.

She was a fighter after all. She always had been.

The binds at her hands reminded her of that.

Abruptly, the rocking came to a stop. She fell to the ground, her shoulder hitting a piece of craggy mountain rock hard enough to send a jolt of pain down her arm. If she hadn't been conscious before, she would be now. Whoever had been carrying her had tossed her aside like a sack of flour. Struggling in the grass, she wiggled herself into a sitting position.

Though seeing in the dark of the woods presented its own challenge, the moon lit the forest enough that she could see the outline of a group of male figures standing nearby. One male stood at the center, barking orders at the others. A chill ran down her spine as she recognized the voice. Donnie, and the other wolves with him were clearly Wild Eight. From the surrounding flora and fauna, they were in the Crazy Mountains, firmly in Grey Wolf territory.

She held no illusion that she could outrun them. She'd tried that before with Wes and hadn't managed to get more than a few feet. She racked her brain for some way out of this, some way she could save herself. Finally, she did the only thing that came to her. She screamed, hoping, praying that any Grey Wolf would hear her. Hell, even Malcolm would be a better choice than none.

The sharp sound pierced the quiet night, but a forceful kick to the stomach silenced her. The air flew from her lungs, leaving her gasping for breath. She doubled over in pain.

"You're lucky we're not closer to Wolf Pack Run, you bitch," the Wild Eight member who kicked her spat out. "Pull something like that again, and you won't have vocal cords to scream with."

The sound of duct tape screeching as it was wrenched from the roll alerted her moments before the sticky adhesive sealed her mouth.

She heard the grin in Donnie's voice as he said, "Much better."

He stepped away from her and pointed to several of his men. "You four watch over her. We need to keep moving. If the Grey Wolves don't know already, it won't be long before they realize we're in their territory. We need to charge them before they can prepare." Donnie glanced down toward her, as if she were nothing more than a bug beneath the heel of his boot. "I'm going to lead Wes back here, away from the battle, then we'll see how quickly that bleeding heart surrenders once I threaten to slit her throat." As Donnie headed into the forest, he shot one last glance over his shoulder at the Wild Eight wolves guarding her. "Rough her up, and make it convincing."

Chapter 22

A THIN STRIP OF PALE-YELLOW LIGHT PEEKED OVER the cerulean skyline, casting grim shadows over the sturdy pine trees. A thick layer of fog had settled over the mountain landscape, the dew and mist brightening the remaining green shortgrass to an eye-popping emerald. Nearby, the occasional singsong call of a meadowlark or the rustle of a rabbit or small fox navigating through the bushes were the only sounds. To the naked eye, the mountainside remained a peaceful, deserted terrain, untouched by man. And the Grey Wolves wanted it that way.

Wes crouched beneath the shade of a large pine and a heavy patch of bushes, gazing out into the open meadow before him. He drew breath in slow, steady movements, careful to blend into the surrounding wilderness. He was armed to the teeth with a blade strapped to each ankle, along with one in his hand.

Several crows squawked their dissent, fluttering off into the air on the other side of the meadow. A sure sign that someone approached. If one remained still, the birds acted as alarm enough.

When the first Wild Eight packmember broke through the trees, Wes recognized him immediately. A wolf named Lawrence, who'd been a brutal but efficient grunt man, the type of man one called when there were bodies to bury. He strolled into the meadow as if there was no reason for discretion or careful footing. A small mob of heavily armed Wild Eight members emerged behind him. Donnie was nowhere in sight.

They would come in waves, small groups of infantry meant to tire out and exhaust the Grey Wolf fighters, saving the vampires and their half-turned monsters for a final sweep. Luckily, the Grey Wolves planned to mimic those tactics, per Colt's orders. But more than several miles from Wolf Pack Run, this first group of Wild Eight had clearly expected the Grey Wolves to still be formulating their plans inside their fortress. It had been Wes who had suggested otherwise. He'd presented the plan to Colt, who'd worked out the logistics. The Wild Eight would reasonably assume the Grey Wolves would take all the time they could to prepare, lying in wait to ambush as the Wild Eight came to them.

Wes waited, still unmoving in the bushes as the men approached the center of the meadow. An arrow swooped through the air, landing straight in Lawrence's shoulder. He staggered in surprise as the wound hissed and sizzled. Eyes wide in confusion, Lawrence reached down to pull Colt's silver arrow from his shoulder as he raised his eyes toward the tree line in alarm.

The first Grey Wolf charged.

The sounds of battle cries, shouting, and feet pounding against cold rock broke the mountain silence. Wes tore from his spot among the trees as he threw himself into the fray, knife drawn and at the ready. As he ran, he noted the tree line in the distance where another surge of Wild Eight emerged. They'd broken from their old tactics in favor of a different approach.

Let them come, he thought.

Knives and fists clashed around him as he tore

through the meadow, past the spilled blood and cries
from both sides. He had only two goals in this fight.
Find Naomi, and kill Donnie where he stood.

A Wild Eight recruit he didn't recognize jumped
in front of his path, slashing his knife in menace. Wes
snarled. If it was a knife fight this pup wanted, he'd give
it to him. Wes brought his elbow down over his opponent's, stepping into the other wolf's attack and bringing
the young wolf down. Wes charged onward. He fought
several more wolves along his way, each time besting his
opponent with skill and speed. The image of Naomi at
Donnie's mercy drove him. He had to find her.

His blade was pushed hilt deep into the belly of a Wild
Eight member when he caught sight of Donnie in the distance. All sound ceased, and time slowed around them as
the two wolves met eyes. Donnie stepped toward him as if
in challenge, and then ran. Coward that he was. Wes chased
after him, running through the meadow and into the trees.

Donnie continued to run, leading him away from
the main battle in order to get him alone. It would have
been a sound tactic if Wes hadn't anticipated it, if the
Execution Underground's intel hadn't already told him
that Donnie planned to use Naomi as bait.

They ran until they reached a small thicket among
the trees, far outside the battle. But the sight before him
wrenched him to a sudden halt. Naomi stood on the
other side of the clearing, Donnie behind her, his knife
poised straight between her breasts, the tip angled for
her heart. From the bruises and cuts that covered the
skin of her arms and face, the Wild Eight had beaten her.
White-hot rage seared through Wes. He would murder
any man or wolf who ever laid a hand on her. A crude

piece of duct tape covered her mouth to keep her from screaming, but her dark-brown eyes met his. A tempest built inside Wes's chest, but on the surface, he remained calm, collected, the eye of the storm.

"I should have killed you when I had the chance," Wes snarled at Donnie. He'd regretted that moment ever since.

Donnie pulled Naomi closer to him, sidling up behind her until she pressed against him. "Don't move or I'll gut her," he sneered.

Wes lifted his hands in a sign of good faith, his blade still clutched in his right hand. "Let her go, or you'll live to regret it."

Donnie scowled. "Perhaps you don't understand…" He reached up to Naomi's mouth and tore the duct tape away. Naomi yelped in pain. The adhesive left her dark skin red and ruddy around her mouth. Donnie's knife pressed into her breast, and she cried out.

"Okay, okay." Wes rotated the blade so that the hilt faced outward. Another Wild Eight member emerged from the surrounding foliage and stripped it from him. With both of Wes's hands empty and a knife at the throat of the woman he loved, Donnie held a distinct advantage. For now.

All Wes needed to do was keep him talking.

At the sight of Wes unarmed and outnumbered, Naomi's eyes grew wide and panic-stricken. She was afraid he wouldn't be able to save her without his knife—foolish, wonderful, knife-fighting woman that she was. He tried to convey everything to her in a single glance, but fear clouded her vision. If only she realized…

"Let her go," Wes commanded again. "I'll do whatever you ask, but don't hurt her."

"Let me guess…because you love her, just as you loved the other human bitch," Donnie spat out.

"No, it's different." Wes meant that he had never loved Delilah as deeply as he did Naomi. The human rancher had been destined for him from the start. He realized that now. He couldn't escape the pull between them if he tried. But as he said this, Naomi's eyes filled with fresh tears, and he knew she'd heard something different, knew what the pain he'd inflicted on her had caused her to hear.

Wes shook his head slowly. If only she knew that he lived, breathed, and bled only for her.

She'd woken him from a life no better than death.

Don't cry, Miss Kitty. It's not what you think, he wanted to say. In a perfect world, she would chuckle at that godforsaken nickname, and he'd pull her close, claim her mouth, and make up for all the hurt he'd caused her, every ounce of pain, because he did love her, fierce and true and forever. Regardless of the pack rules that had forced them apart, she'd made him whole again, and if he had to choose between her and the Grey Wolves, then so be it. He'd choose her, every damn time. But he'd hurt her, and he intended to make it right. Oh, how he wanted to make it right, but now was neither the time nor the place to confess his love, no matter how true.

"You hear that?" Donnie hissed. "He doesn't care for you, not in the way he did Delilah, and look what happened to her."

"That's not true, Naomi, and you know it." Wes stepped forward and reached out a hand. A rustle in the nearby woods told Wes he'd waited nearly long enough.

Donnie dragged Naomi farther backward and shook

his head. "Don't listen to him. He tells a pretty story. A tragic hero framed for the murder of the innocent woman he loved. But she wasn't innocent, and neither is he. There was no knife held to his throat, no gun to his head as he slaughtered our enemies. He murdered in cold blood and just as swiftly took the life of his own father, like the lives of so many others."

So this was how Donnie was going to play it? Draw upon his sense of guilt, his pain, his anger, and convince the woman he loved that he was a monster. Sure, Donnie wanted to kill Wes, but first and foremost, his goal was pain. He intended to hurt Wes in any way he could muster.

But what he didn't realize was that Wes had finally come to terms with who he was. He may not be worthy or deserving of Naomi's love, but now that he had it, it wrapped around him like armor, making him invincible, impenetrable, as long as he had her by his side.

Wes nodded. "You're right. I am a monster."

Donnie's face hardened at Wes's admission, the faintest sign that it had shocked him.

Wes gestured between them. "You and I are cut from the same damn cloth, Donnie. We grew up together, rose in the Wild Eight's pack ranks together, killed together." Wes chanced a cautious step forward, but Donnie was too focused on his speech to either care or notice. "I called you my brother."

Donnie's eyes flared with rage at the reminder.

"I'm still that same wolf, just as violent, stubborn, and ruthless." Wes took another step. This time, Donnie reeled farther back, bumping into a nearby tree.

Just a few seconds longer.

"But the past is the past." Wes dared a glance at Naomi as he said this, urging her to see the truth, the meaning in his eyes. He knew this now. She'd shown him. It didn't matter if he'd been a good man. He could *be* one to her, with her. If she'd still have him...

"I'm stronger now, because there's one major difference between you and me..." Wes continued. One step farther.

Behind Naomi and Donnie, Maverick's face came into view. As planned, Maverick and several other Grey Wolves had followed Wes at a distance, slowly picking off Donnie's packmates one by one while the Wild Eight packmaster was distracted.

Donnie scowled and inched farther back. "And what's that?"

Slowly, Naomi's eyes widened as Maverick slipped his knife into her open hand from behind. Gently, Naomi's palm encircled the blade.

Wes smirked and met Donnie's eyes. "Now, my packmates keep their word."

Several things happened at once. Naomi chose that moment to stab the blade Maverick had just given her into the muscled flesh of Donnie's forearm. Donnie cried out, releasing her. She stumbled out of his grasp and toward the tree line just as Maverick appeared, prepared to guard and protect her. Wes lunged, shifting midjump, and then he was on Donnie. Tearing, pulling, ripping with the strength of his teeth.

Donnie drew his knee up between them and kicked Wes back, using the spare moment to shift into his own wolf form. On their hind legs, they crashed into one another, claws slashing and jaws snapping in a wild, feral battle. Though Donnie had grown in skill over the years, Wes would always be the stronger wolf—by blood, by birth, by character. He knew Donnie's strengths, his tactics. They'd trained together, hunted together, grown together, and Wes knew his weaknesses just as well.

Knocking the other wolf to the ground, Wes came out on top, pinning Donnie. Within seconds, he shifted, gripping the snarling beast by the throat and lifting him high into the air.

Donnie shifted beneath Wes's hands, and once again, they stood in this position. Wes held the power to crush the bastard's windpipe, to choke the life out of him and end his existence for good.

"Go ahead," Donnie rasped, wasting the remainder of his breath flapping his damn mouth. "Kill me." His eyes darted to the edge of the clearing, where Naomi stood watching with Maverick guarding her side. "Show her the monster you really are."

The color in Donnie's face thickened, turning from a pale pink to a breathless red. Every instinct in Wes screamed to close his fist, to crush the other wolf's windpipe, or maybe to leave him like this.

"Wes," Naomi called softly to him from the edge of the clearing, urging him to let go.

If Naomi wanted him to spare Donnie's life, then so be it. If that was what it took to redeem himself, to show her that he loved her, that he wasn't anything like the wolf strangling beneath his clutch, then so be it. Slowly, Wes lowered Donnie to the ground. As he did so, something flared in Donnie's eyes, something like victory.

Let him think he'd won, if it meant one less stain on Wes's already black soul, if it meant the woman he loved thought him less of a monster, if it meant her forgiveness renewed. He released Donnie with a rough shove, causing the wolf to stumble back. Donnie's face contorted in a laugh, and that's when Wes saw it.

The half-turned vampire released a menacing hiss, springing forth from the trees to leap onto the weakest link. It sank its fangs into Donnie's throat, and within seconds, Donnie dropped like a stone, dead at the hands of his own monster. It appeared that the half-turned vampires in all their brute glory couldn't distinguish between a Wild Eight wolf and a Grey Wolf.

"Wes!" Naomi shrieked.

He realized then that she hadn't been urging him to release Donnie and spare him at all. She'd been warning him of the second vampire that approached at his back. The monster sank its fangs into Wes's throat. Pain seared through him, and he felt himself drop, heard the sounds of Naomi's scream and the snarl of Maverick's wolf.

Then everything went black.

Somewhere off in the distance, Wes heard a faint tapping sound. He'd been having the strangest dream. In it, he held Donnie by the throat yet chose not to kill him, which couldn't be right, because in that moment, he fully intended to disembowel the bastard. That was, until he'd heard that *tap, tap, tapping*. As he drifted through darkness, the rhythm remained steady and consistent, drawing closer until the sound pounded in his head, a deafening echo. Suddenly, it stopped, followed by quiet shuffling and then a sharp, searing pain at his neck.

Wes's eyes flew open as his hand gripped whatever

assaulted him, stopping it in its tracks. From the feel beneath his hand, it was another person's wrist.

"I was cleanin' that," a familiar voice snapped. "'Less you want it infected, lie still." The wrist tore away from his grasp with brute strength, and the searing pain returned again. Astringent on a still-healing wound. He'd felt it enough times before to recognize the feeling now.

Vision still blurred, the lights above him swam before his eyes. Wes blinked against the brightness, and slowly, a pair of easygoing hazel eyes in a head full of soft black curls stared back at him. Not the dark, nearly black irises he'd hoped to see, but for now, he'd settle for any but the eyes of his enemies.

"Austin?" he rasped.

"Howdy." The young grey wolf grinned.

Wes tried to push to a sitting position, but Austin nudged him back down. "I said lie still."

Wes followed Austin's direction. The doctor fingered what Wes could tell were several sutures, likely more. As Austin examined him, the events of the battle with the Wild Eight came back.

"How long have I been out?" he asked.

Austin busied himself, still examining the stitches. "Five days," Austin said. "You were in and out of consciousness a couple times from the blood loss, but only for a few seconds. That vampire nearly ripped yer throat out. If Maverick hadn't been right there, you'd be six feet under alongside Donnie."

Wes shook his head. "I can think of far better ways to spend eternity…" He watched Austin as he examined him. If just checking the stitches was taking this long, they had to be plentiful. They would leave yet another nasty scar.

But if he was this bad off, then how would a human…

"She's fine," Austin answered at the sight of the panic on Wes's face. "A little roughed up from the Wild Eight, but nothin' serious. Maverick protected her from the vampires, got 'er back to Wolf Pack Run just fine, and he saved your sorry ass, too."

Wes sat up. He realized then he was lying on the bed in his apartment bedroom. He glanced out the bedroom door toward his living room and kitchen with sudden interest. His vision tilted, and the pounding throb returned to his head, but he didn't care. "Is she here?"

Austin nudged him back down onto the bed with a little less patience and slightly more force than before. "No. If you keep sittin' up like that, you'll tear a stitch. Not to mention you had a concussion, so quick changes in elevation are gonna make you dizzy. You need to rest."

Wes laid back and pegged Austin with a stern glare. "Where is she?"

Austin sighed. "Maverick sent her home. With the Wild Eight gone, she's safe now."

"We defeated them?"

"Just barely, and when the vampires saw it was a losing battle, they fled. There's plenty of them to contend with, and we both know they'll be back. The last few standin' Wild Eight surrendered. Maverick's holding 'em in the cells until he decides what to do with them. I reckon he's waiting on your assessment."

Wes raised a brow. "My assessment?"

"To know if they'll assimilate to being a Grey Wolf or not. Change their ways, and become one of the good guys."

"Ah." One of the good guys? He nearly laughed.

He still wasn't sure that was the case, though he hadn't killed Donnie. Though it'd been for Naomi's sake, not his own. In any case, he intended to be one of the good guys from now on, or at least he was going to try. He'd meant what he said to Naomi. The past was the past, and he held little power to change it. What he could change was the future. That may not atone for his sins, but it was a start.

Wes lifted his arms, stretching until he placed his hands behind his head.

"The stitches," Austin hissed.

Wes ignored Austin's protests and relaxed into the weight of his bed. He had always been a terrible patient. At least Austin always said so. He chalked it up to having little concern for his own fate, and maybe a little to his pride. He supposed that had changed now, too. When the vampire had sunk its fangs into his neck, the only thought that had crossed his mind was that he couldn't die. Not because he cared so much for himself, but because death entailed never seeing Naomi again. Never seeing her smile, never hearing her stubborn but gentle voice, never kissing her sweet lips. And never burying his face in...

"Maverick sent her away," Austin said, breaking Wes from his thoughts.

Wes eyes narrowed. "What?"

Austin shrugged. "You know the rules. No humans allowed at Wolf Pack Run, friends of the pack or not, and definitely no human-wolf relations." Austin raised his eyebrows. They both knew that line had clearly already been crossed, and Maverick had to as well. Yet still, the packmaster had...

Wes tried to sit up again, but Austin shoved him down with a heavy hand to his chest.

"Uh-uh. 'Less you want me to pluck all those stitches out without any anesthesia, you'll rest. You can tear Maverick a new one when you're well again."

This time, when Wes's head relaxed back into the pillow, he didn't protest. Staring up at Austin, he asked the one question he feared most, the question that had pulled him from his unconscious sleep. "What if she doesn't forgive me?" He'd been a downright ass to her. Rough and brutal as he'd accused her of wrongs she'd never committed and swore he couldn't love her.

The way she'd cried as Donnie held her in the clearing, not because of the knife at her throat but because she thought he didn't love her. He would die a thousand deaths—at the hands of a vampire, Donnie, or otherwise—before he ever saw that kind of hurt on her face again. As if the thought was too much for him, a fresh wave of drowsiness crept over him. He blinked several long, drawn-out times, fighting to stay awake.

Austin released a long sigh. "I don't have the answer to that. But if she does forgive you, it'll keep while you heal. Now sleep…"

And again, for one of a handful of times in his life, Wes did as he was told. Lest his reputation be ruined, obedience was becoming a nasty habit he'd need to shake.

Chapter 23

SEVERAL DAYS LATER, WES BURST THROUGH THE door to Maverick's office. He plowed inside, not bothering to shut the door behind him. Fully healed, save for the new scar on his neck, and up and moving for the first time in over a week, he had energy to spare and a bone to pick with his packmaster, his so-called friend. He supposed it was an apt title. The man had saved and spared his life as many times as he'd threatened it when Wes had once called him enemy. At the moment, however, he preferred the latter term.

"I'm leaving the Grey Wolf Pack."

Maverick glanced up from scribbling a letter of some sort to one of the other wolf packmasters in the west. Transportation wasn't the only modern convenience about which the Grey Wolf packmaster proved to be a bit paranoid.

Maverick set down the gleaming ballpoint and assessed Wes with a hard stare. Realizing Wes was serious, Maverick's mouth opened in a small gape. "This is how you repay me for saving your life? No one ever dared call you predictable, Wes Calhoun." Maverick turned back to his papers.

Wes crossed the small space and slammed both hands on the desk. "Why did you send her away?" he snarled. He needed to hear it straight from Maverick's mouth. The thought pained him, but if he was forced to choose between the pack he'd grown to love and the woman he chose to love, it would be her, every damn time. It was a choice he didn't want to have to make.

Maverick lowered his pen again and released an exasperated sigh. "I should have known this was about the woman. It's always the woman, with every friggin' one of you. You know as well as any Grey Wolf that human interactions, human *relationships*"—he stressed the word—"are strictly forbidden."

"And when have I ever listened to any of your damn rules?"

Maverick scowled. "I've asked myself the same question on more than one occasion, particularly when I was saving your life a week ago. You said yourself that she wasn't for you, that you didn't deserve her."

"That doesn't mean I don't want her," Wes snapped.

He wanted her, Naomi Evans, human as she might be, even if he would never deserve her. And when had Wes Calhoun, former packmaster of the Wild Eight and now second-in-command of the Grey Wolves, ever yielded to anyone on something he wanted? Never in his damn life. "If you're going to take that stance, then I'm leaving."

Maverick stood. "Leaving the pack, or leaving to defy me?"

"Both," Wes growled.

He reached for the door, but Maverick beat him to it, blocking his exit. Wes snarled.

"She really means that much to you?" Maverick asked, unfazed by Wes's warning growls. He'd been on the receiving end of such threats plenty of times before.

"She's my mate." Wes spoke the word out loud, finally giving voice to everything he'd felt since the moment their blood had touched when she'd sworn fealty. Hell, before that even, from the moment he'd stumbled into her wolf trap and first laid eyes on her. He'd been drawn to her like to a beacon. Even if Maverick hadn't asked him to protect her, he would still have been unable to let her go. They were two halves to a whole. The rancher and the wolf.

Again, Maverick gaped at him. The alarmed look was startling, considering Maverick wasn't the most expressive of men. The hardened warrior was usually all ice and grim seriousness, not flabbergasted surprise. The most emotive Wes typically saw him was when he observed the subtle twitch of Maverick's eyebrow, just before the packmaster laid his rage into him.

"Y-your mate?" Maverick stammered. "You can't be serious."

Wes scratched at the base of his skull. "Austin helped me do a little digging through the Grey Wolf texts. Turns out a destined mate doesn't need to be a full-blooded wolf to fit the bill, not even half-blooded. If what Blaze found in Naomi's history is right, apparently having a great-great-grandparent who was a shifter will do under the right circumstances."

Maverick swore.

"You can see why I can't remain a Grey Wolf. No matter how grateful I may be..." Wes's voice trailed off, leaving the rest left unsaid.

For saving my life, for making me a better man.

Maverick had better enjoy the glory, because it was the only damn time Wes planned on saying it or coming close, as it were.

The packmaster moved out of the doorway and

toward his desk again, refusing to meet Wes's gaze. Apparently, Maverick was as uncomfortable with the warm and fuzzy atmosphere between them as Wes was.

Maverick blew out a long sigh. "That can't happen."

"Last I checked, you don't have a choice in the matter of who I bed, and—"

A growl of his own tore from Maverick's throat. "I meant leaving the pack. I can't allow you to leave the Grey Wolf Pack."

He couldn't be serious. Prior to the events of the past week, Maverick had made it clear in every encounter between him and Wes that he'd regretted sparing Wes his life and allowing him a second chance. "Who do you think you are, ordering me to stay?" Wes snarled.

"Your packmaster, that's who," Maverick snarled back. "And I won't allow you to leave. For one thing, I've already lost several elite warriors in the past week. I can't afford one more."

Wes paused in confusion. "Several? I thought we only lost Travis from the…"

Maverick shook his head. "No, we lost Marshall, too."

Wes hung his head in a moment of silent respect as Maverick did the same.

"And now with Colt gone—"

Wes stopped Maverick short. "Colt? Where did he—?"

"He tore out of here just after the battle was over. He stayed long enough to make sure his men were tended to, fulfilled his duties, and then he was gone. He didn't take getting passed over for second well."

"Where did he go?"

Maverick shrugged. "Likely somewhere off in the West for a few days, maybe back to his mother's pack.

But if I know Colt, he'll be back, once his ego heals. Until then, I'm short three elite warriors, and I won't lose another second, too. I need—" The packmaster stopped short.

Wes eyed Maverick skeptically. "What are you saying?"

Maverick scowled. "Don't make me say it."

Now Wes was definitely going to make him say it. "I don't follow. You'll have to spell it out for me." A smirk spread across Wes's lips.

Maverick's scowl deepened. "You can have your human woman, but I need you, damn it. I need you here. Are you happy?"

Wes found himself too caught up in the possibility that had just opened up before him to revel in making Maverick confess he needed him. He could have her and still remain a Grey Wolf.

If only she would have him…

Maverick crossed his massive arms over his chest. "Are you listening?"

Wes jolted from his thoughts, back into the room. He'd been thinking about what he was supposed to say to her. He'd been thinking about seeing her for days, but the thought of exactly what he was going to say, exactly how he was going to make things right, hadn't occurred to him until now.

Maverick shook his head. "You're not going to hear a word I say until you've gotten this out of your system. Go." He waved a hand in dismissal before he reached into his desk drawer. "But take this with you." He dropped a hefty bag on top of his desk.

Wes reached toward it. The bag weighed at least thirty pounds. "What's this?"

Maverick nodded for him to look inside.

Wes opened the bag. Inside was a massive pile of bank-rolled cash.

Maverick cleared his throat. "The remaining assets of the Wild Eight. Seeing as you're the only Calhoun left in existence, I figured it was only right it go to you."

Wes had something a bit better in mind. He mumbled his thanks, then turned to go. When he reached the door, Maverick stopped him.

"Wes."

Wes paused without turning back toward the packmaster.

"What I asked you before about blade or gun…"

"Yeah?"

"For the record," Maverick said, "if the roles were reversed, I'd use my broadsword."

Wes smiled. "You wouldn't stand a chance."

With that, he left Maverick's office, tore out of Wolf Pack Run, and mounted Black Jack, settling in for a long ride. He'd weather any length of travel if it meant seeing her again. Over the past several days, he'd ached for her with a constant need. His friend, his lover, his mate. With any luck, he'd reach Naomi's ranch before nightfall.

Deep orange painted the Montana sky the color of sweet tangerines as Naomi rode back toward her house that evening. She'd been out working the ranchland since before dawn, hoping that the never-ending tasks of ranch life would distract her. It'd been nearly a week since she'd left Wolf Pack Run, and though Wes had been stable and projected to heal within a few days' time, he'd yet to show up at her doorstep.

She'd sat at his bedside for several days. But with each day that passed, it became more and more clear that her presence was unwelcome there. Nevertheless, she persisted. It had taken the Grey Wolf packmaster actually ordering her to leave to break her away from Wes's bedside. Even as a pack affiliate, since she no longer needed the Grey Wolves' protection, the Grey Wolf packmaster refused to bend on his rules about allowing humans to stay at Wolf Pack Run. Human relations were forbidden among the Grey Wolves, and even though Wes was second-in-command now, Maverick had made it clear that Wes was no exception.

Naomi leaned into Star as she barreled toward her home in the distance. Star was the only truly good thing that'd come out of this whole ordeal, and if the Grey Wolves wanted the horse back, they'd have to pry her from Naomi's cold, dead hands. She felt a kindred spirit with the animal, perhaps because the equine understood her in a way only one other animal did.

Once again, Wes's handsome face came to mind.

She'd tried to tell herself it was just as well, that even with everything that had come between them, a human and a werewolf simply weren't capable of finding happiness together. They lived in separate worlds, no matter how much she longed to join the adventure and excitement of his. Now, if she managed to get her heart to believe that, maybe she stood a fighting chance of forgetting Wes one day and moving on with her life. All it took was one thought of his hands blazing trails of fiery heat over her skin, lighting her up from the inside out, for her to realize she didn't stand a damn chance.

He'd healed wounds in her she hadn't realized were still open. Helped her find herself, though she hadn't realized she'd been lost. But now he was gone...

She'd been right all along to be wary of loving again so soon after the loss of her father. Now, pain from both losses weighed on her shoulders, keeping her awake at night with tears in her eyes far more than she cared to admit.

As Star drew closer to the house, she spotted something large and dark moving just behind her porch. Pulling the small pistol from her belt, she slowed Star to a halt.

With silent precision, she dismounted, sneaking up to the side of her house until she reached a corner. Quiet and listening. The old rocking chair on the back porch groaned with the weight of its unannounced occupant. She readied her pistol.

Throwing herself around the corner, she held her gun at the ready, only to find that the blue eyes staring back at her from beneath the rim of a Stetson didn't seem the least bit fazed by the weapon.

"You going to make pulling a gun on me a regular part of foreplay?" Wes smirked.

She holstered the weapon as Wes stood.

He watched her as she crossed the porch toward him and came to stand inches away from him. A scar from where the vampire had attacked him marred his neck. Lifting her hand, she ran her fingers across the tender skin. It made him look even darker, even more dangerous. She doubted he would ever look anything but.

She opened her mouth, prepared to say as much, but a fire lit within the depths of those icy-blue eyes at the feel of her touch.

Oh dear...

Wes yanked her into his arms. His lips crashed against hers, and his tongue explored her own. Damn, he tasted fine. Better than any wine she'd ever drunk. As she melted into him, she became aware of a difference in him from the last time his mouth had been on hers. His last kiss had been demanding, wild, unrestricted. This kiss was more reserved, a gentle caress of her lips. An apology kiss, an I-need-you and will-you-forgive-me kiss, or so she hoped.

Before he could kiss all sense out of her, she pulled away, reached up, and swiftly slapped him. Her open palm connected with the side of his face. Stunned, Wes raised a hand to his cheek, eyes wide. Though she knew the small sting of the slap was nothing compared to the sort of pain this werewolf could endure, the action appeared at least to have caught him by surprise.

Though he didn't release her from his arms, he mumbled, "I probably deserved that."

"You more than deserved it."

Until now, she hadn't realized how angry with him she'd been. Hurt? Yes. But angry? No. At the sight of him, it was as if all that hurt somehow pierced through her heart anew, like throwing salt on an already open wound—and damn it, she didn't like it one single bit. How could he ever have believed she was involved with the Wild Eight? Ever thought she would betray him?

"I shouldn't have been so rough with you last time. I—"

She cut him off, though the thought of their last near encounter sent heat blazing through her cheeks. "That's not what this is about. The slap was for not killing Donnie when you had the chance and nearly getting yourself killed."

Wes's eyebrows shot up toward the rim of his Stetson. "You wanted me to kill him?"

She shook her head. "Of course I wanted him dead! When you're a rancher, you come to terms with the fact that some animals simply need to be put down. Donnie was one of them." She pushed away from him. "Not that it matters now."

Wes looked as if she'd just told him the grass was blue and the sky a perfect shade of emerald green. "I thought you wanted me to spare him, to be the better man?"

She crossed her arms over her chest and huffed. "I never said I wanted you to be anything but you, Wes Calhoun. You were the one who thought otherwise." Turning back toward him, she met his eyes. "I know who and what you are. I've seen it in you from day one, lest you forget you knocked me out with the butt of my own gun and dragged me up a damn mountainside the very first night we met."

"Well, I have handsome reparations to pay if that would help make up for it." He nodded to a large bag settled in one of her porch rocking chairs. She looked inside and then up at him incredulously.

"Did you rob a—?"

He shook his head. "It was the Wild Eight's remaining money. Maverick thought I should have it since I'm the only living Calhoun. I have no need for it, and I could think of no better use than to give it to you."

She could save the ranch, complete the renovations she desired, hire extra hands to help. Her father's legacy would be preserved. And she would be free...

Her heart swelled with gratitude.

He opened his mouth to speak, but she raised a hand, silencing him.

A slow smile curved her lips. "Wes Calhoun, I know that you're a stubborn, wild, rule-bending, pompous ass, but despite all that, I also know you're loyal to a fault, a fierce friend, and an even fiercer lover."

If and when you ever allow yourself to love...

She chose her next words with care. "You're a good man, Wes," she said. "I just wish you were able to see it."

Wes swallowed, the Adam's apple in his throat moving in a slow, rhythmic bob, before he reached up and adjusted the rim of his Stetson. He leaned against one of the rail posts of her porch and raked his eyes over her. Even without touching her, he could make her skin burn hot.

"I hurt you," he said. "I never should have believed you were Wild Eight, at least not once you swore to me it was a misunderstanding. I was living in the past. But I meant what I said in the clearing when Donnie had you. The past is the past, and you've taught me better than anyone that I need to let it go. The pain, the guilt I've been living with over the years don't erase my sins, and they certainly don't make me a better man now." He met her gaze. "But you do."

Pushing off the porch railing, he stepped toward her, eyes burning both fire and ice beneath the rim of his cowboy hat. "You make me a better man, a better wolf, Naomi Evans, and I've never told as big a lie as when I said I couldn't love you."

Her breath caught. He sauntered toward her, all blue eyes and smooth, lean hips. She backed into the porch door, but still he kept coming, that damn smirk curling over his soft, smooth lips. Every inch of her came alive, ready and wanting.

"I love you, Naomi. Sure, as the sun sets and rises every day, and I'll never stop loving you. You make me a better man, and I intend to spend every day of the rest of my life living up to the honor of your love. I hope you'll forgive me again, because I've never wanted anything as much as I want you." His hands pressed against the door, caging her in place. He cupped her chin, the rough pad of his thumb tracing over her bottom lip in a promise that reminded her far too much of other, less proper things he could do with his hands.

"I love you, Naomi," he whispered again.

She could hear his graveled voice whisper it a thousand times, and still she'd never tire of hearing it.

"Will you forgive me?" He leaned in to kiss her, but she stopped him with a gentle push of her hand.

"I love you, too, Wes, but I have one condition."

He quirked a brow, clearly curious, despite the way his mouth grazed over her chin, wandering to nibble on her neck and ear in a promise of what was to come. "What's that?"

"In your quest to be a better man, don't completely get rid of Wes Calhoun, former packmaster of the Wild Eight."

Wes released her, pulling back far enough to meet her gaze. "What do you mean?"

"I know you're trying to be a better man and all, but it's just…" Heat flooded her face at her impending confession. "I kinda like the whole rough, angry, unrestricted wolf thing you had going when you…"

Wes's eyes flickered from the blue of his irises to the gold of his wolf's in an instant. From the eager growl that rumbled from his chest, she didn't need to ask twice. He'd cupped her ass and lifted her into his arms within seconds, releasing his hand from her only long enough to push open the door as they stumbled into her house.

Between the rough bristle of his whiskered kisses, his hands gripping her behind, and the hard length pressed between her legs, she was more than ready for him. Each touch, each kiss dampened the lacy black underwear she'd worn today in desperate hope that some mangy wolf might show up at her door and tear them off.

"Wes," she panted in between kisses.

A feral grumble in acknowledgment sent a thrill of excitement through her as he continued to run his teeth over the sensitive skin of her collarbone.

"I have one more condition." He left her so breathless that she could barely get the words out.

He paused momentarily, glancing up at her from where he made his descent toward the sensitive skin of her breasts. "Anything."

This time, it was her turn to smirk. "Don't ever call me Miss Kitty again."

If she'd thought Wes's devilish smirk made her go soft in the knees, the wide, genuine smile he gave her in that moment would leave her wanting for days. Still as dangerous and intimidating as he was with his wolf eyes ablaze and canine teeth prominent and plain to see, his smile delivered a dark, playful promise she knew he intended to deliver, and for the first time since she'd met him, the werewolf didn't chuckle. He threw back his head and gifted her with a deep, wholehearted laugh.

Keep reading for a sneak peek of the next book in the Seven Range Shifters series from Kait Ballenger

COWBOY IN WOLF'S CLOTHING

Chapter 1

COLT CAVANAUGH STRODE ACROSS THE PASTURE, holding the rim of his Stetson against the wind. The heels of his brown leather cowboy boots dug into the frozen ground, each step punctuated with murderous intent. He'd read the note scrawled in his packmaster's hand an hour ago, yet still his anger seethed.

He'd never contemplated disobeying a direct order before, but there was a first time for everything.

The scent of snow and pine seared through his chest as he continued across the Missoula subpack ranch toward the stables. The grunts and groans of his men training their fellow Grey Wolf cowboys and ranch hands to be soldiers grew louder as he passed. Each clash of steeled weapon served as a brutal reminder of his current situation.

Not unless provoked, Maverick's orders had read. During active wartime, no less. What a load of horseshit.

Colt reached the stables and tore open the doors. He spied Silver in the third stall down. The white Arabian stood out among the rows of tamed mustangs. In the glowing orange of the heat lamps, the threads of his coat shimmered and befit his name.

At the sight of Colt, the horse's tail lifted high and proud. The beast shook out his mane with a haughty huff. Silver was a horse more fit for a purebred high commander than the cowboy Colt was at heart, and the animal damn well knew it.

Colt unlocked the wrought iron gate, and Silver trotted forward with show-horse elegance as Colt grabbed an available saddle.

The attention whorse wrinkled his nose in distaste at the old, worn leather. Colt ignored him. He needed to reach the location, scope out the perimeter, and strategize his men's placement before their enemies arrived. Thanks to Maverick and the Seven Range Pact's orders, they wouldn't be running headfirst into battle tonight, but Colt and his men would be armed to the teeth all the same.

Colt mounted and gave the beast a commanding kick. In response, Silver shot out through the open stable doors. They rushed through the camp and into the nearby forest at breakneck speed, rushing past the darkened pines and navigating the underbrush with ease. He'd give Silver that much. He wasn't the most obedient working horse for rounding up cattle on the main Grey Wolf ranch back home at Wolf Pack Run, but his speed was rivaled by none.

As they rode, the setting sun above them painted the skyline over the Montana mountains in shades of vibrant pink and orange sprinkled with violet-blue clouds. The shadows elongated, chasing him like dark, snarling demons as the forest descended into evening, until he reached his destination.

Tugging Silver to a halt, Colt dismounted and scanned his surroundings. The forest was deadly quiet. The remaining late-spring snow blanketed the sounds of even the most dangerous scenarios. He led Silver to a nearby bush, allowing him to graze the frozen grass beneath.

With his horse content, Colt searched for the moon. The white crescent cast a dim glow over the pines. His wolf stirred inside him, eager to be released. His eyes flashed to their wolf gold before he threw back his head and released a long howl.

The sound reverberated off the trees, and his men answered, providing him with a keen sense of his soldiers' positions, and acting as a warning to their enemies. Though Colt was the only wolf in the clearing, he was far from alone.

Maverick hadn't said anything against intimidation.

As his howl ended, Colt inhaled a sharp breath. Three vampires several meters upwind. A low growl grumbled in his chest as the scent drew nearer. They'd agreed to one representative only. He'd known they'd never play by the rules. But they'd made a grave mistake to cross him from the start.

"You failed to follow protocol," he called out in the tone he reserved for those in his charge who failed to follow an order to the letter.

One of the vampires emerged from the trees. He appeared human, but was far from it.

"Given all that keening, I could say the same." The bloodsucker smiled, the moonlight revealing a sinister, sharp-toothed grin.

Colt recognized the vampire instantly. As Grey Wolf high commander, he made it a point to know his enemies. Lucas was a crony of Cillian, the ancient bloodsucking coven leader of the Billings vampire coven. Lucas, neither the most powerful nor eldest of bloodsuckers, was hungry for power and a force to be reckoned with. But what the fuck he was doing all the way out here near Missoula in one of the Grey Wolves' subpack territories, requesting a meeting to negotiate during wartime, Colt hadn't the slightest clue.

"You said one representative."

"You have exactly that, Commander. One representative…and my two guards. We also requested the packmaster, so promises were broken on both sides." That sinister smile flashed again.

A vein pulsed at Colt's temple, but he held his features steady. Colt had learned long ago to hold his cards close, never to betray his emotions.

"Maverick made no such promise. State your purpose or leave," he said.

Lucas broke a piece of peeling bark off a nearby tree, grinding the wood to dust in his palm. "My coven thought we might offer a deal."

Lucas broke eye contact, turning toward the trees in a way that raised the fine hairs at the nape of Colt's neck. The bloodsucker was anticipating something. Colt sensed it.

"We'll cease all war efforts immediately for the span of one year. It will give you time to prepare, rally, and train your subpack troops, and get the other *animals* in that Pact of yours on board," Lucas said.

Throughout Montana, the seven shifter clans that called Big Sky Country home formed the Seven Range Shifter Pact. They agreed to band together as allies in the face of their common enemies and for the greater interest of all shifters. If one of their packs went to war, all went to war.

Lucas's proposition was meant to appeal to a commander like Colt. Strategic, but unfortunately it lacked long-term logistical thinking. This early in the battle they weren't going to strike any deals with the enemy. Furthermore, the very suggestion from *the enemy* to take a year to prepare? Yeah. That raised all types of flags. And what would be coming down the pipeline that they would need a year to prepare?

Colt wasn't keen to hear what came next. He'd rather call bullshit now and rip this bloodsucker's heart out. But there must be a reason the vamps wanted a delay...

"Name your price."

Lucas's face turned businesslike. "Ten of your strongest warriors."

"No deal." Colt's words were cold, distant, betraying none of the hatred he felt.

A smile curved Lucas's lips. "Be logical, Commander. It's only ten men. I'm offering you the lesser of two evils. Think of the lives lost in a year of war. Far more than ten."

"No deal," Colt repeated.

"You can't walk away from this." Lucas's eyes flashed a deep crimson red. "You have an obligation to take this offer to your packmaster."

Colt allowed his wolf eyes to glow through the darkness. "That's where you're wrong." He advanced, forcing Lucas to ease back again. He would bleed this vampire dry for his vile suggestion. He may not have been born a true Grey Wolf, but he was loyal to the pack, to Maverick.

"Let's get one thing straight, Lucas. These are *my* soldiers, and I'd never disgrace our packmaster with such a despicable offer. No deal," Colt growled, low and forbidding.

He and the vampire stood nearly nose-to-nose now. The heat of their breath swirled together in a smoky dance.

"I was afraid you'd say that," Lucas said. "You see, Commander, I really was giving you my best offer, because if you failed to accept, our intent was to take what we need by force. You didn't think I'd play by the rules, did you?" Lucas snapped his fingers and his two bloodsucking cronies emerged from the trees, their intent evident.

"On the contrary." Colt lifted a hand and tipped the edge of his Stetson lower, signaling to his men watching through the underbrush. From beneath the rim of his Stetson, he glared at his enemy. "I counted on it."

The Grey Wolf soldiers burst through the tree line just as Colt tore his blade from his ankle holster. The hilt disconnected to double as a stake, and he intended to use it.

Four of his men took Lucas's cronies, which left Lucas to him. Despite his bravado, the bloodsucker fled. Colt bolted after him. With a quick whistle, he signaled Silver. Gripping the reins, he hooked his foot in the stirrup and swung into the saddle, leaning forward to urge the horse into a gallop.

As Colt rode after Lucas, a howl from one of his men echoed through the forest, cut short by a sharp, piercing yelp of pain and confirming his worst suspicions. He couldn't fathom how the bloodsuckers had managed to get their numbers past his soldiers. But he'd known it would come to this. He should have ignored Maverick and the Seven Range Pact's orders, gone with his instincts come hell or high water, and attacked first.

He would make their enemy pay for the mistake.

Colt steered Silver into the trees, maneuvering the beast into a quick turn, and moments later they burst through the bushes, cutting off Lucas at the pass. Colt dismounted into a drop-crouch with his blade in hand. But as he rose, another bloodsucker lunged from the nearby bushes, colliding with him in a tangle of snarls.

One of those damned half-turned vampires. The half-turned were deranged far beyond the master vampires who controlled them, twice as bloodthirsty and with twice the strength. But feral as they were, they lacked intelligence and fighting strategy. He'd thought they had all but eliminated them at the start of the war.

The half-turned vampire screeched and writhed on top of Colt as it lunged for his throat. It didn't even see Colt dislodge the hilt of his blade, revealing the small stake on the other end. Holding the vampire by the throat, Colt managed to roll, driving his stake into the vampire's pulsing undead heart as he did.

The vampire lurched. Colt shoved the now truly dead bloodsucker off him, stake in hand, but Lucas had escaped.

And whatever Lucas wanted Colt's men for, he wouldn't succeed, because Colt wouldn't rest this night until he found him and bled his enemy dry...

Dr. Elizabeth "Belle" Beaumont had been waiting for this moment, and she'd be damned if she missed this chance. She leaned against the wall of her cell, feigning sleep, the tattered blanket they'd given her draped over her legs.

Tonight, she would set herself free…

The sounds of shouting above the dungeons rang overhead as she listened to the last of the guards abandoning their posts. Whatever had caused the emergency throughout the Missoula Grey Wolf pack had drawn the attention of every guard.

Her breath swirled as she released a slow sigh. The air in the dungeons bordered on freezing. She'd never been more thankful that she was a werewolf than at this moment. Had she been one of the many humans she'd treated over the years, without the benefit of her wolf heating her from the inside out, she would have died from hypothermia days ago.

The hurried voices of the last two guards trailed off as they pounded out of the dungeons, leaving no sounds but the heavy breathing of two nearby snoring prisoners and the occasional shout from above ground.

Now was her chance.

She pulled the bobby pin from the nape of her neck, digging it free from the mess of snarled curls and frizz. Thankfully her bird's nest of hair hid several of the wayward pins when she'd been captured. At first, she'd forgotten they were there. Not afforded the luxury of a bath, let alone washing her hair, she'd found them while finger-combing two days ago and she'd been hiding the contraband ever since.

Placing the edge of the bobby pin in her mouth, Belle removed the plastic cap with her teeth and spit the small piece onto the ground beside her. She leveraged the pin against the concrete and bent it at a ninety-degree angle, then she crept over to the entrance of her cell.

She wiggled the hairpin into the housing of the lock, pressing up until she felt the slight pop of the springs releasing and the lock clicked. With shaking hands, she eased the cell door open. The hinges released a whining creak that echoed through the cavernous dungeon. The light of the torches cast a fading orange glow among the iron cages.

Another round of shouts overhead spurred her forward. She needed to get the hell out of Dodge and fast. Slipping through the darkness, she found her way to the stairs leading out of the dungeons and began climbing.

When Belle emerged into the night, the fresh scent of the surrounding pine forest filled her nose. She hadn't realized how dank the dungeons had been until she was here now, in the fresh mountain air. She scanned her surroundings. To the left were the open pastures and ranch land of the Missoula pack. To the right, lit by firelight, was an army encampment temporarily housing the Grey Wolf soldiers. With the start of the war only weeks earlier, the Grey Wolf soldiers from Wolf Pack Run, the main Grey Wolf ranch and compound, were here in Missoula to train the cowboys of the Missoula Grey Wolf subpack into soldiers. Days ago, she'd overheard the guards discussing their arrival shortly after she'd been taken captive. She would need to take extra precautions.

Shouts and yelling sounded from that direction.

It was now or never.

Belle bolted toward the safety of the forest. When she reached the trees, she continued to run toward the mountains. Toward the safety of the shadows. Toward freedom.

As she ran, her foot landed in a bramble bush, the icy thorns slicing at her leg. She bit her lip to stop herself from crying out but didn't stop to assess the wounds. She needed to keep moving.

Belle wasn't sure how long she ran, but she didn't stop until her legs refused to carry her any longer and she collapsed on all fours in the snow. The cold tingled into her limbs, but she ignored it, staring up at the gorgeous crescent moon shining through the treetops overhead. She fought the urge to let out a victorious howl as she prepared to shift into her wolf for the first time in days. The feeling would be exquisite. She felt the rapid thrum of her pulse as she struggled to calm herself enough to find her focus.

And then she heard it.

A rustling nearby in the trees.

She rose onto her knees. The blanket of snow covering the ground had soaked through her worn jeans, chilling her to the bone. From the close proximity of the noise, her options were limited.

Find or be found.

Lowering herself back onto all fours, she calmed her breathing and steadied herself, finding the place deep inside her where her wolf struggled to break free. In the pale moonlight, her beast came forth with ease. A quick twinge of pain followed by a sweet release and her fur instantly warmed her. Her clothes fell to the ground beneath her. Shaking the snow from her fur coat, she dragged her clothing beneath a nearby bush to cover her tracks and slipped into the underbrush.

Slowly, she prowled toward the source of the noise. Keeping downwind, she zeroed in on the sound. The rustling came from the edge of a nearby clearing. As she peered through the undergrowth, her heart stopped.

The first thing she saw was a horse. From the thin shape of its face, she recognized it as a purebred Arabian. They may not have bred yearlings on her mother's ranch growing up, but they'd owned enough horses for her to tell the difference. But it wasn't the massive horse that caused her pulse to race into overdrive.

It was the sight of the cowboy beside the steed.

In this neck of the woods, if his Stetson wasn't enough to give him away as one of the Grey Wolf cowboys, the earthy scent that drifted on the winter breeze was. She recognized him instantly as one of her kind. He smelled of pine, dark spices, and clove, a warm and welcome scent that was far too pleasant for her liking. But if he was a guard, he hadn't served on her cellblock. She would have remembered, because whoever he was, he smelled divine.

The Arabian sniffed through the undergrowth again, causing the rustling noise she'd heard. Inhaling a steady breath, Belle inched backward. She needed to get out of here before the man discovered her, but the sound of his deep voice froze her in place.

"Find anything?" he asked.

A small band of wolves stepped into the clearing, all in human form. One of them stepped forward. "No, Commander," he answered.

Commander. Belle's fur bristled. These weren't just any wolves. They weren't even guards. These cowboys were Grey Wolf *warriors*.

If they found her, she'd have no choice but to run for her life. She'd never been much of a fighter, and she-wolf or not, her skills would be no match for a well-trained alpha male. Did they know she'd escaped? Were they looking to drag her back to that godforsaken cell?

The fur of her tail prickled. No. She couldn't go back. She didn't belong there. She was innocent, though she knew they'd never believe her. She was a Rogue, an outcast. According to pack wolves like them, not to be trusted. It was the unfortunate way of their world.

The Commander's voice chilled her. "Spread out and cover more ground. We can't let this one go."

The other wolves obeyed without question, leaving the Commander in the middle of the clearing. Her heart sank further as each wolf prowled in a different direction, lessening her chances for an easy escape.

With his back still turned to her, she watched the Commander's wide shoulders rise and fall. For a moment, he leaned his weight against his horse; then he removed his Stetson. Setting it on the horse's saddle, he ran a hand through his short hair, leaving it slightly ruffled. It was pale brown in color, almost dirty blond.

He must have decided to shift and search like the men he'd given orders to, because he chose that moment to reach down and tug the hem of his shirt over his head.

Had Belle been in human form, she would have had to stifle a gasp. The spine and musculature he revealed rippled with sinew, but it was the scars that stole her breath. Even in the dim glow of the moonlight, her wolf eyes allowed her to see. The commander's body was a history of battles won and lost, wars waged on behalf of a supernatural empire.

And then he turned around and Belle's breath caught.

He wasn't just any commander. He was *the* commander. In an instant, she recognized *exactly* who he was. This cowboy wolf was none other than Colt Cavanaugh, high commander of the Grey Wolf armies, infamous Grey Wolf warrior, and one of the fiercest wolves ever to live. Second only to Wes Calhoun, the Wild Eight's former packmaster turned Grey Wolf, Colt had been the Wild Eight's enemy number one. He was more accessible than the Grey Wolf's untouchable packmaster, Maverick Grey, and responsible for countless deaths among the Grey Wolves' enemies.

Anytime one of the Wild Eight had returned to their compound near death's door and clinging to a thread of life, it had almost always been this man who was singularly responsible—and that didn't even begin to cover the damage he'd done to the Wild Eight through the information gathering and patrolling schedules he had directed his men to perform.

To top matters off, his battle skills weren't the only dangerous thing about him. If rumors among the females of the Wild Eight were true, he was also known as an unrepentant rake and womanizer, a man of deep carnal pleasures who could charm the pants off any female he set his sights on and whose intimate exploits were not only known far and wide, but coveted by many…

In graphic detail.

She could see why.

If she'd thought his battle scars made him intimidating, the pair of eyes locking onto the bush she hid in, as if he saw straight through the shrubbery, chilled her more than the snow beneath her paws. Irises the color of steel bore into her, distant and cold.

Those steely eyes framed a handsome yet harsh face. The brown hair of his close-trimmed beard framed his strong jaw and she realized the chill of his gaze made him more rugged than his features should have allowed. With high cheekbones and a perfectly straight blade of a nose, he should have been a charming, handsome cowboy. Yet years of a hard life had roughened him around the edges with a rugged, raw masculinity. Had she not feared discovery, it would have been enough to make even *her* ovaries quiver, and Belle wasn't a woman easily moved.

As he stepped toward her, Belle hunkered lower into the leaves. He drew so close, only the toes of his brown leather boots remained visible. Just as she was certain he had detected her, his horse let out a frustrated whinny, drawing the commander's attention. As he stepped away, she breathed a sigh of relief.

Belle watched as he placed his shirt in his horse's saddlebag before starting on the fastening of his worn, ranch-worked jeans. Oh no. It wasn't as if she could move from her position to look away without rustling the leaves. She *tried* to close her eyes. She really did. Her brain made the signal to her eyelids and everything, yet somehow, the order didn't take. Curiosity got the better of her.

As if the rest of his hardened body and those intense eyes weren't enough to leave her equal parts terrified and wanting for days, the sight of his bare, muscled ass would have done the trick. Never had she seen a more glorious male behind, which was saying something considering that for the past several years she'd worked as an orthopedic surgeon for the rodeo circuit before being forcibly enlisted as the doctor for one of the most notoriously dangerous wolf packs in history. She'd seen hundreds of nice male specimens in the nude—from a physician's standpoint, of course—yet this particular cowboy's behind was worthy of a medal.

What she wouldn't give to see that in a pair of chaps.

She watched as he shifted into his wolf—a massive, gorgeous grey, larger than most others she'd seen of their kind—and bounded away into the woods. It was only once he was gone that the tension in her limbs eased. Slowly, she started to ease backward from her hiding spot, causing the leaves to rustle.

As if his horse had known she was there all along, the beast trotted toward her, sniffing across the ground until the soft warmth of its mouth tickled her paw. The beast examined her with dark eyes, sniffing in her scent. It must have decided it liked what it smelled, because it nudged her with its wet nose.

The horse nudged her again, this time harder, forcing her to adjust her balance. When the horse persisted, she finally shifted into human form and stood, taking in the full sight of the beast and the old worn leather saddle on its back.

Its saddle. Her eyes widened.

Having grown up on a ranch in central Florida, and after spending several years working the rodeo, she was an accomplished horseback rider. She knew her way around a stable well enough that she could tell that not only was this animal well-cared for, it was powerful—fierce in strength, and more importantly, speed. She would move faster on horseback. Deep into the safety of the mountains, far past the Missoula Grey Wolf territory, if she could help it.

What was petty thievery compared to the horrible crimes she'd been charged with? Little consequence, if you asked her. The accusations failed to take into account the truth of her circumstances.

Treason. Murder.

And now...

"Horse thief."

Belle froze. She felt the blood drain from her face as she turned toward the sound of the commander's voice.

Chapter 2

COLT CROSSED HIS ARMS OVER HIS CHEST AS HE STARED at the naked she-wolf holding Silver's reins. "We can add horse thief to your growing list of violations."

He'd sensed a pair of eyes on him from the bushes moments ago. He had passed it off as his own sense of paranoia, anticipation over finding Lucas. It was only when he'd paused while leaving the clearing and heard Silver huff that he trusted his initial impression. He should have known better by now. His time as high commander had honed his instincts into a lethal weapon. Not to mention working a ranch the size of the Grey Wolves' lands tended to teach a cowboy to trust his gut. Colt's intuition rarely proved him wrong.

And neither did Silver's noises. The horse always made that same huffing sound when he'd found a new loyal subject to demand attention from. The horse was the worst kind of bleeding heart. Friend to all and foe to none, as long as they gave him the ample attention he thought he deserved. Apparently, even with lost she-wolves.

He didn't recognize her. Though he knew every wolf at Wolf Pack Run, he'd only been at the Missoula ranch a handful of days and had yet to meet everyone. Between the dozens of Grey Wolf territories with hundreds of wolves at each ranch, it was near impossible to know them all.

Colt stepped toward the pair, shaking his head in disbelief. "Breaking pack curfew and prowling through the woods during a hunting ban, while there's an active vampire threat no less, and now stealing my horse." He ticked off the list of offenses. "Not to mention hiding in the bushes while watching me strip naked like some sort of delinquent. Are you *trying* to get yourself killed?"

Whoever she was, she bristled, changing from terrified to defiant in an instant.

Silver mimicked her outrage, huffing and flicking his tail as he drew closer to the she-wolf, his loyalty instantly gone. Colt shot him an annoyed look. *Et tu, Brute?*

"I...I wasn't watching you strip naked," she stammered.

"No?" He raised a brow. "By my calculations, you've been hiding in that bush since well *before* I removed any clothing. If not from curiosity, why linger?"

She gaped at him as a flush of pink colored her cheeks.

He stepped closer to her, his gaze raking over her nude form, pausing just long enough to make that tantalizing blush deepen. "Typically, when a woman wants to see me nude, she doesn't resort to hiding in the bushes to do so." A wolfish grin crossed his lips. "All she has to do is ask."

Her eyes grew wide. Not that he was able to hold his attention on her eyes for very long. He tried to focus on those beautiful hazel eyes lined with thick, heavy black lashes, but there were other tantalizing parts of her staring him right in the face. Standing where she was, though her lower half was shielded by the darkness, her upper body remained bare, covered by little more than the shoulder length of her dark brown hair. The dark curls, almost black in appearance, glittered in the moonlight with bits of fallen snow. She looked every bit like Eve standing in a wintery Garden.

And Colt would have given anything to be the snake to tempt her.

It was a strange sensation, noticing her nudity. He'd seen hundreds of Grey Wolf women naked after shifting and he'd never stopped to notice the finer details. It was a different experience from having them naked beneath him or in his bed. In the forest, their true nature somehow made the nudity asexual. But not this woman.

Everything about her called out to him in a way that wasn't just sexual—it was *primal*. From the wild, untamable locks of her hair he wanted to grip in his hands to the growing flush spreading across the fair, creamy skin of her shoulders, all the way down to the puckered nipples of her bare breasts, which begged to be licked, teased, tasted with his tongue. The sight alone made his mouth water.

And from the vivid blush on her cheeks, the feeling was mutual.

That didn't even begin to cover her scent. A delicate mix of baby powder, lemon verbena, and wildflowers that reminded him of the mountainside when spring was in full bloom. Between the sight of her naked and her intoxicating scent, his cock was instantly hard and he was grateful his lower half was also concealed in the shadows.

Sure, he worked hard—so he played hard. Colt had a healthy, carnal appetite and liked to take his pleasure among the she-wolves in the subpacks, women like her, but only when he wasn't on duty and was away from the main ranch at Wolf Pack Run. *Like you are now*, his brain helpfully noted. One-night stands at the main ranch quickly became tricky, and Colt didn't do relationships. He always made that clear from the outset. In his position, it was a liability he couldn't afford.

Shaking his head, he tried to clear his mind. He needed to remain focused. Not only did he make it a point to keep his fair distance from the females of the pack while working, but she was in jeopardy standing out here in the middle of the woods during an active vampire raid.

You're meant for violence, not love. The words of his birth father echoed in his head.

Colt cleared his throat, falling into the role of stern commander with practiced ease. "So, delinquent horse thief, what do you have to say for yourself?"

"I…" She stared at him like a doe caught in a hunter's sights.

Suddenly, she shifted into wolf form and bolted into the trees.

Colt swore. He stepped forward, prepared to chase after her, but hesitated. If she wanted to put herself in danger, then so be it. He had more pressing matters to attend to than some she-wolf's disobedience. He turned to mount Silver and continue his search for Lucas, but it was at that moment he caught the scent of a vampire on the breeze.

Headed in the same direction as the she-wolf, but downwind from her. She wouldn't detect it. Instantly, his protective instincts took over.

"Shit." Colt shifted and sprinted after her, running as fast as his four legs could carry him. She was fast, but he gained on her quickly. She dodged left then right, trying to throw him off her trail. Had he been any other wolf, she might have outmaneuvered him. But he wasn't any wolf. He was Colt Cavanaugh, high commander of the Grey Wolf armies, and he'd made it his life's work to be outplayed by no one.

Anticipating her next move, he leaped from the bushes, tackling her. They rolled into a tangle of legs, teeth, and limbs until Colt came out on top, pinning her underneath him by biting onto the scruff of her neck as if she were no more than a pup. Even in wolf form, he outweighed her by at least fifty pounds and was nearly twice her size. Dragging her by the scruff, he pulled her back into the bushes with him and into hiding.

The vampire likely drew closer by the second.

Under the cover of the brush, he pinned her on her back, using his weight to keep her down and still, before he shifted into human form. She followed suit.

As his fur receded, he clapped a single hand over her mouth, silencing her. She struggled against him and let out a strangled cry against his hand.

Lowering his mouth next to her ear, he whispered, "Vampire. To the left." The bloodsucker was still a considerable distance off. But that didn't mean it couldn't turn in their direction.

Immediately, she stilled.

As if in confirmation of what he'd said, a hiss sounded far off in the distance. Her head turned toward the noise and he felt her breathing quicken.

Slowly, he removed his hand from her mouth, assured

she wouldn't make further sound. As they lay there together, naked bodies tangled in hiding, he watched her face. Adrenaline heightened every sensation, and her hazel eyes entranced him, urging him to draw closer, though he didn't dare.

She clutched his bicep like a vise, and braced her other hand against his chest, desperate and eager for something, *someone* to hold on to as her eyes urged him to help her in a silent plea.

Another flicker of sound rustled off to the west, moving away from them. It could still circle back, but for a moment, they had a reprieve.

He leaned down until his lips brushed her ear. "I'll protect you," he whispered. "You have my word."

At his promise, she relaxed against him.

It was a gloriously awful mistake. Her acceptance of his touch changed the situation entirely, bringing a whole new awareness to the feel of her against him. The smooth, creamy softness of her skin. The hint of wildflower that lingered in her hair. The mounds of her naked breasts pressed against the hard planes of his chest, deliciously warm and soft. The feeling instantly stirred something low in his belly. He could feel every inch of her—the hourglass shape of her waist, the wide curve of her hips.

He tried to fight his arousal, but he couldn't. Not with her naked up against him. The tantalizing scent of her filled him with longing. He ached with it. Her scent drew him in like a siren. His cock stiffened until his length brushed against the warm crease of her thighs.

Her breath caught, and her eyes grew wide in surprise, before they quickly began to narrow into a heated glare. Her mouth drew into an angry, annoyed pucker. If he didn't know better, he would have thought his body's reaction to her had pissed her off. But her eyes betrayed her, filled with another emotion, one that only served to worsen the situation at hand. Because what Colt saw reflected back in her golden wolf eyes wasn't rejection, anger, or even surprise. It was desire, unmistakable.

Pure, animal, raw.

He felt his own eyes flicker to the gold of his wolf. Her sharp breath told him she'd noticed and slowly he shook his head, urging her to remain quiet. In response, she bit her lower lip, drawing his attention there. Their mouths were only a hairsbreadth apart, so close to touching he could practically taste her on his tongue. If their lips touched, he wouldn't be able to hold himself back. He knew that without question. He'd take her, rough and hot, right here in the bushes like the animals they truly were.

If only she granted him permission…

They lingered, minutes seeming to stretch into hours as they slowly drew nearer. Just when Colt felt certain he couldn't take the torture a second longer, that he would close the gap between their lips and kiss her, the rustling of the vampire drawing closer to them once again broke the silence. They both froze, the spell between them instantly broken. He felt the terrified thrum of her heartbeat against his chest at the vampire's nearness. It was now several meters to the left, but they were still downwind, hidden. The forest had been prowled over by so many creatures tonight, Colt hoped it was enough to mask their scents.

The bloodsucker lingered for a moment, then pivoted

north. It must have decided to follow a different scent. After several minutes, when Colt felt certain the immediate threat had disappeared, he whispered, "It's gone."

Immediately, he released her. He pushed into a plank position and lifted himself off her. Like a bat out of hell, she tore from the bushes, brushing the mixture of dirt and snow from her behind. He tried not to notice how her ample round ass and hips swayed as she did so, but it was a lost cause.

Colt mimicked an owl's hoot, ordering Silver to return. A minute later, the steed trotted through the trees toward them, having been trained to follow close by whenever Colt made chase. When the horse came to a halt, Colt opened his saddlebag, digging inside. He retrieved the extra pair of pants from his bag and slipped them on, eager to cover his massive cockstand.

Locating an old T-shirt balled at the bottom of his saddlebag, he extended it toward her. He half expected her to refuse it, to shift again and run, but she didn't. Instead, she accepted the shirt from his hand. Once his jeans were on and fully fastened and he'd given her sufficient time to cover herself, he turned around to find her standing, arms crossed. The shirt proved just long enough to cover her most intimate parts. Not that he wasn't well acquainted with the feel of them by now.

"Did you just touch me with…?" She gestured to his lower half, struggling to find the words until finally she settled on glaring at him.

It had been a necessity to keep her safe. Plain and simple, and she had to know that. It wasn't his fault his body had reacted that way in the process. She *had* been naked beneath him after all, and it wasn't as though he could have prevented it. Engaging in a battle with the bloodsucker would have made her a target as well.

He would have said as much, but something about those narrowed eyes sparked the pleasure of a challenge in him, and he found he didn't need nor *want* to explain himself.

"I'm not certain what you mean." He knew exactly what she meant, but whoever this she-wolf was, he wasn't going to make it easy on her.

A defiant spark lit in her eyes that made him want to bend her over his knee and make that gorgeous behind of hers as pink as the blush on her cheeks. She indicated the lower half of his body again, making some bizarre signals with her hand as she pantomimed. She had to know how ridiculously amusing she looked from the way the fire in her eyes grew with each passing second.

He watched with silent amusement as her frustration built.

"A mongoose? An eggplant? I'm not very good with charades," he said. A wicked grin crossed his lips. He enjoyed watching her bristle.

Her hands clenched into fists. "You know *exactly* what I mean."

"My cock…" he finally offered.

The blush that burned on her cheeks and spread down the length of her neck caused the appendage in question to jerk in response. She had looked downright delectable flushed pink and bare in his arms. At least this time, the evidence of his thoughts was safely tucked beneath the fly of his jeans.

"Yes… Yes, *that*," she finally managed. "First you

accuse me of stealing your horse, and watching you strip nude, and then you mount me with something that may as well have been attached to Biscuit over there," she cast a quick wave toward Silver.

Colt didn't know where to begin. He wasn't certain which part of that sentence he was hung up on more. The fact that she *had* been trying to steal his horse and watching him nude, that she thought Silver's name was something as ridiculous as Biscuit, or the fact that she'd announced *he* may as well have been part horse between the legs.

At least the last point was a fair assessment.

"You *were* trying to steal my horse," he said, deciding to start there.

The horse in question gave a small, enthusiastic shake as he lifted his tail and batted his large, dark eyes. He puffed up like a damn peacock, eating up all the attention like it was sugar cubes.

She released an impatient huff, as if he were slow on the uptake. "That's beside the point."

As far as Colt was concerned, that was *entirely* the point. But as amusing as this frustrated little she-wolf was, he didn't have time for this. "Look. I don't know why you're running around the woods during a vampire raid and stealing horses, but I won't allow it. Not in my woods."

"Your woods?" She looked at him as if *he* were the insane one. "Last I checked, I had every right to be standing on this mountainside, no less than you do, and I didn't steal your—"

"That's beside the point." He turned her own words against her.

Already this woman was pushing his buttons. But Colt was controlled, calculated. He wouldn't rise to the bait, however difficult he found it not to.

Releasing a steady sigh, he raked his fingers through his hair. "Let's start with something simple then. What's your name, sweetheart?"

"I'd prefer not to start there, Commander." She uttered his title as if it were little more than a participation trophy. From the way she said it, she knew who he was. She simply didn't appear to give one flying fig.

Colt fought down a growl. He wasn't used to being defied, and he wasn't sure he liked it. The woman was as frustrating as she was beautiful, and she had the saucy little tongue of a viper to match. In any case, he needed to get her to safety and fast. It was his duty to protect the pack, even viper-tongued she-wolves.

"Fine," he said coolly. "But you're still going to march that sweet little ass of yours over to *Biscuit*," he said, highlighting the absurdity of the name, "and get on the godforsaken horse, so I can take you to safety."

At least Silver had the presence of mind to look confused at the unfamiliar name. He stared at them while chewing on a blade of grass.

The she-wolf looked at Colt as if he'd grown two heads. "No one has ever called my ass little."

That's what she'd gathered from this? He couldn't help raking his gaze over her. She was fuller-figured than many women of their kind, but to him, she was perfect. All luscious feminine curves to his hard muscles.

"No, I'm certain they haven't," he said.

Judging from her frown, she hadn't caught the hint of appreciation in that statement.

Ignoring the comment, she nodded toward Silver. "What if I don't get on the horse?" she asked.

His cock gave another eager pulse. Maybe he *did* like the defiance—at least from her. From the growing ache in his jeans, his lower head had different opinions from his ego.

Colt was about to tell her that if she didn't get on the horse, he would take one of each of her ample ass cheeks in his hands, bend her over, and give her a proper spanking for disobedience as any good cowboy would—a spanking that would leave her thinking of him with every bounce of the ride back to the camp—but as he opened his mouth, a familiar scent on the edge of the breeze alerted him, and Silver let out a warning whinny.

Instead, he only managed to breathe out one word to her before the vampire came crashing into the clearing.

"Run."

About the Author

Kait Ballenger hated reading when she was a child because she was horrible at it. Then by chance, she picked up the Harry Potter series, magically fell in love with reading, and never looked back. When she realized shortly after that she could tell her own stories and they could be about falling in love, her fate was sealed.

She earned her BA in English from Stetson University—like the Stetson cowboy hat—followed by an MFA in writing from Spalding University. After stints working as a real vampire, a.k.a. a phlebotomist, a bingo caller, a professional belly dancer, and an adjunct English professor (which she still dabbles in on occasion), Kait finally decided that her eight-year-old self knew best: she was meant to be a romance writer.

When Kait's not preoccupied with writing captivating paranormal romance, page-turning suspense, or love scenes that make even seasoned romance readers blush, she can usually be found spending time with her family, being an accidental crazy cat lady (she has four now—don't ask), or with her nose buried in a good book. She loves to travel—especially abroad—and experience new places. She lives in Florida with her doting librarian husband, her two adorable sons, a lovable, mangy mutt of a dog, and four conniving felines.

And yes, she can still belly dance with the best of them.